V.M. MOUCHAS

MEMORIES OF A MAD MAN VOL. 1

Published in 2020

Special thanks to the following

Jessica Green
Izaiah Fergusson
Emma Newton
Rose Styles
Elise Flory
Bob Dylan/Blackmore's Night

CHAPTER ONE: Y'VONNE

Somewhere on the planet Laguna, 1435 ATC

  Two masked guards led by a tall, muscular drow with a pure white ponytail who wore a cocky smile walked into the dungeon. The guards carried with them a bloodied man wearing a very unusual outfit made of a very unusual material. His armor seemed to be molded to be muscular and anatomically correct, with rubbery nipples and a comically supersized codpiece. He wore maroon leather boots caked in mud, a battle skirt, and a turquoise and gold cape over his right shoulder. The guards opened the cell across from the pale woman and slammed it shut.

"This one again..." The drow with the ponytail said to the single drow talking to the only other prisoner in the dungeon. Jaelna, the one with the ponytail carried the other prisoner's confiscated items. A unique looking short sword with a painted white blade, a utility belt with many pouches and vials, and an odd metal device in a holster. He threw these items on a table and began to walk away with his guards. The bearded man in the weird outfit laughed as he rose to his feet inside his cell. "I'm not done with you!" He yelled to the guard, gripping the bars with bloodied hands. "Come back and be my pretty little girlfriends! Ha ha ha!" Annoyed, the guards walked to his cell and opened it. "You'll have to bathe for weeks!" One of the guards punched him in the jaw, knocking him over while the other guard kicked him. The man did nothing but laugh.

"Thank you sire may I have a- Ooh!" The guards kicked him once more and left. "Jaelna... I've been here more than once. I oughta have my own private chamber!" The lead drow merely spat in his face and slammed the cell shut.

"Annoying worm..." Jaelna muttered as he left. The man in the cell laughed and sighed looking out of it. "What a lovely place."

The bearded man in the opposite cell stood up and patted himself down. "Why do they never take the stuff in my pockets..." They weren't very visible on his battle skirt. He brushed back his hair, smiled, and waved to another pair of passing guards. His gaze then went over to the fedora like hat with the giant white feather sticking out the top on the table with the rest of his stuff.

He held out his left hand through the bar, a strange glowing green white brand on the back of it emitted steam, and then the hat began to float from the table over to the cell trapped in a green aura. "Prisoner again... Sort of. Heh."

A snicker was heard from above as she saw the hat start to float toward the man, she would crawl from the corner off ceiling and wall. A creature with a naked woman's upper body on top of a demonic spider couldn't help but crawl down onto the bars of the man's cage. She stared at him with a soft smirk upon her lips as her legs were clinging to the bars "Prrisonerr you say?" She grinned, her teeth were sharp and jagged.

The bearded man stepped back a bit and chuckled a bit, placing the hat upon his head. "Prisoner, more of a guest from time to time really. Who are you?"

She chuckled as she looked down at him "I... like your hat..." She swayed from bar to bar, her human half just dangling "I seeee youu behind bars. Soo... You are prisooooneer." She started to climb down the gate, a toothy grin leaked some in between her teeth. She got to the bottom, not getting off the gate as she started to weave her web, slowly closing him off from the outside with her sticky yet thick webbing.

Venser backed away further from the bars. He was a tad creeped out, but yet he kept his arrogant manner intact. "I can get out whenever I like." He cocked his head to the side, looking to her, then looking up to his crimson fedora like hat. "Ya got a name?"

The spider woman chuckled as he backed away, a lot of people were creeped out by her "Whhhy is my name importttant." She hissed before she dropped down, and opened the gate. And slipped into the room, closing the gate. The web spun over the door trapping them in together "Mm..." She purred and stared at him.

He smirked arrogantly and gestured to the webbing that kept the cell sealed now. "It seems I'm stuck in here with you." He took a few steps back, looking to her lower body. "So why don't we get to know each other a bit?"

She chuckled as she got closer to him, "Can I have your haaaaat." She smiled almost innocently as she closed the distance between them.

Venser found it odd that she dragged on every last word she spoke. Her mere presence he found equally as odd. "Uhh...You can try it on. But not keep." He said, backing up some more. Only to hit the stone wall of the cell.

The spider woman grinned, her human hands coming out to grab the hat as one of each side of her legs slammed into the wall on each side of him "I like itttt." She grinned and took the hat off his head, placing it on her own before she suddenly started to spin her web ensnaring his ankles, her webbing slowly going up his legs trapping him to the wall.

Venser watched her remove his hat and put it on her head, and then he looked down as she webbed him to the wall. "Lemme guess, first you're gonna suck me dry and then eat me? I've seen this before." He clenched his left fist, the mark on the back of his hand glowed greenish white and emitted steam.

The spider woman chuckled at his words, she looked positively silly in his hat. "Mmmmmm noooooooo." She snickered and ran her tongue over his face, her saliva burned a bit on his skin but not doing any real damage "Mmmmaybe I plan to keep youuuuu?"

"Not gonna happen." Venser said, wincing a bit when her saliva burned his face. It felt good though that she ran her tongue over his face. "Tell me, miss. What would you intend on doing with me? Sing and dance for your amusement? Strip for your pleasure? I mean... Just ask."

"Of course... I don't know how you get pleasure. I know nothing of... Spider sex organs." He cringed saying that aloud and mentally beat himself over the head. As much as he loved women, now the thought of female spider sex organs disturbed him. But, he was willing to give anything a try once.

She snickered at his words, her webbing now at his thighs it split to keep his groin uncovered "Perhaps something like tthhhaat..." She purred loudly and stroked his face.

She snickered at his words, her webbing now at his thighs it split to keep his groin uncovered "Perhaps something like tthhhaat..." The spider woman purred loudly and stroked his face. She smirked softly and covered his form up with her webbing before laughing "I am a Queeenn. You will become part of the dungeon for others to play with..." The spider woman grinned before she walked away, her legs tearing at the web and unblocking her path as she opened the gate. Swiftly closing it and locking it, she spun another web over the entrance to his cell "I'll come check on youuu when you learn to behave." She snickered and started to climb on top of the webbing, burrowing into a small hole in the ceiling and disappearing into it.

"Sounds lovely." Venser said as she watched her leave, once more blocking the entrance with more webbing. He sighed and tried moving his hands, they barely budged. He tried to extend a finger and he managed to nearly get it fully extended. A small fork of bright green lightning shot out from his fingertip, burning a hole where his hand was, the edges were singed, allowing him to move his hand around until the hole grew larger and larger. He held his hand out and trapped the sharpened femur on the skeleton he stashed in the corner and pulled it over to him in a green aura, cutting himself free. Once he was free he casually walked over to the bars of the cell, looking to his utility belt on the table near the torture devices. "Be a dear and fetch my belt, will ya? I'm in the mood for a cigar." The spider was gone; its traces was still there.

''By the void... No damsels to rescue right now.'' Venser thought burning a small hole in the webbings that covered his cell. He peeked out and then disappeared in a puff of thick red smoke. Reappearing by the table and grabbing his utility belt. He retrieved a small pack of matches and a silver tin from his belt and teleported back into his cell, starting to clear the webs and hoping more lovely maidens would be dragged in today.

Venser was a man that had just turned thirty-one, with fair skin, a messy black beard that really needed a shave, and long black hair tied back in a ponytail. He stood there, flicking a match and lighting a green cigar, inhaling and exhaling a dull shade of smoke that had an earthy, citrus scent to it. The flame from the cigar casting a small glow upon his face, showcasing his eyes, which were like pools of emerald and were slitted like that of a serpent. Oddly enough.

A figure padded gently against the cold stone, shoes clicking lightly as it continued the long descent into the dungeon. Upon closer inspection, one would find a woman, with golden milky skin and almost neon blue eyes dressed in one would call noble robes with an intricate headdress adorning her head. No doubt she stood out against the murkiness of her surroundings, much to her displeasure. Summerland, why was she hear? She had no idea. She hated crowded areas, but her father had insisted they come here.

Normally, her twin sister, the more agile one, would be the one accompanying their father on such travels but her sister was not here, where as she was. Mental note: Never tell father you are bored and wish to travel to faraway places, for he will take you to places such as these. Finally, she made it to the bottom where the endless steps ended and found herself in a dark place.

Her face blanked and she stuck to the wall. She almost looked like a wallflower, perhaps just as pretty as one but her face held an unamused look, like she wasn't afraid, but not completely comfortable either for her nose wrinkled on her gentle face. Her crimson hair, tied and styled neatly on her head, stood out boldly against her almost golden skin, would catch on the sharp texture of the wall as she tried to slide by without being noticed by anyone. Trinity above, why her?! She was the God Queen of Pryldahn, not an errand monkey.

Through the bars of the cell he caught notice of the well-dressed woman with the headdress move by his cell. He craned his head to the side and leaned forward a bit. "What's a gorgeous, high class woman like yourself doing in here?" He asked with a smile despite his situation. "Have you ever had a Kullero before? What's your name?"

The woman continued to struggle with her hair, fumbling with the long, rebellious strands. Blasts! She liked her hair better when she was younger. It was shorter then, easier to handle. Finally, she managed to 'detach', dare say, herself from the wall huffing a bit before a voice of a man behind bars spoke to her. Oh, good Summerland, her father has mentioned to her about men like him. Don't look him in the eye, she thought. Though, she did for a few moments, taking in his odd clothing but then turned away, staring at nothing in particular. "It is not by my choosing, sir." She replied in a voice that had a tad bit of annoyance laced within. A Kullero? What in the Trinity's name was that? She crossed her arms and stood straight. "Afraid I have not." Her voice was respectful and practiced, as if the art of communicating with charisma and etiquette has been drilled into her very being. Then, someone else asked her name. Summerland above, why not. "... Y'vonne." She replied with a bit hesitancy in her voice.

Venser merely scoffed at her and watched while he smoked his cigar. "You don't partake? You sure? This is very fine cannabis."

The woman scoffed, as if offended by having the thought of someone thinking she would do such a thing; smoking. "I do not sir. For diplomatic reasons that I cannot share, I have come here to spread the news of our great land... You... You don't know who I am?" She trailed off, her glance now casting downward at the stone floor.

"But, alas, he has abandoned me." Y'vonne seemed a bit upset by this, but she hid more than she felt. Surely, as soon as she made her way home she would give him an ear-full. Suddenly, she was being dragged and then hurled into a cell. She clumsily stumbled, appearing like she would fall over but, she was fast on her feet. Once she found her bearings she turned sharply only to have the cell door closed in her face. She blinked, everything happened so fast she didn't... What?

"Excuse me." She counted the creature whom imprisoned her. "Didn't know they were so touchy, apparently." She spoke in a matter-of fact tone.

"That was fast... Oh, so you're looking for castle workers then? Mercs like me?"

Y'vonne scoffed again, something she did quite often when annoyed to bits. "My father the God Emperor has an established kingdom, so yes. Strange you've never heard of it..." She then leaned against the cage and crossed her arms, looking less like a noble and more like an upset child.

"My, prissy, aren't we?" Venser said with the cigar dangling from his lips. He took it out and exhaled some smoke. "What are you and your father looking for? I've been looking for a new one to serve. Find a decent place for me and my children to live in. I mean... Like, I don't think like, a tavern is a good enough place for them."

Prissy? Excuse me? She took a deep breath, and exhaled. Manners Von, manners. Suddenly, the woman's back straightened. Here comes the diplomat side. "That would all depend on what you have to offer." She held her hands in front of her, her face unreadable, her eyes almost uncaring. Though, this was the way of diplomatic negotiations.

The man clicked the heels of his maroon, leather boots together and did a little jig. "I was the court jester of Hempteth Keep! The fool. The only one who got to use comedy to tell the truth in front of the queen. I was also a storyteller, and they gave me the position of keeper of the house." He shrugged. "I didn't want it. But it involves organizing events, something I was never good at. But that was a few years ago, right now I'm a tavern keeper part time as well as merc and explorer part time!"

The woman would suddenly blink as the same set out on some sort of... Dance. A...Jester. Great. Her eyes gave an unchecked twitch so she shook her head to wave it off. Her crimson hair flowing with the movement. "Alright..." She started, unsure of what to do with this information. She racked her brain for a little, causing for a few minutes of silence before finally, clearing her throat. "We'll have something for you I am sure about that sir." Y'vonne then quirked an elegant, crimson eyebrow. "May I know your name first before doing any further interrogations?"

"Venser. Tybalt. Karrrrrrrrrrrrrrrrrr... Kaldwin." He disappeared in a puff of thick red smoke and reappeared sitting up against the wall near the skeleton. "Hold this for me Phil." He said putting his cigar in his bony hands. "Every kingdom needs a jester and a storyteller. In Hempteth Keep I had applauses from the royal courts." He sighed blissfully, remembering those days. They were truly nostalgic, for Venser was a born entertainer. "May I ask what your kingdom is called?"

The woman jumped as the man vanished and then appeared near the wall where a decayed skeleton lingered, placing a hand over where her heart would be. Phil? She counted that skeleton lucky, not many beings receive a name beyond the grave. How quaint. "I am sure you were quite popular; you smell well..." She paused for a moment to find the right words. "Ahem. Informed on your subject." Truly, if she were to hire anyone, they would need to be a professional. "Tis a pleasure to meet you Sir Venser, though I wish it were in... Better conditions." The woman looked around and sighed audibly.

"The name of the kingdom will not matter if we are stuck here for too long." Her ears, adorned with expensive jewels and metal suddenly twitched in thought. "Say... That little act you just did..." She gestured with her hands a bit. "The puff of smoke thing... You know teleportion? Could you perhaps get us out of here?"

Venser merely laughed at her, with a loud cackle. "Of course! That's how I always escape. And then get thrown back in here." He coughed a bit, picking up his cigar and taking a puff. "I'm here on my own free will..." His eyes were glazed over and faintly red as he exhaled greenish white smoke. "We get some lovely maidens in here sometimes." During Venser's small high, the skeleton he often hid many objects underneath suddenly spoke to him. "I haven't had sex since the year three hundred forty-two." Venser jolted and looked to the clearly dead skeleton. "By the void Phil! I'm so sorry... We can take you to the Witch's Wiggle. Lots there." He turned to the royal woman in the cell with him. "Ever been to No Name Port before?"

''Why on Laguna would you stay here on your own free will?" She asked, with obvious shock and annoyance in her voice. But, for as soon as he gave his reason about maidens, her face literally fell into a frown. Oh, she should have known. She lifted a nimble hand and rubbed her temple. "Alright, well-" Once the skeleton spoke, the one officially named Phil, Von screamed. Outright screamed. It was high pitched, and girly, and echoed in the cell and down the hall. She inwardly cringed at it herself. She quickly thinned her lips, cutting off her voice as soon as it slipped out. Her eyes were wide, her blue orbs darting back and forth between the now two characters that she shared a cell with. But, Venser appeared to be talking to it. "Summerland... My sister does these kind of things to me constantly..." She could barely handle her, and now possibly him? Mercy, her heart wouldn't be able to take it. "No, I have not been to No Name Port." Von all but snapped, still a little shaken from being spooked for she let out small breaths of air.

"Because of the lovely maidens." The smoke must have been getting to her, as the contents of the cigar being burned induced hallucinations sometimes. But mostly calmness. "I met my Arielle in here a while back. Normally I meet plenty-yyyyyy of women in the tavern or off on an adventure somewhere…"

She had managed to calm herself, flicking a handful of her crimson hair behind her an elegant shoulder. "Arielle?" Y'vonne tilted her head, the delicate jewels from her headdress dangling as she did so. "Might I ask, who that is?"

"One of my squeezes." Venser said picking up his cigar once more. "Are you sure you don't want to try it? It's a delicacy from my homeland."

"Your… I'm sorry, squeezes?" The noble woman was obviously confused. "No, thank you sir." She was still suspicious. Though the man did not appear to cause her harm, she still did not trust him. Not fully anyway. She heard unnatural sounds coming from the other room. The woman turned to stare off in the distance, her brows furrowing as she searched for the cause of the noises. It sounds like two voices, perhaps arguing?

"Aight." Venser said smoking more of it, then placing the light green cigar back into Phil's skeletal hands. "I'm sure you don't wanna be here anymore. Wanna come back to my place for a drink?"

As the winds of change come full circle the demon Shatael, decided to go to the dungeon once more to see what fun we going on there. Normally he would look more human but this time he decided to go a differ way. He demonic tattoos was showing and this skin was midnight black. This one's claws were long and black as charcoal. His hood and scarf had his demonic symbols on them. His outfit was those of the Ancient Reapers of his old world. As he gets to the dungeon he kicks the door open with his feet and makes his way down the steps. Shatael would walk around and then come to a dark part of the dungeon… He sniffs the air and catches a scent. Something human… Something… Godly. Something fleshy. Something tasty.

For a drink? Y'vonne wasn't sure about a drink but she did want to leave this place. "Absolutely." She breathed out, though her head turned again as she heard something large coming towards them. "Did you hear that?" She questioned. She then stood straight, her eyes searching and confused as a humanoid, demonic figure turned the corner and grinned at them, causing Venser to immediately throw out his left hand at the giant demon and shot multiple forks of bright, light green lightning at him.

Shatael would turn and raises his arm, taking the magical green lightning as it began to burn his blackened skin, taking a few steps towards them slowly. He looks to the redheaded woman and smiles, letting out a loud cry as chain like tentacles appear and hit Venser so hard he went through the wall leaving a decent sized hole.

His body became black and skin smooth like shark's skin... But harder than dragon scales, a tentacle now black with silver tips. Wings now emerged from his back. He lets out a loud roar that shook the walls. His crimson eyes now set on the mad mercenary in the strange red outfit. With a split second he runs towards Y'vonne and grabs her would grab her by the throat. He would look at Venser and smiles.

"You dare stop me from my fun?" As he looks at him one of the tentacles would start to rub over Y'vonne's body.

Venser was thrown through the wall and into an empty storage room. "Ah!" He yelled loudly hitting the floor with a loud thud, lying still for a few moments. He winced in pain and then laughed, coughing a bit as he felt his bones ache. He should have been dead. But, he was no normal man. He was much tougher and always kept going until he wore himself down to the very bone.

"Rescue the damsel..." He mumbled trying to rise to his feet. "Yah!" He flicked his left wrist and summoned a massive horde of bloodthirsty, carnivorous rats at the creature's feet. They squealed loudly and ran at him. Venser disappeared in a puff of thick red smoke and reappeared beside Y'vonne, extending his right hand. "Take it! Quick!" He backhanded the air in front of him, blasting the creature with a powerful gust of wind strong enough to knock him back.

As the gust of wind knocked the demon back one of his tentacles still had Y'vonne by the waist. As he flies back her goes with him. He stays on his feet whilst kicking away the swarm of rats and then looked at him. ''If you want her so bad, all you had to do was leave." He looked at Y'vonne and then licked the side of her face and let the woman go. "If you ever get involved into my affairs again you will die, human." Shatael would walk away from the both of them started to walk near one of the guards who had rushed in. As he gets to the guard he ripped his head off and tosses it to the side as he watches the guards body fall to the ground before leaving with a laugh.

Y'vonne was disgusted once she felt the cold appendage of the demon's claw wrap around her neck. How dare he... Such filth. For a brief moment, the neon blue color that was the woman's eyes began to illuminate even brighter, pupils disappearing. She'd take care of this worthless shit. Ancient millennia of pure dragon blood pulsated through her veins, though she was hesitant to use her powers, for it caused her extreme pain afterward, she knew how to use them well if needed. Though, her concentration broke once the human, the jester tried to help. She blinked, her glowing eyes gone, back to their normal blue. She was then set down. She made to speak, perhaps to say an angry outburst most likely but was cut off but the wetness of a tongue licking across her face. Oh... Summerland... Her face scrunched up, as well as her shoulders. Well that was... Gross to say the least.

"Now-now see here." Once the demon walked off, Y'vonne was angry, confused, and wanted to give him what for but he had attacked a guard, decapitating him in front of her. She blinks, her face holding a glare. How childish. She scoffed, a disgusted noise blowing out from her nose before she turned and made her way over to the jester, Venser, to check on him. To see if he was well. "Are you alright sir?" She inquired. She kept a respectable distance between them, wanting to see if he was badly injured.

"Perfect... Heh heh." He hobbled to the side a bit and nearly fell over, having to use the wall as support. He let out a groan and cracked his back. "Fuck me... I need to lay down..." He held his left hand out to her once more. "Let's get you somewhere safe, shall we?"

As the first sign that he was hurt, she was at his side. "Perhaps we should get you somewhere safe, neh?" She placed a hand on his shoulder, her eyes glazing over for a brief moment. She was searching for something, but what? "You have a fractured skull and an unstable spine at the moment." She said in a monotone voice. She then released him, not really knowing what to do at this point. She wasn't the healer of the gang, no, that was her sister. Perhaps she could find a way to get him to her? To heal.

"Ha! Naw. I'll be fine once we get to the Dragon's Head..." He muttered slumping against the wall. "I just want a drink and to be back in my own bed now... I ha-babaobobbeeadbop..." The red merc mumbled gibberish. ''... And a cabin by the lake...''

She nodded her head in understanding. "I know; rest would be good for you...but you need a healer." Von reached out for Venser, but then stopped. She hesitated for a bit, as if struggling with herself before finally taking his hand in hers. "You really need to have your skull healed."

''Ehhhhhhhhhhh sure. I've had sooooo many blows to the head I've lost track! Heh heh!'' Ven grasped Von's hand and the two disappeared in a puff of thick red smoke. The redhead was confused to say the least, when a puff a red smoke, the same smoke see's seen the man use from earlier, engulf their forms. On instinct, she moved closer to him, covering her face with her hands. She didn't know what to do, this has never happened to her before. She leaned her head against his arm, her hands still shielding her face.

For the God Queen, it felt like she was lost for a moment, flung across space and time at a million hours per hour through a potato and then suddenly stopped a moment later, finally uncovering her eyes.

CHAPTER TWO: THE DIVIDE

???? ATC

This was the day she really felt like the dirt had swallowed her up and dumped her somewhere, heels digging in the mud she raised with a groan. Muscle and bone aching, the clamp of the binds around her arm.

"Shit zey ahre tight." She thought. Whispers of lilac hair danced over her lashes, glitters fell from them framing her eyes, an icy opal, misty and lost. Down the bridge of her delicate nose, a silver scar streaked trailing its way beneath her whiskers and to her jawline. Punishment. Her top worn and muddied pants just about fit. The air was cold, frosty of sort. Drafting through it like a lost lamb she tried focusing on her sense, the vibrations beneath her and the touch of the trees to her fingertips guided her to the kingdom. Splashes of crimson trickled down her collar and side, small cuts and open as stitches now come free.

It stung, like alcohol on a wound, the touch of dew upon her pearlescent skin, Fleur had to stand back, her boots thick in mud as they scraped the floor once again.

"Dammit..." her mind uttered as she palmed herself on her forehead, hands painted with dirt, the mud run into her hair. She was tired, but still going, pushing away from what was behind heading back to her home.

"Ahlways so cahld..."

Words uttered from her lips, thick like honey the accent had a swirl, soft and young but old and wise. A roll off the tongue. Moving up to the now near buildings her feet found stone as her feet begun tapping on the cobbled stairways, her eyes darted about, the kingdom was so quiet, so empty... As usual. Walking the lost corridors, she was looking for a place she could pause at, the kingdom was once full of such laughter and love, but torn apart it left Fleur on her own. Still carrying on the hope that once more this place would rise and prosper like it had done previously, that she could build it back. But things kept happening to her, she slept, but never woke up where she rested, just like today with the new addition of tight clamps around her arms she'd often return injured and her mind blank of where the last few hours were spent. Stress, she thought quite possibly. But it couldn't be. The scars now trailing across her collar and shoulders, reaped over her hips and bare exposed skin, something wasn't right.

As the neko girl walked, a breeze blew throughout the area, increasing in temperature and speed as time went by. A blinding flash of orange and purple lit the sky for a mere second. A massive wall of dust and sand, nearly a thousand feet high loomed in the distance, bearing down on the sea. The heavens twisted, bolts of lightning flashed inside the swirling sandstorm, and the drumming of a thousand hooves upon a bloody world and noisy metallic groaning rang out loud enough for all to hear.

She felt the wind sweep past, her body curled letting the streams of air rush over as hair tangled and danced before her. Ears standing on end she looked about, her eyes retained the purple and orange flashes which sparkled in her opal hues. The dust caused her to cough, now holding onto her chest the kitten dropped behind the wall, looking out the tips of her ears perked forward as she peered out.

BOOM!

A fiery flashbulb went off inside the tornado. Sand, metal, fire, blood, and distinct bodies of several humanoid figures of several creatures were thrown out of the storm. Among the bodies of the unknown, was a half elf wearing tattered leather armor over the remains of simple steel armor, messy, long silver hair that fell over his head like a platinum waterfall, and orange sunset eyes. Several of the bodies plunged into the deep ocean, one was crushed by a giant object covered in a giant tarp, and several wound up on the sands of the beach. The half elf laid on the beach, unmoving for several long seconds until he pushed himself off the ground with a loud gasp. "Flop!" He gasped out looking around at the strange, new setting. He had never seen so much water before. At east in a few years. "Nugha! Narghhfr!" Down the beach was a deformed, heavily scarred orc that carried a crude club in one arm, and her other arm was withered and useless.

''Reeee! Reee!'' She screamed and swung the club around.

"There he is! That metal rat!" A shrill female voice said, that came from a ragged, wild eyed woman wearing tattered leather armor with multiple bottles and flasks hanging from her belt and her chest. "Hea they come again..." The half elf mumbled looking to the few fluid raiders that had survived.

Fleur watched, her eyes widened at the sight before her it'd been so long since someone had arrived here and now there seemed to be a fight about to play out. Standing tall the kitty stretched her figure out, head held high as she moved from behind the wall, careful for those not to see her. Darting from once place to another she was a little closer now, hidden behind a tree as her tail ribboned behind and sneaked up her thigh. Reaching for her moonblade with the additional limb the opal hues gained brightness, reflecting the light spectrum as she watched these beasts before her. The man who stood alone caught her attention. Watching the silver shine of his hair dance behind Fleur realized it was him against those. "Fuck." She thought. Now trouble had come to her land and she still didn't know who this lone man who'd seemingly been at the center of this mess. A streak broke through the atmosphere, a blinding flutter of crystal like shards trailed like a river. She stood behind him, silent her feline senses taken over as breathing slowed down and her body streamlined. She was a cat now. Soft hairs decorated her body as on her forehead a crown of symbols swirled painted into her fur as she stepped a paw beside him, ready to defend her land she was still unsure of this one. She could take one on her own, but the group in front of unwelcome visitors were the current priority.

"Fluids! Fluids! Fluids!" A mad, snarling man yelled loudly stumbling to his feet, sprinting towards the lone half elf. The half elf reached for his kukri that was sheathed to the left of his hip, it's blade gave off a pale orange color and the black hilt had grey cloth draped around it. He turned to look at the human fluid junkie running right at him and noticed a small cat with what appeared to be a crown on her head.

"Wha- Arghhhh...!" A searing, mind pounding pain came to his head and the raggedy man fell to his knees."Leave and fade from the memories of those- Fuck. Need water. Caught opening the book must be- Fluids! Fluids! Kill me! Kill the world!" He heard all the thoughts of those around him.

"Friend!" A monkey wearing a vest with several pockets jumped onto the back of the mutant orc and covered her eyes. The mutant orc screeched and hit the wild eyed woman with her club, sending her flying into a tree up the beach and killing her instantly.

She couldn't quite just figure out what had happened, orcs, mutants had crossed onto her land. The kitty started running forward, her feet pressed into the soft earthy ground as her body phased with a slow motion. During the cats run her full figure appeared to those who looked closely. A slender frame danced in the air above the feeling, dressed with thick black trousers torn and frayed, midriff showing her body glittered with a fine dust. White cropped top contained her upper half, pearlescent skin tainted with the pink painting of scars. Her light lilac hair danced, curls caught in the wind, her short sword, it's magical blade black and edges white, drew to her hand and ready in the cats tail it headed for the creatures preparing to propel off the ground and vortex up the mutant, scratching skin with a sharpened slice it cutting peel she climbed up the deformed woman injuring as she went.

Flop the monkey tugged at the golden earrings on the mutant orc's head. She was in poor health and Flop tore them right out. A loud, deep cry was heard, and worsened when the cat began to slice her up. The mutant orc was staggered and had trouble keeping her balance, Flop noticed the cat with the blade and covered the mutant's eyes again while she recklessly swung the club around, trying to smash the cat. "Fluids! Fluids! Fluids!" That was all on the wild man's mind. The raggedy man raised his kukri and the wild man kicked it out of his hand, it impaled itself in the sand. He was disoriented as the thoughts, his inner thoughts, the thoughts of every living thing in the land filled his mind to a point where it was nothing but static. "Where is it! Where's it!" The wild man yelled grabbing the raggedy man, groping him all over. "Yah!" The half elf swung his fist at him and knocked him over.

On his left arm was a metallic sleeve that ran all the way up to his shoulder, a modified part of the steel armor he wore underneath. The palm of the glove glowed light blue and imprinted on the side of his shoulder was bunch of falling stars and barely legible letters. "Yous gimme fluids or I'm gunna-" The half elf held out his metal arm and activated a gravity beam, which pulled the man right towards him, then there was a spark and he was blasted back with a large force of electricity. "Ahahahaha!" He laughed in an insane manner sliding along the sand to a stop. The half elf grabbed his kukri from the sand, ran at him, jumped, and then brought the pale orange blade down. Silencing the fluid addict.

Liquid poured from the beast as she sliced with a curl, running down the orc's skin as she reached the throat. Slicing without a thought or notion, she didn't stop to consider taking a life. Especially while she was in this form most coherent thoughts vanished from her mind. The thick skin flapped from the neck, the creature's words garbled and spilled a mucous lather. A shine struck her eyes, gemstone cracks glittered hidden deeply. Avoiding the monkey, the kitty fell to the floor as the orc dropped. With her landing she appeared back in her humanoid form, slightly breathless her frame grew as she stood. Fleur turned to the monkey, looking for guidance on her next move.

The monkey jumped up and down on the dead orc's head, then blew a raspberry in a mocking manner. "We sure showed them!" Flop exclaimed, from down the beach the raggedy elf heard his thoughts. "What?!" He yelled, hearing that single voice in his head when all the others had gone silent. Flop the monkey looked up at the cat who had morphed into human form and smiled, he hopped off the orc and tugged at her pants, then took off running down the beach.

Her head tilted in an innocent manner seeing the little padded hand grip at her trousers. Watching the monkey head off Fleur decided to follow, it had been a while since she saw such a beautiful passage of water, her favorite element. Her footsteps imprinted over the monkey's, turning back once more to a feline she sprinted up beside him, catching up and nearly overtaking at a pace.

The ragged half elf fell to his knees once more and grasped a handful of sand in his metal glove. The light blue glow from his palm lit up the sand and he extended his fingers, allowing the sand to slip through them. He turned himself around and sat down on the beach, the water almost touching his feet. He heard the small pattering of paws running towards him and he craned his head to the source of the noise. His loyal monkey companion, and the seemingly

magical cat from earlier. He also noticed a light grey, single strapped backpack floating in the water. "Flop! Get tha bluey!" He yelled in a strange, thick accent pointing to the floating bag. Flop knew how to swim. Primo didn't.

Flop took a detour and ran into the water to retrieve the bag. He raised a light silver brown at the cat and straightened up while sitting. What was it?

The figure in front of the neko girl stood so proud and tall, but it wasn't long before she met his level. Her bright opal eyes stared straight at his as her feline body become humanoid. Walking around him her footsteps in circles Fleur held a defensive stance. The other issue had lessened and this man was now what intrigued her. The scar across her face now clearly visible as it shone a satin look trailed across her face. Pale lips pursed as she kept watch of this man her hand still with her magical stone blade ready to defend her home.

The ragged half elf brushed back his silver hair and grabbed his kukri, staring into the girl's opal eyes with his own bright, carrot colored ones. He was growing stubble, appeared to be in his late twenties, and had garnered a scar on the left side of his cheek and another small one on the left side of his nose. "Now stop raight there." He said in his strange accent, not saying the R's at the end of his words. "Just whoin Shaelyn's name ae you? And whea am I?"

"La question est... Aho, ahre you? Fleur often changed from her native language to the common language of the other lands, mixing up her languages it was a result of her many mindless nights, ones she couldn't remember but always returned from. Injured and lost herself, it was rather repetitive. So she wasn't that sympathetic. Awaiting his answer her heels came to a stop, in front of him she stood ready to engage in battle, soft ears fluttered back and forth, batting hair with its swipe, Fleur's gripped tightened around the blade.

"Just anotha wandera. Who comes from a world of metal, and blood. Not liek those bushrangers we just kilt." He replied still keeping eye contact, and holding his kukri tight. For a brief second his eyes flicked over to the corpse of the mutant orc before going back to the woman who stood in front of him. "Now, ah asked you first so I deserve ahn answer."

"Fleur, of Kundaland." She didn't refer to it so much a kingdom these days, empty barren lands were what's left. Fireflies filled the halls at night illuminating the beautifully aged stone structure. The thrones coated with a cuddle of dust as fires forever lit burned embers into the wind. The man hadn't attacked her yet, and in all her years if he wanted to hurt her, he could have done so already. The tenseness eased off, looking away to the grounds behind her eyes never once pondered over the body beside them.

"Why ahre you here?" Her accent was still heavy she tried speaking the tongue they mutually understood.

"Fleu of Kundaland?" Again, he didn't pronounce the R at the end of it in his own accent. He lowered the Kukri and flop washed up on the beach with the grey backpack, he began to drag it to his companion through the sand. The half elf examined her closely. She wasn't hostile. Not like almost everyone he encountered in the land where he came from. Almost everyone had gone out of their minds, and he was afraid of having to live out there with him he'd end up the same as them. He paused before answering, "Primo Shando, of Nomerhia."

"Nomerhia." She pondered over those words, her finger rested on her bottom lip as this brief moment went over her. The thing is, Fleur didn't move. She literally looked frozen on the spot. But she didn't notice it, she was wandering in her mind wondering where this familiar words come from. "Nowhere?"

"Land of the downed stas? Evah heard of it?" Primo asked grabbing his bag that Flop had brought him. "Thanks mate." He said patting his small monkey companion on the head. Flop nodded at him then flopped over onto the bag, relaxing on it as he let out a sigh. "Something wrong Fleu?"

Her body sprung back into movement, she had no clue she'd been stood still for so long. "Ah étoiles!" The neko girl loved stars, their gentle beauty always graced a night, reflecting in her crystal eyes they drew her like warm fire. "You weesh to rest here?" She walked over, looking down to Primo her bare feet strong and steady.

Primo had no idea what she meant and stared at her with a dim, cow eyed look on his face. Half was her odd language and question, and the other half was of awe of her opal eyes, and Fleur herself. She was beautiful. He had to draw her. "Resting here? I don't even have a matilda... Or..." He gazed back at the ocean. "The Sand Stalka is gone... And I don't know how to get home-" Primo paused at what he had just said. Kundaland. From the trees, from what he had seen. He had always wanted to leave Nomerhia behind, cross the ocean, and live a life as... Maybe a bodyguard. Not some scavenger hireling. Anything but that. He wasn't quite sure.

"Cohme, I'll show you." Her tail swept in the sand, waving a little over his feet as her direction alternated and she was heading back to her land. It seemed like her body faded, left behind was her tail swinging in its hypnotic motion before vanishing too.

"Show me what?" He asked rising to his feet, grabbing his backpack and slinging it over his shoulder. Flop climbed up his back and perched over his shoulder as Primo followed behind Fleur, glancing down at her tail for a brief second. "What are you?"

A hand poked out gesturing him over, she stood in the now shadowed land. Fireflies glittered the dew damp grass. Before them would be statues of the nameless stone gods, protecting the land once and proud Fleur's eyes gazed to them. Head falling back her ears flopped aside, she brushed her hair away, revealing the full length of her scar.

Primo's jaw unhinged and he and Flop gazed in amazement at the many fireflies that glittered. Flop cupped his hands around one and it shined, he smiled and then shifted his hands into a ball, occasionally making a small hole to peek inside. Primo glanced up at the statues as they passed and ran his hand along them. He noticed the scar but didn't say anything about it. "I'll be stuffed..." This land reminded him more of the fabled lands beyond Nomerhia.

"Ma terre." The neko girl said, meaning "my land" this place was hers to protect, this little space of now silence was everything to her. Fleur looked at him, noting the equal amazement he had for this place. The fireflies swarmed around Flop, scooping the little fuzz ball up under their gained wing. Like a golden carpet they carried him across. She smirked, a little fangs showed with this gesture, whiskers tickled her cheeks as a hand raised to paw at them. Swatting the blushed skin, she allowed him to continue his awe, not wanting to break the tranquility.

Primo watched the fireflies swarm around his loyal monkey companion, and then carry him through the air. He then dug his foot into the ground. Grass. Dirt. Not sand. He bent down and then began to pick at it. "Grass... I could use a rollie sooner or later..." Primo then stood back up and began to eat the grass that he had picked out of the ground.

"Smohke?" Her expression a little hesitant, she creeped down and prowled almost over to him. Now she could register his scent, the tip of her nose gently poking his silver strands before she pulled back. Sitting away from him her legs crossed over on another in a meditative position, a curious kitten stare flourished over and lips pouted.

"Aye. Keeps me from losin' it." Primo turned to look at Fleur feeling something lightly touch his hair. From what Fleur could see, Primo was a tall, tan man with leather armor that was dried, ripped, and torn in several places. The steel armor wore underneath was beaten and scratched and was barely hanging on by a thread. In his carrot colored eyes were half awe, and half curiosity. His eyes looked much older than he was. His ears were pointed, but more rounded and less pronounced, telling Fleur that he was only half an elf.

"Ah…" Rummaging into her pocket she pulled out a small wooden box, filled with tobacco and cannabis. Small papers littered the inside and wood carved into hollow roach all prepared inside. "Help yourself, mahn ahmie." The neko girl scooted the box across the floor, allowing the newcomer to join in a smoke, tobacco or not, giving a little smile as her tail swished back and forth.

"Gunna need a way to light it." Primo said sitting down on the soft grass in front of her. A small smile ran across his neutral face before it disappeared. He scooted side to side feeling the green softness. "Do ya know of any inns or something nearby? Maybe a cave?" He normally camped outside or in the Sand Stalka, but his camping gear and his motorized carriage were both lost at sea now. All he had were the clothes on his back and everything in his backpack. He recalled the state of the statues he had seen just a minute or two ago. " Wait no... Ruins?"

"Ruins, such a hahrsh wahrd, mahn ahmie." Fleur chuckled to herself, her approach more relaxed as she handed him a grinder from her pocket. Made of wood with spikes in the middle it perfectly ground any herb inside. "You cahn stay here, weetheen ze wahlls" Nodding to the tall building now towering over them she sat back, tail curling up beside as she allowed him to roll.

Primo took a few herbs and three pieces of rolling paper, then closed the box and placed two papers face down. "Within the walls?" He asked looking up to the tall building, before going back to rolling the joint. He stuck the third paper in the back of the first two and added the herbs.

"My hahme, ziss buildeeng" Laying back on the ground her tail waved with a roll, hair scattered in the grass she stared up into the sky. Crossing one leg over another Fleur relaxed a little. Finding an odd sense of comfort and company with this handsome, rugged half elf. Something about his aura was soothing, settling. Looking up to him her hands rested beneath her head, the tightened thick binds making it difficult to raise the limb Fleur grunted.

"Ya don't even know me. All ya know of me now is that I'm just some dero. Could be some root rat or something." Primo said sitting legs crossed at ankle level watching Fleur relax.

"Well. Ah am a dero. I rarely go into cities." The half elf admitted. More of a nomad than anything else.

"Zen I'll keell you." She said with her thick unusual tone, her words did not hesitate and her eyes didn't flutter. Losing herself to the skies above Fleur nearly froze for a moment. "Zen ziss plahce should feel like hahme, yes?" Behind her little ear she rummaged for a nestled joint, bringing it to her lips she searched for a box of matches. Lighting the end, she took a few draws, letting the smoke fill her lungs as her chest rose.

Primo had never been offered to stay anywhere before. Aside from that small community he had saved from a roving bands of bandits armed with weapons they had scavenged by nearby ruins. He turned them down so he could complete his job. "I've only seen forests in books." He replied taking on of the matches to light his joint.

"You cahn explahre zese lahnds zen, ze centrahl point of ahll plahces... Sahmewhaht. you see, Kundaland... Eet's so much beeggair..." Sitting up smoke clouded from her lips, dancing over her cheeks and spreading between her whiskers. She concentrated on blowing smoke circles, letting them hoop in front and distort in the wind.

"What can ya tell me about... Kundaland?" Primo asked inhaling the smokey goodness in, before blowing it out slowly. He let out a deep sigh afterwards. Recalling the events of earlier now, and how he thought he was going to die in the lightning, fire tornado. "What a lovely day..." He said in a sarcastic manner.

A bitter smoke surrounded her, thoughts crossed her mind as he asked about her home. Filled hallways and conversation echoing throughout, sights of people grouped together. She smiled.

"Ziss ees my hahme, ze spahce between spahces where people dahn't often pahss. zough, eet wahsn't ahlways like zat... wance... befahre we gaht cut off frahm ze rest of ze wahrld... befahre we were trahpped here, een ze spahce between spahces. hence my surprise aht your ahrreevahl." She offered him her joint, either letting him two toke or simply enjoy the variation of herbs she'd acquired. "Ahnd you ahre a smohker too, I like zat." Her smile turned to a grin.

Primo pinched the joint and smoked two at the same time, he removed them and held one in each hand. "That's relaxing..." He handed Fleur hers back. "So, how many people live around hea?"

"Just me, ahnd ze others een my mind." She said with a playful slur, her mind relaxed as an effect of the smoke. Continuing to take a drag little puffs of smoke left her mouth. "Ziss plahce ees ahs you see eet, left fahr nahture to decide eet's fahte."

"What happened?" Primo asked exhaling a bit more of smoke. Flop scurried over and sat down beside his companion. He glanced at the two, then took Primo's joint and took a puff.

She choked back her laughter seeing the monkey take the spliff, ears flickering back and forth she couldn't help herself. "Lahng stahry, one wheech well, you know how eet goes." Fleur didn't speak about what happened, betrayal and blood soaked the land. Her palm touched the ground, she pulled it back and the mud turned red. Closing her eyes she let the joint hang from her mouth, smoke taped around before she looked back to him.

"And so... You've been here, alone, for how long?" Primo asked taking the joint from Flop. Flop reached out to take it again but he smacked his hand away. "Wait yer turn ya bugger..."

She leant over, almost a crawl. Handing the joint to the little monkey, Fleur nodded. "Knahck yourself out...well, naht literahlly." Sitting back up her arms stretched out, a hidden wince at the tight clamps on her arm she still hadn't got round to figuring out what had happened. "I've beeeen hereeeee, eh, few full moons, I sink." She had no track of time, hadn't wanted to keep a record as it recorded the time spent memorizing her past. And also the time spent where she couldn't remember it at all. She'd lied, Fleur didn't know if they were alone, she was going somewhere of a night, things were happening and she was feeling more and more drained.

Flop took the joint with both hands and heavily inhaled it. He then let out a few really loud coughs. "You don't know do ya? Are ya already baked out of yer mind?" Primo asked with a small laugh. "Gods... This grass is so soft..." He mumbled fondling it with one hand.

"'Ze lahnd ees reech here, Mahthair Laguna blessed us weeth such fertile soil..." She run her hand through the grass, fingertips stroking the dewey leaves. "ze ahtmahsphere wahs cahlm, drowsy aht times; ahnd sings like zat." Fleur flashed a wink, standing up her body stretched out as she reached for the sky, tail unravelled behind like a roll of satin. Her tail swished with excitment and she was quick to grab Primo's hand with both of hers and tug at him.

"Cahme, cahme! I must show you ze rest of my hahme! Let us go dahnce een ze moonlight, weareeng weeld flowers een our hair!"

The neko girl had the feeling she and this ragged half elf would be good friends. And couldn't wait to show him everything. Maybe they'd be even more than good friends, in time.

"You must understand the whole of life, not just one little part of it. That is why you must read, that is why you must look at the skies, that is why you must sing, and dance, and write poems, and suffer, and understand, for all that is life." - Jiddu Krishnamurti

CHAPTER THREE:
THE LIBRARY OF
INFERNAL WORMS

1445 ATC

What a perfect place to escape to! The light storm had passed and now the afternoon sky over the Kingdom of Arinova was absolutely, perfectly clear, with nary a cloud aloft to mar the bright azure sky over the city. A dull grey mare, a knight atop it strode through the city looking about. The riding knight was covered completely in armor. Though, only simply chain mail, covered by a split white and red tabard, a crest of a bell crossed by two swords stitched into the front of it, along with a helmet that obscured his entire head. The only parts of him visible were his hands as he watched many people pass by, many of them done with their duties in the city and leaving for home. "Hello! Hello! You ever get that feeling of deja vu?" He called and greeted to almost each and every passing person as he rode by on his horse, all before stopping in front of the rather large library.

"Public? Yes! A place of knowledge!' Maybe I can find someone to help me here!' The knight rode around the large library, looking for a place to hitch his horse. "Stay here Grace...That's a good girl." He said petting the mare softly and feeding her a few oats, all before moving in front of the library again and looking up at it, the building dwarfing him and his horse and the buildings surrounding it completely. He gave his horse a gentle pat again before digging through his saddle backs, retrieving an unusual dull brown book. Curious, the knight pushed the large double doors open, and entered.

Rota Frey had been perched in a chair, book in one hand and head chin in the other. It wasn't often that she went into town anywhere. She normally stayed to herself and kept to her own. Still, she would lounge in the chair, ready to be seen by anyone. Her blue eyes flicker to the occasional fire, and she would nervously chew the inside of her cheek. Hours before she had been on a task for seven hundred silver to kill the Grand Duke of Elsburn. Now, she was relaxed. Her eyes lit up with curiosity when she realized someone had entered. She kept in the chair because it was the least of her worries considering she was in a public library, but she was a little curious on who it was. She turned a little to see what looked to be a knight walk in. She chuckled to herself, brushing back her long silver hair. A knight in a library? Then again she was an assassin in a library herself. And looked the part too with the adventurer's leathers that almost screamed rogue.

Libraries offer a place of rest for the wandering fire mage Aithne who made a career in pyromancy both working for law enforcement and academia. Having been disbarred from both offices her reputation is all that is known. A quiet thing whose age remained a mystery and who has no doubt indulge in forbidden rituals in the pursuit of raw and unlimited power. The stigma of her moral crimes is worn in the form of arcane animality in the likeness of the hyena with ruby red eyes. It worked wonders for the mind to wear humbler clothing, not quite rags but hand me downs nonetheless. Keeping her eyes hidden beneath the shade of fiery orange hair is a prerogative for Aithne at least until she can become at ease with the locals who with good reason were sometimes jumpy. Upon entering the library, she took a moment of pause to enjoy the smell of dusty books and the sound of silence before starting to peruse the history section of the isles.

He continued moving down a row of bookshelves lined with tomes from throughout the ages. The knight seemingly spent a lot of time looking over them, reading the covers. "Places of Power, The Golden Wheel, Hmmmm." He raised a hand up to scratch the back of his helmet and looked around still, lingering on the many books. Some of the titles were way too tough to pronounce, for him, at least. A few weren't even in the common language. All this was history so it seemed. He took a step back and help up his dull, gilded book, which had a golden seal on the front, of which depicted a golden war elephant grabbing the sun. And then quickly put it back underneath his arms, looking about and noticing a group of scholars, all clad in blue robes. "Oh, hello! Can you-" The scholars ignored him. A group of monks passed by. "Hello there can you-" The white clad monks ignored him too. The knight let out a sigh, walking over near the fire and accidentally bumping into something. "Ah! My humblest apologies! Whoa..." The faceless knight bent down, looking to the small, beast like woman, looking her right in the face. "I've seen something like you in a dream once! You are... Something. Ah, perhaps my dream has brought us together?" The knight briefly looked past her at a silver haired woman sitting by the flickering flames. Looking at her from behind, the knight spoke aloud, "Ah yes, the elderly are wise! Maybe she can help!"

Instead of acknowledging his mistake, she looked in his direction as he spoke. "I wouldn't." Rota told him. She knew the lady sitting by the fire wasn't kind to nice strangers, and that's exactly what he was… A nice stranger. She sat upright and closed the book in her lap. "She's not very helpful, and trust me I'm not either. I'm simply visitor. All I can tell you is I've traveled a long way and the nearest inn was full." She stood up and went over to the nearest table where different wines were displayed. It had been funny that alcoholic beverages were displayed in a library setting. What, did they want you to get drunk reading about demonic beings and then lash out at the people around you? Did they realize that most who went to the library were unarmed? Rota played with the blade attached to the sheath on her arm. "What is it you are looking for?" She finally asked.

"I am Aithne." The humanoid girl with cat like features answered the knight in a broken, soft and slightly raspy voice as though cursed of plagued. There is a long pause between sentences meanwhile her ears displayed an energy her vocals didn't quite have. Seeing all of the monks and long robes caused her anxiety as she feared too many questions and then spots the silver haired woman by the fire eager to take her attention away from the scene unfolding. "Ah yes…. Unicorn poaching… Eherm. Unicorn poaching, texts on the matter. Controversies, resolutions… Locations." Having to speak up after the first line of speech was so soft the draft had carried it away. She seemed very troubled and distractible in the moment and slowly made her way over toward the fireplace. There was a wand that helped tie some of her fiery orange hair onto a cascading tail behind her head. This wand being her primary weapon but currently in the safest position.

"Ah, apologies my lady! Silver hair is often associated with the elderly or… Elves. Or… Other kinds of mystical beings. Moon elves! I have never seen nor met a moon elf but that might be another story! Or reality… I often travel to strange places and stay among strange beings." The eager knight plopped himself down beside the silver lady and looked to her, placing his own book in his lap. Oddly enough, the holes in his helmet, no matter the lighting or even the golden, flickering flames, the eyes in his helmet were simply black voids. "The nearest inn is full eh?" The knight let out a chortle. "There is nothing wrong with camping out beneath the stars outside the city!" He shifted where he sat looking to the many bottles of wine. "Oh jolly good! Is it on the house?" He cleared his throat. ''Aithne, Nicholas of Grigwald, follower of the Divine and an adherent of Pathfinder Lhikan!" He extended a large, bare hand to the little redheaded thing. The hand was the only visible part of his body, and it happened to be a strong human hand.

Rota hadn't come for conversation but knew the stranger had been nice. She sipped at the wine she had poured into her goblet and walked off towards one of the shelves. Then, a small copper colored lizard poked her head out just then. Once Rota realized what was above her she chuckled. Meesha the miniature wyvern landed right onto her shoulder in a very smooth manner. She had found Meesha and a few others miles south from Arinova abandoned, and even though sometimes she found there frustrating, she did love Meesha with everything.

"If ever you wish to see... Lunar elves..."

WHEEZE.

"The moon would be a good place to venture. Sir with many titles... What do you think of unicorns? She did not maintain eye contact long enough to get any answer but her ears did listen. Her eyes went to the new arrival to the library and then to the alcohol on the shelves. Hopefully no one would get drunk or start a fight with her. "I hear elves and unicorns are of the same ancestor. They both eat the same stuff and speak the same language." It was hard to tell if she was being disrespectful to elves or very smart cryptically speaking to an observation no one had the time to really make or care to consider.

The airheaded warrior did not answer, and was distracted by the little copper dragon, drawn to it instantly. "A dragon! Ha! They say that the rulers of Pryldahn are dragons and human form, and direct descendants of the Almighty Dragon Gods. That's..." The knight stood, placing a bare hand where his chin was, then snapped to the redheaded mage. "Rather small." This library really was something! "Elves and unicorns... The same race?" The faceless knight was bent down to match Aithne's level. "Unicorns are creatures of beauty, and the kind of beauty most men never see in their lifetimes. They say the old king of Grigwald rode one into battle... As did the Pathfinder Lhikan with his Sunblade! I have never heard of such a thing Lady Aithne." He stood back up and looked over to the wine, trying to contain his excitement at the thought of dragons and unicorns being common in this new foreign land. "Are you thirsty? I shall pour the wine for us."

Aithne shook her head in negation, red locks flowing everywhere. "I don't need any drinks. I have... alcohol on my person always.... Germs." She could only stare at the dragon.

"Oh." And the faceless knight bowed back to the little dragon, extended his right arm out and glancing to Aithne as he did. Then rose back up and reached his fingers out to pet Meesha, fingers brushing over her scales. "A truly rare and beautiful creature." He glanced down to the little cat like girl again. ''Have you ever seen such a creature, up close? Being close to the gods of Pryldahn almost...''

Meesha had sneezed and flames danced everywhere, causing the knight to recoil. The flame mage was apathetic, cocking her head to the side and frowning a bit. Quickly, Rota had watched it hit a few books in which she had dusted off so the fire didn't spread. "Meesha..." She sighed and picked up the books that had fallen and appropriately put them in their places. She then scooped up her small lizard who crawled onto her neck and nuzzled into her. She filled another goblet of wine and overheard the conversations between the guests in the area. Her return to the library frightened her but she wasn't sure if she was supposed to be frightened.

"Aye, I have. Very few roarbooms... Dragons. Even in this primitive state exist anymore. I remember the higher dragons like the God Queen Y'vonne... I remember them before they all disappeared. It's a sad story I don't want to go into. As you can see... I am cursed... You know what happened to the dragons.'" She was implying their use in rituals. After saying that Aithne l walks to a shelf pulling out a random book and she started to read it not caring much about the contents too much. It was druid's take on the story of the Trinity, St. Holly the mother of life and forgiveness, and the other gods of Laguna, almost like a satire.

"What do you mean? The stories say only the God Queen and her family survived the Cataclysm and that the higher dragons disappeared long ago?" Nicholas asked, looking down to Aithne as she walked away, grabbing a book off the shelf at random. The two women had walked off to read their own books. Scholarly women? Even better. And the flame mage was implied to have ancient knowledge. The faceless knight went back to his seat and picked up his dull brown book. "Do you know what these things are? It's a code of sorts, I know that much." The contents of the old book contained intricate golden pictures of the gods and miracles. along with text containing a code of odd bumps.

"I believe those bumps... Are intended for those without sight." The book still in hand looking into the fires which she knew very well personally "I need help with a corrupted Scaley Roar-boom... Soul of one and the ashes of a unicorn" The Scaley Roar-boom is what she called a certain dragon, one that should have died or disappeared long ago and now suffered a fate worse than death. She couldn't slay it on her own as it would just end in a literal ceasefire as neither of them could really be burned or get within melee range of one another. No one wanted to help her though as the journey there was no easy hike.

Rota, who paid little attention to their conversation, walked back over to where the wine was and sat down, crossed legged and removed her Arinovian knife from the sheath she had it in. She began twirling it between her fingers and every so often, one side of the blade would be clean enough to see her reflection. Her silver curls had been twisted into a bun, which was normal if she knew she'd be physical with another person, and her pale features looked tired and exhausted. She licked her chapped lips and took a deep breath, beginning to listen in on their conversation, without putting much input in.

"How do you figure?' He asked looking at the book again. "They could have at least made these bumps in the shapes of real letters instead of... These dots. Dominos! Are you sure these are not..." He scratched the top of his helmet, where a black and white feather stuck out the side of the top. "No this is not a book about the game of dominoes, silly He looked down to the little furry thing. "Help with the scaly roar booms? Whatever do you mean?" He turned to Rota and opened the braille tome again. "Do you know how to read this?

"An old mine housing... The forge guardian Frignitrigoth. This roarboom had been selectively bred to have two heads and breath a bloody red flame that not only..."

HUFF.

"Burns but inflicts a poison and causes a fever to those touched that survive the heat to cook them well after being licked by the fire. And somehow... It became a host for a colony of magical parasitic worms. But, deep within it is power I wish to collect if you... Would be so kind." Aithne explained. "And if you help put down this suffering creature, I will help you decipher your bumpy tome. And we'll be able to help ourselves to all of the loot down in the mine."

Rota's face scrunched into a weird look. She got up and got closer but not too close. "I've yet to know anything about this... Stuff." She bit the inside of her cheek nervously and slid her knife back into the sheath. "A long time ago, my great grandmother who was a witch in her own right, had books and books on knowledge of witchcraft.... That is if that's what this is." She thought.

"In this odd bump code for the blind? I've not heard of... I suppose it's not exactly common." He said, his hands trailing over the said bumps inside the book, trying to comprehend the writing. The faceless knight turned and looked to Aithne. "Are you asking for my help in a jolly adventure?" Hearing of such a fate, being cooked alive and licked by fire... It sounded exciting. Though, a part of him felt guilty for helping, as he knew that was blasphemous to kill a dragon. Only on the continent of Pryldahn, which he was not from. And right now the prospect on an epic quest really overtook his eager mind. As well as loot. Sweet, sweet loot. Which would keep financing his trip around the world. "If you wish to engage with me, then I accept!'

"Thank you. Your reward will be great... This is indeed witchcraft and your grandmother was no doubt a great witch but... "was" is not... "is" which means that any texts lack the ambitious depths I am seeking because somewhere along the line the... Pursuit of power had come to an end and thus the books have their limits. We are past any book in academia and those I seek aren't allowed to be written, their authors killed at the block and words devoured by flame. These burned books... I have found... A way to unburn and call back to my hand that which has been claimed by entropy but it takes time and... Lots of energy." The redheaded mage has extracted an unholy level of forbidden fire magic by communing with the spirits of the dead and condemned in order to describe their research which had been burned after the contributing spirits resulting execution. It was a type of necromancy that would no doubt see her burned or beheaded.

Rota narrowed her eyes at the girl and once again, removed her knife, playing with it. She certainly wouldn't seek solitude for a kitty fight. Her grandmother wasn't only a witch; she was one of the most powerful battlemage's that Arinova had ever experienced. Meesha hopped down onto her lap and curled up. She used her other hand to pet her creature and soothe it to sleep. Opting to stay in the library while the two set out just like that on a quest to kill a parasite ridden dragon.

"The greatest reward of all! Glory, fuel for my heroics and the favor of my goddess! Sna ha ha!" He pounded his chest. Nicholas didn't understand a word the little creature told him, aside from the part about it taking a lot of time and energy. Most importantly... "Just as any jolly great adventure does! Yes! Engaging in jolly team up to reap the rewards! Where would we be off to?"

''Follow me outside, Sir Knight.''

CHAPTER FOUR: THE DRAGON'S HEAD

The Dragon's Head Tavern and Inn, Vorland, 1435 ATC

It was the dead of night when Venser and Y'vonne appeared out of a puff of thick red smoke in the middle of the rustic, wood and stone tavern. "And this is it! Home sweet home." He said letting go of her hand, taking a few steps forward before collapsing.

"Ahh...! I think I might have broken something..." He rolled onto his back on in the middle of the floor and looked to the noble woman standing before him. "Hey, are you-" He paused and winced, wriggling slightly. "Are you fine? Most people usually blow chunks and fall down after teleporting for the first time."

And, so here they were. Y'vonne kept her eyes squeezed shut, her nose and brows crinkling. For a moment, she stood there. Unmoving until she heard a thud and opened her eyes to see the man that brought her here rolled onto his back. He didn't look so good. And, then the nausea hit her. Like a wave crashing down on a shore. She swayed a bit the veil the fell behind her back swayed gently with the movement. No, she was stronger than this. The God Queen shook her head, her strong will trying to focus in on the injured man before her. "I am fine." She said with such tranquility that surprised even herself. Soon, she was by the man's side, settled down on her knees and looking down upon. "But you, I'm afraid, are not." Pointing out the obvious, she knew that. But, this man needed medical attention. "Right away..." She finished her thought out loud. "Is there anyone here a healer?" She asked the man, he was obviously well acquainted with this place, he would know.

"Roselie is... But she's on her honeymoon... And I've had worse than being thrown into a wall. Far worse." Venser's usual outfit was merely for show. The only real protective parts were just the codpiece, knee pads, and the single shoulder pad. A wonder why a man would walk around in such a ridiculous outfit. And fight in it, or tend a bar in it. "I'll be fline, just a night of laying on my back and some cider. Why don't you go have a seat at the bar? And I'll figure out a way of getting over there without much pain involved."

The crimson haired woman smirked. Honeymoon? That didn't help at us all. And did he just say fline, rather than fine? Y'vonne sighed heavily. "How about I help you to a bed?" She woman then stood, the simple movement seeming unnaturally elegant and quiet. "Come," She held out a hand, though was prepared take his full weight in assisting him to where ever he's lead her to go. "you've helped me now I shall help you." She curled three of her fingers back and forth, encouraging him to move though she knew how painful it would be. "Can't have you lay on this hard, uncomfortable floor now can we?"

Venser raised a brow and chuckled lightly, looking to her. "An obnoxiously thin small fry like yourself? We'll teleport. I've teleported in there so many times I've lost count." He shifted slightly and raised his right hand, offering it out to her.

Smallfry? She was a few inches taller than him. Her eyes squinted at the man beneath her, somewhat offended by what he thought she way. Though, it wasn't his fault. In this more mortal form, at least. So, she did not bother to correct him. There was no reason for him to know what she really was just yet. "You know how to teleport?" Y'vonne hesitated and glared evilly at his hand, as if it was the root of all evil. She'd rather walk, honestly. But, eventually she settled her hand in his as her body stiffened, mentally and physically preparing for the uneasy feeling she might feel again. ''Only about the hardest spell to learn… If you're capable of learning magic.''

"Don't want to? You get used to it after a while." He sighed and rose to his feet, groaning slightly and ignorant of how his comment slightly offended her. "Follow me then." He said using a few tables for support as he walked down the hall. "We'll have to get you a room of your own to stay the night in."

She reached out to him as he made to stand, unsure of where to help, unsure of how to help. She felt frustrated with this feeling. "Let me help you, Venser." She made to stand close next to him. "I'm… Stronger than I look." Stay the night? Her family would worry about her safety, but they knew she could take care of herself if necessary. It was late after all. "Alright," She agreed with a nod. "Lean some of your weight on me." It wasn't a suggestion but a command, like she was use to giving orders. Looking around the empty, rustic tavern she blinked her electric blue eyes. "What about the patrons who wake up and want something in the night? Or people who come in this late?"

"Eh. The shadow tendrils will get to them. I'm usually the captain runnin' dis ship but they do it when me or any other employees aren't around." The handsome bearded bartender explained leaning her weight onto her just a bit. As they walked down the hall, Venser stopped at the sixth door on the right. "And here's my room." He gestured to the one on the right of it. "Soarin and Lucinda sleep in there when they stay with me." He smiled slightly and pushed the door to his room open. Venser's room was fairly big. A queen sized bed lay by the windows, and it was covered in turquoise silk sheets and he had about a dozen pillows all with furry gold throwovers. Off to the left was a wardrobe with a few dresses hanging out, some spilt onto the floor as well as a white theater comedy mask. To the right of the bed was a desk with a bag of silver in it, a mirror, and a few pieces of jewelry and some small boxes. Right beside it was various papers and pieces of art. Above Venser's bed was a multicolored painting of a woman's vagina, and below that his signature double bladed sword, the Dual Personality.

She helped him make his way down the hall, stopping when he stopped. "Soarin and Lucinda..." Von repeated to no one in particular.

"Are they your children?" She asked, starring at the room that lingered with emptiness. As he mentioned his room, she guided him to it, then once inside, a B-line for his bed, not even bothering with taking in the details of his room. She took his frame and settled him the soft cushions of his bed gently, making sure not to exhaust his body in any way. She looked him over, checking to make sure she didn't cause any further damage before running a hand over her dress, brushing out any wrinkles or smudges she have acquired on their little adventure in the dungeon. "Well, I do hope you feel better." She said, her cobalt eyes staring down at one of her hands, checking her fingernails for dirt. Finding no smudges to fix, she lifted her gaze, flicked a handful of her crimson hair over one shoulder before now taking in her surroundings. Her electric blue eyes scanned the walls and simple furniture and, her nose upturning at the messy sight of clothes dangling from a wardrobe in a messy manner.

Tsk tsk. Briefly, she held the smiling mask in one hand. Though, the various papers with drawings and paintings caught her attention. "Oh, " She started and strode over to them for a better inspection, setting the comedy theater mask down on his desk.

"You paint?" At the time her eyes caught the artwork of the inappropriate painting of a female's genitalia. Her mouth then dropped to a frown. How... Lovely.

"Yeah. They both turn three in a couple of months." Venser said plopping down into his bed, making himself comfortable as he rolled over onto his back, watching Y'vonne inspect his room. "On occasion. Haven't had much will to do it lately... With various plotting, going out, and taking care of the twins. Oh! And work, of course, I take my job very seriously here. When I am here." He cracked his neck side to side and rested his head on his pillow, closing his eyes and going still. "The shadow tendrils can hook you up with a room here. Unless you'd rather travel at night. Don't know how far away your kingdom is away from here. Or if it's even on the same plane. My homeland isn't, nor are the other isles."

Y'vonne turned now, her dress ruffling with the movement. "Twins are a handful..." She smirked at this. "For I am also a twin." She brought a small hand up to her mouth and chuckled. "Thank you, I think I will take advantage of this tavern's hospitality. And you know Pryldahn is only north of Vorland right? Just over the bordor." She strode over to the right side of his, her head inclining back at him. "Perhaps, do you need anything before I take my leave of you?" The sound of sirens faintly hummed in the background but she ignored it, thinking she was just hearing things.

"Errr, yeah right. Really? You must tell me about your family tomorrow, and Pryldahn... I suppose I need reminding and a more detailed history from one of the royals themselves." Venser said with a smile. He shook his head and said, "No. That I can think of. So I guess this is goodnight."

She blinked at the man and then nodded. "Yes. The land of Pryldahn. If you wish." She then strode out of the room but stopped at the near the door. She placed a hand on the frame and turned back at him. "Goodnight Venser." The woman bowed, and then quietly left his room as her light footsteps carried her down the hallway.

The shadow tendrils heard all in the tavern. Behind the bar, the pool of shadows behind the bar manifested themselves into a silhouette version of Venser. Complete with the battleskirt, suit, shoulder pad, cape, and even his fedora like hat. It held a small, silver key out to Y'vonne. "Left hall, second door on the left." It said mimicking the serpent eyed bartender's voice, albeit with an echo like twang to its voice.

Y'vonne De Seraphim all but jumped as the shadowy tendrils formed into the man she was just speaking to, her heart jumping a bit once she finally made it back into the main area where everyone gathered. She placed a hand over her chest, releasing a deep sigh before taking the key that it offered. "Th-thank you." She said and then bowed. She didn't know how to interact with such a thing, she's never come across anything like it. So, she just settled for scooting aside, trying her best to blend in with the other late night patrons. Though, it was hard. With her noble attire and striking colored hair. Y'vonne looked misplaced, like someone plucked her from a doll house and settled her in this tavern. She sighed, tired now that the unfortunate events of the day now caught up with her. She needed time to think over her thoughts, perhaps write down some of her findings. So, with her mind made up, she found an empty table and lowered herself onto a chair in a very lady-like manner. Back straight and face stoic, she pulled out some rolled up paper and a feathered pen from a deep pocket that she kept under one of the many layers of her skirt and began to scribble.

The next day...

The woman sat, cleaning no doubt. Crimson hair, styled up and out of her face. A change of clothing that didn't expose much of her title as a diplomatic figure, but was still overly decorated and eccentric. Much like how she was. The sun fresh in the shy, the morning still chilly with the night's grasp. Today would be a good day for her to start traveling back to her kingdom, she thought. She had enough of going on adventures and venturing out from her safe castle, out from under the protection of her father. She's grown accustomed to it, and a bit spoiled by it. She missed her family, her twin sister even, though the woman was practically her opposite and drove her mad sometimes. With a cloth she found behind the bar in hand, she ceased wiping one of the tavern's tables, her actions slowing before coming to a complete stop. The tavern was empty when she woke, and still remains so, which caused the noble woman to grow bored and anxious. Y'vonne would notice some sections of the tavern needed cleaning, and though the odd shadowy vectors did the best they could to keep the place tidy, she battled with the dark mass into letting her help clean. She couldn't just sit here and do nothing. Finally, they had given in to her whining and pushing before eventually handing over a rag, which she has been using efficiently since. The regal redhead stood and then straightened her back from her hunched over position sighing once again before one of the dark vectors slithered into her range of sight and made a grab for the dirty rag she held in her hand to only be replaced by another wet, clean one. The woman chuckled and thanked the vector, smiling at it before gliding over to another table to clean.

Suddenly, while the noble woman cleaned the tables inside the tavern, a variety of exotic and sweet aromas entered the room. Something was cooking downstairs, and it smelt good. A few minutes later Venser appeared at the top of the stairs wearing his usual outfit. Red rubber suit with rubber nipples and an oversized codpiece. "Morning." Venser said holding a silver platter with a lid, looking to the woman work. "Ya know the shadow tendrils can do that, Von." He set the platter down on the table she currently worked at. "Hungry?"

She stopped and eyed the man that she has known for a few days now. "Good morning." She replied. The silver platter caught her eye's attention before she returned them to her working hands. "I know..." She started and then stopped her administrations. "But, I had to do something." Honestly, the woman hadn't eaten for days. Twelve to be exact. But her kind could go without food longer than most. Doesn't mean she didn't get hungry every now and then. "Quite." She retorted. "Do you always prepare food in the morning?"

"For breakfast, yeah. I knew you were getting up, so I decided to make some extra. And sometimes I starve myself for some days so I can just eat an entire feast all by myself later." He said grabbing the lid and lifting it aside. On the platter were a few pieces of fried catfish, with some salt, paprika, and pepper added to it for taste. Along with a few hash browns and some freshly cooked bread. "Did you enjoy the room?" He asked picking up a bottle of hot sauce and dumping some of it on the fried catfish, then he looked up to her and blinked his unnatural, snake like eyes.

"That's... Interesting." Starving oneself? Huh, she's never heard of someone doing that before. She looked at the food and smiled, the sight of the pepper catching her attention but she didn't move to reach for it. Not yet anyway. Y'vonne would have to wash her hands first. "The room was well enough." She smiled at the man, though the smile did not reach her eyes. In front of her, she began to neatly fold the rag she was cleaning with into a perfect square.

"I must...thank you again for the other day. Your efforts in saving that girl was admirable." Von folded her hands in her lap in a proper manner.

"This all looks delicious." She added in a side note.

"Pantian cuisine, the best. Sometimes I think it trumps the food from Kupidnos." Venser said taking a bite of fried catfish, moaning slightly as he chewed it. Sitting down and reclining lazily, opposite of Von's regal manner. He nodded his head and looked to her. "Thank you. Remind me again why you were there?"

"A-Ahh..." The woman breathed. "My father had urged me into going." The obnoxiously thin redhead shivered a bit, turning her head to the side at the memory of the place. "Last time I venture out on one of his errands you can be sure of that." With that said, the woman stood, bringing the folded rag to a waiting tendril before finding a place to wash her hands. After a few moments, she came back to the main area and sat back down where she was before, her movements quiet and gentle. "Though, unlike you, I do not think I would enjoy the company of a companion there." The woman smiled. She smiled. She was trying to jest, show some humor. Little amount of humor that it was, she was trying.

"You woulda think he'd send two body guards along with you." Venser replied with a small chuckle, a bit of hot sauce dribbling down his chin as he ate. "Or... I don't know if you can use magic or not." He shrugged and picked up another piece of fried catfish. "I used to be a merc, still am at times when I wanna go out and have myself an adventure. Not so much anymore. Here and there. Like last night."

"When I was young I was in the Pantian Legion as another mere grunt. But they kicked me out for mouthing off one too many times and ignoring orders. And I was just a recruit... While I did learn several valuable things, it just wasn't for me. Namely, not being able to have a mind of my own. But... Ya know. Soldiers can't I suppose." His mind flashed back several years back for a few fleeting moments, before he dismissed it. That was another life.

The God Queen chuckled at his statement as she reached a slender arm over to the silver plate and picked up the pepper. "One would think so. Perhaps if I was younger." The woman shrugged her shoulders before she took a small bite into the pepper, listening to his words. "It would appear you've had an interesting life, sir." She wanted to avoid the comment made about the possibility of her able to use magic or not. She took another bite and chewed. "Surely someone with battle knowledge as yours would not settle for being a jester?" Her tone was like and questioning. She did not want to offend him in anyway.

"Ehh... I prefer entertainment. I always wanted to do that in my youth. Always had a thing for the theater." He shrugged. "My magic and skill makes me good for merc work, and the pay is good. I don't do it so much because I don't want my kids to worry about me." He looked over to the shadow tendrils. "Cider! And..." He turned to look at Von. "What do you want to drink? Anything you want."

''O-oh..." She pushed some of her bangs behind a pointed ear. "Glass of water, please." She looked over at the man. "I bet you have stories." She smiled. "You seem like a man who cares deeply for his children. What happened to their mother?"

Venser nodded in affirmation as two snaky, shadowy hands slithered over them setting down a bottle of cider in front of Venser, and a glass of cool spring water in front of his new regal friend. "Lots. That's why I was also the royal storyteller. Kari... She's still around. We just live in different places. Since she's the guardian of her village and I have a tavern to look after most days. Soarin and Lucinda are bastards too. We..." He wasn't sure if he should say it or not, but he was honest.

The bearded man shrugged. "Had em out of wedlock. No. I don't like to call them that. Fuck my cock." Not like it mattered, as taking care of his children had really started to bring the mad man around and help him on his journey of redemption. He loved them, along with their mother, as well as the other women he met and bedded at the tavern and all the other bastards Ven had out there.

She said a polite thank you to the tendril that get her water down, still quietly listening to the man speak, nodding every now and then. "She sounds like a very busy woman." Von quirked an eyebrow, curious at the man's hesitation. "Do you wish to marry her?" Von was nosy indeed. For she highly enjoyed getting to know people better.

The bearded man shook his head. "Naw. Maybe. There's a lot of odd things said about me around the village. The age difference, really. Besides, I love being a bachelor here."

Von smiled at this. "Of course. Where I come from, our people partake in polygamy, as there is a disproportionate female-to-male ratio. It's even as far as honorable, marrying multiple women and taking good care of them. A married bachelor, is common, quite." The woman then took a sip of her drink before settling it back down. "At least the children have a mother." She said. "My siblings and I grew up without one." She eyed the man a moment and then said, "My father, the God Emperor Cervial ate her."

Venser nearly choked on his sparkling green cider and looked to her. "Huh?"

Von brought a hand up to her mouth, chuckling, her small shoulders bouncing up and down slightly. "I only jest."

"That your father ate your mother?" He was skeptical whether or not she was serious. "He sounds rather demented... And I thought I was demented! Oh the stories I could tell you... All of them true!" The man in the strange red outfit then mumbled a bunch of incoherent nonsense under his breath. Such as "stabbed with pitchfork" and "relation with horse." Along with "fire" and more interestingly, "coven of vindictive witches and a dead man with a hot sword."

"Oh, you have no idea." She laughed a little louder this time, but then tried to cover it with a cough. "Though he can be punitive, he is a very good man. Especially to his children. As you are with yours." Von then smiled at Venser and reached for a hash brown, figuring they have had enough time to properly cool down now.

"So, you gonna tell me about your kingdom, the royal family."

"There is my father... Cerviel De Seraphim. A great man with terrible power and then my twin sister and I..." The God Queen cleared her throat a few times. "God Emperor Cervial is away most of the time up above, and my sister chooses to assume a form much like mine and travel the world. Leaving me to rule my country in their places most of the time. Perhaps I can show you? It's north of here, far north along the coast, but I can tell you, Pryldahn is truly an amazing land."

"The land of dragons..."

CHAPTER FIVE: SHAE'LYNN

The Dragon's Head Tavern and Inn, Vorland, 1435 ATC

"So, can you carry all of this for now?" God Queen Y'vonne asked handing her new friend Venser a simple burlap bag as they stood outside in the field behind the tavern. She was standing tall and erect, with practiced posture and etiquette, striking red hair was settled in a neat bread and dangled over her golden shoulders. Her naked body was tall, too thin, a little over six feet and had patches of shiny golden scales on her arms, legs, and shoulders. "Venser? You're speechless." Her lips were perfectly shaped, with a perfect arch, with a perfectly light and natural lipstick that soon curled into an amused smile.

The bearded man stared at the nude queen in front of him, completely enamored at her naked body. He licked his lips and finally reached out, taking the bag containing her clothes and jewelry. "Let's see it then." Sip. It was barely past noon and he had already been drinking.

Y'vonne's head dipped low causing crimson locks to fall in her face and sway lightly in the cool breeze that felt good against her unnaturally hot skin. Her other arm draped over clutched at her side. Her hand turned claw like as her shiny silver scales began to spread all over her body now, armoring her. Nails scratching at her sensitive skin from underneath as she began to grow several feet in size, causing Venser to take a few steps back and look up at her during all of this.

A haggled breath fell from her lips, her head shooting up as the crimson haired woman inhaled a deep breath, her slitted electric blue eyes wide as her ribs expanded. Her body was stiff like a statue before but now it appeared to have gain a sense of mobility, a pair of great leathery wings emerged from her body as she completed her transformation into a massive gold, blue, and silver dragon.

"Ready to get going, Venser?" She asked beckoning the man to climb atop her back, and the man replied with a quick nod and eagerly climbed atop her back, making sure to grip the spines on her back tight along with the burlap bag containing her clothes as they took to the sky above.

The sky was a soft golden with grey puffs of clouds slowly passing overhead. The land was a bright green, the color scheme almost colliding with the black magnificent castle that sat upon the tallest of the mountains and capital city by the sea that surrounded it.

The two flew over a mystical land filled with many secrets and challenges to be overcome. Pryldahn. Which lay in a mountainous region of the planet known to most as Laguna on the continent of Posiil. Pryldahn was located in the coastal mountainous regions of Posiil, and is characterized by its high peaks, vast forests, and low valleys. At the center hundreds of feet above their subject was Y'vonne's home, Castle De Seraphim. An impressive, towering structure above the capital decorated with ancient, draconic imagery and radiated godly beauty and wonder.

"Whoo! What a ride!" The bearded man exclaimed sliding off her back when they touched down in the wide open courtyard, and the God Queen began to shrink in size and revert back to a more humanoid form.

Venser appeared alongside her and was fazed, and felt very dizzy. He wobbled and stumbled as he walked forward, tripping over his own feet. He let out a cheerful laugh before hitting his head hard on the stone steps, spilling the bottle of cider he still held in his free hand and knocking him out cold.

"Oh Trinity." The woman had the unconscious man moved to a resting chamber in the castle by servants as she stood to the side, watching over the proceedings carefully. It was nice to finally be home with her family. Once Venser was well taken care of and settled into a bed Y'vonne spoke the head caretaker, asking for his wellbeing and if there was any long lasting damage. He did hit his head pretty hard on the stone ground when he slid off her back and stumbled. Perhaps he had been smoking one of his cannabis cigars earlier before they took off as well. "Nothing to worry about dearie, it wasn't anything too substantial." Von let out a sigh of relief and nodded, glad in knowing that her new strange friend was not badly injured.

"Thank you, ma'dam." The courtly woman did a bow, and the servant bowed back. "Trinity be praised." And immediately thought of her father. He would want to hear about this new arrival. He had been ascended as of late, and she was quick to rush to the chapel to converse with him via his shrine.

Sometime later Venser that day was awake with a bandaged wrapped around his head. He walked down the halls, running his gloved hands along the stone walls. "Well hello beautiful..." He said popping his chest out, standing against the wall as a good looking, black haired elvish slave girl passed him by. She gave him an odd look before continuing on her day. He shrugged and moved down the hall. "Oh hi Y'vonne!" He chirped cheerfully seeing her.

Yvonne turned once she heard her name called and turned. She blinked wide, seeing Venser up and about. "O-Oh, Venser. You are awake already." She offered the man a smile, her eyes roaming over his bandaged head with an apologetic smile. "I trust you are feeling well?"

"Yeah. Fantastic. Eeeeeyuppper doodles I've got a high endurance, even with all the blows to the ol' cranium over the years! Ya know you got some really good looking servant girls around here." He looked about and seemed somewhat happy, peppy, and energetic after his long rest. Venser reached up and scratched his head, muttering to himself of how itchy the bandage was. Along with lamenting the loss of his hat. The red wide brimmed one the unnamed centaur spider woman had taken from him. "So, 'How about a proper tour of this place?"

The crimson haired woman rolled her cobalt blue eyes at the man's words, her mouth turned into a frown. "I am pleased to see you well." He was well alright. He seemed quite alert and active. "Of course. Follow me." With that said, Y'vonne turned, her noble dress dragging behind her slightly as she strode down the hallway she walked, her arms folded in front of her as she walked in what one could all but call a throne room. At the end of it, four regal thrones rose like a spire above all else, truly the highest point in all the land as they were symbols of authority "One of our main halls," Y'vonne said, pausing a bit so the man could take his fill. "My family and I often converse here, when we can." The God Queen said, sitting atop one of the thrones.

Then, another red head, her hair was pulled up into a tight ponytail which then was brought into a braid, the sides and back of her head shaved. With each step, the sound of her intricate blue and gold scalemail jingled against her frame. Her steps where a tad louder and slower than the other red head, for she carried much more weight around with her. A sword on her hip, heavy boots strapped to her legs as a light flapping noise from her miniature wyvern, Nessie, could be heard. He chittered to her softly in her ear that had quite a few piercings in it, a gauge in her earlobe. Her blue eyes where ahead of her, scanning the hallways as she could hear the presents of her other always busy other half. Before Y'vonne was even in her sight, she moved in front of the two. As she turned the corner, Shae'lynn bowed her head politely to her, "Sister." She said to her, looking to Venser after her. Nessie chittering in Shae'lynn's ear again, "Yes yes, I know, Ness." Her hand went from the playful greeting dropping to the sword on her hip. "Who are you?"

"Shae..." Von began but trailed off. She knew her sister didn't know the man who was going to move into their father's castle, and that this was the first time she's seen him. Knowing her sister, she would reach for her sword, and then ask questions later. And, of course, she was right. When she turned her eyes back to her sister, she noticed Shay's hand was already on her sword. "Wait, he is not a threat." Von walked over to her and gently placed her hand over her sister's. They now stood next to each other, and looked exactly alike. They were twins after all. But, they were still so different, in their individual ways of movement, taste, and even the way they spoke.

He moved back a bit seeing her raise his sword him, but lower it to her hip. The man was in his early thirties, with fair skin, a messy beard, and unnatural emerald serpent like eyes. "Ah! Your sister!" He smiled, well, then again he was always smiled and walked over to Shae'lynn extending his right, gloved hand to her.

Shae'lynn watched him carefully as he extended his hand to her, her draconian hues narrowed as he spoke to Y'vonne with friendliness. "Mmph." She resheathed her sword and stood there, beside her sister, staring at him for a little before extending her hand to him, "Shae'lynn De Seraphim. The Psychic Dragon Twin." Nessie chirped on her shoulder, lifting himself off for a moment to chortle and bark at the male before returning to Shae's shoulder, glaring at him. And as a demonstration, she placed two fingers on the side of her head and her sword came unsheathed, levitating above her and spinning in a quick circle, then back and forth, all before sheathing itself.

Von stood straight and smiled a bit, glad that this little exchange didn't break out into a bloody warm. "It is quite alright Venser." Her eyes fell between the two people in front of her. "Yes, indeed this is my LOVELY twin sister." The word lovely was over dramatized, almost like she didn't mean it. "Shae, darling, this is Sir Venser, the new jester of the court. He and I met in... Unfortunate standards but, it has all turned out for the better He did save me from a terrible creature. A tentacle demon." She made a scoffing sound that crinkled her nose. "Disgusting creature."

Venser took her hand and shook it quickly and vigorously like a child. "Shae'lynn! Lovely name, and I'm Venser. Or VenVen. Or Venny. Or My Little Vensie. Whichever you may prefer." He let go of her hand and looked to the small pet like dragon sitting on her shoulder. "Cute." He said reaching his hand out slowly to pet it. He retracted it though and saluted Shae'lynn when Y'vonne mentioned that he was the new jester. "Yeah. The tentacle demon through me right through a wall. But," He paused and gestured to her. "Saved the damsel in distress."

The man in the strange red outfit then disappeared in a poof of thick crimson smoke, the scent of freshly cut roses and wine lingered in the air for a moment before he reappeared in the middle of the throne room. "I gave it some of this!" His left hand shot into the air and a web of supernatural green lightning erupted from his fingertips. Before he teleported again and appeared in midair, kicking it wildly. "And some Kicks McGee!" He rolled on the floor in front of him. "Then, I summoned rats to distract him before I stunned him with the Heart Punch! Yeah I really did serve him a spoonful of whoopass and Von can speak as a fist hand witness!"

Not a trickle of amusement would pass Shae'lynn's eyes as the two spoke of the unfortunate event. "Hm... This man is a Sir?" Was her only response as he pulled himself into a salute. Inwardly cringing at that gesture and the way he spoke. "Very well then." She looked to her younger sister before she turned away slightly, "I just came to do my monthly patrol, before I wander off again. You look great sis, keep up whatever it is you do." And with that, she turned from her sister, All the while, Nessie sat perched on her shoulder, staring at the male that called himself "Venser". How old was he? He was an adult with a beard clearly. Was he insane? Or was it just smacking his head on the pavement?

The God Queen laughed half heartily at the comment her sister gave her about looking well. Truth is, she did not feel well. Haven't slept for weeks, her skin always warm to the touch with a fever, her body aching. With that though, Von coughed a single cough and sniffled before sighing tiredly. "Lies, dear sister. Have a good patrol." Always hard working, that one. She honestly had nothing to say, for she was the same way. Though, her sister preferred to travel, fight. Anything combat related.

Venser chuckled, looking back at Y'vonne before looking over to Shaelynn as she walked away. "When you're done with your patrol, we must all have a drink together. I'll whip us all up my signature drink, Pink Footed Booby! I happen to be a tavern keeper along with mercenary and nowwww your jester!" He did an improvised jig on the spot, flailing his arms while he did. "Spaw! Pew pew! I also play guitar!"

Shae'lynn stopped dead in her tracks when he called out, turning to glance at the jester. She didn't say anything, just stared coldly at him. Nessie perched silently, gave him the same blank stare before she continued on down the hallway A small smile sat against her lips, he was an interesting one.

Venser's smile faltered a bit staring back at her as she got farther and farther away. He craned his head to Y'vonne and said. "Not the actual name... I just like saying booby. Actually, that should be official name. It's quite interesting."

Von's eye gave an unnatural twitch once he called out and she had to physically restrain herself from facepalming. Oh, her sister must think lowly of her at this moment. "I am sure you do."

The bearded man shrugged and threw his shoulders back, then threw his side cape over his back and poofed over to a nearby balcony, looking over it at Capital De Seraphim below, and then to the ocean. Where three massive statues of the Trinity themselves stood vigilant in the harbor. "Still haven't gotten a proper tour. But I know where my room is, I know where to find you. And if I am going to be staying in the castle part time..."

"Then I need to get to know the land better. The city. Oh yes I am going down there to the city..."

"Will you need an escort around our capital, Venser?" The God Queen asked, slightly concerned about the man making a fool of himself in public. Especially the way he was dressed. What even was that material of his outfit?

"An escort? Ha! I am an escort! Another one of my many occupations!" And with that he jumped from the castle that towered a hundred feet off the ground, much to the shock of everyone, Y'vonne, guards, slaves, that had just witnessed the scene.

"... That was unexpected." This Venser Karkaldwin was truly an interesting one.

CHAPTER SIX: THE LAKE OF INFERNAL WORMS

1445 ATC, Nillheim Forest

Aithne left the library and not even a few moments with the eager knight there were three mercenaries looking for her. The sun beats down on the steps of the grand library and thankfully the town in which this is all staged was mostly vacant and those attending were all in the library fixed on what it is they were there to do. They had plate armor on that shone with ornate etchings and what appeared to Pryldahnian repeating crossbows. Their horses looked to be the best of the best and the leader of the groups who had a red feather in his helmet rode a black steed. "Halt! Aithne the Wanderer... The game is over. Stand down, overturn your casting aegis and come along. If you come now it'll be a clean beheading and not the gallows. More dignity at the guillotine."

"Are my crimes that vast?... Am I truly that wicked?... Then..." She replied, before handing her new companion a slip of paper from her clothes with the name of the location on it. She nods and approaches the group.

"I request execution by fire. It's a religious rite... Family custom." The hired but noble contractors nod in understanding. "If so then there should be no problem. But where we are taking you it might be outlawed by the time you get sentenced... Sorry it had to be this way." She overturned her wand and boards the wagon leaving the knight with the instructions to meet her at the volcanic mine.

And there they were, off on a grand adventure! Nicholas tucked his divine braille tome underneath his arm as the two walked out of the front, mildly disappointed that the assassin would not join then in their journey. After all, it was the more the merrier! Quickly after stepping out they were confronted by three glorious knights with odd weapons. And then... It happened all so fast! The faceless knight took the note and watched as the wagon set off, confused. "Hey, wait!" It was no use as he watched it disappear into a crowd of other wagons and many people walking about the village.

"Come Grace, come along." Nicholas of Grigwald mounted his black and white horse, dropping the divine tome into the saddlebags and opening the note as he sat atop Grace. It was a very long journey to a volcanic mine. It'd take a day and a half. Aithne promised however to be there though. Perhaps she would reason with them? Or more likely she already had an escape plan before they were confronted.

Grace nickered and kicked at the cobblestone. "There there..." Such a short journey for something of this description... Yes. He had had of something this close, along the coast. Sulfur mining was it... Or was it some other place? He shrugged, studying the map provided on it. "Let's go!" He whipped the rains and the horse of black and white took off, weaving through the crowed the faceless knight threw both arms up above his head, darting through the exit gate much to the confusion of the city watch. "I'm going on an adventureeeeeeeeeeeeeeeeeee!" Nicholas of Grigwald had stepped out over the threshold of the city of Arinova, and out into the wilds of the wide open world.

When he reached the wilds it was getting dark. The sky was orange and it was about time to set up camp but the day had been a little too peaceful. No one had ever taken this route to the mine it was deemed not safe for people coming back from the woods insane or not at all. They simply called it Nillheim forest. It seemed that not even animals lived here despite the beauty of the verdant forest and lush vegetation. There are many other horror stories that come out of this location and on most maps its marked black. Aithne had seen many things but she had no label for it. A lot of the trees around are nice and leafy but there are an abundance of branches lying about. Many are razor sharp and nearby was a pond surrounded by collapsed trees covered in moss. Save for a bit of algae, as the fading god rays of the setting sun shine through the green tree tops the bottom of this pond can be seen however there is an ominous antithesis to its captivating beauty that stood like a barrier keeping anyone to behold its magical facade from getting too close but if an adventurer so chose to they could defy their natural inclinations and bring themselves to get closer. Regardless it was a source of water.

The occasional hare dashed by... One he had seen since he entered. It was brown with a tan spot on its flank... Was it stalking him?

"Oh no, oh dear lords." The faceless knight chuckled as he rode along and onto a lesser traveled route without much thing. Jolly old Nicholas, always doing things on a whim! He recalled the assassin told him that all of the inns in that part of the city were all full up, and then he made mention that camping outside the city wasn't a bad thing. And here he was... Not exactly camping, but wandering into an odd part of the ancient forest.

"Hello little bunny! Hello!" He called out gleefully to the little forest hares he passed by, letting out a sigh and taking in the scent of the fresh air, eventually riding towards a lake. The sun was going out, and he needed to find shelter. Perhaps there was a cave near the lake? Grace stopped at the edge, and the knight took a look around.

Once at the pond they see an ancient frame of what looked to be a shrine or summoning altar covered in vegetation. There is a cave under this water's surface but the water is too pure to be... "Right" There is a toppled sign warning not to even touch the water. On the map it appears as the only water source for a very long time. They can see remnants of another bonfire right nearby. Well a clearing but the ashes are old. Nicholas didn't need binoculars to see decomposing corpses almost skeletal lying there in a circle and when the breeze comes from that direction the stench of rot becomes apparent.

"Hm. Good thing I brought drinking water. Knight's motto... Always be prepared!" He had hoped for a cave to make camp in, but outside in the open would do. He hoped it wouldn't rain. He took the reins of his horse and led her over to the remnants of the bonfire, wincing as he noticed all of the corpses.

"Oh dear lords..." Nicholas dug into his saddlebags and removed two leather gloves, starting to move the corpses over to the bonfire where he would burn the bodies. For he did not have time to give the bodies a proper burial, though, this was as equally respectful. Even if there was no funeral pyre.

As he moves the bodies he can see a trail of pink slugs that come out of their nose. They looked to be living brain matter. Some of the bodies even involuntarily thrash at him as he picks them up. These brain slugs endlessly come out of the nose, ears and eyes of the victims and all crawl in the same direction... Back to the water of that pond. The bodies burn on the pyre for a while but the ashes and smog started misbehaving. Soon a black vortex formed in the center of the clearing and as it spins faster and faster, red lightning forms when a red flaming core takes the form of a human heart. Forming around this is a dense shell of ash that forms the effigy of a person.

It was an Aithne statue.

The shell of this statue crumbles off like a crust revealing the now dirty ash covered fire witch with thankfully all of her clothing and all of her skin thanks to the corpses burned. She started dusting herself off but can't speak for a while because of a coughing and dry heaving fit. She had to purge all of the coal and ash from within her body that was excess.

When this was done she said, "My apologies for the delay."

"AH!" Nicholas drew his simple steel sword and swung wildly at the pink slugs of living brain matter, good thing he put on gloves before disposing of the corpses! No no no... A long sword was not the right weapon for dealing with such things. He winced and shook his head, feeling the need to vomit or pass out seeing such a thing. He walked over to Grace, about ready to remove his sheath before turning back, watching the scene before him. "Why I've never..." The signature weapon of a proper knight, or the armor smasher? He already had the long sword. He grabbed a badge shaped shield from the many items Grace carried and held it in front of him, prepared for the worst as the statue before him crumbled and the girl from earlier emerged. "... What?"

"Did you drink any of that water? I'm sorry. I didn't put that in the notes." Aithne checked on him looking at his eye holes. It didn't help because he was essentially faceless. "I did.... I regret it... even now... Worms, all of it is worms and part of an ancient parasitic demon." She picks up a sharp stick and points it to what looked like the upper half of a woman's face peeking up from the surface of the ponds water at them both. Its eyes wide open as it watches them in curious study.

This demon had long blonde hair with short pointed ears and green eyes like the forest. It looked exactly like a teen woman with her face half submerged from where he and Aithne stood. "The biggest force in... These woods and its fabrications. Animals that look safe to eat but they too... Are full of worms."

And again, despite the lighting, the holes in his helmet were always just... Black voids. "What?" The world was spinning again... Nevertheless, through thick and thin, it all amounted to glory! Oh, this would be a tail to tell! He would have to tone it down, for the children of course. Though, most stories he knew had different versions depending on who they were told to. "Just don't... Leave the lady in peace." He turned away and turned his badge shield to the side, sliding it down his arm, the sharp end pointing forward. He placed his long sword among his saddlebags and removed another one containing a simple steel mace, pretty much just a decent metal ball with small studs on the end of a stick. "I suppose the armor smasher would be best for this... Worm demon, yes?"

Nicholas let out a shaky sigh, examining his mace, not looking over to her. "That whole show... How... What was it?" He spun the mace about.

Aithne trusted him. "Death by flame, life by ash. Call it a curse, but before this It required an ability called entropy undone which can restore that which was burned from the ashes. Death by flame life by ash allows the spirit to bind with carbon ash and reemerge from any ash source. This combines the eternity of the phoenix with the godlike will to manifest from nothing. If the ash is minuscule they will materialize as an ash golem and would have to devour flesh to get skin and nerve back. The ritual to make it so that my non corporeal form *Cough* Could cast entropy undone... So that I didn't rise from cold ashes as a baby was so excruciating... The pain and screaming left my voice as it is now... I tried suicide to extinguish the burning. I'd just reform to burn more until the pain stopped hurting and my spirit and flame were as one."

The knight turned and gave the girl a blank stare. Well, his helmet was pretty much expressionless. He held the mace in both hands, one hand on the head. "So... You chose to be burnt alive so you can come back as you were, as you are now. Good, good, tis better to be flesh and blood than a golem of ash and stone." Nicholas took a few steps back away from Aithne, visibly disturbed despite the girl not being able to see his face. Or any part of his body, for that matter. But he couldn't imagine what it was like to die, only to come back. Over and over again. It'd truly be a curse to be alive at that point.

"I threw myself onto their bonfire on the way to town. Luckily you had burned bodies here making the materials for flesh sufficient and have a location." She had clothes too as those were also burned. She'd look over to the demon, the new stick she had picked up would have to serve as her catalyst should Nicholas want to take this monstrosity on.

"Right, yes." The knight could not wrap his head around everything she was saying. "That thing, that demon in the water... Should we take it on? Hmmm..." Knowing now that everything around them was infested with demon worms, he wondered what else he would need. A mace would be best for smashing them to pulps so there was nothing left. Would he need oil? Not sure. He knew of one thing he did need though. He walked around Grace and rummaged around in his knapsack. "Ah, here it is." If they did take on this demon, he wanted his loyal steed to be a safe distance away. Nicholas led her a few feet away to a collection of trees, a shadow was cast over them both as he twisted his helmet to the side and removed it, his entire head again obscured. He replaced that helmet with a completely identical one. Though, this new one had a few unusual attachments to it. On both sides were holsters where two vials of healing potions were stored, one on each side. And Nicholas could drink the potions from straws attached to the helmet. And on top was a miniature lantern, enclosed in a glass cage. He stepped out and directly in front of her, mace in hand. "I will let you lead us on. After all, it is the knightly thing to do."

Aithne made her way to the front of the demon thing. with the tree stick wand. "I'm worried...." She was very fearful of it even though she can now easily destroy this demon with her arsenal but it had damaged her brain in the past. Aithne did a twirl on the balls of her feet to cause the orange dust that lined her hair to go airborne. This orange glowing dust stays in orbit around her head forming eight small glowing orbs of flame. The demon rises from the water and it was a horrifying spectacle Its long blonde hair was endlessly long and drapes over a seat composed of a giant human shaped brain. Her hands are very long and clawed and instead of a lower body, she just had red root like tendrils that caress the massive brain the size of a small home. A hare, the one he had seen leaps to try and disarm the girl but her flame orb generates a bright beam cutting it in half and burning it to ash. She had four left... Around the brain from the margins of pond raise clear amoeba like tentacles there were hundreds of them it looked like and they creep like a wave homing Nicholas along the ground seeking to ensnare him if they succeed. The woman lure had more a mandible set than a lower human face.

The only sounds to be heard were the sounds of the water crashing and dripping as the large brain worm woman... Thing. Emerged in her full glory to tower over the two adventurers.

"BY. THE. GODS."

The knight looked up to it as a fireball soared over his head, spars and cinders falling from it as it struck the demon, causing her to rise up even more, and then the odd worm hare was burnt to ash just as hundreds of clear tentacles tried to sweep Nicholas into the lake. The knight raised his badge shield and backhanded it at the tentacles, running to the side and swiping at a few with his face. "What's your plan of attack?! I should have prayed before we did this!"

Aithne casted a fire bolt at the tendrils that chased Nicholas and when it hits he can see the violent bubbling and expansion in the long amoeba like worms. They are boiled dead and explode in a steamy blast allowing him the mobility to get distance and cast something or buff up if need be. the remaining four flame spheres produce their powerful rays that cut deep into the Neurophage Woman. The brain platform it was on started to edge closer to the water now possibly in melee striking range but as it is prone a multihorned eyeless stag the size of two bears charges through knocking trees over to get at the small fire mage, and she rolls to the side causing it to skid and slide in an effort to change direction for her keeping her away from the worm monster.

"Uh, yes. Magic was something the knight was not skilled with. He struggled to learn even the most basic of magic, though he could sometimes. "Aithne?!" The knight blocked with his badge shield and crushed more of the tentacles into pulp with his mace as his furry companion dodged about. Nicholas saw an opening on the brain platform, deciding to rush right at it. With a burst of strength, he pushed an incoming sweeping tentacle off to the side. Then surged out of the grass, already gripping the armor smasher before springing forward. In a few bounds, the faceless knight closed the distance, his strong arm coiling back for a heavy strike.

The heavy strike does quite the number on it and the injured top part wakes up and moves back to the center of the water with the now bleeding brain platform to charge up a ranged attack. The fire neko used her wand to draw a diagonal slash on the ramming stag using some of the ember dust from her hair to cut it in half in a cauterizing horizontal wave of strange lilac plasma heat. Its dispatched and psychic energy causes an assortment of sharp sticks to levitate near the Neurophage Woman. Extra branches and stubs are smoothed off and a glowing lilac psychic energy coats these wooden and now perfected projectiles.

"Shield!" She rolled behind Nicholas for some cover.

"Hiya!" When the studded head of his mace collided with the membrane he fell back just as it moved back as well into the water. The knight fell to his knee, planting the head of the mace into the grass in the midst of the chaos. That felt great! His first hit on his first worm demon! Infernal thing! "Shield!" He yelled holding it in front of him with all the strength he could, shifting his feet into the grass and putting all his weight into his arms.

"Augggggghhhhh...!" Straining.

The force the sticks are thrown is explosive with the branches and twigs bursting on impact denting the shield and sending sharp fragmentation everywhere. luckily no one was in front and at this point Aithne's hair is fading to brown as the emberdust was wearing off. Her abilities are weakening and after the next, three more flame spheres can manifest from the dust and after the tendrils break Nicholas's poise, they caress him and lift him trying to find a way into his nose but it was not easy with his armor. This gives her to merge the three spheres into one large glowing fireball and cast it forward to blast the humanoid part with a violently explosive attack destroying the upper part entirely. The brain platform coats in the membrane of amoeba slime and drags itself onto land now with its psychic abilities now voided with the loss of the humanoid upper half.

"Ah!" Nicholas recovered and recomposed himself into a defensive stance, peering over his badge shield at the worm demon, being pushed back he waved his shield at the tendrils, and then striking back at it again with his mace. There was a burst of light and he felt the heat around him, stepping back more as the worm being began to drag itself onto land. "Give it everything you got! Push it back!" The knight kept his shield in front of him, only swinging his mace when the tentacles neared him.

Aithne found herself relying on the old cantrips with no more fire in her hair. She throws sharp sticks and stones doing cumulative damage to the brain monster which thrashes her with its tentacles knocking her back onto the sharp sticks causing cuts and puncture wounds. Eventually though Nicholas gets an opening at what appears to be a medulla its weakest point.

Peering from behind his shield he saw the big pulsating gland. That looked vulnerable!

"Aithne!"

Nicholas had to kill this thing now. In one fluid motion he ran forward and lept, grasping his mace in a difficult manner all while holding his badge shield, putting all his strength in both arms as he dove right at the weak point, bringing the hard, studded mace head down with as much force as humanly possible.

"Eeeya!" And with a mighty blow from his mace, the thing went pop!

It started to bubble violently and collapse withering away like a rotten fruit and fading to nothing. But before it all disappeared, the fire mage held out both hands and slowly brought them towards her chest, making a crushing motion. Black flames with white outlines burned in her palms, trapping it's very soul into physical form, splitting it. There is now no water in the pond and both of them are free to go down if they were feeling curious as to the treasures hidden. Both of them get a piece of Neurophage soul Aithne already knew what she'd do with it and would sort that out at the next bonfire.

"Ah! Ah!" He quickly got to his feet and swung his mace around recklessly, dropping it as the worm flesh began to fade away from his body. "Ooh! Ah!' He dusted himself off and hopped about, kicking his legs before it was all gone. Aside from battle damage. "Good, good... How's that for testing your might?! Sna ha ha!"

The knight beat his chest with one hand. In front of him, was a wild sphere of fire. Dull oranges and yellows twisted into a floating golden flame. "'What is this... This thing?" He asked bending down to pick it up, holding it in his hand before him.

"This is the soul of the Neurophage Matriarch. Its wisdom contained in a golden glow. Wisdom and will." She slides down into the bottom of the pond to get a look at the cave.

"So... What do I do with it?" The faceless knight asked, mesmerized by the soul. Nicholas leaned in close, the bright yellow glint catching the front of his helmet. The soul in his hand danced around his fingers, the soul clung to his outstretched limb, seeking out life in any way it could. "Is it trying to possess me or something?"

"It's like it wants me to consume it... Or is it the other way around? Either way this thing can't be safe, coming from that demon. It almost seems... Wrong. A soul."

The fire neko returns to answer his questions with a ring that she studies. It doesn't suit her so its tossed to Nicholas instead. "You can merge it with your own to increase your will to manifest however you choose. Are you a creature of strength? Speed? Health? Intellect? Things to reflect on as you make its soul... Part of you. If you hold onto it great demons will often manifest themselves as an object submissive to its wielder"

Nicholas extended his hand out and caught the ring in his free hand, opening his palm, scoffing a bit. As if consuming a soul... An actual soul would make him smarter. "Thank you." He looked up at the little furry thing and if she could see his face then it would be blank. Well, his helmet was blank. "So, I just eat it and I gain its power?"

"Ye." She nods but doesn't use hers right away and follows Nicholas around. Its nearly midnight.

Nicholas looked to the soul in hand, and the ring in his other. He slid it onto his right hand and now with a free hand he raised it up and opened a small hatch about an inch long where his mouth was, and directly consumed the soul, pushing it into the small mouth hole of his helmet.

"I could've cooked that. I think." She makes her way over to the bonfire and rekindles it. Aithne could use the fire to extract more emberdust for her hair but now it was her turn to make use of the soul she had gotten. Perhaps it would be a spell kit, or maybe a weapon. Time would tell and she was excited. She begins preparing everything, the clearing and dirt and drawing a very complex symbol that took quite a while to finish. "Hm." She sat crisscross, currently drawing stuff in the dirt around the bonfire.

"Mhmhhhm!" The faceless knight smacked the metal collar where his neck would be, swallowing it down and falling to his knees, feeling as if suddenly he had inhaled a gust of air, and he could feel something warm and wriggling inside him. He shot up. He felt stronger, faster. "Should we rest for the night then?" He asked, clenching both hands and staring off into nothing.

The soul she had slowly drifts off to hover over the bonfire... Once its situated it started to pulsate and change color and the etchings Aithne carved into the ground started to glow a bright red. With a crackle like fireworks the light of the soul fades leaving a beautiful looking wand. With a two pronged tip and spindly length like dancing roots. This resembled a synapse and is wrapped in a light feathery tissue fiber for a grip. Its color was a beautiful shining silver and red. The glowing etchings fade and the roaring bonfire settles as the new aegis wand flies to the girl's hand and the stick she was using is cast aside. "I think now is a good time for rest."

The ring looked like a skullcap for a gem slot with raven's talon texture decorating the metal that caresses the finger.

Nicholas hopped about, feeling almost light as a feather and like he could do anything. He walked off to where his horse was, oddly calm after the giant battle. Taking her reigns, he led her over to the bonfire. "Here Grace..." Grace nickered more and kicked at the dirt, falling forward and resting near the bonfire. Nicholas looked to the new ring on his right ring finger. A ring that looked like a skullcap for a gem slot with a raven's talon texture decorating the metal. Kind of... Dark. Boy that made me hungry... Thirsty too.' He said rummaging around in his packs, before his attention was drawn to the bonfire, the crackle of flames and the soul morphing into a beautiful looking wand. "Amazing!"

"I too am hungry. Did you bring... Any food?" She'd hope there was enough. With the Neurophage Matriarch dead though It was safe to go out, and get food but now it was very late at night and Aithne did need her sleep too but preferred napping throughout the day. Her eyes close mostly and shed set up her spells waiting for his answer on the food issue.

"Knight errant's motto, always be prepared! Let's see, salted meat helps with the wolves, dried fruit, nuts, dried berries, bread and cheese... Bit of everything! Sna ha ha!" He slid his hand into his saddlebags, grabbing a small handful of oats to feed his horse, sitting down beside his faithful seed. "What do you want?" At the same time Nicholas removed his shield and set it near the fire, then removed his mace and inspected the head, grabbing a rag to clean it off.

The neko girl helps herself to the dried nuts, fruits and cheeses and a little bit of bread to help it down. She was a fast eater and makes a quick shelter with time to curl up in. They had plenty of time to talk now and if he needed anything she would be resting in a crudely made tent.

The knight gave her a blank look from how quickly the furry thing ate most of the food he had offered. He himself had a drink in an odd metal mixer, raising the mixer to to his helmet the metals collided. Nicholas attempted to pretty much shove it into his face, all before reaching into another one of his bags and pulling out a straw. Opening the small hatch in the front of his helmet, he stuck the straw in there and began to sip. And then she was quick to set up a tent. "... That was fast! What exactly are you again, Aithne?"

"I am a person from a faraway land long forgotten... My race, where I am from is inconsequential. My tail. My ears... My ears let me hear all verbal magic and my voice is shared... Only a chosen few can hear the other.'" Nicholas wouldn't under-stand it or perceive it but every word she says or mutters it repeated by a much quieter almost ghostly whisper of everything she says in reverse. This is why she makes room for pause. The practical implications of this is that every magic she casts verbally is cast twofold with the delay being a change in syllables. She had been seen casting fireballs at a rate so fast it looked like a steady stream of inferno of overwhelming power.

"So, like a panther person I've heard legends about? But like, human kinda mostly? The ears and the tail are... Yes. They also help with magic." The knight continued to sip the drink from the mixer through the straw, looking to her and sitting Indian style in front of her. "How did you learn all that magic and trap that things soul? Isn't that necromancy? Oh Oh Lhikan's sword I ate it... How did you become this way?"

"Trust... I was given a glimpse and gateway to the forbidden arts. Our school for graduation had us bear witness to. the fate of all who broke the sacred vow of those who practice the arts forbidden. I got to speak with the prisoner alone... he wild me that for the wicked death is but an interval, that execution meant nothing because... We the Magi Anathema ensure our own beyond the grave through a ritual in common one you saw tonight. With the soul."

Nicholas could still barely understand a word the girl said to him, sitting there staring at her with his blank helmet. He scratched the back of it and said, "That's some school... And some ceremony." He crossed his arms. "It does mean nothing if you can come back like that. The question is, at what price? At what consequence?"

She nods. "Everyone will seek to kill you for money or fear that you will kill them. Your loved ones may die as blood sacrament for a curse and they would know this and so you are disavowed by all who claim your blood. The pains of growth... They drive you mad but it's like alcohol. Each new bit of knowledge fills you a little more... Save for what learning fills all else is empty "

"A terrible price for all of that... Never the less. There is more to this life than knowledge, Aithne. As addicting as it is." The knight said simply. "Do you know your purpose? What do you truly wish to do with everything you've obtained?"

This was something she had never really thought of or questioned and many of her kind didn't. "I think I want to be an entertainer and do... Impressive things with colorful fire, or, able to be the prime authority in the pyromancer arts."

"You are young, as am I." He clenched his left hand and threw it up triumph. "This is our time to work towards those dreams, and to get out there and see the world! This is our prime time to adventure and step into the annals of legend!"

"I but with unlimited power?" She was trying to have a sense of humor, smiling a bit and backing up. "I'm not as young as you think. Or maybe I am? Who says? Ha!"

That didn't sound like the common language to him. "Yes! Adventure with unlimited power! For glory!" Nicholas finished the last of what he was drinking, popping a few walnuts into his mouth and washing it down with some water. The knight errant let out a tired yawn and began to set up his sleeping bag directly across from the girl's crude, quickly set up tent, used to sleeping out in the open.

"For glory..." The fire mage repeats softly back in her emotionless voice but being friendly for the first time in a long time. He could know that she was smiling on the inside. Her flickering ear and beating tail compensated laughter as she settled in, ready for the next day. Before she fell asleep, she let out a long sigh.

The knight laid down and spread out his limbs, making himself comfortable and throwing his right hand up in a sort of hurrah gesture. "For glory... And for a good night's sleep after an epic battle."

That night, Nicholas had a most unusual reoccurring dream that first manifested several months back before he left Grigwald. He dreamt of a young neko girl in hiding, similar to his current companion. Though she had a very kind face, opal eyes, lilac hair, and white ears and tail. Though there was something regal about her despite the fact she wore a very simple white dress. He dreamt he was in a dark, wispy stone corridor, and she was calling for him to help. Him. Nicholas. She ran, and he followed, and he found himself in a bell tower. And the bell rung, and called to him...

The call to adventurer, and the young knight answered.

Who was that woman? Why was she calling for help? Why was she hiding? Nicholas had to know! He knew she was out there, and something was guiding him. He wasn't sure the path, but he knew he'd eventually stumble across the destination.

With that dream he felt something, the girl pulling him not only towards adventure, but he reckoned Sunlight Falls, the place where he wished to travel to make pilgrimage in the first place.

Could the visions about The Girl In Hiding, his worldwide journey to find the fabled Sunlight Falls, and this meeting of the rare neko girl all be connected?

It had to be.

All the while Aithne secretly kept a close eye on Nicholas as he slept, and soon, sleep's comfortable embrace took her too.

CHAPTER SEVEN: THE ENTERTAINER'S TUNIC

Capital De Seraphim, 1435 ATC

"Whoo! Wahoo! Banana! Whop!"

Fwip.

Bip.

The bearded man ran along the rooftops of the large capital city, disappearing in a puff of thick red smoke and reappearing on another rooftop as he parkoured and teleported his way to the harbor. Leaping down from a local seaside tavern and off a dock. Landing in the sand as the tide came in.

The coast was something on this early night as the man walked along the sand, looking out at the statue of the Trinity that watched over the harbor. The waves crashing against his burgundy leather boots and the bottom of his leg, a slight breeze caused his already messy hair to dance in the wind. Swaying back and forth. He had a slight smile on her face as he smelled the crisp scent of sea water, and the booze and smoked boar of the local seaside tavern. The bearded man glanced down as another tide passed, and looked at his wavy reflection. Hmmm... Perhaps it was time to go shopping for a new outfit. Maybe. Maybe yes, at least buy some. Didn't mean he had to wear them the very next day. Perhaps he would buy some clothes and wait a while before wearing them.

Wandering the streets of Capital De Seraphim, Venser was dressed in a strange red rubber suit with rubber nipples and an oversized codpiece, and his messy head of hair atop his head made him stick out like the sorest of thumbs, and he caught the eyes of various cityfolk who seemed interested in the strange man in the almost alien outfit, but were hesitant to say anything to him, which was fine with him for now. Venser had a few stops to make if he was to regain some semblance of what he had lost in his time away. Or, at least, to blend in. The bearded man had armor and outfits that fit the setting but often chose not to wear them. And often just flat out forgot about them.

The first stop was the blacksmith's, where he was able to purchase some pieces of armor at a fair cost, finding the older gentleman he was haggling with to be a lovely soul, and after a bit of small talk he had paid for light, simple metal armor that would fit over his shoulders, legs, and a chest piece. And a bit of extra coin to have the man begin working it into the measurements he provided as he stepped back out with armor in a bag and moved to the next stop. Which was just the bakers. He took a few minutes to browse but ultimately he decided he was not hungry, but noted he would come back later.

One minute after stepping out of the shop, he had stepped back in, now spending his time slowly walking through shops and stalls, taking in what's available for purchase and trade. All while munching on a multilayered, laminated sweet pastry with cheese in the middle. He avoided overly active areas for now so he could explore a bit easier and purchases just basic supplies, such as dried rations, crossbow bolts, and adventuring supplies in various shops. Though he required very few of it as most of his days were spent tending the bar at the Dragon's Head Tavern and Inn, and now part time jester for the De Seraphim family.

Going down an alley and into another big marketplace he passed a pair of gnomish entertainers dressed in lavish colors, both of them with a lute and singing together in harmony for a small crowd.

"Dear Gods, I was terribly lost when the galaxies crossed and the sun went dark. Dark, dark darkkkk. But, dear Gods, You're the only star I would follow this far. Da da da da da da da da da. Da da da da da da daaaa... Through the galaxies!"

Clapping as they both did simply played along to the beat and didn't sing, and Venser couldn't help but toss a few silvers their way.

The man passed by them and right beside the signing gnome couple he saw it. Staring him right in the face. A gnome merchant woman selling the same entertainers tunics the singing couple wore, in all shapes and sizes, and all colors. Though, he didn't see any purple or yellows. As both of those required very expensive and rare dyes, especially the former which was worth its weight in gold. "Hehh... These... Actually look nice. Like something I'd totally wear. Like..." Venser picked up a turquoise and crimson entertainer's tunic and curled it up into his fist, feeling the light, comfortable fabric that would really breathe like the softest, most luxurious cotton in the world. All before holding it up in front of his chest and checking the sleeve length with his own arm. It was perfect.

"Do you like?" The gnome merchant woman asked who was several inches taller than the two entertainers who were wrapping up their song. "You have to pair that with these!" She offered him a pair of baggy red pants and some funny looking pointed blue shoes.

"Hm. I... Ermmm..." The bearded man bit his lips, tempted to buy the ridiculous looking shoes but cleared his throat. "Just the tunic and the pants for me!"

"Another satisfied customer!"

Venser handed the gnome woman a small sack of silver and stuff the clothes into his large burlap sack along with his pieces of armor. Though, he couldn't help but open the bag as he walked and peer down at the crimson and turquoise entertainer's tunic and baggy red pants.

He had the feeling he was truly going to enjoy wearing this outfit, and he considered going back to buy out all the pairs of this color they had. Crimson, like his own unusual outfit, and turquoise, like the cape over his right shoulder. And it was an entertainer's tunic, so it would be quite fitting when he was jesting to Y'vonne and her sister, the court, his family, and his own patrons back at the tavern.

Truly a match made. Venser had a really good feeling about this.

CHAPTER EIGHT: THE OASIS

1435 ATC

A man in a red rubber suit with rubber nipples and an oversized codpiece wandered through the endless desert, transverse dune after dune for a story he thought of writing.

"Heh... Yeah... Could do that... I'd be easy to make money in Pantia writing about... Naw here as well I'm sure..." Venser didn't know why he was doing this other than a story, and for experience. And he had wished he had different attire. The suit was getting pretty damn hot. After stumbling down a hill the man saw an oasis, a pool of shining, blue water. He ran towards it and got to his knees, cupping the water in his hands and drinking it down greedily. He was happy, and it was the first time he had been that parched. "By the void I'm hot..." He mumbled removed his codpiece and the rest of his suit. Leaving him completely naked as he began to wade into the water.

"'Uh! Guhuh...'' He had wished he had cut his hair now and actually tied it back, and worn that new tunic he had bought recently rather than the ridiculous out-fit he wore in a place like this. ''Fuck, yeah! Oh I need this... Bah... Hydration is important!''

It was a hot day in the desert sun. In the sky above, a red dragoness was very lucky she could fly as her she feared the sand would roast her alive. In the distance she began to see water. A sign of hope as she was beginning to get thirsty after flying for days. Water...

The dragoness landed in the pool of water and made a realization that it was ice cold. Perfect. She smiles softly as she relaxes in the water, standing on both legs and rubbing her thighs together. Her unusual non-mammaled nipples suddenly hardening. She was so enthralled in the water she completely ignored the fact that there was someone else there. So long was her journey that she almost felt like she was the last being on the planet out here. She remained in the water. Her body naked and her rump very curvy. Nivarah was seven feet tall, and had a mess of raven black shiny hair atop her head that resembled an undercut in between her horns. Looking over her body it was very feminine yet muscular, a small waist which curved with her luscious wide hips, topped with two plump butt cheeks delightfully squeezing her ass into a perfect heart shape. Her tail was a foot longer than the well trained but still feminine legs, long and beautiful.

Venser stopped, the water up to his knees as he waded into it. The man was in his early thirties, with fair skin, a muscular body with faint scratch marks on his chest. He had a short, black beard neatly cut, long raven hair that nearly reached his shoulders, and green serpent like eyes. "By the void..." He said watching the humanoid dragon figure splash around. Her body was curvy, and looked fairly soft from where he was, and her breasts were huge. He stood there watching her splash around while his member stiffened up and hardened.

Nivarah closed her yellow eyes and laid her head against the soft sand as she lays on the shore. She heard splashing other than her own and a deep voice richer than most human's ring out from nearby. "Oh... Um... Hello there human " She looked at the man who seemed to be looking at her with a bit of a strange glint in his eyes. "Welcome to the pool. Wish I had some food we could eat but nothing beats this water, eh?" Her forked tongue licked her lips as she writhed a bit.

"Yeah, wanna join me?" He asked wading deeper into it, the water going up above his waist, hiding his rock hard cock as he looked to the wet, naked humanoid dragon lying on the shore several feet away from him.

She smiles softly as she walked into the water with him and her tongue flickered a bit. He seemed harmless so far.

The muscular naked man was confused as the naked dragon creature joined him in the water. "What brings you here?" He asked, looking down to her large chest and finding himself unable to stop looking there. Despite the fact that she was larger than him and had a humanoid figure, two arms, two legs, two giant wings jutting out of her back, she had clearly defined breasts. Hers, from what he could gather, appear to be at a nice, firm C bordering on D.

"Probably the same thing that brought you here. This place is hot as hell, just like you, and there is not a drop of water for miles. I came here to find some relief from my heat. Er... I mean the heat." She blushed, somehow, as she didn't want to give away that she was a bit in season. The scaly dragoness was rather relieved she wasn't here alone as traveling was really boring, and at the same time, a good thing. Though, being on the run at the same time and she wasn't sure how long she could keep going…

''You're in heat?" He asked looking to her. "Oh. The heat, right." Venser dunked his hands into the water and then ran his wet hands through his hair. "Bah… And could use a bit of bathing, been almost a day since I started walking." He swam forward and around the dragon thing, inspecting her body. "So, tell me… You got a name?"

"Nivarah. My name is Nivarah… And yours, human?" She gave a toothy smile softly as she bends over and lifts her tail diving into the water first then slowly swimming downwards before standing up. The water began to drip down her body and pool in her navel. Some of it dripped freely off her erect nipples.

"Nivarah. Lovely name for a lovely dragoness. Just what an oasis paradise in the middle of nowhere needs…" The bearded man said still circling her. "Oddly enough," He paused and looked around, "There's an abandoned building, trees, a bit of grass, and cover over there with a carpet and pillows. Heh, perfect right? The name is Venser. Venser Karkaldwin."

''Yes. If I didn't know any better, I would say this is a slave trap… But what slaver in his right mind would drag people through the desert? " Nivarah thought for a moment. She cupped handfuls of water and poured it over her head, wiping her curved horns down, washing the small spikes that studded her back, cleaning her tail and between her taloned toes. She was careful of her wings, gently fluttering them in the water until she was ready to get out, which she did after a short while. She stood at her full height and flapped her wings, attempting to dry them and herself at the same time, looking calm and serene as she lifted herself into the sky and brought herself down near some blankets.

"Naw. Seems like some sort of post people pass through to me." Venser said shrugging his shoulders, following Nivarah as she crawled out of the water. He snuck a few glances at her curvy round rump, hidden at times by her swaying tail, walking behind her. His cock throbbed as he laid down next to her, grabbing a pillow. "Ah… Paradise, right, Nivarah?" Venser asked with a smile rolling over, his muscular naked body in full view for her.

"Sure is? Only thing that is missing is… Hmm… Maybe some food?" She relaxes and stretched. as she does her soft pink slit can be seen. She was rather too oblivious to care as she looked around for a moment. Her tail trying to reach a branch to fan herself with... She grabbed a palm leaf and began to fan herself as well as Venser, all the while soft glimpses of her pink sex could be seen.

"Closest thing that comes to food, well, food are those." Venser said pointing across the water to a lone apple tree, seemingly the only tree fruit grew on in the surrounding area. He disappeared in a puff of thick red smoke and reappeared on the other side, hopping up to grab a few red, juicy apples. He teleported back in front of Nivarah and offered her one. He was still wet and a few drops slid down his nude, muscular body as he stood above her. He licked his lips slightly sneaking more glanced at her nice, pink slit.

"I don't like apples. But you can catch me some fish if there are any in there later."

"Oh yeah, and then you'll easily be able to cook them. Must be fun having a spark box. Heh, figured I woulda found figs out here actually..."

"Human anatomy is so strange in comparison to dragons. You either don't know how to mask the pheromones from your attraction, or don't wish to, and your members are so... I don't want to say small, but they aren't intimidating. But it looks like it'd do the job." Nivarah scratched her throat. "It's not something I can control just yet. I don't even know if fire is the element I'm supposed to wield. It might just be there temporarily, and might go away once I find my element. Anything could happen."

"Humans normally cover themselves." He glanced at her darkened peaks of nipples that rode high on those large mounds and let out a soft moan. "Because of this... I mean... I know your kind doesn't-" he cleared his throat a few times and his cock twitched, still staring at her chest. "You just told me about masking pheromones..."

"Masking pheromones requires extreme concentration, self-control and willpower." Twitch. Nivarah rubbed her thighs more. She was going to say more when she stiffened and spun on her heel, looking skyward, her keen eyes searching the sky as her nostrils expanded, sniffing the air delicately, processing the information. "Dragons. Five of them. Male. Correction. Three dragons, all males. At a distance. Heading this way. Hide." She dropped onto all fours and began running to the other side of the lagoon, sweeping the sand clear before returning to Venser's side. "Quickly. We can hide before they get here and I'll mask our scents. We need to hurry."

No no, I'm sure I'd still be able to aside from smell, I would be able to tell just by looking..." He licked his lips a few times and took a few small steps towards her to close the distance, stopping when she lifted her head to sniff the air. "Eh?" He bit his lip and let out a sigh. A gang of male dragons eh? No females. Shame. And they most likely were closing in fast. He cracked his neck a few times and merely walked back, disappearing in a puff of thick red smoke and teleporting to the other side with her. "Er, hide where? Not many good spots around here." He looked about the desert oasis.

She nodded and stood tall, her tail swishing as he closed the distance. "It's not uncommon to find a gang of males seeking females to take with them. We can either hide from them or try to fight them off." She watched as he quickly cleared away his things and made her way over to the thin forest, poking about to find anything that could help them hide. "I don't know where we could hide, but I don't know what else to do."

''You wouldn't happen to be in heat, would you?" He asked looking at her lower lips again. "Pheromones and all, looking for a nice round of mating and tracking the scent... Mhmmm... If we had time to look I'd suggest a cooler. But..." He thought quickly and suggested, "Would the water mask your scent?"

''... Unless you want to witness a very violent dragon orgy, it might be best if I remain undetected. I believe the water might mask my scent, but we'll have to move quickly." She spread her wings and flew to her rock pool, diving below the water to fetch a large rock with which she planned on sealing the entrance to the pool.

He shrugged.

"Well do you want an orgy?" Venser watched her dive into the water beside her and took in a deep breath, before diving down with her, swimming quickly to catch up with her and resisting the urge to grab onto her leg so she'd drag him down faster.

She used her tail to grab his wrist and used her wings to propel them through the water. The rock pool was made predominantly of rocks and dirt, but the floor resulted in nothing useful, so using her claws, she began to dig into the wall as fast as she could, quickly creating a short tunnel until she fell into a decent sized cavern, which she dragged Venser into. Glowing crystals jutted from the ceiling, it was cold, and they were both wet. "This is the best I can do for now. Aroused male dragons can be... Aggressive, and I wouldn't be surprised if they ended up hurting either of us, and they'd tear you to shreds... I'd rather be down here with you than up there with them." She let go of his wrist, leaning against the rocky wall as she relaxed.

"MHMMM!" He breathed loudly as he was suddenly snagged and opened his mouth, choking on the water as they sped through it. When she dug up and into a small tunnel he was disoriented, shaking his head and blubbering a bit. Sitting and falling against the dragoness, his face going right in between her scaled breasts as he sputtered up water. "Gahhh... Yeah..."

Her breaths were even as she leaned against the wall, seemingly asleep. Her wings were crumpled behind her, her legs spread open with her tail drooping on the ground. The sound of running water filled the cavern, muffling the sounds from above. "You are actually really warm..."

"Gahhh... I think we coulda fought them off... Woulda been fun," He coughed a few times still with his face right in between her cleavage. "I remember now... Explored an underground treasure chamber... Stood on a cloud and pissed off of it... And if I fought greentusks... So many adventures...."

On the ground above the dragons got closer, and closer.

"If I know my kind, they'll rip you limb from limb if you go up first. They'll rape me 'till I'm bleeding from every orifice if I go up first. They'll kill us both if they find us. Honestly, none of those ideas are preferable. Perhaps if I go up first and make it look like I was swimming. Worst outcome is being raped, best outcome is being left alone." Nivarah scratched her throat, trying to think of other options, then looked down at the bearded man in her chest. She had to admit, heat or not, that he was handsome for a human.

"No no I got an idea... That just might work!" Still sitting down in front of the dragoness, he wrapped his fingers around his hardened cock, rubbing the shaft up and down as rapidly as he could in front of her, moaning and breathing heavily.

Yellow eyes wide. She licked her lips again. "I have the same idea."

She began to move away on all fours, her tail moving slightly to show the soft lips of her sex as she headed toward the center of the cavern, lifting her tail for the human. Staring back at the muscular human with this certain yearning, predatory look in her eyes. Her reptilian pupils thin and slitted. "I am in heat... And you're good for a human. Better you than those up there.'' Nivarah back up into Ven, lowering her rear for him and moving her tail to the side.

His emerald eyes became hungry, wanting this honestly attractive dragoness so badly. Venser's hardened length dribbled a bit of pre-cum from the tip as he slowly rubbed his dick against the smooth skin around Nivarah's hole drenched in arousal. With his dick in position he could feel it press against the hot entrance of Nivarah's dragogina.

There was a brief moment of suspense as the bearded man pushed into her moist love tunnel, causing both of them to moan out inside the cave.

''Ohh...!'' Actually, he was so beautiful. Fair skin painted with streaks of varying reds and pinks, from scabbed maroon scars to raw pink healing wounds. On all fours, the dragoness craned her neck and she let her eyes rake over his muscular form. Taking in every detail of the man she was to mercilessly take. Her chest swelled with a big gulp of air as he pushed in as deep as he could. And despite he was smaller than a dragon, he felt very nice.

Nivarah gasped as she felt him starts to frantically hump his hips, his supple, fertile balls slapping against her ass. She moaned louder, her walls massage and suck his cock much like her mouth and tongue would only it was a three sixty all around his shaft pleasure.

The bearded man began to pull his hips back, Nivarah making strained half moans as his impressive mast withdrew. With each of her inner wall's ridges that his head's sides brushed against on its way out, her claws would rake against the stone floor of the cavern, digging into it. Pulling back again, enough of Venser's length had been pulled out to the point where only the head remained within her, still basking in the satisfying warmth her body provided.

Nivarah backed into Venser again, carelessly plowed down to impale herself with his thick member, knees wobbling a bit. Her head slumped to the ground, ragged breathes sucking in oxygen as every beat of her heart was accompanied by a ravenous contraction of her dragogina.

"Rahhhhhh... Rahhh." She managed in a breathless heave, followed by a short roar. ''Venser, hurry!'' Above them, the male dragons landed with a whoosh of wings, scattering sand everywhere. They were majestic creatures, all eight feet tall with ten foot wingspans. One black, one a mossy green and the third a burnt amber color. They could smell the female, they could smell the male with her, but they couldn't see her or her companion. They began sniffing around as Nivarah and Venser his in the tunnel beneath the oasis.

"Already there...!" His balls tensing up ready to unload everything he had into her, along with every inch of strength. Released in short volleys, rope after rope of Venser's seed fired deep into the dragoness's cunny, mixing in with her own juices before seeping out from around where you were both joined. "Mhm! Mhm!" Splattering his highly fertile seed against her walls and shooting it deep down for several long moments. Pulling out he could actually see the torrid human dragon concoction slowly leak from her entrance and pooling onto the cavern beneath them.

"Now, I think we're ready to confront them..." Venser approached Nivarah and kissed her on the cheek, felt quite hot and she smiled and slumped forward a bit.

'Stay here, I got this." He said breathing heavily. "You'll be safe from... What you said, what they'd do to you the second they saw you." The bearded man then disappeared in a puff of thick red smoke and reappeared on the surface, his bare feet digging into the hot sand as he walked into the oasis again as the ale dragons searched the area. "All of you!" Venser announced loudly placing his hands on his sides, looking to all of them. "Nivarah is mine! I have mated with the dragoness you seek!" His cock had gone flaccid now, but his cock still leaking seed as he looked to them.

"I have claimed her, so I ask that all of you leave! Fuck off! Fly! Be free!" He pointed to the mossy green one who appeared to have nose tendrils akin to a Chinese dragon. "You! Mustache! Go back to your cave and suck more cock! Show some respect! I have showered her in my coconut cream pie!"

He tried not to laugh at his own sentence.

The dragons looked from the scrawny male to his flaccid member and laughed loudly. The mossy green one leered at the male and spoke. "A frail human? Hmmmm... Something about your eyes you aren't entirely or... No matter. Where is the female? We wish to enjoy every curve of her if she allows us..." Nivarah had exited the tunnel, broken through the rock pool and was now emerging from the water, sheets of moisture falling from her body, droplets curving around her breasts and down her body. She went to Venser's side and wrapped her arms around him, running her fingers over his lower abdomen, his seed still leaking from her cunny. "He's right, although what happened between us was a little more than just mating. Master..." She nibbled on his ear before looking at the stunned dragons. "Did you not hear us? This is our spot, get lost." She pulled her top lip back and growled menacingly, pulling the bearded man closer.

He gestured to the many faint scars that adorned his chest, as well as the giant slash across it clicked his tongue. "Right here bucko. So take your kin, companions, whatever and-" Venser stopped talking feeling the dragoness's arms wrap around him, her dragging her talons along his stomach. He moaned in pleasure and smiled, licking his lips. "Yes... You see now? She chose me, a handsome human... Now go."

The dragons snarled back at her before lifting off the ground and flying away, their wing beats growing softer. Nivarah let go of Venser and stepped back, heading back to the pool. "Thank you... That was really brave. And what we did in that cave I... I just want more. Master." She winked at him as she felt oddly, powerfully attracted to Venser, almost as if she belonged to him and wanted to keep being around him. It felt oddly satisfying to call him that. She was being playful bit part of calling him that made it just feels right.

"Anytime my fair dragoness." Venser said cracking his neck a few times, staring at her ass again as she walked away. "And now the two of us can go back to just frolicking and enjoying life." He quickly teleported all over the lagoon, before finally reappearing near the shore, lathering his nude body up in oil. "Come here. I wanna try something."

''What is it, Master?''

CHAPTER NINE: NIVARAH

1435 ATC

The red dragoness was waist deep in the water, her tail floating in the shallows and she watched as he teleported around the place, finally staying still near the shore, covering himself in a shiny substance. She slowly waded towards him, her tail swaying in time with her hips. She stood in front of him and looked at his skin, seeing her reflection, running her large, taloned hands all over her smooth red scales.

"Just curious... Curious." The bearded man moved closer, closing the distance once more and rubbed the oil into his hands, slowly he extended them both out to her. "Lovely name. Nivarah... Nivarah." He smacked his lips a few times and nodded. "Really rolls off my fleshy lips. Oh." Venser gestured to her chest. "If I will..." He placed his hands on her breasts and began to rub the oil all over her scales, making them shine like never before.

"Ohhh..." His hands were gentle and the oil felt nice on her scales, so she stayed quiet and let him continue. Her breasts weren't breasts as such, they weren't used to feed hatchlings like normal breasts. They were simply fat storages for when winter came, and the scales had nipples used to attract mates. And the large globes were firm, yet slightly squishy and Venser would be able to feel the muscles beneath that allowed her to walk on all fours. "Not that I'm objecting to this because it feels nice... What is this supposed to achieve, Master?"

"Just look at how shiny your scales are now, and..." Venser's hands trailed down her slender body as he continued to rub her down, pretty much just nicely polishing her scales, his hands rubbing against her thighs, brushing against her pink lips and then moving behind the dragoness, rubbing her shoulders and then bending down a bit, kneading around the joints of her wings in small circles with his thumbs, massaging away at certain sensitive spots.

Nivarah closed her eyes and let him continue, her smooth scales rippling under his fingers, the way it did when she warded off flies. "And what? We're now in a dilemma, we can't sit in the sand without it sticking to us, nor can we go in the water without polluting it. What else can we... Ohhh." Venser had reached her wings and she hung her head, his hands rolling away numerous knots that had developed over her years of flying.

"How's that feel?" He asked as he continued to let his hands fall all over her back. "Ease your back. It'll help..." he chuckled slowly working his way around, gently kneading each point of her wings, massaging the tension knots away. "Figured you'd be used to heat."

"Duck for a second." If he ducked, she'd shake her wings out and make a motion similar to a jab with her wings, effectively popping the joints. If he didn't, he'd get smacked in the face. Which is exactly what happened. Bending down for a mere second before standing back up. "Oof!" He got sent flying back on his ass in the hot sand. "Ah!"

The red dragoness heard him fall and turned around, offering a large, taloned hand. "Sorry about that. I should have been more explicit and told you what I was going to do." She helped him up and stretched her wings out away from him, sighing as her joints popped.

"And I should have taken it more seriously." The naked bearded man said taking her hand, feeling her talons dig into his skin as he got up, looking to her wings. "Is that all you were gonna do, stretch em? Stretch em and spread emm... Mhmmm-mhmmm...''

"You know when your elbows or hips pop? I need to do that with my wings sometimes, otherwise they get sore." Nivarah bent forwards and stretched them to their full length, a whole eight feet in length.

"Mhmm... Beautiful. Majestic." Venser actually said aloud admiring her wings again, his ween twitching and starting to harden again. He almost seemed mesmerized as she kept her wings spread out to the sky.

The red dragoness jabbed out with her wings again, crying out as a loud POP came from her wing joint. "Agh! Oh Fblthpr's scales, that hurt." She stayed bent over, making half-laughter half-moaning sounds. Her wings were spread to their full extent, fluttering slightly in the soft breeze.

"But it feels much better, yes?" Venser gestured to one of the beach chairs left behind in the oasis, walking over to it and lowering the end so it was now flat. "If you lay down I can make you much more relaxed, and I'm sure this thing can support your weight." He teleported away and returned with a table with different bottles and tins atop of it. "I mean, you never did say if it felt good, but by the look on your face. I'd say yes. I trust you've never had a wing massage? Especially by... Someone like me." Ven narrowed his attack eyebrows in earnest.

"No, it hurts. It really hurts. I haven't heard it pop like that in a while." She straightened slowly and gently moved her wings, delicately folding them up before moving towards the beach chair, looking it over.

"So, you don't want me to rub them?" Venser asked as she looked over the long, white, and simple folding chair.

"Oh no, please do. It felt so good, I've just never had someone get the knots out of my wings. Um, how do I use this? Do I lay on my stomach, or...?" She gestured to the chair.

"You simply lay down, but I'd have my head just at the center so all your weight is right in the middle. Otherwise you're going to fall forward or backward."

"Oh, okay." She climbed onto the chair, wobbling slightly and hearing the painted wood begin to crack a bit as she settled down on her flat stomach. "Like this?"

"Flat on your stomach, relaxed..." He said climbing on top of her, glancing off to the side and looking over all the bottles and tins. Half of which he had never actually used before. He squinted, pointing at them, before settling on the same oil he applied to himself and her. "Alright, ready for me to touch you?" Venser asked hovering his hands over the base of her wings, and couldn't help but stare down at her ass in the most obvious way.

Nivarah nodded before realizing that she was laying on her face. "Yes, I'm ready. I just need to move my tail." She slipped it out from under his leg and lay it across his lap for him to move how he pleased. "So, do you massage every dragoness you meet, or am I special?"

"A few in my time... Recently became friends with one... Such rare creatures... I am somewhat trained to do this, mostly self-taught... And ... What was I going to say?" Watching her move her tail, feeling it brush against his hardened member and having it block her nice, tight rear no longer. "Ah ha ha... No no but I have massaged one or two... I know my way away- I mean around wings. Interesting things." Ven leaned in to rub small circles, pushing his thumbs down as he did so. He kept his touch gentle, his fingers caressing her scales. "Mhmmm..."

"So you've met dragons before? That's interesting, though I figured as much when you didn't completely freak out when you met me... I'll have to take you home with me and ask you to teach others how to do this one day, we don't have this kind of thing at home. We come from far east, there's little like, crack in the world where we travel through from ours. Some of us settled around it into tribes." She felt his hardened member against her tail and quickly moved it, relaxing again as she listened to him speak. He hit a particularly stubborn knot and she moaned throatily, missing everything else he said aside from the last part.

"What's this about being naked?"

"No, I was more..." He paused for a moment trying to find the word. "Intrigued." Venser started to slow down as he felt her back, stopping at the base of both wings, before moving his fingers in between them, pressing down. "Take me home and teach other dragons how to do this? Hmmm... Would be different. Considering I lack claws. And scales. So, my fleshy hands against your scales... It would be different." He shifted again sitting on her legs as she laid down, his member brushing against her rump now.

"Being naked is simply one of the greatest things in life. The perfect world would be where everyone has no concept of clothing, grooming and bathing is an important part of daily life... Almost essential. Like eating and drinking. Living life peacefully and without want, having no concept of war, money, possession or government. Spending all the time farming, singing, dancing, frolicking, mating, drinking, trying new things. Where I came from, nothing but greed, cynicism, and hypocritical prudeness."

"Wouldn't matter if you didn't have claws, if you taught one of us to do the same." She moaned again as he pressed down on her back, enjoying the feeling of his hands too much to realize where his member was. Nivarah let out another satisfied groan and blew smoke from her nostrils, wiggling her rear a bit. "Unno what government is... Like, tribe? That concept of life is nice to think about. But there would always be conflict, people scrapping over mates, over food, over anything they can."

"Hey, sharing is caring. Ask any of my other loves." Venser grabbed a heated tanning oil and rubbed the hot liquid all over his hands, leaning in again to trail up her wings now rather than massage the muscles at the base, the part where the wings were actually attached to her back. Smoothing out her plumes, focusing on the right wing and working along it. "Not exactly hidden. The shape of your body. The breasts." As he moved forward to trail up her wings it was apparent his member was poking against her rear now. "All we can do is dream of said perfect world. Especially with my kind."

''Sharing isn't always the way to go, even in a perfect utopia. Um, just mind the webbing of my wings, I'm a bit paranoid about keeping them clean because I've heard of dragons who had mold growing on their wings that then rotted the webbing." She felt the warm oil on the stems of her wings and wondered at the warmth. "My breasts aren't used for anything, and the shape of my body only comes about because I'm female. I train myself to stay slim." She could feel his member sticking into her rear. "What do you mean by your kind?" Nivarah moaned yet again as he rubbed her shoulders, her tail shifting and stiffening as he ran over several hard knots.

When he was done massaging her lower back, just above her tail he awed as she lifted it, allowing full access to her rear again, and seeing her pink lips beneath it as she laid down. He took one hand off her, using it to slowly rub his shaft up and down again staring down. Oh how he wanted to slip it in and take her from behind... Venser let out a sigh, taking his hand off and using both hands to caress her round, scaled ass.

The tall red dragoness felt his hands on her rear and shifted her tail again, tapping his leg. "Could you stand up for a few moments? I really need to stretch, Master.''

His cock resting in between her cheeks beneath her tail now. "Uh, sure." Venser said then getting off of her, wincing as his feet touched the hot sand. "And then I can work on the other side of you'd like? Your limbs?"

Nivarah stretched like a cat, lifting her backside into the air as she stretched her back out, groaning in a satisfying way as her back cracked in several places and giving Venser a face full of bountiful dragon ass. Much to his delight, giving her ass a smack and trying not to hit her tail. She shook her wings out and winced as several loud pops exploded from the base of each wing before sitting up and stretching her arms above her head, slowly bending from side to side. She looked at him, and shrugged. "If you want to work on my limbs, I won't argue, but I'll have to sit up since." She gestured to her wings. "... I can't lay on my wings at all, otherwise I could do all sorts of damage..."

"Weren't expecting this today, were ya?" He gently put both of his hands on Nivarah''s left wing and applied a small amount of pressure, slowly running his fingers up and down the length of the wing, periodically squeezing lightly. Bit by bit as he moved around, getting the knots out of both of her wings before moving in front of her, sitting down on the chair in front of her. Applying more oil to his hands he placed them both on one of her thighs, slowly rubbing up and down, up and down..."

"Well, considering I thought I wasn't going to wake up this morning, this is certainly a more pleasant outcome." She let her head hang and closed her eyes as he massaged her wings, eventually getting all the knots out. She kept her eyes closed as he moved in front of her, placing his hands on her thighs. Nivarah remained silent as she thought and allowed him to massage her thighs, her yellow eyes flickering with satisfaction.

He took his left hand off her thigh and looked to a nearby cooler filled with cider bottles, most of the ice had melted but nevertheless the cider it contained was still cold. His mark flashed greenish white and he pulled a bottle over to him in a green aura. He popped the lid off and trailed his fingers along her shined scales, brushing past her draconic womanhood again as he massaged her other thigh with one hand. "And what then when I'm done relaxing you?"

''Master... I had been alone for six months and was unused to companionship. Even though I'd only been in your company for a few hours before that I felt lonely for the first time in my life. I don't have any friends bar you. I genuinely like you and I don't want to be lonely anymore." As she spoke, Nivarah sat up and ended the massage. ''Do you live in the lands close to hear? I could easily fly both of us there right now!''

''I live about errr... In Vorland, close to the border of that and Pryldahn... The Land of Dragons! And I live in the Dragon's Head Tavern and Inn, have my own room a bungalow near the lake.''

She raised a scaly brow, intrigued The red dragoness opened her mouth to speak before Venser stood up with her. ''Though, I don't think you'll fit in my room... The barn, maybe?''

"I suppose I could make my own cave somewhere out of the way, or I could just build a large bonfire somewhere in the forest to sleep." She sat down and dipped her tail in the water, swishing it around as they stood near the lagoon. Venser offered his hand to hers. "We'll figure that out when we get there. So, shall we?"

"What is this, Master?" Nivarah asked taking his smaller fleshy hand in her large, smooth taloned hand, a bit puzzled. Could the bearded man fly?

"We are about to teleport, my fair dragoness... And I can already feel that this is going to be a relationship, with a wonderful start... Who woulda thought?"

CHAPTER TEN: SEDNA AND THE FAWNS

The Dragon's Head Tavern and Inn, Vorland, 1435 ATC

"So, you ready for camping?" Venser asked lugging a big backpack out to the bar area of the Dragon's Head Tavern and Inn, carrying a second, smaller bag with him. The soft leather of them both gently sliding across the wooden floor. "I know just the perfect place, overlooking the lake. At night when the moon is out and reflects off the lake? Something you must witness, Sedna."

"Venser, we've been planning this trip for weeks, of course I'm ready."

From the left hallway where some of the rooms were, come a rough yet noble looking woman carrying a backpack of her own, Sedna dashed into the room struggling with her hunting dress. She was about the same height as him, five eleven. Her long straight hair was blacker than black. Like the void Itself lived upon her head, her eyes big blue and almond shaped, though the lids didn't fold as much as those with actual almond eyes. Added with high cheekbones, slightly pointed jaw, ending in a delicate chin, she was one beautiful huntress. An exiled princess turned huntress, but still. Such a beauty.

"Has it been weeks? I assumed it'd be overnight, but sure. Or.... Habababoob-boptits.'' Gibberish. ''What? I nearly forgot... With everything that's been happening lately. And a lot HAS happened. Been very busy." He grumbled to himself not packing enough food. Then again, all he'd have to do was teleport into the tavern and done. When she came back wearing a hunting dress with a bow slung over her shoulder he raised a brow. "Oh! Later..." He thought forgetting his own bow. Of course, the bearded man had his wrist bow but that wasn't really suited for hunting. It was, sort of, but a bigger bow or an actual crossbow would have been better to bring down game bigger than a rabbit.

''That busy? Never a dull day at the Dragon's Head huh?'' Putting her bag and weapons down, the noble huntress zipped up her dress and put her cloak on, hiding her raven hair. Opening small pockets within her dress, she packed most of the contents of her bag into her dress and slung her bag over her shoulders under her cloak and picked up her quiver and bow, checking that her arrows were still in good condition. "You don't need to worry about food, Venser. I've brought down deer for myself, often. You could say it's my life now. It won't be a problem hunting for the both of us"

"Actually it's been happening outside of work and home. Traveling as I do a lot... Yeah. Ahem. Right... Well, do you have everything?" Venser asked watching her check her equipment. As usual, he wore his red rubber suit with no weapons on him whatsoever. Except for the metal wood thing he always kept holstered to his right thigh. Which he never took out.

Lifting her skirt to above her upper thigh, she strapped a small dagger to it, and hid another inside her boot. noticing Venser watch her, she replied. "I have everything I need for travelling light, so I'm good. Do you have everything?"

"Everything except for my spearbow... Heh... Got a wristbow and a spearbow I got from serving Hempteth... But... Fuck me I really should use it. I can come back and get it soon." Venser said offering his left hand to her. "Ready to teleport?"

Securing the pockets in her dress and dropping her skirt again, Sedna took his offered hand and squeezed it. "I'm more than ready, Venser."

"Hold on tight." The handsome bearded man said grasping her hand and the reigns. They all disappeared in a puff of thick red smoke and reappeared right below a hill near a cliff overlooking the lake. "We get a great view from up here. That's why I love this area." Venser said holding her hand, looking out at the great blue lake beneath the setting sun and orange colored sky. "What a lovely day." Looking around and feeling a bit nauseous, she gasped in delight at the beauty of the area. "Venser, I can't begin to describe how beautiful this place is... How have I never been up here?"

"Yup. Lovely." Venser said letting go of her hand, walking over to the cliff and looking out with his arms crossed. His foot slipped and he suddenly fell over the edge of the cliff. "Ahhhhhh!' And out of sight.

Sedna's bright blue eyes shot wide open as she ran to the cliff as Venser fell and began climbing down."Fuck, Venser..."

As soon as she said that, Venser poked his head over the edge of the top off the cliff, having teleported back up there. "Gave ya a real scare didn't I?" He asked with a laugh reaching his arm down. "Come back up love."

She scrambled up the cliff, tackled him and began pummeling him with her fists. "That wasn't funny!"

"Oof!" He fell onto his back and blocked her punches, most of them at least. "Alright! Alright! I'm sorry! Void, fuck my ass with a loaf of bread!"

Venser got up from the grass and brushed himself off after Sedna had repeatedly punched him for fake falling off the cliff. "Why's your hair black and not some crazy color?" He asked starting to unpack his things and set the tent up. Pausing for a moment to make odd, squeezing hand gestures.

After snapping her fingers, magical sparks flying from her fingers and starting a small fire, Sedna started bending some saplings over to create a frame for her shelter, still peeved at Venser for tricking her. "Black is easier to conceal when I'm hunting. It's a rather interesting kind of magic I've always known... Just... To change my hair color. Why'd you let your hair and beard grow so scraggly? You almost look like a completely different person!"

''I don't want to talk about it.'' As Venser set up the tent, accidently dropping one of the supports and causing the whole frame to collapse, he looked over to Sedna who seemed to be making her own. "Hey, I thought we were sharing a tent. And a sleeping bag."

Looking over her shoulder at Venser's collapsed tent, she smiled to in mirth. "This is just a shelter for the food. I'll dig a small pit and wrap all the meat that is hunted in leather and bury it. After it's buried, I'll pour a little water over it and that will keep it cool. I'll also put any other food we have in the shelter, out of the smell and reach of animals."

Blink blink. Venser gave her an odd look, ignorant of how people stored food like that. He figured they'd eat it fresh, but they had to do something about the leftovers. "Right. Maybe we'll snag ourselves a big kill tonight, huh Sedna? Sednnnaa Roseriann." He asked going back to setting up the tent.

Blink blink blink. Why'd he say it like that? Venser was a bit strange at times, less than usual today but that's why she liked him. Going over to the fire, she used a stick to stir up a little ash and using a blackened wooden spoon, ladled a little ash onto a small piece of leather, which she set down to cool. "Yes, hopefully the woods will be filled with game, and we will eat well"

"I brought some sau..." He decided not to speak of the sausages he had brought to cook on the fire. And rather allowed both to have the thrill of the hunt later. Once he pitched the light brown tent he grabbed the bag of sausages from his bag. "I'm running back to the tavern to grab my bow." He said before disappearing in a puff of thick red smoke.

Watching Venser disappear, Sedna began to smear the cooled ash on her hands, face and bow disguising her scent so as not to disturb the wild animals. Rummaging in her backpack, she pulled out an outfit that was more like a bush than clothes. It was just a simple dirt-brown tunic and leggings, but she had woven bits of grass into it and tied small switches of plants, so that she wouldn't stand out in the forest. Sitting down by the fire, she pulled out a small container that was full of grease and applied a small amount of it to her bowstring as she waited for her friend, the bearded bartender and traveling mercenary.

While still waiting Sedna watched as Venser disappeared in a thick cloud of red smoke and went to her pack, retrieving a fawn-colored hunting outfit, with leaves attached to it, making it look like a small shrub. She quickly undressed and got into her hunting clothes, slipping her feet into a pair of dirt-stained foot coverings. Sitting down by the fire, she retrieved a blackened wooden ladle and a similarly blackened piece of leather and scooped out some of the ashes, leaving them to cool on the leather. Picking up her simple long bow, she began to smear a thin layer of grease over the string and frame, waterproofing it and lubricating the bowstring. Using the small amount in her hands, she smeared a little grease on her face before rubbing the cooled ashes onto her skin and hands.

Venser asked suddenly right behind her, holding a rather long crossbow, with three bolts knocked on top another, and each appeared to be at least two feet long. "Nice make up. You look like you've been making out with a chocolate mousse moose. It's... Well I don't think you know what mousse is."

Snorting at Venser's remark, she crumbled up a small handful of dead leaves and tore strips from a small handful of green ones. Using her dagger as a mirror, she placed the pieces of brown and green leaf onto her mostly grey face, giving her the appearance of tree bark. Wiping her greasy hands on the grass, she took her raven locks in hand and swiftly braided it, sticking leaves amongst the hair and tying it with a small strip of leather. Picking up her bow, she nodded at Venser and melted into the forest. ''I'd recommend you do the same… You really stand out in that ridiculous thing Ven.''

''Ermmmm… How about no? Or maybe another time. You know how much I love this outfit. And I know you do too…'' Venser followed her wielding the long crossbow, crouching down and peaking glances at her ass as he followed, keeping an ear open for any quick noises or crunches.

Keeping her ears open for noises, she heard footfalls and slowed her pace. Crouching down and moving slowly, she looked around a tree and spied a deer, drinking from a small stream. Drawing her bow and nocking an arrow, she felled the deer. Smiling at Venser and drawing her dagger, she ran over to the deer's body, thanked it for giving its life and slit its throat, letting the blood drain into a large flask she had brought with her.

Venser applauded for her, walking over to Sedna and smacking her ass. "Good kill! So, shall we…" He paused and watched her collect its blood in a flask. "Uhhh… What are you doing? That's not how you skin a deer! I think.''

Sedna almost dropped the flask of blood when Venser smacked her ass, and quickly caught the last few drops. "I'm collecting the blood for two reasons. One is so that the blood doesn't spill all over the ground and lead wolves to our campsite, and the second reason is because I want to make a sauce with it." She looked over the body as she tightened the lid on her flask and noticed an abnormal swelling in the stomach area of the felled deer. Pulling out a small length of leather, she crouched down beside the body. "Venser, could you please hold this bit of leather? I think the deer we just killed was pregnant, and I want to see if the baby survived or not."

Venser nodded silently and took the bit of leather, looking to Sedna with a worried expression. "Right… This is why people back home only kill the ones with horns… I… Ugh.''

Slitting the stomach open and moving the intestines out of the way, she finally found the womb of the deer, and found not one, but two deer fawns. They were moving a little, and were the right size for birth, so she carefully slit open the womb and amniotic fluid came rushing out, covering Sedna. Gently picking the fawns up and cutting their umbilical cords, she placed them in the bit of leather Venser was holding and swaddled them up, rubbing their fur to dry and warm them.

"Oh void." Venser almost vomited and looked away, dropping the leather.

Giggling at Venser's displeasure, she pulled out another bit of leather and began rubbing their faces, gently trying to get all the blood and gunk off them. As she wiped, one of the fawn's eyes opened and slowly blinked. "Come on Venser, it's not that bad. It's just blood and fluid. Surely this isn't your first delivery?" Snickering at Venser, she began to softly sing to the alert fawn, who began to sniff at her face and hands.

"I didn't look when Soarin and Lucinda were born... You just cut them right out like you were stealing them. I know you're not, just that sight. " Venser was slightly disturbed looking at them. And he had seen a lot of fucked up things in his time. There was once such a time where he actually ate people. It wasn't until a little over two years ago, with the birth of his twins that he really started to regain his sanity and turn things around. Venser the Mad they always called him... Venser the Mad... No. He tried. He really did.

Wiping her hands on the scrap of leather, she turned to the bearded man.

"Venser, if I didn't cut them out, they would have died a horrible death. They would have suffocated, as well as starved to death. If I can prevent death, I will, no matter how horrible it looks. I killed their mother, so I'm going to take care of them until they are weaned. Then I will let them go live in the forests of my home. But look at them. They're so cute and sweet, and they're alive. They get to have a future now. Doesn't that count for something?"

She lifted the fawns and set them on her hip, using a long bandage to tie them to her. As she approached their mother, she placed another piece of leather over their heads, and gathered up the kill, wrapping it up in the biggest piece of leather she had, and lifting it onto her shoulder. Without looking at Venser, she set off in the direction of their camp, still crooning to the fawns on her hip.

And the bearded man followed, nodding his head in affirmation. "Did a good thing... Two little fawns, yeah. They remind me of my own twins."

"I've only met them once, I think. They live with their mother?" Sedna asked. "How often do you see them?"

"Soarin and Lucinda live with Kari." He confirmed. "And they come to the tavern sometimes or I go visit them in this village a few miles away from the tavern when I can. When I'm you know, not out exploring adventuring or whoring or working... The last two can be considered the same thing."

The noble huntress giggled. "It's always good to go out and do something with you, Ven."

CHAPTER ELEVEN: THE GOLDEN GYPSY

The Dragon's Head Tavern and Inn, Vorland, 1435 ATC

"So, how much length does Venven want to be kept on the beard?" She asked him, before she continued on. "Thorn thinks you should trim it all the way down! Not allll the way down but still have some beard! Make it neat!" The pink haired demoness barmaid asked twitching a bit, her blue eye going in one direction her red going in the other. Thorn went through life with an almost innocent persona, wide eyed and bright. She appeared to be in her early twenties, but was much older than that.

"I don't mean to say it again but VenVen looks like a vagrant! Or a silver prospector!" She smiled, her mismatched hues going off in two different directions again, her spiky, shovel headed tail swishing back and forth and her long elf like floppy ears wiggling a bit as they sat in Thorn's room. The bearded man let out a sigh and blinked his emerald eyes a few times. What she was saying was true. He had seriously let his raven hair and beard grow much too long.

"Yeah just… Yeah. Just short. I don't know, around half an inch. Three fourths." Venser said sighing. "What you're saying, do it."

"Oh this is going to be fantabulous!" Twitch. The pink haired demoness heard the front doors open on the first floor and called out, "Welcome to the Draggy's Head Tavern and Inn!" She wanted to work fast, knowing there was a patron in the tavern who was coming to the bar soon. She began to work quite rapidly with the scissors, and her hands almost became blurred, due to the speed she was going. Soon after, those scissors came to a stop, and he was left with a short, neat trimmed, beard. She spun the chair around, so he could face the mirror on her dresser. "And before Thorn thought it was a spider eating VenVen's face! Ha ha!"

"Looks lovely. How about the hair?" He asked feeling his face. "Or I might just tie it into a ponytail. Never done that before."

She pondered a moment, running her fingers through his hair. "Could do." She reached to the side, and grabbed a simple hair tie, and began to put his hair into a ponytail. The pink haired demoness hugged him from behind, looking into the mirror. ''VenVen looks so handsome! He's going to look good for tonight when it gets busy!''

''Thank you, Thorn.'' Venser said rising from his chair, heading for the exit to go back out into the bar area. ''I have a good feeling about tonight!''

Thorn giggled. "Anytime Venven!" With that being said, she also left her room, and followed shortly behind him, moving behind the bar, humming to herself, playing with those pink dreads. ''Cheer up! VenVen hasn't been like his normal self lately! Maybe tonight? Hmmm? Good night!''

A few miles outside of the small trader's port that the caravan was headed to, wagons and horses alike drug slowly through the mountains. There were a few stragglers that were stubborn and continued to walk on foot, though there weren't that many due to the mixed weather. Volcanoes to their immediate left, mountains behind them and a lake that seemed to be frozen solid through... It was no wonder the little ones were so fussy. The head of the caravan called out the signal of a nearby town as they passed beyond said lake, bringing many to cheer with relief. They'd be able to sleep in warm beds tonight. When they arrived they immediately set out to putting up the booths and setting up their wares, though one woman deviated from the group to venture further forward on horseback. This woman with perfect golden skin was usually garbed in silks of red, though they were covered now by a burgundy overcoat that was only a few shades darker, and the staff she usually had with her was what she used to guide the horse due to its length. Intense, bright green eyes looked forward to the Dragon's Head with a sense of relief as well as exhaustion and the horse seemed to huff in agreement toward her sentiment, causing her to chuckle and pat her mane. "It'll be nice to get inside, I know. You'll be taken care of too, especially if they have the oats you like so much." A happy neigh from the horse caused her to smirk as her staff tapped against one of the beams of the stable, making her bring the horse to a halt and hop off. She tied him inside where it was warm and went inside the tavern, using the cane as a bit of a walking stick as she shut the door behind her and removed the overcoat. Brilliant scarlet silks adorned a lithe frame, accented by the occasional well-placed jewel, and a shawl to match rested on her shoulders to cover what needed to be covered for the most part. The tanned woman was dressed as a dancer, yes, though that was only one of her small group of talents. She draped the coat over an arm before walking up the stairs with the aid of the staff, tapping her way to a table before taking a seat inside the rather busy tavern.

Laughter filled the air as patrons gathered around tables, the many lanterns along the walls lighting the rustic little place up. The bearded bartender was hanging out pamphlets titled "Guide to Pryldahn" to many of the patrons while he flipped bottles around and did flair tricks with them. "Could I have one more ale over here!" Called a patron. "Coming right up eight now!" Responded Thorn who clapped a few times watching Venser do tricks with some of the bottles. A small leather pouch of silver landed right in front of her.

"Drinks for everyone!" Venser flailed his arms and grabbed that woman's glass, refilling it with bourbon since it still had ice. He slammed it down in front of her and pointed to his merc friend Ivy, some man at the door, the woman in the lovely red garb of silk who sat at another table. "You get a drink! You get a drink! You get a drink! Oooweee! Ooooweee! I'm taking all orders now. Or how about I serve everyone my special cocktail? Pink Footed Booby! You won't find a better drink anywhere people!" He lowered his voice and bent down to speak to Ivy. "Yes. Yes I am. Keep reading." He flicked her nose softly with one finger. "Maybe you can do guard work or something?" She rolled her eyes. "Boring."

The silk-clad was surprised by the rather jolly demeanor of the barkeep, as the ones she was used to were typically the burly, angry type that would sooner throw you out of a window with a collar on your throat than make a drink for you if you were a woman. It was a pleasant surprise, though. Rather than call out her order like a loudmouth, she stood from her seat and walked over to the bar, leaning against the counter just slightly while adjusting the shawl in order to assure no… Unneeded hilarity would be had over a garb malfunction. With a voice sweet on the ear and endlessly patient in tone, she spoke. "I'd like to have an ale too, if you would. Nothing too terribly strong; I don't handle drink well." She produced a few pieces of silver and placed them on the counter before taking a seat, brushing a few stray strands of hair out of her face.

"An ale? How about something way better?" Venser set three bottles on top of the bar, one full of clear liquid obviously vodka, one full of light red liquid, one full of yellowish green liquid, and a small vial of neon pink liquid. He set one glass in front of the woman, and one to the right of him. He poured the three ingredients into a silver cocktail mixer. "Oh shit. Hold on." He disappeared in a puff of thick red smoke and appeared a minute later, opening the shaker and dropping some of the pink liquid into it. He shook it vigorously for a few long moments then poured a glowing, neon pink drink into the woman's glass. "There we are! Pink Footed Booby. Give it a taste. C'mon! Try. Boobies!" When she would drink it, she would find it tasted exactly like a Strawberry Starburst. Only liquid. And if Starbursts existed in this universe. "Perfection." The man said with full confidence, pouring Ivy a glass and passing it down the bar to her. Thorn shook her hands above her head. ''That's the VenVen Thorn knows!'' It truly made her happy to see her dear friend like this again, knowing what had happened weeks before. But she both knew they didn't want to talk about it. And now was not the time to recall it.

"Not bad.'' Ivy admitted. "I suppose there's alcohol in there aplenty." She sighed and looked at the glass sadly. "I don't often pity myself for being a silver elf, but barely being able to get drunk is a stupid thing."

A tilt of the head gave the notion that she was curious, though before she said anything she decided to watch as he set up the bottles and the glass in front of her, one to his right. The golden gypsy chuckled lightly as he seemed to just poof nothing but a cloud of red smoke in his wake, and return quite quickly with yet another bottle. Resting her hand over her lips, she tried to hide her amused chuckling. Somberness had been all over her features before due to travel, though now her face came alight with a grin as he mixed the strange drink. Her eyes widened slightly at the brilliant coloring as it was poured, and the name made her almost fail in stifling a giggle. "Such a strange name for a drink... And a peculiar color," she said, though her tone was very much one of a woman impressed. She brought the glass to her lips and savored the taste for a moment...and one could swear they watched her bite her lip in the wake of the flavor. This was indeed much, much better than ale. "Fute zeii... I do believe ale has been outmatched for me!" The tanned gypsy woman grinned, taking another sip.

Venser flailed again. "Not bad? Not bad? It's like an orgasm in your mouth. An orgy of orgasms in your mouth." He flailed again. "Orgies! Orgies!" He grabbed himself a glass and poured some of the neon pink drink into his glass, gesturing to the silk clad woman. "She's got it right. Wayyyy better than any ale." He turned to her and asked, "What's your name?" He examined her closely. Surely she the wealthy sort, royal at best.

The mention of orgies had the already-red garbed woman blushing worse than a virgin in a nunhouse. She'd been mid-sip and she quickly swallowed to avoid spitting out her drink in a giggle... It was too good to waste like that. When he turned to her again and asked her name, she smiled with a respectful bow of her head. "Sanna of Krimeakhet, good sir, is my name. I'm a dancer with the caravan that's come to town a few meters down the road. She gave a kind smile, enthralled by the bartender's pretty emerald eyes.

Venser nodded and sipped his drink, glancing over at Ivy as she read the pamphlet. He laughed and took another sip. "So, a gypsy huh? I mean, dancer, but still a gypsy." Ivy put down the pamphlet. "Venser, you have to be kidding trying to recruit me for this. Me, a guard."

"Of a sort, yes. I'm their healer when they need me; otherwise I'm simply entertainment. I'm decent with a quarterstaff, though, and a bit of fire magic here and there." Taking another sip, Sanna felt her head fuzz over a bit. She figured now would be a good time to finish this drink and not have anymore.

"Healer? Entertainer? Decent with a quarterstaff? That's two things we have in common! But like, sometimes I use a sword since I need one hand free to use magic! And I like to change it up!" Venser offered Sanna a warm smile and opened his mouth to speak, but was cut off by Ivy's voice. He craned his head to her and asked, "Why would I be kidding? You've been to the castle before. And we need more staff. Like a healer... I mean, why not? The pay will be good."

Taking yet another sip, Sanna wasn't truly able to stop as the drink was that good, the tanned gypsy tilted her head some as he mentioned things they had in common. "Well this is certainly a welcome change from the bars back home," She mused. "Last I saw, if anyone needs any wares, my group was setting up their booths alongside the north road."

"Lovely, I'll have to visit them eventually. Maybe that's where Juliette went this morning... Fellow gypsy... Arielle too..." Venser said looking back to Ivy, disappointment plastered on his face. "Well wouldn't it be nice to be a part of it, be around for half the time, and then travel the other half?" He sighed and turned back to Sanna, looking to the man briefly who had yet to order something. Food he had heard him say. What kind of food? Spotted dick and BLUE Footed Booby?

"So, Sanna, what can ya tell me about yourself?" He said with a smile leaning against the bar, looking down to her. Venser was a man in his early thirties, with fair skin, odd serpent like eyes that were like pools of shimmering emerald, and dark hair. He sported a neatly styled beard, courtesy of his pink haired demoness friend. On top of that he was also quite handsome, his voice rich and deep. "Oh now he wants something." Venser nodded and grabbed a glass, motioning for the shadow tendrils to get the other half of the order. Downstairs, the shadow tendrils began to cook while they set a plate with a few pieces of bread down in front of a patron who requested it.

Sanna finished the last of the drink before setting the glass down, leaning on her arm for support. Her head was damn-near swimming, though she hoped it would clear some. She heard his question and started to answer just before another ordered something, and she let him tend to him before answering. The tanned gypsy smiled a bit, having to brush hair away from her face again. "Well, I'm from across the sea as you probably assumed. Common is not my first language, though I've spoken it enough that I'm semi-fluent, and I have travelled to the East. It's how I met the caravan, actually. I was sold to them as a dancer and they've been my family since then. Other than that, I'm simply what you see before you."

Ivy pulled a face of disgust. "Yeah, but… Swearing loyalty? I'm not very good at that. That's why I'm a sellsword." She put the pamphlet down firmly again, shaking her head, now looking amused again. "Besides, I think you have no shortage of recruits, do ya?" She winked at him.

''You speak fine for someone who claims to be semi-fluent in it." He said with a chuckle. "But being sold to them and considering them family, you're happy with your life, yes?" He asked looking over to Ivy as the shadow tendrils set down a plate of roasted boar down in front of the man. "Actually, we do have a shortage. A big one since most I've asked are also wanderers. It's not that hard to swear loyalty." He saluted Ivy and said, "I swear my loyalty to you. Now look both ways before crossing my- my- My penis.''

"Can I get you a refill?" Venser asked casually spinning to the side to face Sanna again.

The jewel on her forehead jingled a bit as she bowed her head with a blush, chuckling. The drink had been strong, but she didn't mind. She was also very flattered. "I appreciate that. I work hard at it, and sure." She answered in response to his question of a refill, offering the glass to him. "It's delicious. As far as being happy with my life, I am more than so. It'd be nice to settle down with a proper job, though."

Ivy laughed loudly, shaking her head once again. When she caught her breath again, she said: "Sadly, I think swearing loyalty and all that is not a small matter for me. It's a big thing for my kin." Stared off into space for a second. "That's probably why I left home. I don't like having to swear loyalty to anyone."

Venser refilled Sanna's glass to the brim with the lovely, addicting, neon pink drink and said, "Settle down with a proper job? Well I have an offer for you..." He set the glass down in front of her and handed her a pamphlet identical to the one he gave Ivy earlier. "We need anything we can get for our kingdom." He said with a smile craning his head to Ivy. "Well, give it some thought. At least. If you worry about your kin wouldn't you think you're loyal to them?"

Sanna took the glass and pamphlet with a smile, nodding in understanding as she read over it. This was where the semi-fluent seemed to show most, one would notice, as she occasionally had to struggle to pronounce a word every now and then. She took another sip of the drink, mainly to keep it from spilling as well as to savor its sweetness.

Ivy pulled a face again. "I sure hope not; otherwise I would be back there and not here, travelling to my heart's content. Apart from the," she smiled a sarcastic smile, "Belonging to a group' and 'feeling at home', what's in it for me?"

Venser looked over Sanna, examining her outfit, her features, every curve of the dancer's body. He let her read as he continued to speak to Ivy. "Well, a place to call home, of course. Purpose. And they have some pretty sexy servant girls in the castle."

"And let's just assume, hypothetically, that I'm not looking for a home, a purpose, or, as you so eloquently phrased it, 'sexy servant girls', what can I expect in return for my service?"

"Cake." Venser said, a small smile forming on his lips.

Sanna's brows relaxed as she finished reading and she leaned back, taking another sip as she grazed her eyes over it again. It was definitely something to consider. Having been so focused, as well as tipsy, she'd not heard his comment nor noticed his way of looking over her, and so when she looked up it was as though they were never said. "It is definitely an offer to consider, one worthy of acceptance so long as I'm not mistaken for a slave."

Ivy's grin widened. "While cake and girls obsessed with sex is, of course, a very good incentive, I was looking for something with more... Universal value."

"Cake, being a metaphor for money. I'm sure you'll be paid nice being a part of Pyrldahn." Venser said to Ivy looking to Sanna. He refilled his own glass and took a sip. "Of course. We can put you in as the healer, and both of us can be entertainers." He said laughing at Ivy's comment. "Like gold? Golden cake..."

"That seems reasonable. What sort of entertainer are you, if I may?" Sanna asked him, taking a bit of a bigger sip this time.

Ivy yawned. "You know what, I'll think about it. No promises. But it's something to consider, especially with this blasted weather. Oh well, I bid you goodnight." She got up and disappeared down of the halls, closing the door behind her.

Venser did a little jig behind the bar. "The jester! The fool! The only one who's allowed to use comedy in front of the queen. I sing, too, and I was once a thespian. A born entertainer!" He said grabbing his glass, splashing the whole thing at his mouth. He wiped the drink off the lower part of his face after drinking down some of it. "Whoooo...! Nother glass." He refilled his glass and pointed a finger to Ivy. "Yeah. Think about it." As she walked away he glanced quickly at her rear.

She chuckled. "You're definitely talented in that respect. My prowess in dancing, I hope, is welcomed as well with this kingdom." She got about halfway through her glass before digging for a few more gold pieces, setting them down on the counter. "I think I'll have a room for the night... I doubt I'm able to go anywhere in this state," she laughed a bit.

"Good good. So, you'll think about it? Or later we'll go see Y'vonne about you." Venser said bending down to retrieve the room cards. "We can go back to my room if you'd like and continue drinking." He stood back up and asked, pointing to her briefly, "Do you like wine? I have a Kupid Red I always keep around for guests. Now, Kupid Red is probably the finest wine you'll ever find. Costs me a fortune just for one bottle."

"Ooh! And because I sing along with ya know, be an ass in front of everyone I can sing something for you? And play the guitar!"

"Kupid Red... Now that's a name I haven't heard of in ages. An odd trader woman came to our caravan once, garbed in black, and sold us a bottle. That was the only time I tried it... Can't remember her name, though. Poor woman's dead by now, I"m sure." Sanna shook her head at the thought, sipping some more. "I'd like to see Y'vonne about it, honestly. I'm interested in this kingdom. As far as going to your room, I think that would be very kind of you." She smiled warmly. "Of course you can, if you'd like to."

Venser just raised his glass and cleared his throat, setting down the room cards. He just decided to sing right now at the bar for the whole tavern to hear. "No onessss-sssssssss slick like Venser, no one's quick like Venser, no one's dick is incredibly thick and big Venser's! For there's no man in the country half as manly. Perfect, a pure paragon! You can ask any Julie, Thorny, or Kari. And they'll tell you whose side they'd rather be onnnnnnnnnnnnnnnnnnnn...!"

The brightest blush one had ever seen blazed across her face like a flame. The golden gypsy listened to the lyrics and tried not to spill her drink as she laughed softly, shaking her head some as she set it down. "Brilliant song, my friend!" She applauded, clearly intrigued and clearly more than just tipsy at this point. "Oh, Gods forgive the lack of courtesy, but what is your name? You asked me, yet I've no idea what to call you." She truthfully couldn't remember if he'd told her already, or if she'd asked before.

That was only the start of Venser's song and he froze, and it looked like someone had whacked him in the face with a frying pan. She didn't even know his name yet? Dafuq? How couldn't she? He was handsome! He chugged down his glass and slammed it down, extending a gloved hand to Sanna. "The name's Venser Karkaldwin. Or VenVen. Or Handsome Venser. Or Ven. or Venny. Or My Little Vensie. Or whichever you prefer."

Thorn butted in, nuzzling his head. ''VenVen!'' Before she went off to another table to continue her story about being away from the tavern at sea for a month.

Another blush was granted across her tanned cheeks as she hoped she hadn't insulted him. She took his hand with a bit of an apologetic smile, squeezing lightly. "It's a pleasure to meet you, VenVen... Ahem. Venser. I'm sorry if I hadn't asked before.''

Venser took her hand and shook it vigorously. "It's- What the void is going on ov- Ah fuck!" He disappeared in a puff of thick red smoke and reappeared a few seconds later seated beside Sanna when the shards hit some of the bar and the floor and the wall. He sighed and stood up. Offering a hand to Sanna. "So, shall we go have some of that Kupid Red. Hopefully those people don't wreck the tavern." Venser didn't even notice some of his cape was torn.

Sanna squeaked and ducked at the sight of him poofing as well as the crash of glass that followed, eyes wide. She was definitely somewhat sober, and if she wasn't it was a miracle. She took his hand with a nod, not even questioning. "Preferably before we wind up shredded apart," she mused with a chuckle. ''Tipsy gypsy.''

"Never a dull day at the Dragon's Head." Venser said with a laugh taking Sanna's soft, tanned hand in his, guiding her down the hall to his room. "Thorn you got this!" He called back to the bar.

"Thorn has this VenVen!" The pink haired demoness called back, waving to her while holding a small wooden boat in that hand.

CHAPTER TWELVE: SANNA

Venser's bedroom, the Dragon's Head Tavern and Inn, Vorland, 1435 ATC

He led Sanna down the hall, holding her hand as they came to the sixth door on the right, and then pushed the door open. Venser's room was fairly big. A queen sized bed lay by the windows, and it was covered in turquoise silk sheets and he had about a dozen pillows all with furry gold throwovers. The royal colors of his homeland. Off to the left was a wardrobe with a few dresses hanging out, some spilt onto the floor. Beside that was a mannequin wearing nothing but a white porcelain comedy mask from the theater. To the right of the bed was a desk with a bag of coin in it, a mirror, and a few pieces of jewelry and some small boxes. Right beside it was various papers and pieces of art. Above Venser's bed was a recently acquired multicolored painting of a woman's vagina, and below that his signature double bladed sword, the Dual Personality. The bed though, was very inviting...

"What do you think?" He asked moving over to the desk in the corner, opening a drawer and picking out a bottle of the Kupid Red he spoke about.

Sanna's silks flowed like water as she walked, the true grace of a dancer showing in every step as she followed the man forward and gazed in awe as she saw his room for the first time. Her fingers had interlaced with his gently and despite her slight shyness, she was not trembling in the slightest. No, in fact she seemed bolder than she had been when she first came in, though no one could say for sure how long that would last. Her hand rested over the desk, a smile breaching her features as she looked over the bed with many a thought as to how she'd like to be in it. Preferably not alone. Her gaze fell to him then as he spoke and she approached, that same gentle smile remaining, though it was laced with something a little more fun when matched with how she looked at him. "It is very impressive... The make of your furniture is astonishingly craftful. Where is it you are from, the kingdom? The colors." she trailed, blushing as though she'd spoken too much and feared she'd rambled.

"I come from the isle of Kupidnos. It's... Far, far away. Very." Venser said standing up, sitting on the bed. He poured her a glass of the bright, ruby red drink and offered a glass to her, returning her gentle smile. "Though, I live here a majority of the time. But Kupidnos... It's warm all year around, golden beaches, excellent cuisine and culture, the best cannabis around. It's paradise. Like this." He said shaking the glass a bit.

The tanned woman wrapped her fingers around the stem of the glass, raising it slightly to him in respect with a bow of her head. "Kupidnos... I have never heard of such a place. It sounds beautiful. Much like a place near my homeland, if I remember... Krimeakhet. We had no such things but when I was sold, I saw them all the time. The shipping crates full of things like wine, silks, and even other women. I mainly hail from the mountains, though, the Charpathians." She tipped the glass to her lips, and if she were a cat she would have purred in savoring the flavor. Warmed her thoroughly to the core, and that showed in how the slightest hint of her silks seemed to poke out a bit due to her nipples hardening beneath them. "Kupid Red... Mhm."

"Well, they do call Kupidnos the jewel of the south." He said with a chuckle. "I've never heard of either of those lands, but... Not to sound rude or anything but glad you were sold. You're here now," He gestured to her outfit, "Wearing fine silks, looking absolutely gorgeous in them, and sipping fine wine with a very handsome man."

Sanna chuckled slightly, resting the glass aside after taking another sip. "I'm quite glad I was sold myself. For many reasons, but none so evident as the current situation. I'm very flattered you find me beautiful, and I do agree... You are handsome. I hope that my... Curiosity was evident." The bearded man scooted closer to the gypsy woman and took a big swig of his wine. "It was. Now, speaking of curiosity, what do you think of the wine?" He asked.

She offered a playful smirk as she too scooted a bit closer, the shawl dropping from her shoulders. "It has a full, seductive flavor to me. That combined with the drink you so eloquently called a... Pink Footed Booby, was it? They accent each other." This time her intense, bright green eyes wandered for a moment before coming back up to meet his pretty emeralds.

"Yes, they do." Venser said with an equally playful smirk. "It has the same flavor to me as well. The Pink Footed Booby in particular has a... Secret ingredient that gives the drink its unique glow." He took another sip and played with her locks, twirling some of her hair with one finger. "I imagine you're quite warm right now."

"What manner of ingredient is it? You've intrigued my curiosity," Sanna practically did purr then, her head leaning into his hand as it twirled a long strand of her hair in one finger. Sanna had to admit, he was right. A slow heat had been circulating throughout her figure, though she'd not truly noticed until her mind was a bit more... Focused on one subject. "You would be right." She said, her tone softening as soft fingers reached up to graze across his cheek, running through his raven hair for a moment, noticing a subtle green tint to it. She wondered what it was.

"Something I created years ago." Venser said running his right hand down her back slowly, caressing her with his gloved fingers. "A strong type of aphrodisiac. It's strength though, relies on your race. A normal human as I don't need so much of it to become..." His voice trailed off as she ran her fingers across his cheek and through his hair. "Doesn't seem..." He moved his head closer, his lips almost touching hers.

"I am as human as you, though... I have the ability to use magic within my blood... That, and when one is distracted by socialization... Tends to distract one from the feeling..." She'd trembled at the touch on her back, the caress bringing an infinitely stronger effect than mere proximity, and it was then she felt the effects of the aphrodisiac. She didn't mind, though, not at all... Her lips barely grazed his until she moved forward to press them further, lips meeting lips. She shifted until her legs rested across his lap, reaching up to move the jewel from her hair and set it aside. No sense in losing them.

"And I don't have the ability to learn new magic... I'm quite limited." Venser said, shuddering a bit as his body heated up. He breathed slowly as her lips grazed his slightly, blood flowed rapidly in his cheeks as he wrapped his arms around her, pressing his lips against hers in a passionate kiss as he held her close. He planted several more on them, ranging from soft to rough.

No words were left on the gypsy's lips, only feeling as he wrapped his arms around her and hers made their way around him to rest against his back. Sanna parted her lips for him for a moment, grazing her tongue over his lower lip before he pressed several more kisses to her, some that made her gasp, others that drew the softest of moans and the pressing of fingers against his clothes. The room felt as though the fireplace had been turned up if there was one, though she knew by his words that the heat she felt wasn't due to any flame. Her fingers trembled lightly as she shifted as though to fumble with the strings that held her silk in place, her breath a little heavy due to many things. The main one being this was her first experience with an aphrodisiac.

Venser bit her lower lip, tugging at it as they kissed. His outfit was made out of an unusual, stretchy material as she pressed her fingers against his suit. "Yeah... Why don't we get these silks off? Should cool you down...' He said running his strong hands up and down her body, feeling all of its curves. Then his fingers began to undo the strings of her outfit.

A soft, surprised "mn" fell upon the lips that bit and tugged, her head tilting back some as he spoke and she gave a nod. "Aye... Please, though aren't you warm...?" Sanna asked through breathlessness, her cheeks flush as she felt his fingers untied the top of her outfit.

The silken skirt would slide down as the top fell away, revealing tanned and golden skin. Skin that bore no tattoos, no sign of touch, no scars, nipples that were indeed perked fully to accent full, medium sized breasts that have never nursed. It was clear that she was either untouched or simply new to this by the way she grasped him, the way the feeling of his fingers seemed to make her come to life.

"Oh yes..." Venser said softly as her clothes fell away. He took the time to admire her perfect, luscious skin, her wonderful breasts. He raised a hand up and grasped them, fondling them lightly. "These fell so nice..." He began to harden up with every second he caressed them. "Yes, I'll be getting out of my clothes too..." He said standing up, undoing the zipper on the back of his suit and kicking off his maroon leather boots. He moved it down, revealing a leopard print thong and nothing else. His body was muscular, and he was barrel chested. His hardened member was fully erect beneath the thong, and it made the fabric stretch very, very visibly.

Sanna's head did not tilt back this time, but instead leaned forward to rest on his shoulder with a more audible whimper of pleasure. Her hands rested upon his biceps for a moment before he stood to undo his own clothing, her eyes fully delighted as she caught sight of what was beneath. Her hands then rested upon his chest, feeling the hard muscle beneath her fingers... Before those fingers steadily and slowly drifted to relieve a bit of the pressure on his end by simply sliding down his thong over his erection. She gasped with a blush as she realized how hard he truly was while learning fingers slid along his shaft before fully wrapping around it. "How can the body become so rigid." She murmured, blushing at her own comment. "I-I'm sorry. I've not... Um."

''You haven't done this before?" Venser asked sliding it down his legs, kicking it away too. He stood in front of her, naked completely as she rubbed his shaft up and down. "Well, there's a first time for everything..."

Sanna pressed a kiss to his shoulder then, trailing such gentle and fleeting traces down his chest and abdomen before her lips met the tip of his cock. "I'm curious." She murmured with another blush as her tongue slid out partially and she licked there, just across the head, slowly. She smiled a bit and her lower lip could be seen being bit before she drew the tip of his cock into her mouth, giving a soft moan to the taste of him. She didn't know why she'd done it, but she was truthfully glad she had... Perhaps instinct.

Venser moaned a bit when she just licked the tip, placing a hand on her head to guide her mouth to his hardened cock. "Let's get your curiosity satisfied, yes?" With his other hand he rubbed his cock up and down very slowly in front of her, inviting her to suck it.

Her hand moved forward to entwine fingers with fingers as she granted his stroking with her lips, sliding her head further down until he was almost fully into her mouth. The only thing keeping her from taking it fully was the fact that the tip was at the back of her throat. Sanna moved her head back and forth then, a gentle but strong enough suction applied with movement as she felt tingling between her thighs. She pressed them together and squirmed a little in response, a darker blush falling upon her cheeks that was a signal of her furthering arousal. In common terms, she was getting soaked from simply sucking his cock.

"That's a good girl..." Venser said with a soft moan petting her hair slowly as she went down on him. He held her head with both hands now, slowly thrusting his member in and out of her mouth. Both his lust and arrogance flared up. He just wanted to pin her down on the bed and dominate her.

A tremble emanated then as he held her head and thrusted, soft whimpers of need - need for him to go further, need for a firmer hand despite it being new, vibrating around his thickened shaft. Finally, she moved her head up and away to kiss him deeply, whispered words against his lips sure to be music to his ears. "Amazing... T-though I'm new to this... I want more of you."

"You'll get better with practice, Sanna." He said kissing her back just as deeply, placing his hands beneath her arms to lift her up. Venser playfully licked at her lips and laid her down in the middle of his bed, right atop his soft, silk turquoise sheets. He then laid on top of her, his lips tracing along her jaw, from her ear to her collar bone. His stiff member poked teasingly at her crotch as he did so.

Sanna licked his lips in return as he laid her down, a faint blush upon her cheeks again as she felt how comfy the sheets were. As he laid upon her, as though in instinct, her arms wrapped around his to draw him close. The way his lips traced along her jaw and from her ear to her collarbone elicited further trembling, though this was slightly nervous trembling. She wasn't afraid, Gods no, though the sensation of his erection poking against soaked lips made her gasp a bit, and barely resist jumping in surprise. She willed herself to relax as she knew very well she was safe, parting her legs a bit more for him and wrapping one leg gently around one of his. "Is it painful?" She finally asked, though the words were so soft only he would hear.

"Only for a second. And then," He paused breathing heavily as he felt their soft skin collide together, his member teasingly making circles around her wet flower, pushing at the opening of her lips, "It's a painful pleasure." He locked his lips with Sanna's and pushed himself into her slowly, thrusting in and out slowly but gradually speeding up.

The tanned woman pressed another kiss against his bare skin, this time to his collarbone as she felt circulating tingles of pleasure come from where he rubbed against her, then their lips locked and the quickest instance of pain, much like when one is pricked with a thorn, pun not intended but welcomed, graced where their hips then joined fully. She gasped and only gave a soft cry in surprise for a moment, though the pain had passed as quickly as it was brought... Just as he told her. "Mnn...!" She moaned against his lips as her hips rose partially to meet his as he began thrusting, her skin prickling with goosebumps as she arched up against his body.

"Mhm!" Venser moaned into her lips as she felt the short pain of being entered for the first time. He kissed her roughly and thrusted his cock in and out of her in increasing speed as he pinned her down with both hands. "That's it... Yeah...' Mhm!" He gave her one hard thrust and paused briefly, rattling his cock around in her inner walls before returning to the good thrusting. He craned his head to the side and kissed her neck, he placed his lips there and began to suck in like a vacuum, while biting her neck at the same time.

Oh, with the way he'd pinned her... That had unlocked something. Definitely a good thing. "Ah...! Gods above, Ven..!" She'd cried out as he pinned her hands to the bed, the way he thrusted... Especially when he'd given one firm thrust that she swore made her head spin... She felt as though her body were tightening, then releasing. At his kiss to her throat she tilted her head aside for him, gasping with a mewling cry once more as he began sucking and biting. Her walls definitely welcomed him, especially with how they rhythmically squeezed him and the way her thighs seemed to be soaked in a mixture of her wetness and the small, barely there drops of blood as proof of her virtue.

Venser left several love bites on the right side of her neck as he had his way with her body. "Mhmm ah... Yes yes yes!" He increased the pounding, then flipped them over with surprising strength so that he was now on the bottom, and Sanna was on top of him with his member still up inside her slit. "Ahh...!" He groaned and bucked his hips, quickly placing his hands on her sides. "That's It! Ride me hard!"

The bites made electricity-like jolts shoot through her body and her hips began rolling against his thrusts, grinding against him before he'd suddenly flipped them both. Her gaze met his with a sultry smile briefly before she felt him buck his hips, gasping in a squeal of delight while her hands rested on his. Her hips instinctively kept moving, rocking and thrusting him in and out of herself as though she couldn't control her actions. She cursed aloud in a foreign language as he could feel her walls tightened, her cries becoming more frantic... More frequent. She was getting close, not surprising, this was new to her after all. "Don't... Don't stop!... Something...!" Sanna tried, her very tone indicative of the coming orgasm that was clawing its way up her body.

The handsome bearded man rocked his hips back and forth as Sanna bounced up and down on his cock. The sounds of their bodies colliding, her rear slapping against his thighs filled the air. He moaned in pleasure running his hands down her back, resting them on her ass. He gave her a hard with each few thrusts. "Ah yeah! I'm not gonna stop!" He pounded her harder and faster now. "Lean forward.... I wanna taste you..."

Her nails pressed into his chest and dragged down a moment, leaving small impressions as he began pounding harder, faster within her. His request was met with instant gratification as she leaned forward, her hair draping to cover their faces from outside view, scented like western flowers. Her lips pressed to his just as she lost control, her screams of release muffled against his lips only partially while her body clamped down around his cock. Limbs and back trembled though didn't stop moving, instead moving faster as if to bring him with her.

Venser groaned and smiled feeling Sanna's nails drag against his skin as they made love. He gave her one last hard smack, leaving red marks on her rump as he brought his hands up to fondle her bouncing breasts as she bounced up and down on top of him. He allowed her to scream into his mouth, and her speeding up made him do the same. He felt close now.

The gypsy had definitely not complained about the roughness and even wiggled her ass in response to the last hard swat, gasping with a long and exasperated moan as he'd began to fondle her sensitive breasts. She quivered and sped up as fast as her body would allow, nibbling his lip just slightly as she bounced upon him.

"Yeah... That's it... I want to make you mine..." He said licking at her lips. Venser pushed his face forward and took one of her nipples into his mouth, sucking and nibbling on it as he slowed down a tad. His cock twitched and Venser held back, continuing to ram his nice, meaty cock into Sanna's sopping wet virgin cunny. "Gah, need to cum soon..."

She purred against his lips softly as he licked hers, a soft pleasured squeal escaping as he took one of her nipples into his mouth. Only then did she realize how sensitive they had become... It felt as though when he nibbled and sucked a thousand jolts at once were rocking through right to where they joined below. She felt him slow down as well as the twitch and gasped a bit, trembling strongly herself... In his slowing down, the twitch had hit a spot she didn't know about that made her walls squeeze him tightly. She ran her fingers through his hair. "You... Already have, Ven... It's okay, please. Don't hold back, okay..?" She whispered against his head, pressing a kiss there as well.

Venser stopped sucking on her lovely nipples and looked up, breathing heavily and sweating. "You want me to- Mhmmm...!" He shot glob after glob of hot, sticky cum into her. With each shot his cock rammed into her slit, then calmed down, then rammed again like a slow moving piston. "Ah..." He let out a relaxed sigh and pleasure ran through his body as he went calm with Sanna on top of him.

Just before he finished his sentence she felt the heat of something fluid shooting into her, gasping with a surprised and delighted cry as the sudden nature of it caused her body to have a second orgasm, not as strong as the first as her body was a little tired from the first, though definitely impactful. Her walls held him tight as he rammed into her slowly, rhythmically while they both calmed.

"A-Ahn... M-my Ven.." She murmured softly as she rested her head on his shoulder, holding him as close as she could with him remaining inside of her. Already so captivated by the handsome bartender.

"Did you have fun?" He asked kissing her softly on the cheek and laying his head back on a pillow. "And do you wanna get off me?" Venser asked inhaling the scent of their sex, smiling more and looking up to her, admiring her body.

She adjusted so that she lay beside him with a chuckle, pressing another kiss to his jaw this time. To be close to him, she rested one hand over his heart. "I've never had so much fun in my life," she admitted, eyes meeting his. "Perhaps the stories are true and I am a fool, but I sincerely hope this is not the last time."

Venser wrapped the silk sheets around them and cuddled close to Sanna, resting his head on hers and smiling. "Stay with me, here in this room, and we'll have more fun times... What do you say?"

Sanna thought about it for a few moments. "It's an honor I'm more than happy to accept." She answered with a nuzzle of her head against his chest as they cuddled close beneath the silk. "I'm quite lucky to have met you."

"Me too... Goodnight Sanna." Venser gave her one last passionate kiss on the lips before wrapping his arms around her waist, slowly falling asleep with his naked body pressed against hers.

And Sanna returned his kiss and was soon to follow him in sleep, her lips just above his heart.

CHAPTER THIRTEEN: BLACKENED ALLIGATOR

The Dragon's Head Tavern and Inn, Vorland, 1435 ATC

''Venser?''

"Huh?" The bartender was in his early thirties, light skinned, with messy raven hair, a neatly trimmed beard and eyes that looked like they were plucked from the skull of a snake. "Certainly." He said snatching up the coins in front of a brown haired traveling adventurer woman. He met her eyes with his emerald ones and turned around. "So, grapefruit beer this early huh? And the shadow tendrils downstairs can do the cooking.''

Due to many things, including the brief bout of interesting commotion that had since died down earlier, Sanna woke and shifted herself up from the sheets. Once-pristinely slicked back locks were cast astray to cover her eyes with a sort of forgivable messiness that slid against her bare back as she stood, bending to retrieve the fallen silks that had been set aside. She went ahead and put them on though did not seem to bother with the shawl she had before, combing out her hair to a favorable degree mainly to get rid of tangles. She made her way from his room to the bar then, offering a playful smile toward Ven. "Good morning."

Looking into his bearded and handsome face she was struck by the preternatural brightness of his unnatural, slitted emerald eyes, meeting their bewitching stare with her own grey ones she nodded. "Aye, sir, the best you have, and mind you do not water it as those of your profession are wont to do." Hanna smiling slightly her own jest she looked around.

Ivy smirked as she looked from Sanna to Venser. "Well, this is an interesting place indeed. Got any more recruits, Venser?" she asked with a grin while she took another gulp of her drink.

"Well hello beautiful." Venser said to Sanna brushing back his messy hair back. He still wasn't dressed. And anyone who walked up the stairs could easily mistake him for being naked behind the bar. He then burst out laughing at the woman who ordered wine, laughing for several long seconds in almost a cackle. "Oh no no no no no. We don't water down anything here. You see, we care about our customers. We never try to rip them off like that." He grabbed a bottle of Kupid Red he had on the top shelf and popped the lid off and poured her a glass, passing it to her. "Not yet Ivy. But..." He turned to his newest lover Sanna and asked, "Want some of this? It's not as nicely aged as the one you had last night. But this wine is still a very good quality."

Chuckling at the bartender's humor Hanna took the wine gratefully and took a long draught of the heady liquid, feeling its heady warmth course through her body and calm her mind replacing the goblet on the bar, "another" she said, "I will divest myself of my armor before eating if you will kindly point the way to the bedroom."

Venser quickly gave the woman a refill and nodded. "Very well. Give me a minute to find the room cards." He yawned and bent down to grab the room cards from beneath the bar, he began to flip through them and yawned again, passing the armored woman a silver key. "Right hall, third door on the right." He said.

''My right or yours?" Hanna asked, brushing her dark brown hair back a bit asked, raising a quizzical eyebrow.

"Your right. Once you come up the stairs, take a right and down the hall," The bearded bartender said.

Sanna chuckled softly, tucking some hair behind her ear for a moment. "I would love some, and perhaps we can share a meal together later on," she offered with a smile, soft and warm. "My treat this time."

''So what do you usually do, as a recruit, anyway? Does Queen Y'vonne send you on quests or something?" Ivy finished her drink.

Bowing to the company, reserving a particularly low and formal courtesy to the tanned beauty who had returned to sit at the bar beside herself, she picked her way in the direction he had indicated and found her room, where she began the tedious task of removing her armor from her travel weary limbs

Venser was mentally undressing Sanna as she once again stared off into space for what felt like forever. "Huh? Oh! Uhhhh, how about I cook for this? I make the best blackened alligator. Took me years to perfect." He said shifting where he stood. "I... Uh, what was your question again, Ivy?"

"What I would get to do as a recruit, if I were to become one." Ivy asked sitting back lazily in her seat.

Sanna had indeed noticed this time and had given a respectful flattered bow of the head toward the woman that walked away, her eyes drifting back to Venser with a grin, she'd caught his gaze as well. "I'd be honored," she said softly, having to stifle a chuckle and a blush as he'd had to ask Ivy to repeat herself.

He clasped his hands together and said, "Whatever position you plan on doing at the castle. If you're a healer you'd be healing, studying, whatever." Venser cleared his throat and took a breath while speaking to his new lover now. "I'm going to have to make a quick run to the market in town." He felt for his utility belt, but alas it wasn't there. "Be right back!" He then disappeared in a puff of thick red smoke that dissipated quickly.

The tanned woman chuckled a bit as he disappeared so quickly, a deep and dark blush replacing the one she had before. One of this shade would actually cause her scarlet shawl some envy. She seemed to try to think of something to say to the other two that sat beside her, her gaze meeting theirs for a moment before she blushed and looked back at the counter. Still, the smile never faded.

Ivy smirked and stole a furtive glance at the lone company, she said pleasantly, "If the vintage of last night was better than this, it must have been special indeed,"

Sanna's intense bright green eyes went as wide as dinner plates for a moment. "O-Oh... Well... He was my first, actually." She managed. "Definitely something to remember."

The silver haired elf guffawed loudly, snorting a little of the wine she was drinking and slapped her hand loudly on the bar to steady herself, "No, no, no, precious one! I was referring to the wine you were drinking last night, the vintage of which Venser spoke earlier." Causing Ivy to snigger a bit.

And there came the blush to follow. "... Great Gods, I'm a bit more sheltered than I thought."

Silent for a moment, admiring the deep rose tinted hue her skin had betrayed, she smiled, "No matter, my dear, a mistake easily made and one that only serves to highlight your charm."

Sanna chuckled and smiled again, this time a bit softer. "I apologize. I only came here last night to get away from the caravan and became caught up in drink. I sincerely hope I made no fool of myself. My name is Sanna," she extended a hand to shake the other's, another nod in respect given. "We're set up in the town not too far from here if you need any wares."

She turned slowly on her stool, curious as to the noise of footsteps and mutterings below. "Interesting, you are travelling folk then? Did I already ask this last night?"

A few minutes later, Venser appeared out of a cloud of thick red smoke behind the bar holding a meat tenderizer in one hand and a pamphlet with a royal seal on the front in another. "Gimme ten to fifteen minutes dear." He said leaning over the bar to quickly peck Sanna's lips. He then teleported away in that usual puff of thick red smoke, downstairs to the kitchen.

"I am, aye. We're a caravan from Krimeakhet, across the Slender Sea originally, though I'm hoping to break away and find a home. Though, I may have already..." The golden gypsy answered, eyes catching the puff of smoke with the suddenness of Ven's reappearance. She smiled at him warmly and returned the quick peck as he passed on the pamphlet, just as quick to poof away as he was to return. She smiled, though this one was a more caring, fond one. Much like one would see on a young girl with a crush.

Ivy noted the looks that passed between her and the man who had just returned. Sweet, she thought, but the sweetness of a kind that she had long forgone. "And what wares do you carry to market? I guess they must be expensive and of exquisite workmanship." She asked as her eyes moved languidly over her body. "I've heard of such people."

"We carry all sorts of goods. Silks, women, wine, tobacco, herbs from the mountains and the desert alike... There is much more, as well as entertainment. Dancers and flute players are among the few gifted. I am... Well, was, their healer and one of their dancers." She chuckled. "I am hoping to work for a kingdom that Venser introduced to me."

"I am sure it would be a rare pleasure to see such dancing, alas, I have seen little of the courtly arts for many months." The silver haired elf said blinking a few times.

The bearded man appeared several minutes later seated at a table in the corner, setting it with plates and tableware. A silver platter of buttered, spiced blackened alligator with leeks laid in the center of the table. He made a motion with his left hand and trapped the shutters in a green aura, slamming them to darken the corner of the tavern in which the table sat. He set a single candlestick next to the silver tray and lit the candle, smiling and turning around. "Sanna! The alligator is done."

The tanned woman perked her eyebrow slightly as one of the women shifted to guard her for some reason, taking a sip of the glass of Kupid Red that had since been resting in her hand untouched, save for a few sips every now and then. She closed her eyes to savor the flavor again, and one would swear she'd purr. "Perhaps I would be granted the permissions to perform here, thoug- Oh!" She stood slowly, hearing Ven's prompting and chuckled as she'd heard the commotion of him setting up a table. Sanna walked over to meet him and blushed, pressing a kiss to his cheek. "Ohh...Thank you, dear one.." She said softly, her smile bright and no longer shy, though she was immensely flattered. No one had gone to such lengths for her. "... I am truly honored to have met you last night, and to have tried that drink." She chuckled playfully.

Venser smiled and kissed her back, wrapping an arm around her. "I'm glad you feel that way, now, sit." He moved the plate and silverware beside hers, and let her go, taking a seat. He turned back and trapped the bottle of Kupid Red in a green aura, then pulled it over to him. He grabbed it out of the air and set it down on the table, tethering a glass for himself.

Sanna chuckled and took a seat where he prompted, eyes curious at the green aura that encased the Red for a moment as he pulled it forward. "The magic you use, I'm curious… Why is it green like so?" She asked him, her hands rested upon the table and folded gently. Then she had an idea... Opening one palm for his view, a small flame erupted and flickered, though remained in the confines of her grasp. It was a simple trick, but one she hoped he'd like. "Does it work in the same way as mine does?"

"I don't know." Venser said with a shrug wrapping an arm around her, nuzzling Sanna's head and kissing her softly on the cheek. He watched the small flame erupt and he asked, "Well... What else can you do? My magic is limited in a sense, but being here," He paused and gestured around him. "There's so much mana in the air! I have unlimited power here! Not like in the isles where I have to rest and drink spiritual remedies to keep my power up. There's just so much mana here!" He took a fork and placed a few pieces of the blackened alligator down on Sanna's plate.

"Go on, give it a taste."

The golden gypsy nodded in understanding, nuzzling his head in return before turning to meet his lips in a brief kiss. With a flick of her wrist, the flame was gone as quickly as it was ignited, and a pleasantly warm palm rested against his cheek for a moment as he asked of her magic. "I was born with the blood of a phoenix, if that makes sense... Very, very rare. Though I am a human, I can use their fire and their healing," She explained, listening to him as well. Taking a piece of the alligator into her mouth, she quivered a little bit with a happy "mm". It was very different, but very good. "Talent in both food and drink... Now that is something I will have to learn as proficient as you have," Sanna chuckled, taking another bite to savor.

Venser playfully kissed her cheek a few times and pulled back, pulling her a bit closer as he had one arm wrapped around Sanna. "It's good right?" He asked with a chuckle. "When you run a place like this you have to learn it. Besides, ladies love a guy that can cook. don't they?" He asked taking a piece and popping it into his mouth.

Sanna smiled ever still as she rested closer against him, bare back against bare chest. "It's very, very good, Ven. I hope that I can learn how to cook as well as you. I can, though not a great deal many things." She chuckled a bit, embarrassed by the admission. "I suppose they thought me best for dancing rather than serving meals, but that's alright." She placed another piece in her mouth, leaning against him gently.

"I can teach you." Venser said as she rested against him. He gawked, only did he realize he had done all his cooking in nothing but his leopard print thong. And he was only noticing this now. Somehow. "It's great to have many skills. Be right back." He kissed Sanna on the cheek and disappeared in a puff of thick red smoke.

The tanned woman had noticed the particular lack of clothing and covered her mouth to stifle a giggle, managing a wide grin. "Take your time, dear one" As he puffed away again. Sanna shook her head a bit with a softer chuckle... She must have had an effect on him if he'd forgotten most of his clothing after the night before.

Venser reappeared beside Sanna again, dressed in his usual red rubber suit with rubber nipples and an oversized codpiece, with a crimson and black tri cornered hat atop his head. "There we go." He said pulling her close as he popped another piece of blackened alligator in his mouth. He chewed and swallowed, then picked up his glass of wine and began to chug it down.

Sanna smiled as he returned, this time looking over his outfit. It was interesting, and she figured she'd have to go to the caravan to get her things once she'd found a place. She had a great many silks that she was sure he'd appreciate, as well as other things. Then again, she figured he preferred her best in a lack of attire. She kissed his cheek as she popped another piece into her mouth as well, finishing it before taking a sip of the wine. "Did you sleep well?"

"With you, I slept wonderfully." Venser said refilling his glass of wine, only half-way. "Sleeping with someone, their warmth pressed up against yours keeping you safe and comfortable is the best feeling you can possibly come across in life. I didn't experience it until I was twenty, to be honest Sanna."

"Really?" Ivy looked at Venser incredulously, butting into the conversation out of boredom. "I thought you would've gotten that pleasure of life a lot sooner, Venser."

She flushed a bit gently and sipped her wine as she listened, though set it aside before resting her hand at his jawline. "You were the first to give me that experience, Venser... Truly, I had never slept so calmly. Thank you... For more than just the wonderful night."

Venser waved Ivy off so he could focus on his own conversation. Looking to Sanna and then Ivy he shook his head, then nuzzled Sanna's. "You're very welcome... And there will be many more nights to come..." He looked up to Ivy and asked, "How old do you think I am?"

"Not a clue. I'm really bad at estimating ages, even within elfkind."

Sanna returned the nuzzle sweetly. "I look forward to them," She mused, a playful look in her eyes. When he asked the question of how old she thought he was, she chuckled some. "Enough to be experienced in such pleasures... I would say twenty and eight. Nonetheless, I am younger than most here. Only twenty and three."

"'Gimme a few months and I'll be thirty-one." Venser said running his hand down the side of her body, caressing the fine silk outfit she wore. "With time, Sanna, you'll be as experienced as I."

"Is thirty-one much for your kind?" The silver elf asked.

The tanned woman seemed very impressed when he gave his true age, her other hand taking the free one of his and entwining their fingers. "I'm truly blessed... Most men are already mated in our culture by your age. It is an honor to be as young as I am in your company." She took another sip of the wine, smiling warmly. "I do hope so... I'm definitely eager to learn."

"Truly blessed despite I'm ten years older than you?" He asked with a laugh looking back to Ivy. "Well, the average human's lifespan is a hundred. Middle age if fifty so... I'd say, kind of."

''Ehhhh kinda not really.'' The bearded man said with a dismissive wave.

Sanna laughed a bit. "Where I am from, we are married off early unless we are sold. To actually find one a woman wishes to be with is rare, if that makes sense... So yes."

Ivy frowned. "Only a hundred years? That's barely enough to do anything!"

''Glad we met." Venser said with a laugh looking over to Ivy, gesturing for another plate and giving her some of the blackened alligator as well. "That's why you make the most of it when you're young. I actually can't die, but... Old age might actually be able to kill me. It's... Complicated. And I don't like talking about my curse."

The silver haired sellsword turned to Sanna. "What do you mean, ''Unless you are sold? Like how they practice slavery up north? Curse... Okay." She made odd gestures at Venser's eyes, before dismissing it altogether.

"I have a different life cycle, oddly enough, it's difficult to explain." She chuckled some, turning to Ivy. "Before I came here, I was actually sold to the caravan I accompanied to the town near here. I was a slave dancer in the far west, and I was sold in trade. I've been treated as family by them ever since and I am free."

Ivy shook her head. "Slavery... That's one of the few things I really hate about travelling around in these lands, especially up north. I had never even heard of it before I left my home."

Sanna smiled. "I am not a slave any longer, though one could say I serve in a different way." She chuckled a bit, tossing a playful smirk at Ven.

Venser let out a chuckle and let the two talk among each other, eating the blackened alligator he had expertly cooked. "You should show Ivy a dance."

She grinned, finishing another piece of the delicious alligator before standing. "I think that's a pretty good idea, actually," She said as she disappeared to his room for a moment, retrieving the silk shawl she used when she danced. Returning to them she stood in an area where there was no table and nothing to really bump into and closed her eyes, her hips sashaying slowly from side to side, similar in the way that a belly dance shimmies, but not as erratic. Wrists and hands twisted and slid along abdominal muscle hidden by smooth skin as her left hip bucked up every now and then, a gesture that had she been wearing her jewels would have given the softest of jingling noises. Then she truly came to life as her waist twisted, silks flowing and flying around much like hair moves beneath water, her chest and hips arching and gyrating in circular motions. Unbound hair moved as freely as everything else, though there were times she tossed her head back to lick her lips at Venser or to throw a wink toward Ivy. She was quick and light on her feet, though had a distinct sense of control.

The silver elf was reluctantly impressed. She got an idea, she picked up her pack and got a flute and started to accompany Sanna with a tune she'd picked up on her travels.

Venser watched her with awe, his mouth slightly ajar. The music made the dancing all the way better. He smiled widely and picked up his wine glass, taking a sip while ogling Sanna as she danced.

When the music hit her ears, a sweet laugh erupted, and then song, in a tongue she'd not used often. A very old language not unlike what the priests would use, though Sanna seemed more fluent than even they. Her waist and hips moved slower, more sensual in nature, speeding up at times, there was even a moment where she slid to the floor suddenly in a split and began using naught but her stomach muscles to sashay her chest back and forth. Fingers traced over legs as they slid to meet each other before she drew herself up to her knees and leaned back until her head touched the floor, coming back up slowly to end the dance. She stood with a blush and bowed at the hip, a low and respectful one.

"By the void..." Venser began to applaud quickly for Sanna as she finished the dance, he then stood up to clap for her. "That was fucking hot! Bravo Sanna!"

Ivy chuckled and clapped, putting down the flute again. "Impressive. I haven't heard that language in a looooong time. You have a lovely voice and, to be honest, you are one of the best dancers I have ever seen in my life." She smiled to Sanna.

Her dark hair had brushed against the floor when she'd bowed, sliding into place against her back as she walked over and kissed his cheek. "Thank you both very much... I haven't been allowed to sing in that language in a very long time. As far as dancing... It's been, again, some time."

Venser wrapped his arms around her waist and pressed his lips against hers after the dance. "Truly wonderful." He said nuzzling Sanna's forehead.

She returned the kiss and wrapped her arms around his, comforted by the nuzzle. "Much like the Pink Footed Booby?" She jested, chuckling.

"Yes, much like Pink Footed Booby." He said with a laugh. "Why don't we go lay down? I'm sure you need a short rest after your spectacular dance."

She giggled a bit. "Aye, on that note... Though I figure you're as tired as myself given your travel. Is there anyone to help your shift?"

"The shadow tendrils always serve when I'm not here or any other employees. Thorn is usually here, Roselie is on here honeymoon Kojin just disappeared... We've been meaning to hire on some more tenders and servers." He snapped his fingers a snakey, shadowy hand popped out from behind the bar. "Get rid of this." Venser said pointing to the silver tray and the dishes on the table.

"Shadow tendri... Oh, how lovely!" She gasped, a delighted smile on her features as she watched the shadowed hand pop out from behind the bar. "Another form of magic?"

"Not mine. But I end up being their master most of the time." He took her hand in his, linking his fingers between Sanna's. "So, shall we go to my room?"

Sanna weaved her fingers in his as he did, nodding gently. "Aye... The one with the beautiful sheets," She recalled.

"Well let's go then!" The bearded bartender ejaculated scooping up the tanned woman in his arms with surprising strength. Sanna laughed and wrapped her arms around his neck, holding him close and tight as he carried her bridal style down the hall. "You can have everything that's left, Ivy!"

Once they disappeared out of sight the silver haired mercenary sat herself down and picked up a fork, rubbing her legs together a bit.

"Fuck. I should have asked to join them. Dunno if I really should..." Ivy could have, recalling a few of the nights she spent in Venser's bed in the past. Though they hadn't slept together in what seemed like forever. And she was very well aware of the other women he met here and bedded, and they often rented out the many rooms of the Dragon's Head. She sighed, and rested one hand on her chin, staring at the piece of meat on the end of her fork.

CHAPTER FOURTEEN: THE CAPTAIN AND THE VENGEANCE SEEKER

The Dragon's Head Tavern and Inn, Vorland, 1435 ATC

A man in an unusual red rubber suit holding a medium sized wooden box to him appeared out of a puff of thick red smoke behind the bar, letting out a yawn and looking around the tavern which was somewhat busy. "Evening. Anyone need anything?" He asked looking about, setting the box down and grabbing him a bottle of his usual cider.

"Thorn has this handled!" A familiar pink haired demoness bartender said with a twitch. "Where is VenVen's dancer lover? Or his other lovers or the kids?"

Venser shrugged as he began to stock the shelves behind the bar, and would have the check the barrels on tap later. "She's out for the night visiting her gypsy family, they've been here for a few weeks and they are getting ready to leave soon. And Juliette is liking the gypsies and Arielle... Dunno. Kids are with their mom and grandmother."

Downstairs, a mercenary captain entered the tavern, with her right hand glued to the hilt of her sword. The calvary saber rattled against her side. Her ginger hair trailing behind her as she ventured through the tavern.

Clunk, Clunk

Her boots hit the floor and her spurs jingled as she walked swiftly and finally settled herself on a seat at the bar, her hands cupped her chin in thought. Alexis raised her pale hand in greeting before addressing the bar maiden directly. Her voice was husky and deep; she wasn't as feminine and 'oh woe is me' as other maidens who only wanted to be courted by their prince. Alexis just wanted a drink. "I'm looking for a wench or a man and a wee' bit of ale. And maybe some grapefruit beer later." She said whilst pointing toward one of the biggest mugs. Her right arm was permanently held against the side sky blue uniform in order to ensure no one saw the dark blood droplets splattered on her shirt. It was no one's business. Briefly she took it off to adjust the black cape with dark blue inner lining over her seat as she settled. When she stood, the cape would reach just below her rear, a rather short yet somewhat elegant cape.

"Welcome to the Dragon's Head Tavern and Inn!" He called out his usual line, watching the woman with the auburn hair walk to the bar. "A wench? A man?" He looked back at the mug she pointed at and chuckled. "Well, there's a wench. And a tavern wench..." He said pointing to an unnamed woman from the local town, and then Thorn. "Uhhh... I think it's just her. Lot of guys today." He grabbed the mug and filled it to the brim with the finest ale they had on the tap, passing it to her. "Two silvers miss."

Alexis glanced to where the lad had pointed, "Oh well." She said trying to focus on the ditzy pink haired wench carrying a tray of mugs. "Maybe not" Her dark brown eyes briefly scanned the lass in disgust. She turned back to the barkeep and gulped down a few sips of her ale, before sliding two polished coins from her pocket onto the table. "Keep em comin', my good man" she lifted her glass in thanks.

The serpent eyed bartender blinked a few times and looked down to his outfit. He wore a red rubber suit with rubber nipples and an oversized codpiece with a red and black battleskirt, maroon leather boots, metal gauntlets, a shoulder pad, and a turquoise cape over his right shoulder lined with gold fabric. "I always wear this. Either that or I go nude or put on some pants or a shirt... Boring... I have these nice tunics I'm not wearing." He took the mug back and refilled it, passing it back to the unnamed girl and swiping the coins away, tossing them into the coin jar. "There ya go miss. Need anything else? Like food or a room?"

Not long after the red-haired female entered than another woman came in after her. Margot was clad in a soft leather jerkin and hunter green trousers wetted with a deep dark slick that stretched from over her chest, down her arms and over most of her torso. Bloody red fingerprints dotted her cheek, in startling contrast to her ivory colored skin. She walked swiftly and purposefully up the stairs in pursuit of one person and one person only the red-haired bitch, Alexis. She had to pay. Stopping at the top of the stairs, Margot's gaze swept over the room until it stopped on the unmistakable figure of the red-haired female sitting at the bar. Closing her eyes, Margot clenched her fists at her side and took a deep shaking breath before approaching her. Stopping just a few paces back, she spoke in a low hostile tone, heterochromatic eyes flashing seething rage. "You." She said tightly, spitting with rage as her hand moved to grip the top of one of the daggers strapped to her thigh. "You did this."

"Uhhhh..." Venser leaned against the bar and pulled the wooden box atop the bar close to him, looking to the woman that had entered and then to the red haired woman behind him. "Whatever this is, take it outside. I had an angry mob in here earlier and I'd rather not have to do any cleaning up again."

Rubber nipples. Hot. After the bearded barkeep mentioned his clothes, she raised a brow in pure amusement. "You must get a ton of 'Tips'." She muttered and grinned at her own joke, though she had a tiny feeling inside of her it was actually true. Unfortunately, her 'hilarious joke' was rather inaudible as she slowly became aware of the current situation. "Maybe I'll take that wenc-ch... Now" she stuttered as Margot's scent filled the tavern. "For Fucksakes." She hissed. Once Margot was in her vicinity and started bellowing, she tapped her fingers on her knee before turning around very slowly. In her head, this scène couldn't get any more dramatic. "I do this for a living." She said getting up and unsheathing her sword slowly, and undoing her short cape and letting it fall back. "Sorry weird nipples," she whispered apologetically at the barkeep "So... Come at me then", her hands motioned toward the girl's petty dagger as she was busy unsheathing her polished saber. "If you want to run with the wolves, don't piss like a puppy." Alexis was calm, but seeing Margot turned her on more than anything. She could give less of a shit about whose blood now stained her uniform. Everyone in the tavern went quiet. Somewhat. They lowered their tones and continued to socialize a bit all while watching the scene play out.

Slowly tiring from her long walk she looked into her water skin, seeing it dry as a bone as usual caused a long sigh. Looking up she spotted a tavern along the path, gritting her teeth the centaur began to remember her last run ins with humans. An angry sounding growl from her stomach rose to settle her decision for her, sighing again she took one reluctant step after another toward the tavern. Opening the door, she peered inside, before coming in fully. Soft thuds from her hooves echoed around the room. Oh no stairs... She slowly tried her best to climb them. Looking to the people by the bar she folded her hands in front of her and smiled kindly. "Um, not to be a bother. But could I ask for some water? Oh!" She backed up a bit, blinking her strange, reddish blue eyes that looked like a chemical spill.

Venser appeared near the wall out of a puff of thick red smoke, dragging the couch downstairs with him as he watched the two women in anticipation. He had a bottle of cider in one hand and a bowl of kettle corn in the other. "Punch her tits off!" He called to the red haired woman, setting his concessions down. He clapped his hands twice and the shadow tendrils manifested themselves into two shadow versions of the head bartender himself. One held a broom and the other a mop. "Huh? Water?" Venser asked looking to the unusual looking creature. "Oh! A centaur. Wow, it's been about... Four years since I've seen one in here. Welcome!" He mentally facepalmed. "Water! Uh, there's a horse trough by the stab-" He cut himself off and disappeared in a puff of thick red smoke, reappearing behind the bar and grabbing a glass. "One moment! Have a seat!" He quickly froze and mentally facepalmed again, letting out a sigh. "Take a seat..."

"You talk a big game for a backstabbing cunt," Margot spat acidly as her fingers wrapped around both daggers strapped to each of her thighs and drew them quickly, keeping a tight grip as she bent her knees and watched the woman with fiery eyes, each of them a different color, one blue, flashing pure hatred. Lifting her daggers before her, the blades pointed outward as she gripped them tightly in her fists and squared her shoulders. Rolling forward on the balls of her feet, Margot bent her head slightly as she watched Alexis' posture. "Fight me... And maybe you can die with the honor you lack, you scummy merc. And you call yourself a captain!"

Raising a brow, she watched the stuttering man quietly as he puffed around the room. Folding her ivory arms across her chest she continued watching him in amusement, "Not used to my kind here I see? Eh puffy?" Chuckling she simply relaxed herself onto the floor out of the way of anyone, "I'm sorry for the trouble it's just been days since I have had water at all. I've wandered so far from home and I thank the stone gods I have not been killed yet." The centaur woman reached up and began to fiddle with her neon blue hair.

Venser teleported away from the bar and near the couch against the wall, walking over to the centaur with the glass of water extended to her. "No problem here. Just those two fine ditties over there." He said gesturing to the two women who were yay close to mauling each other to death. "I don't know about you, miss since you just got here but I haven't been excited to see a fight since... Hmm, Chippy Dee and Ana Lee." He brushed her off and chuckled. "Uhh... Wrestling. Made those names up! Have you ever be- No no, I'm sure you haven't? What brings you here, miss" He asked the centaur woman. He leaned in close and whispered, "Between me and you my coin is on the red haired woman."

Taking the glass from his outstretched hand the centaur woman nodded to him in thanks. Looking over to the two bickering women she raised a brow in confusion, "You are quite right, it's been awhile since I have seen such a tiff. Not as bad as the one I saw last though, I swear you could not even recognize my brother when he was done with his fight. Kicked, stomped and mauled as he was..." Shrugging she raised the glass and took generous gulps of it, quickly finishing off every drop of water in the glass. "To answer your question, I have simply been walking to see where the road leads. Ran out of water and came here in hope to get some." Setting the glass down carefully on the floor beside her she sighed in relief, her throat no longer feeling dry as a desert.

Alexis glanced back to her ale and then to Margot. It was a really hard decision. "Right." she nodded, and leaned back on her seat, whilst crossing her arms. Her curved cavalry saber lingered against her barstool. Suddenly she felt the cold sink into her boots and glanced at the man offering them employment. "If you want a wench" she pointed to Thorn, who smiled and waved. "All yours". Why would a stranger take the opportunity to ask for sex during their fight? Strange things have been happening since she saw the bartender with the rubber nipples. Maybe Alexis would ask him for sex. Her eyes narrowed on Margot. "Now, I'm stuck against the god damn, motherless floor besides that, I have beer over here. The option of moving toward your stupid ass isn't really viable, you cocksucker."

"Do you need a canteen or two? A belt? We sell those here. Well, at least I do. I used to sell lust serum and grey amber before Roselie threatened me with my job." Venser said crossing his arms, watching the centaur set her drink down on the floor. "We have tables ya know, come, join me." He walked back over to the couch against the wall and pulled up a table next to him.

No sooner had the words left her mouth than Margot felt the chill permeate the thick leather soles of her boots and hold her to the floor. "Ah, hell..." She muttered to herself as she pulled uselessly against the force binding her to the floor. Her skin prickled with rage as she heard the other woman speak. "Well, really now? Well aren't you a genius; I certainly hadn't fucking noticed that." She snapped sarcastically as her hands, still gripping her twin daggers, lowered a fraction. Looking back at the man that had them stuck to the floor, she glared at him and pulled futilely at the force holding her again, her expression a mixture of exasperation and rage she practically trembled. She couldn't let the bitch get away with this and this bearded man was making it impossible for her to exact her toll.

Letting out a chuckle the blue haired centaur woman shook her head in response.

"No, I don't need any thank you though." Getting up carefully as possible she picked her up her glass while standing up, walking to the table he had pulled over she set the glass onto it. Settling herself back onto the floor again she folded her legs more comfortably beneath her. "Thank you, I didn't want to possibly break one of the tables by accident..." Giving Venser a sheepish smile she pointed to the glass which now had tiny cracks here and there. "I'm sorry about that, even if I try to be very gentle I can unintentionally break things... This is why I don't go outside my land."

He chuckled and said, shoving a handful of kettle corn into his mouth, offering the centaur the bowl. "Setting a glass of water down on a table don't break it. No matter how strong you are." His attention was quickly turned by him misunderstanding what kind of job the man was offering the two women. "Ooh! I'm interested in sex right now!" He yelled raising his free hand. He turned his head to the two women.

The centaur woman's eyebrows raised at the man's declaration to the others, shrugging. "What an interesting scene this is."

Alexis tried freeing herself by subtly pouring the warm mead into her heavy boots. It was futile "If you can stop me dead in my tracks, why can't you do the work yourself" she said spitting on the floor. "If I wanted your money, I'd kill you." She hissed. Alexis didn't quite enjoy being forced into a situation. "Margot-t" she said, her voice cracking "I killed that slimy fucking brother of yours, a horrible frail man, after I saw you two fucking in that filthy shed by the river." She turned to both of the men, her frustration visible as she tried to kick the gold satchel towards them. "Weird Nipples, help me. Out of this predicament and we can fuck like rabbits."

"Right away!" He handed the centaur woman his bowl of kettle corn and hopped off the couch, teleporting over to the red haired woman, standing between them with both arms extended out, taking Alexis's side. "Let's talk about this. She can't undo what she saw, and you can't undo what... Yeah."

"Step-brother," Margot corrected tersely, baring her teeth as she struggled against the bind again, glaring alternately between the gold on the floor and Alexis as she continued, her struggle evident in her tight tone. "And it's not as if I had a choice, he would do what he wanted, bastard he always did..." Her voice trailed off as the bartender in the strange outfit stepped between them and she leaned to the side to glare through him almost. "You know that just as well as I do, Alexis, maybe even better."

Noticing her glass still lying on the table she stood, picking up the glass she walked over to the bar setting on the counter to be taken away when someone wished to. Heading back to her spot the centaur woman settled herself back onto the floor, picking up the abandoned bowl of kettle corn she popped a few pieces in her mouth while quietly observing the room. So many interesting people in one place today...

Alexis watched the strange man in the rubbery material immediately take control of the situation. "Dammit." She uttered, she didn't really take cognizance of the fact, that he might actually take her offer seriously. Alexis only started realizing she was free to move at this late point and started undoing the top buttons of her blouse immediately. She motioned the barkeep to keep smoothing the situation over. Alex put her ankle of the sack of silver coins, just to ensure the wench wouldn't attempt to steal it. "If you didn't have a choice, then why are you angry that I forced my blade through his disgusting frame... Over-r and over an-nd over again-'n.''

"That wasn't your choice to make! He was my brother! That was my revenge and you stole it!" Margot's heterochromatic eyes shined brightly with the shimmer of angry tears as her entire body trembled with pent up emotion. No matter what her pathetic excuse for a brother had done when he was alive, he was still family and he was hers to kill, no one had any right to take that away from her. "You have always thought you could do better than me, haven't you? Do you think I need your protection, Alexis? That I can't fight my own battles?" She hissed angrily as she moved back a half-step, tightening her grip on her daggers as she raises them once more watching for any sudden movements as she stayed at a more fortuitous angle.

The man blocking Alexis shrugged his shoulders. "Despite what happened in the past... You're free to part ways. Wander alone and truly fight your own battles." He glanced back at the woman he was defending.

Alexis took off her blouse, the soft material slipping off her scarred skin. The pink flesh lines from her healed wounds ran all over her pale white skin. She wore a flimsy shirt underneath her blouse, the material hardly covered her chest. Her nipples were erect and visible through the thin fabric. She quickly slid her curved cavalry saber back into its sheath. Before gulping down the rest of the ale. "Margot, I CAN do better than you. I killed him because I could, kill me or leave".

She cracked her neck from side to side, "He seduced a noble man's daughter, I got paid. And I would do it again. All that matters." At this point, Alexis was calm.

Watching her disrobe, a soft pink flush spread over Margot's cheeks. Is this seriously necessary? She thought to herself, shaking her head after a moment to collect herself. The self-aggrandizing cunt wouldn't distract her. Rolling her shoulders, she bounced ever so slightly on the balls of her feet before she hissed low in response to Alex's words, her heartbeat thundered in her ears. Margot's passion had always been her greatest boon and her biggest bane. Without another word, Margot gave a low almost inaudible growl as she lunged forward, moving toward the redheaded woman; spinning her long gnarled dagger in her hand so the blade pointed straight out as she aimed for a right hook into the woman's side, between her ribs. With her other hand, she kept her other fist gripped tightly around the hilt as she held it up toward her face.

"Oh... Nice..." Venser said licking his lips at the sight of Alexis disrobing. He turned back to the woman as she growled, the mark on the back of his left hand glowed greenish white and emitted steam in case she tried anything. And she did. "Ah!" He yelped and moved back as the dagger came at him, throwing out his left hand at her. Suddenly, the dagger was trapped in an eerie, glowing green aura same as his mark as it hovered slowly towards Venser, where he caught it.

"Throwing knives. Cool, but impractical. A waste of perfectly good metal, and you just gave me your weapon."

Blinking rapidly when the green light made contact with her body, her breath was knocked out as she was forced back another half step. Growling in frustration, Margot seethed with irritation as she got more and more frustrated. "You can't even fight me by yourself. You have to hide behind our friendly bartender!" she hissed as she rolled her shoulders again, not willing to give up yet.

"Ladies, ladies." Venser waved his hands, his mark stopped glowing and the steam quickly dissipated. "I think just sitting down and having a lot of wine will be better than this little... Cat fight that clearly isn't going anywhere. Sound good?"

Alexis cocked her head to the side watching the fiasco. She glanced to the man in the rubber outfit, whilst standing on one leg, stumbling by taking off one of her boots. "Where the rooms in this joint at?" She raised a brow before glancing at Margot and shaking her head. "We can talk tomorrow."

"Well miss, I'd have to check the room cards before I rent a room out to you."

Venser said brushing back his messy black hair, stepping out from between them to focus on Alexis. "But you can stay in my room if you'd like for no charge..." He said with a low, seductive growl.

Shaking her head, Margot shook her head in disgust as she dropped her hands to her side; this was obviously not going anywhere and it was pointless. Sheathing her daggers, Margot stepped backward. "Yeah, whatever," she said bitterly. "I see you've still not changed, Alexis. Still the same whore I knew before." She said, giving her head a jerk in the direction of the man. "Maybe he can give you another job."

The redheaded captain kicked the sack of silver up towards her and caught it in her left hand, whilst carrying her shoes and blouse in her right. "Let's go sunshine." She gestured toward what seemed to be the bedrooms. "I keep my word". Margot's words rang in her ears. "At least I ain't fucking my own brother you cocksucker." She hissed as she walked towards a corridor in the big tavern, her belt dropped to the floor as she disappeared into the darkness, hoping Weird Nipples was smart enough to follow her.

Venser watched Alexis walk away and he turned to Margot, nodding his head and offering her back the dagger he caught. Before dropping it to the ground with a clatter. "Well..." He gestured behind him. "I wish you a good night. And so sorry for what happened tonight." And with that, he disappeared in a puff of thick red smoke, reappearing in the middle of the hall, following Alexis from behind.

''What. The. Fuck?!'''

The centaur woman shrugged, happily eating kettle corn with the pink haired barmaid. ''Thatttttt's VenVen! Thorn is happy no one got stabbed or killed until they were dead.''

Margot gave a frustrated sigh, threw her arms up, and headed down the stairs to the exit.

CHAPTER FIFTEEN: ALEX

Venser's bedroom, the Dragon's Head Tavern and Inn, Vorland, 1435 ATC

Venser's room was fairly big. A queen sized bed lay by the windows, and it was covered in turquoise silk sheets and he had about a dozen pillows all with furry gold throwovers. The royal colors of his homeland. Off to the left was a wardrobe with a few dresses hanging out, some spilt onto the floor. Beside that was a naked mannequin wearing a white smiling mask. To the right of the bed was a desk with a bag of silver in it, a mirror, a hand crossbow, and a few pieces of jewelry and some small boxes. Right beside it was various papers and pieces of art. Above Venser's bed was a multicolored painting of a woman's vagina, and below that his signature double bladed sword, the Dual Personality. "Ya know... I never did get your name." He said opening the door to his room, gazing at her with a sly smirk. "What is it? My name is Venser Karkaldwin."

Her dark brown eyes scanned his room, before placing her clothes on the floor near his wardrobe. "Alexis Bonneville. Just Alex is good though." she said softly. Alexis had never really cared about much in her life she thought, as she dragged her finger against the wardrobe whilst moving closer to the painting, her eyes zoomed in on the layers of flesh. "Hmm..." She hummed and turned to him. "A deal's a deal, isn't it", her hard nipples were still visible through the thin layers of fabric as she brushed her palm over her left breast, her hand sliding down her chest toward her hips. Her sheath and saber dropped to the floor with a hard 'thud' as soon as she loosened the buckle. Alexis had always been rather rough woman, her eyes settled on his crotch as she bent a little forward to help her wiggle out of her beige uniform trousers.

The handsome barded man removed the maroon colored codpiece and tossed it aside, walking over to her. He gave Alex a gentle push down onto the silk sheets of his bed and growled a bit more, undoing his suit from the back after tearing off his gloves and kicking off his boots. "A deal is a deal indeed..." He said as the red rubber suit fell to his ankles. Venser's nude form was muscular, he was barrel chested and had faint scratch marks all over his chest and body. His hair was brushed back his beard neatly trimmed and his jaw chiseled. Despite the scars, he was still quite handsome. "Let's get you out of these clothes..." He said unbuttoning her pants, sliding them down.

Alex fell down onto the cold sheets, and squirmed. Her small breasts brushed against the cotton material of her shirt as she curled into the cold sheet. The woman's slender frame was promptly exposed by Venser; who swiftly undid her trousers and exposed her soaked white undergarments. Her pantie clung to her wet lips and emphasized her pussy, a soft small clump of hair visible where her lips met. "Fuck-k." She muttered in whilst exhaling deeply. Her body was toned with a healthy amount of muscle. Her skin was pale and cuts ran all down her body, she had no shame for these scars. They made her real. And seeing Venser's now, she admired them. As soon as he finally moved her trousers past her ankles, she licked her harsh lips and reached down toward her boney hips, she started pulling at her shirt. Her cheeks turned crimson and she was quickly started wiggling out of her shirt. "Your-r turn." She whispered. She arched her back to expose her average sized figure. Alexis's brown eyes immediately locked with his when the shirt reached her neck.

Venser stood before Alex naked, his member stiffened up as he gazed over her body. "Let me help you..." He said placing both hands on her shirt, removing it. He tossed it aside near his suit and wrapped his arms around her body, locking his lips with hers as one hand trailed the side of her body, feeling every curve of her body, a warrior's body, every scar until his fingers gently rubbed against her clit, then to her womanhood. He rubbed it slowly as he planted kiss after kiss on Alex's lips. "Feels great... Doesn't it?" He asked in between kisses.

"Yes it does Ven..." Alex pushed herself forward, puckering her lips and giving the handsome bartender a kiss that warmed them both from the inside. There was a certain taste from behind her lips; sweet, yet strong. Rough. Her tongue pressing against his lips. Venser's tongued danced a romantic, well-practiced routine that his many lovers knew, while the captain's tongue flickered in and out and flopped about inside his mouth like a dead fish, showcasing her inexperience.

"You like that?" Breathed Venser, leaning in to plant firm kisses against her neck, even nipping at her ear a bit before pulling away. Alex's mind was so awash with pleasure that she wasn't capable of coherent speech just then, so she made do with an unrestrained moan and a gentle nod. She couldn't believe what was happening and was now captivated by his handsome visage and his muscular body. And if there was one thing Alex valued, that was strength. She placed one of her hands on his firm tricep, squeezing it before trailing her hand down his arm.

''Mhm. I do...'' Her hands trailed over his body, down his stomach and wrapping around, grabbing his firm butt cheeks as the captain writhed underneath Venser. "Don't be gentle." Were the last words she'd say before drawing a breath in anticipation for what was to come.

''Your wish is my command...'' Without warning, he gripped his length and slowly guided himself into his Alex's snug, tight pussy. ''Mhm!'' Alex let out a sharp cry and gripped his buttocks harder, raising one hand, curling it into a fist and smacking his back. ''Ahhh... Ven!'' Noting its tightness as he licked his lips, closed his eyes and began pumping in and out at a rapid pace, just rocketing away. Venser sat up a bit held her by the back as he laid into her with a swift, steady rhythm of fast thrusts.

Her mouth formed a small 'O' as Venser's thickness went in and out of her by only a couple of inches. "W-Wow... Oooh, gods!" Alex huffed, gripping his butt harder and raising her hands up, her fingernails digging into her back. "Fuck, you're so hard!" Her entire body was rocked with pleasure. She moaned as her entire body concluded around the handsome bartender's thick shaft, stars dancing in her vision with each deep stroke. Subtly her legs wrapped around his body now, her perky nipples brushing up against his barreled chest.

Venser started slow, still enjoying the feeling of the redheaded captain's legs holding him close, easing his way into Alex's tight hole, gently gripping her back as he slid his thick cock slowly into it. Burying himself inside her momentarily before moving his hips in hard thrusts, pummeling her insides in the most delicious way, groaning in pleasure from her tightness and loving the feeling of her immediately. Wrapping his other arm around her.

The mercenary captain let out a shivering, breathless moan, melting against the bearded bartender with each sharp buck of his hips. Her entire body felt aflame, every touch and graze feeling like lightning bolts of pleasure coursing through her body. Venser's head would then lower itself, his lips parting as they trapped one of her perky nipples between them, sucking on her flesh with his warm mouth, leaving behind his drool and saliva to cover her rosy nipple, and pale skin, all while he penetrated her.

Her hips moved slightly against him, legs trembling as she held onto Venser's back, nails digging into his skin and adding to his scars. Cries of pleasure erupt from her Alex writhed more and tried to control herself. Feeling the warm mouth and the beard hair tickle her skin on tender breast peak, she groaned louder in enjoyment. Dark brown eyes rolling backwards into her skull for a moment in pleasure as she parted her legs wider to give him full access to her.

"Fuck! Shit!" She hit his back again. " Cocksucking bastard!"

Venser kissed her breast, his tongue swirling in circles to caress her nipple as well as her tender skin, playfully, he'd bite her breast ever so gently before kissing it with a loud noisy kiss, pulling away from it, a strand of his saliva that attached her breast to his lips breaking as he moved his head away, sitting up a bit and gripping her legs.

The redheaded captain sat up as well and pressed her palms to his chest, giving him a push and scurrying back a bit. Venser slipped out as Alexis quickly got on all fours, gripping the sheets and spreading her legs a bit more. "I want you to give me everything you got! Hold me tight and fuck me like a horse."

He blinked his slitted emerald eyes and a sly smile spread across his lips, moving forward and giving her a harsh smack on the rear, then he lined himself up again, smearing pre-cum all over her inner thighs before pushing himself in again. Venser's legs locked around Alex's as he continued to pound away, his fertile balls lewdly slapping against her ass with each thrust. Every impact causing the captain's ass to jiggle deliciously as he mechanically pistoned her pussy, the bed creaking a bit underneath them as Venser took Alex from behind.

The strong, bearded bartender bucked his hips faster, harder, he could feel his cock twitching as his strokes became shorter and more brutal, hilting herself and causing the thick base of his shaft to jackhammer her abused hole. The motions slowed, if only for a moment, prior to the sound of a loud smack. The noise was unmistakable; it was the clap of a spanked ass cheek. "Oh ah Ven hit me again!" Alex cried out as he delivered another firm, harsh smack to her ass, followed by another, and another until he left a bright red mark, causing the captain to grip the sheets with one hand and punch at the wall with the other.

Alex could feel an orgasm building as body succumbed to the pummeling of the strong bartender.

"Ulp! I gotta- Nghaaah- aaAAAAH!" She cried out, her spine arching as she felt him increase in speed. She could barely feel him tense up as she gripped around him, his body clenching inside hers as his cock throbbed freely in her vulnerable body, forced to spread against nothing more than her untouched inner walls. She did so love the manhandling. Being taken from behind like this was captivating beyond belief, and it only added to her excitement.

"I'm right there too!" Fully hilting himself, the man's nuts contracted, sending a torrent of his hot, stringy cum deep into the captain's inner walls. Every shot through the man's length caused the organ to throb violently, only adding to the redhead's enjoyment.

"Cocksucking SHIT Venser! Ahhhh! Ohh!" Alex squirted her climax all over Venser's cock right after he came. Clear nectar erupted from her pussy, spraying his lower body. The captain's whole body shuddered as she rode out her orgasm. Her spent muscular and toned slumped flat on the sheets in order to better enjoy her afterglow, Venser's seed and her juices dripping from her cunny.

Venser let out a satisfied sigh and pulled the silk sheets back a bit, wrapping the covers around the both, and the two enjoyed each other's body heat. She didn't need words to convey her next message, but a gentle nuzzle and a satisfied sigh as they both lie there together, waiting for their shared tiredness to lull them into a slumber, ending the night with a bang. Literally.

Alexis yawned and rolled over. "Ahhhh..." She ran her two fingers against her lower lips and sat up, kissing Venser who looked up at her with his pools of emerald. He returned the kiss, there was a pause, and he was met by a punch in the face.

"Ow! What was that for?"

"Sorry Ven. Just had to do that. It felt too good."

CHAPTER SIXTEEN: THE CAPTAIN'S DUEL

Venser's bedroom, the Dragon's Head Tavern and Inn, Vorland, 1435 ATC

The rays of the beautiful sun shone through the blinds of Venser's room, lighting up the beautiful golden and turquoise silk sheets of his bed as the two laid beside each other, The serpent eyed bartender held Alexis close as the two slept naked. "Nurfpgh... Mer..." He yawned a bit and moved, groaning. He let out a small chuckle moving one hand down his chest, feeling all the new scars the girl made.

Alexis growled at the bright light peered in through her closed eye-lids. She wasn't ready to face the shit she had gotten up to last night, she purred against the warm frame beside he before slowly opening her dark brown eyes. "Owhhh..." She said, feeling a surge of pain ran through her frame. She had been fucked ruthlessly by the sturdy man next to her. She felt the wetness under her lower back, the sheets were still soaked from what happened earlier that morning. She rolled onto her stomach and wiped her eyes to try and regain focus.

"Well hello beautiful..." Venser said fluttering his eyes open, wrapping his arms around Alexis's naked frame. He nuzzled his head against her back and planted a few small kisses up it to her neck. He chuckled again and said, "Slept well? By the void you were rough..." He began to play with her hair and said, "Long, sweaty sex... I like the rough ones."

The redheaded merc captain felt two strong arms wrap around her slender frame, normally Alexis would fight it, but she just cuddled deeper into the warmth of his body. His presence was comforting and she rubbed her thighs together, trying to resist the urge to beg him to fuck her raw. A deep crimson color sank into her cheeks as he spoke and she looked away trying to play it off. "Well-l... Yeah" She uttered before maneuvering a hand under the sheets trying to feel for her underwear. "Thanks, I guess" She uttered as she managed to persuade herself to sit forward instead of staying in his arms. His smell and touch was starting to haunt her.

Venser sat up with Alexis and wrapped his arms around her again, pulling her down with him as they laid in bed. "And how are you this morning?" He asked cuddling into her. "I never did get to ask what that uniform is for... A soldier of some kind clearly. Officer, since usual soldiers get chainmail and actual protective gear... Those. Those are fancy commanding clothes." He pulled the sheets down and ran his hand down the side of her body gently. "These scars... The body of a warrior. A rough one." He said again, giving her rump a nice, hard smack. Afterwards, he rested it there and gazed into Alexis's brown eyes with a smile upon his lips.

"Dammit." She muttered to herself feeling Ven pull her into the sheets again. "I'm good-d-d.." her breathing increased as she attempted to create even the smallest distance between the two of them. She pushed her palms up against his chest, landing on her side toward him. Her heart was racing her hands settled on his muscular frame. Alex cursed herself under her breath as she felt the texture of his muscle under her palm. When Ven smacked her rear, she tried to resist squirming at his touch, but comfort filled her when his palm rested on her soft mound. "I used to be, it doesn't matter now does it," she said sharply, before feeling wetness drizzle down left leg. She hadn't laid naked next to a man in several years, her toes curled as she tried to ignore her indecent urges. "What do you want?" Alex immediately regretted this question, confusing filling her expression.

Venser shrugged and he laid down next to her, looking into her eyes. Unlike her, he seemed completely calm. He took her hands gently and pressed them to his barreled chest, running them up and down it slowly. "Simple. Just to... Heh. Well the morning after I just like to cuddle and talk after sex." He smiled and extended a hand out to her cheek. "Why don't we just make ourselves comfortable and get to know each other better. Would you like that, Alexis?"

Her cheeks were flaunting a bright red color as he proceeded to place her hands neatly against his chest. "The morning after." The woman whispered, there was a brief replay of how he had rammed his hard shaft into her. The sound of flesh on flesh contact rang between her ears. She had screamed loud enough to wake up the whole town over whilst smearing her creamy white cum all over his bedding. A shrill ran down her spine and she licked her rough lips. "You first." She managed to say. She had calmed down slightly; relieving the pressure by sinking her pearly whites into her bottom lip.

"Well... What would you like to know first? You know my name and that's just about it... And I'm the head bartender, and I'm handsome and charming and- Oh."

He waved her off and chuckled, stroking her hair. "I could go on forever of how great I am. I'm more interested in you going first..." He gestured her clothes on the floor beside his. "So tell me about what you fight for."

Alexis sighed and trailed a finger down her bare chest and over the pink scars that stretched across her slender frame. "Let's just say," she hesitated, "I might have lead a decent sized legion into their own demise..." She cleared her throat. "knowingly". She leaned forward lifting her blouse with one fingers, the epaulettes hanging onto the material for dear life. "Hypothetically speaking, of course." Alex crushed her forehead between her palms, "Hypothetically there might be a large bounty on my head". She pulled the sheet over her head and sighed, hiding her guilt behind the flimsy fabric. "I might or might not, wear it out of respect for those who lost their lives", she cleared her throat before narrowing her eyes. "They'll find me someday." Her smile turned into a displaced smirk. "Ven, I share, you share. Like we did last night." She mumbled the last bit under her knuckles.

"So you were a commander?" He asked listening to her closely. He lifted the sheet up slowly to look at her with an equally displaced smirk. "What? Well, stick around... And I'll protect you from anyone who comes seeking the bounty. "Or I could offer you a job..."

A rare sweet smile crept onto her plump lips. "Captain, actually. The rank of commander belongs to my father. Even though I lead and managed on the front lines more than him. And I can protect myself." She said defensively, but quickly backtracked, "But-t err... Thanks." His words rang between her ears and she lifted her brow in amusement. "A job?"

"My kingdom is recruiting, and we need all the help we can get." Venser said throwing the sheets down a bit to reveal her upper body. "I'm sure you'd fit in just right with the other warriors there. And I've been wanting to adventure for some time. And I'd like a companion who'd kick ass. Would you be interested in being my companion?"

"What kingdom?" Alexis asked whilst shifting on the bed. "Do you often fuck women for recruitment?" another question followed promptly after the first but this time with a more serious expression. "What is your... Err" The young girl glanced at his half bare torso, imagining him as the gigolo of some sorts. "Position in this kingdom?"

Venser chuckled and shook his head in negation. "No don't be ridiculous. Well, sorta. My position is the jester. The fool, the only one who's allowed to use comedy in front of the Royal Family of Pryldahn!" He said with a hand pressed to his chest. "Also, Von, who's the God Emperor's daughter and head of household has tasked me of being a recruiter."

"Pryldahn. They make some damned good crossbows. Pffft. I would be fired and kicked out of Castle De Seraphm for fucking the jester" She chuckled and scratched her head. Alexis couldn't believe she was smiling genuinely for the first time in a decade. The situation was a bit hysterical. "Companion, I don't need to make an ass of myself do I?" It was a rhetorical question. She offered palm for a brief handshake. "On the condition that, we repeat last night on a weekly basis."

Venser let out a loud, raunchy laugh. "Why not a daily basis? I have a saying that I invented myself, like my signature drink. Sex everyday keeps the gloom away."

She shook her head in disbelief of being recruited whilst naked. "I like a daily basis better. Where next, my friend... Probably best to put on clothes on first." Alex grinned. "Or maybe not"

"No... Let's stay here for a while..." He said wrapping his arms around Alexis's naked body again. "You're not allowed to leave this bed. You're my prisoner." He said playfully, flicking her nose and pressing a quick peck against her lips. "The kingdom can wait. We're not so busy these days..."

Alex purred into his ear before sinking her pearly whites into his earlobe. As she exhaled, with teeth lightly pressed against his tender flesh; her warm breath brushed against his ear. "I've escaped many a prison but." She trailed her finger across her bottom lip, the feeling of his tender lips against hers lingering as she spoke "You have yet to tell me of your past..."

"And you have yet to do the same. I've been around for a while... I've got lots to tell. My early years though, before..." He moaned and nuzzled her head in response to her warm breath against his skin. "Look my eyes." He looked into her brown eyes with his green, serpent like ones. "Didn't always have these. Or my powers. But... That's complicated. Curses... Basics. Tell me about your home, Alexis."

The captain never really noticed his eyes until she gazed upon the green orbs directly. "Must have hurt," she said as an observation. "We are both in the same boat regarding our past, it's too complicated to explain and a brief summary of events wouldn't do our history justice" She trailed her cold tongue over his collarbone. "How about..." She said sweetly before straddling his hips. "We just continue where we left off." The words escaped her lips slowly whilst she grinded his crotch.

As Alexis sat on his lap and straddled him, his member began to stiffen up. He placed his hands on her rear and gave it a nice squeeze, moaning breathlessly. "Afterwards... How about I cook you breakfast? Would you like that?" He asked brushing his lips against hers, teasingly slapping his rock hard member against her cunny.

She felt his shaft harden between her thighs and smiled from ear to ear. "Breakfast sounds..." She whispered whilst suckling on his neck, leaving dark blue bruises in numerous places along his neckline. After a few more prompt bruises, she forced her lips against his; her tongue slithering into his harsh lips. Alex kept thrusting her pelvis against his thick member, her breathing increased, forcing her to stop kissing for a brief interval. "A man who's good in bed and can cook... I think I'll keep you..."

Venser shoved his member into her sopping wet flower without any warning once their lips met. He groaned into her mouth loudly and pushed his tongue inside her mouth, flicking it around in there, poking at Alexis's tongue opting a game of tag as it retreated into his own mouth. "Mhm!" He gave her rump another hard smack, leaving a red mark as she rode him.

"Ohhh... One more thing I want Ven..." She breathed.

"What's that?"

"A duel."

Alex's rippling short black cape lined with blue velvet fluttered in the light breeze as she and Venser stood outside in the clearing behind the tavern. Fully dressed now, with her auburn hair tied up, there was a fire in her dark brown eyes. "So, you think you can beat me?" She asked, Alex drew her cavalry saber from it's flashy, decorated brass scabbard, making a loud SHING noise when it was drawn.

Venser wore nothing but a pair of baggy red pants tightened with a belt, and from the belt hung a polished silver and mahogany sword hilt that was clipped to it. He unclipped it and twirled it around in a three sixty motion, allowing the short blade to telescope from inside the hilt. The blade's mechanism was both strong and resilient. This utility combined with its dense metal made it perfect for de-fensive maneuvers, and easy to conceal and carry. "I think I can. Even without magic or without my usual double bladed sword."

Alex scoff. "Double sided swords! Talk about impractical. Strange you haven't cut yourself in half earlier using it. But I am glad you're using a better blade. One I've never seen before..."

"So, are we gonna fuck?" Venser asked leaping back into a proper fighting stance, his blade positioned defensively in front of him with one hand. Alex did something similar, holding her saber pointing right at him, and Venser noted that her form was impeccable. Oh, and her stance was perfect as well. And the man normally relied on magic more than his swordsman skills so she really could beat him easily.

"Let's fuck." Smiled Alex.

The two circled one another warily. Quick as a whip, Alex lashed out, closing in and slashing at Venser's chest. It got no further, however, as the bearded responded quickly, batting away Alex's sword with his unique folding sword and returning them to a neutral position. "Heh." Alex launched her own flurry of probing attacks as the two took the measures of their opponents. "Scared, Venser? Come on, be more aggressive."

A familiar woman with long, glossy black hair, an olive complexion, a slim but voluptuous physique heard the commotion and walked around the back of the tavern. Sanna had said farewell for now to her gypsy troupe to live with Venser in the Dragon's Head Dressed in brilliant scarlet silks, accented by the occasional well-placed jewel and letting her hair down. She saw Venser fighting a redheaded woman with a short cape and sat down on a bench nearby, watching the two for now.

They swung through the air and clashed against one another. After a full minute of fierce blade combat and blocking each other, the two backed away from one another warily. Alex's dark brown eyes widened peering over to Sanna, and Sanna's intense, bright green eyes did the same. "She's beautiful." They both though. Before Alex narrowed her eyes again. Win. She swung at Venser with her narrow saber and he parried it, knocking it to the side with his own blade before grabbing her arm. "Ah!" She did the same, grabbing his arm and holding it up, while he held hers down and the tip of the saber dug into the grass.

"Argghhh... Nhnhhh!" The two struggled, before the handsome barkeep closed his eyes and locked his lips with Alex, giving her a deep, passionate kiss, causing her to drop her saber. The captain then brought a single hand up and let it travel slowly over the bearded man's side.

'W-who is this, love?" Sanna asked standing before the two. "She's beautif-" SMACK. Venser was decked straight in the face by the woman in the blue uniform, causing the man to fall on his rear. "Venser!"

"You have a lover?" Alex asked, that fiery look in her eyes again.

"A lot and I have kids... Soarin and Lucinda... Possibly many others."

"And he has kids!" She threw her hands up and let out a hard sigh, blinking a few times and looking up to the tanned beauty.

"Yeah I do, and I haven't told you yet but... Yes. It's all about the togetherness, you see."

Alex could feel her stomach growl and started to calm down just a tiny bit. "Did you just call me beautiful? You mean it?" The gypsy Sanna gave her a soft, warm smile and nodded, approaching her and giving her a soft kiss on the lips, causing the captain's pale cheeks burn red with a blush now. "Ohhhh well uhhhh... To tell the truth, I like women as much as I do men." Her voice bashful.

"Perfect!" Venser picked up his sword and opened one of the handles of his folding blade, allowing the blades to collapse into the hilt where he hung it back on his belt. "I say we should all do breakfast and get to know each other better." He took Sanna's hand in one, and Alex's in the other, and the three of them began to head back inside.

"Oh wait, my sword." Alex let go and rushed back, picking up her blade and sliding it back into the brass scabbard, before moving past Ven and taking Sanna's hand, causing her to blush. "Oh, hello... My name is Sanna." The tanned woman said.

"I'm Alex. And I have this weird feeling we're going to be good friends..." The captain purred mentally undressing the gypsy now.

CHAPTER SEVENTEEN: SANDALWOOD

The Dragon's Head Tavern and Inn, Vorland, 1435 ATC

The tanned gypsy woman had slid past the door as he had and now undressed for a bath, languishing in the warm water only for a moment before cleansing herself and stepping out. She draped a black silk over her body after drying and combed out her dark hair with her fingers, smiling with a soft hum as she rubbed sandalwood oil into her tanned skin. It was something she'd retrieved from the caravan, one of the possessions she held dear mainly due to its unique scent. She walked back out to the main bedroom, sitting on the edge.

"Someone smells nice, and looks nice too..." Venser said with a smile, sitting up in his queen sized bed. He wore nothing, always more comfortable this way. Occasionally, and much to the displeasure of his boss and a few others he would tend the bar in the nude, with the bar itself hiding his lower body. "We could have bathed together ya know..."

Sanna blushed a bit and smiled warmly, sliding into bed beside him with a kiss to his chest. "I wanted to surprise you with the oils," she mused. "Sandalwood, from what I have heard on the road, is an arousant itself."

The bearded man ran his hand down her side, leaning forward to inhale her scent. "Of course... I could have rubbed the oil all over you myself... Massaged your body..."

Sanna closed her eyes then, one hand merely tugging at the corner of the silk to untie the loose knot, allowing it to fall off and away from her skin. She had only seemingly put the oil around her throat as a perfume, though the rest of her was still wet from the bath. "I didn't rub it all over, dear Ven. I've never had a massage in that way."

'I'll give you one later then." Venser said nuzzling her head softly, wrapping his arms around her. "Gotta love air drying... Oh! Can ya sit up for me real quick? I have something for you."

The tanned woman sat up as he asked, a curious chuckle leaving her lips. "A gift? Goodness, I will have much to repay you for." She jested. In truth she was honored, crossing one leg over the other.

The bearded bartender sat up too and placed both hands on her cheeks, leaning in for a smooch. "My gift to you. Muah." He got out of bed and stretched out his muscular, naked body, then placed his hands on her sides and ran them down her. He stopped on the side of her hips. "Alright." He walked over to the wardrobe and went through a box, taking a few seconds before grabbing something and walking back over to Sanna. "This." Venser smiled and offered her a red lace thong with the words embroidered in green fabric in the back, "Venser's Property."

Sanna pressed her lips against his as he leaned in for a kiss, biting her lip just slightly as his hands ran down her sides to rest at her hips. Then she watched as he walked over to his wardrobe, retrieved something, and then came back to her with a rather strange, though not unfamiliar fabric. She grinned at the words as she took the thong and stood, sliding it on to show it off for him a little. "It's very fitting," she grinned, her voice slightly sultry as she wiggled her ass a bit, letting it jiggle a bit.

"Yeah... And it suits you very nicely." Venser said giving her ass a nice, firm smack. He laughed and plopped down beside her. "Sanna, tell me more about where you come from. Like, what was it like?"

The tanned woman's ass cheek bounced back against his hand mildly and she squealed with a laugh, sitting back down before resting her head in his lap to look up at him. "Very... Cold, I remember that much. There were lots of trees, a few rivers and lakes though they mostly stayed frozen in winter, and the castles were the highlight of it all... I never saw beyond their gates, though always admired them."

"I thought you said you come from a desert region." Venser said running his fingers through her hair, blinking his eyes.

Sanna tilted her head some. "Ah, forgive me... I was born in the desert, and then... Ahem. Originally, before I was a slave, I lived in the region of the Charpathian mountains. The desert, however, was very much a culture shock. Many women wore the silks I do rather than furs, the men were round and fat and it was overall a wealthy place. Amunaptra was more reserved, though the one. I suppose one could call it a tavern... That I performed in briefly was specifically made as a... Hmm. How to put it... Pleasure house? I was their delicate flower, their..." She said a couple of words in an ancient tongue, struggling with describing the region.

"Their leading lady." Venser said listening to her. "Interesting that no managed to take your virginity before me but, you were just an exotic dancer." He smiled warmly at her. "An exotic, very attractive dance. Now my dancer..."

She nodded as he found the right descriptive term. She rested her hand on his cheek as he spoke, blushing just a bit. "They would have had the man who took it killed if I had been deflowered before my given time. I was considered to be much like an Art Woman. Since I was young I spent many years learning to play various musical instruments, sing, dance and be the perfect hostess in a party of men.

The perfect woman. And her body, her face... Yes. He nodded in affirmation. "Regardless you had a wonderful first time." He said placing a hand on hers.

She squeezed the hand that rested on hers gently. "It was more than wonderful, Venser. I can't thank you enough."

"May I ask what you brought back from your caravan aside from that oil?" He asked.

Sanna nodded, standing to retrieve a small box before sliding back onto the bed aside him. She opened it and retrieved a leather corded necklace that held something of an old religious symbol, albeit a rough make of it, with a few beads that were handblown. There were also a couple vials of different scented oils, a pouch of fine southern tobacco, and an ivory carved pipe with the decorum of a snake on the side. "Some gifts of my own, for you."

Venser smiled and picked out the pipe, examining it closely. He kissed her softly and said, "We'll share all of this. What's mine is your, my dear. So, I take it you smoke?"

"Very rarely. It's mainly the men who smoked, but I was given a taste every now and then by the traders. It's a fine cut if you're the one for smoking." She kissed him in return, hand grazing over his shoulder as she watched him examine the pipe.

"Oh I am. I smoke Kullero cigars every now and then, but this pipe, hmmmm..." He paused and continued to examine it, running his fingers over it. Upon closer inspection, there was an odd black tattoo on the back of his left hand. While on the back of the right was the letters, "RG". On the left and right palms were, "AV" and "AK". On the left and right wrists were "AN" and "TD". Just burnt into his skin.

She tilted her head slightly when she saw the marks, though she was slightly afraid to ask. If the brands were painful memories, she didn't want to upset him. Instead she kissed the wrist nearest her, then pressed another to his jaw. "I'm very glad you like it."

Venser smiled and kissed her back, setting the pipe on the nightstand near his bed right beside the angel feather that sat there. "Tomorrow I get the kids back from their mom." He said not having mentioned them before. He placed a hand on her stomach and gulped, staring at it.

Sanna's expression seemed in awe then, the deepest compassion in her eyes as he spoke of his children... Her hand moving to cover his as it rested on her stomach. She saw how he stared and blushed, pressing a comforting kiss to his cheek. "Children are a wonderful blessing. I am glad that you have had that experience, as I have not. I've wondered upon a family before, though."

"I was actually... Well, I remember the other night clearly." He said still with a hand on her stomach. "Do you know if you're fertile or not?"

She nodded. "I am a very healthy woman, yes." She never moved her hand away, leaning against him after shifting to sit in his lap.

"Well... I shot my load into you last night... And the nights before that. No." He shook his head. "You were a virgin. I don't think I can get you pregnant the first time."

She shook her head. "My time for being fertile this month has passed. Don't worry," she assured him. "Would you be afraid, were that to happen?"

"Has passed? Like in heat?" He honestly had no idea how it worked despite having twins already. Venser opened his mouth to speak, then closed it, shifting slightly as Sanna sat on his lap. He rested his other hand on her thigh, still the other one on her stomach. "No, I wouldn't. Honestly I've been wanting another child."

The tanned woman shook her head a bit. "I don't understand it myself, though the women in the caravan say that there is a certain time that a woman has the best chance of becoming with child... Something about it being a few moons after the woman's bleeding passes. It's confusing, truthfully." She trailed off slightly and leaned her head into the crook between his neck and shoulder, deeply blushing in embarrassment as she attempted to explain. In honesty that wasn't how it worked at all, though she wasn't aware. She heard his latter statement and her heart jumped in her chest, a barely audible "really?" whispered against his neck. It sounded almost hopeful, though she had quickly cleared her throat and nibbled her lip some. "S-Sorry, I..."

"You don't need to be sorry." Venser said resting his head on hers as they laid in bed. "But yeah... I can understand them." He chuckled and said in a joking voice, "We must get you pregnant lest your womb shrivels up and dies."

She laughed and nibbled his neck playfully, weaving her fingers in his. "If you truly wish me to mother your child, I will do my best. I have no doubt that you are a wonderful father." He could tell she meant those words as she sat up and kissed him tenderly, parting her lips just a bit to flick a curious tongue against his lower lip.

"Well you can ask my kids that when you meet them." Venser said holding her hand as they laid in bed. "I'm glad you're so positive about it. I mean... Most aren't ready or don't want a kid so quickly. And we met only a few weeks ago."

Sanna met his eyes with her own, a sort of knowing in them. "Time is short in the life of a human... Life is still fleeting. I have grown close with you in these few days, though if you would like to wait a while and get to know each other further then I am more than happy to. As long as I'm at your side," She said, resting her head back on his chest.

Venser kissed her forehead softly. "We can get to know each other all along the way." He smirked and ran his hands all over her semi-golden skin. "We'll try for one... I say, a day without sex is a day wasted Sanna."

She nuzzled against the lips that kissed her forehead, smirking back as hands wandered over her skin. There came the heat again, slowly, this time without the need for any aphrodisiac. "I can agree to that," she purred against his chest, running her fingers through his hair for a moment as she enjoyed how he touched her.

'Heh. I don't even know your last name and we're talking about a baby together." Venser said with a chuckle nuzzling her again. "You're right. We're close in two days. Very intimate... I could spend all day in this bed with you..."

She nuzzled against him as he did, tracing her fingers over the muscle in his chest and abdomen. "I actually have no last name," She admitted. ''It really just is Sanna of Krimeakhet.''

"So it's just Sanna and where you're from then?" Venser asked looking down to her, a bit confused. "Like... Shit. I can't think of anyone back home with no last name. My one friend Musea doesn't have one either."

She nodded. "The desert tradesmen claim it a good thing. Say it makes it easy on whomever were to marry me, since I would simply be taking their name." She chuckled a bit.

He flicked her nose playfully and smirked. "You're welcome to take my last name if you'd like. Sanna Karkaldwin. Has a nice ring to it, doesn't it? Oh!" Venser snapped his fingers and shifted. "How does your family back at the caravan feel about you staying here?"

"Sanna Karkaldwin... It sounds wonderful" she said with an honesty in her voice that was akin to wonder, chuckling as he shifted. "They are glad that I have found a place to start my own life. I am more than old enough and they have taught me all that they can, and so they are very happy for me."

"How do you feel about... Well, I'm sure they'll be around to visit." He said clearing his throat. "Yeah, you're old enough." Venser caressed her cheek and said, "You're independent. You can do anything you want. Learn anything you want."

She nodded in agreement as he caressed her cheek, leaning against it softly. "Aye. I've learned a rather important lesson from you already... they've already said they will come to visit from time to time when they are in the area. How do I feel about what?" She asked, curious as to why he'd cut off his sentence.

He shrugged. "A travelling band of gypsies. And here you are snuggling up with a naked handsome guy whom they've never met."

Venser then playfully flipped her onto her back, looking down to Sanna, then quickly pinning her down to kiss her neck. "You're my prisoner here in this bed... Rawr."

She squealed a bit and laughed softly as she was flipped onto her back and pinned, biting her lip with a tilt of her head as the kiss was placed to her neck. Her toes downright curled as her eyes met his. "Ah, but you cannot imprison the willing, love."

''Rawr...'' He playfully growled, biting at her neck. "I don't want either of us leaving this bed..."

The bite drew out a sighed moan as her leg wrapped around one of his, her nipples already hard against his chest. "I certainly agree with that sentiment." She whispered, lifting her hips slightly to press on his.

"Ooh... Someone is excited." Venser said feeling her hard nipples against his chest. He grazed her lips with his and asked, "Like I said... A day without sex is a day wasted... We'll always fuck before we go to sleep. Sound good?" He asked, his member beginning to stiffen up.

"This time there is not an aphrodisiac to prompt me... It is because of you entirely that I feel like this, as it was last night." She murmured against his lips, giving a fleeting kiss as she felt herself getting slick between her legs. "Sounds very good to me." The golden gypsy answered, nibbling his bottom lip a bit.

"You find me very handsome, charming and desirable. Don't you?" He asked rubbing his hardened member against her cunny teasingly. Slapping it a few times. "If only I met you years ago..."

The tanned woman gasped a bit as she felt him rub his cock against her, sliding her hips up against it every now and then and biting her lip again with another moan as he slapped it a couple of times. "I found you that way from the start."

'"And I found you beautiful and exotic from the start. I wanted you the moment I saw you and I did..." He said placing the tip of his member at her entrance, poking it a few times. "Are you ready for me?"

"Always," she answered as he poked at her entrance, taking a breath while trying to hide a broadening grin.

"Uh! Uh! Uh!" Venser moaned in pleasure wrapping his arms around her waist as he held her down on her back, breathing heavily against her bare neck. "Maybe we'll keep trying for a baby..."

She rocked her hips against him as he held her down, her lips brushing against his ear softly as she moaned against him. She arched her back a bit until her body was up against his, as close as they could be. "Mn! A-Ah, I hope. So..."

Suddenly, the door opened and a drunken redhead wearing a short black cape that had blue fabric on the inside. Her dark brown eyes watched the two before closing the door, walking over to the night stand and setting a bottle of whiskey down that was three fourths empty.

"Nuuhmmm... Mhmm... Hey Alex..." Venser moaned as he and Sanna made love right in front of her.

Alex undid the golden buttons of her uniform top and began to undress. "Time for a little fun..." She drunkenly mumbled.

"Perfect... Fun."

CHAPTER EIGHTEEN: SANNA MEETS THE TWINS

The Dragon's Head Tavern and Inn, Vorland, 1435 ATC

It was a depressing day in the tavern. The skies were a stark white in the winter cold, and the wind howled outside in the afternoon outdoors. The tavern was pretty empty, except for the man and two children seated at a table in the corner, several platters of pizza on the table and all of them were shoveling as much as they could.

Sanna had woken to a comfortable, but empty bed. She figured she had slept far too late and sat up with a start, blushing darkly as she slid on a well-covering dress with a fur overcoat. The weather more than permitted it, given how dreary it looked outside, and she was thankful she was not with the caravan anymore. Bare feet padded against the floor as she walked from his room, still brushing her hair slowly, to the main tavern area - and was greeted with the sight of two children, an empty tavern and a strange food being devoured in hastened pace. A smile graced her otherwise curious expression though she didn't interrupt, merely setting the brush aside before approaching the table with a soft amused chuckle.

"Sanna!" Venser said with a mouthful of pizza waving to her. "Mhm." He gestured to the many plates of pizza. The children glanced at her for a second and waved too. "You're pretty!" The girl with shoulder length black hair exclaimed at the sight of her, some pizza falling out of her mouth. "Eww!" The boy with messy silver blonde hair exclaimed. "Yucky." Both twins were barely three years old, and both wore matching bright red sweaters. Their father motioned for Sanna to sit down.

Giggling she kissed Venser's head, smiling fondly to him as she sat down and ran her fingers gently through the little girl's hair. "Aww, you're so sweet little one! You're a beautiful young lady yourself," she said warmly as she took a slice, biting into it...and she gasped with an "mmm". "This is amazing! We didn't have this in the caravan!" She said in awe, chuckling a bit at the response of the two boys. "Aww, you two are so handsome as well - just like your father, yes?" She smiled brightly.

"Yeah!" The boy said happily nodding his head, stuffing another slice of pizza in his mouth, moving back and forth a bit, his stomach made funny noises. The girl smiled and set a tiny hand on top of hers, then took Sanna's dark hair in her hands and said. "Braid?" Venser held his stomach and pointed to them, "That's Soarin and Lucinda. My lovely children." Soarin pipped, "Lady are you one of daddy's girls?" He asked.

She ruffled the boy's hair a little playful, looking sweetly to the little girl as she asked if she could braid her hair. "Of course! Would you like me to braid yours as well?" She asked her, eyes raising to Venser as he introduced his children. The smile never left her face, through her eyes came alight, what beautiful names. To Soarin's question she gave a nod, taking another bite of pizza. "Yes, I am. Your father is very kind to me."

Somewhere out in the forest... This is was HORRIBLE. She was cold, was bleeding profusely from her side with possible broken ribs and for sure right wrist was broken. The only companion she had was her horse, Ellie. They both were wasting away slowly, not eating anything for a while. But Ellie wasn't as starving as the woman was. Her usual, thin, but lean figure was thinner. Her bandaged chest that had blood bleeding profusely from it, was the only top she had other than her cloak. Her ribs were clearly visible. Even though she was hunched over, there was barely any fat rolls on her stomach. Ellie whined slightly, the woman patted her neck, "it'll be okay girl, we'll be there soon, I promise." She said soothingly. An almost right away, her thoughts had been answered. A brightly lit tavern stood in all of it glory. The woman urged her horse forward. And Ellie, sensing the excitement, obliged. Soon they were up ahead of the porch. Dismounting quickly, but painfully, she walked up the stair as Ellie looked around the ground, scavenging for any plants or grass. The woman, holding her side, pulling the cloak tighter around herself, she pushed the door open, the warmth bombarding her, making the heat sting slightly, but it was pleasant to the woman. She let out a breath she didn't she was holding in, and fell to the floor, sitting upright, happiness flooding her body.

"Okay lady!" Lucinda pipped letting out a burp, moving closer to Sanna. Her brother laughed and then placed his hand underneath his chin so that his fingers were dangling and spread out. "Like my beard of testicles? I'm an octopus! Ha ha ha!" Venser raised a glass to his lips then set it down to look to his son, while Lucinda began to braid Sanna's hair.

"Son," He spoke slowly, "Tentacles. Not testicles." He said with a laugh, looking up to the general direction where the door was. "Welcome to the Dragon's Head Tavern and Inn!"

Sanna had been midbite with pizza when his misphrasing caused her eyes to widen and her to quickly cover her mouth to hide the laugh that sprung forth, nodding in agreement as his father corrected him. She tilted her head back some for Lucinda as she'd begun to braid her long hair, though it was more than long enough for the girl - it rested at her hips, after all. Her eyes shifted over to the downstairs area where the door had been opened, followed by a prompt /thud/. She perked an eyebrow with another chuckle. "Welcome," she called out to the woman below, though seeing her was a task at the moment with her head tilted.

Lucinda stood up on her chair and began to work on a ponytail like braid on Sanna, smiling while she did. "Me and Soawin are gonna do the pizza eating contest ad Chipmunk Chawlie's." She said in her tiny voice as Soarin looked up to his father his summer grass green eyes. "Test- Tentacles." His father shook his head. "Good." He scooted closer to Sanna and kissed her sweetly on the cheek, looking over the railing again. Either the person was lingering at the door or they were injured. Always an injured patron some time during the week. Or day.

Ellie could barely hear the words that were directed at her, the happiness flooding through her was overwhelming, but soon the pain in her side and wrist was also becoming unbearable. Attempting to not pay any attention to the pain, she struggled to stand, and she looked to the railing, seeing someone looking down at her. "Uh, hiya, sorry about barging in, mate, but, in a bit of a shambles, if ya' know what I mean." she said, showing her bandaged and bleeding side and then her right arm that was in a makeshift cast made from string and cloth and a stick or two.

"Oh? What is this place you called... Chipmunk Chawlie's?" She tilted her head a bit toward Venser, as if to ask if she was saying it right. Her accent had been thick around the words. She bit back another chuckle as Soarin struggled with the word 'tentacles', nearly making the same mistake twice, and turned her head just slightly to kiss his cheek as well when he kissed her. She heard the woman's words and frowned in some concern, though not moving from the child who braided her hair.

Both children started to sing, almost in sync. "We are the monks of Chipmunk Charlie's we will give you food to eat! And once it's in our tummies we will move our chipmunk feet!" They giggled afterwards and looked to Sanna, giving her and their father and odd look when he kissed Sanna passionately, biting her lower lip and suckling on it for a few seconds. "Oh!" He broke the kiss suddenly and looked to the woman who suddenly spoke. He disappeared in a puff of thick red smoke and reappeared behind her. "Are you alright miss? Hold on I'll go get some healing paste and elixir!" He then disappeared in a puff of thick red smoke again.

The tanned woman chuckled a bit as they sang but was caught off guard when Ven's lips stole a kiss, making her purr a little as she returned it and shivered as he bit and suckled her lower lip. She watched as he poofed away to tend to the woman injured, smiling to the two children. It was then she realized they'd seen the kiss and she turned all sorts of scarlet. "How does he do that thing, with the smoke?" She asked them, giggling a bit, trying to bring up another subject.

The girl smiled slightly as he poofed away in a thick smoke of red. Fanning the smoke away from her, coughing slightly, she looked up at the railing, hearing other people up there but decided to stay down here for the better good. Being pale, and extremely thin and with blood all over her clothes she didn't want to scare anyone. Even though she was the sweetest person you can think of Unless if you get on her bad side. Shouldering off her cloak, she set it on a chair, nothing but the dirty, bloodied bandage that covered from the top of her chest to the bottom of her ribs, and a shoulder vest to keep the bandage secure. She cracked the finger in her left, examining her swollen fingers and hand. The pain pulsing throughout her whole arm.

"Magic!" The both said at the same time. "Lewcinda was born with magic and I wasn't." Soarin said with a jealous pout, while braiding Sanna's hair his sister stuck her tongue at him. "Fuckass!" Soarin yelled throwing a slice of pizza at Lucinda. She squealed and tried to block it but it hit her in the chest. She grabbed it and threw it back, pretty soon the twins were having a small food fight.

"Alright," Venser said returning with a wet cloth and healing paste. He applied it to the wounds on her arm, and washed off the blood.

The tanned woman smiled slightly as they both spoke at the same time, then tilted her head a bit as she heard the bit about Lucinda being born with magic, yet Soarin was not. She caught sight of the peeping tongue from the little girl and was about to chide her gently until she heard the rather foul word that left her brother's lips, causing her to gasp some as the food fight began. She rested her hands on top of each of one of theirs with a sharp-tongued "Enough!" in a foreign language, though it was gentle enough not to be seen as too rough and her tone was scolding, her volume unchanged. She hadn't yelled, didn't need to. "Now that wasn't nice, either of you. Sweet girls don't stick their tongues out at their brothers, Lucinda, and Soarin... Where did you learn such a foul word? Your father wouldn't approve of you calling a woman that, now would he?" Her eyes were kind throughout, and her tone eased slightly. "Now let's both hug and get along, aye? No reason for fighting, tis only the fates...one born with magic and one not. Soarin, you will grow to have many gifts as your sister does, though they will be your own alone. I have magic too, but my gift lies elsewhere. Do you understand?

''Alright." Hearing the commotion upstairs, she couldn't help but giggle slightly. When did they learn a curse word like that? Cracking her neck slightly he let out a groan as a sharp crack reverberated from her neck. "Sorry about barging in like this, I've been wondering when i would find salvation again." she said, chuckling a bit at the end. 'Do you got a place for my horse? We're both underfed, but my first concern is her." the woman said, her mind now turning to Ellie. The beautiful black horse with socks and brown tipped ears and a large white diamond on her forehead.

Soarin shook his head in negation, his hair so blonde it looked white bounced around. "Daddy said fuckass was my first word." He said in his tiny voice. "Daddy said mine was goat." Lucinda said finishing the braid.

"Yay!" The final part was a thing braid around the front of her head akin to a headband. She then hugged Sanna, Soarin stood up in his seat and hugged Sanna tightly too. "Totally fine miss. We have lots of injured people barge in like this all the time." He said offering her a silver vial full of dark red liquid. "Drink this. And yes, we have stables on the side of the tavern. Hmm... What happened to you? Might need my..." He trailed off for a second. "Um... My- The- My sexy lovely friend who I am sleeping with take a look at you." He then facepalmed. "Fucking void."

Sanna couldn't keep the stern tone then; she laughed as she heard what their first words were. "Ahh, goodness...how funny! Mine was...hmm...I believe it was bell, like the bell on a dancer's skirts," she chuckled to herself as Lucinda finished braiding. She brushed her fingertips over it lightly and her heart warmed, returning the hug to both of them with strong, yet gentle arms.

"You two are so sweet... Your father does so well to raise you," she murmured as she rubbed their backs, then blushed scarlet as she heard Venser mention her in a rather unique way. She chuckled and stood slowly, taking both of their hands and pressing a gentle kiss to them. "I will be back in a moment, I have to help the woman downstairs," she said before letting go and taking small steps down the stairs to greet them both. "How bad is she?" She asked Venser, the gaze falling to the woman with a visible wince. "What in the world... Stay still! Venser, love, I need a sturdy plank and cloth long enough to make a splint with."

Ellie nodded, hearing the odd explanation of seemingly his lover. Taking the vial, she downed it without an ounce of trouble. When she started to move towards the door, she heard another voice, a woman's. She could hear her wince from hear, her elf ears poked slightly out of her, which was a mess. She understood why anyone would wince. She looked horrible. She had blood all over her, her side was bleeding, and the only top she had on was bandages that was dirtied beyond recognition. Of course she didn't do his. She woke up one day to see that someone had bandaged her up, leaving her in the forest alone with nothing but a very small bag of food and gold. the woman didn't remember anything about it, before, after, or during the time. she turned around to face the woman, silver eyes inspecting everything she could see. She felt almost subconscious. To look like this compared to anyone. A thin, ugly mess, or so she thought. her pale face, and silver eyes were paired perfectly with high cheekbones and full lips. But she thought the opposite. "Oh, hello." she said, waving her left hand to the woman awkwardly.

"Bad!" He snapped his fingers. "Yes! Lover. She's my lover. I'll go get it!" He disappeared quickly in a puff of thick red smoke while the children hugged Sanna back and smiled, then decided to play tag in the top part of the tavern. He returned a minute later with a pair of scissors, some plain white cloth, and a plank. "Here, take this." He said handing off to the golden skinned beauty before him.

Sanna chuckled as he poofed away again, returning momentarily with the supplies needed for a splint. She kissed the hand that offered the supplies and smiled to him with a nod as she got to work on splinting the woman's hand, seeing as how it was the worst, though she was taking that at face value. She then scooped her up with the lightest bit of struggle, holding her in her arms while scanning over her other bandages. "They're going to need to be replaced," she said, nodding to the bandages, then looked to Venser. "I'll need to lay her down comfortably so I can further work on the wounds beneath the bandage, as there's a high likelihood of them being infected... Is it safe to use the rooms and baths?" She asked.

"Yes yes, we have a room just for the injured." Venser said pointing up the stairs.

"Right hall first door on the left." He teleported away to find more bandages.

Panicked a little at the sudden movement of being picked up, she made an odd squeak, and felt pain in her side again. She shut her eyes, trying to keep the pain subside. "Wait." she said, suddenly remembering Ellie, "Wait-my horse! What about her?" she asked looked to the woman who had picked her up. Her silver eyes widened with fear. Again, Ellie was more important than her needs. She needed help first. She tried to move out of the woman's arms, attempting to least put her in the stables where she will be warm and there will be more food.

"Your steed will be tended to, now don't move so suddenly! Easy. You're safe, it's alright. These wounds need immediate aid," she chided as she gave a nod to Ven's words. "Thank you, love," she said, giving him a soft kiss before heading up the stairs to take the woman to the injury room. "Would you tend to the horse so she doesn't worry herself to death?" She called out before entering said room, setting her down.

"Sorry!" Venser said appearing out of a cloud of thick red smoke beside Sanna. "The room is prepped, and I had to put the twins to bed since their tummies were act-ing up. Too much pizza!" He laughed and nodded. I'll go find her horse and have him taken to the stables. Miss, can you describe it?"

"Oh don't be sorry, love. Poor little ones ate so much of... What was it, pizza? Such a strange, doughy dish she had only come across about once or twice in her own lifetime. That I'm not surprised they ache. You did too, come to think of it." She chuckled, waiting for the woman to describe the horse to him.

Nodding, she described it, "Black with white socks and a large white diamond on her forehead, with brown tipped ears." She said quickly, the slight pain exploded through her. "And she responds with Ellie." she added quickly

"Ellie. Black with white socks and a white diamond on the forehead." He repeated. Venser gave his lover a quick kiss on the lips, then a second, softer one on her jaw-line. "You tend to her and I'll meet you in our room, alright?" He nuzzled her head with a warm smile, before disappearing in a puff of thick red smoke.

Sanna returned his kiss, nuzzling his lips lightly as another was placed on her jawline and she nodded to his words. "I will see you then, love," She said before he disappeared, relief all in her expression. "Now then, do you know how you were injured or shall we begin unveiling?" She gestured to the bandages, knowing that such was going to be painful nonetheless. "I can't truly help with the pain, but I can potentially give you something to sleep."

Ellie looked to the woman, unsure what to say. "I don't know..." She muttered, heat rushing to her cheeks. In all honesty she really didn't know. She remembered yelling and someone putting her on Ellie to get away from the yelling, and the trees and birds, and that was it. Nothing else. It was odd, not knowing or remembering something that is so crucial to you. It was odd. finding help from a complete stranger. Someone who doesn't know anything about you or what you've done. "Why do you help people?" she blurted. "I mean; you don't know who they are or what they've done. Or if they are ever going to repay you at all." she said, it really was a very jarring answer that not a lot of people answered

Sanna nodded a bit and took a breath, very gingerly beginning to cut away at the bandage. Sweet gods, she hoped it wasn't so infected that the bandage would be stuck... She heard the question and paused, giving her a kind smile. "I don't expect repayment at all. I just do what I know that I should. People have cared for me in my past and asked nothing in return, and so I give what I have been given to those that need it. Does that make sense?"

Later that night...

Sanna had been tending to the girl in the injury room for most of the night and when she'd finally gone to sleep, she slid into the bedroom and pulled off the overcoat she wore. She took the jewels out from her hair and set them aside, doing the same for the earrings before remembering he'd said something about the children being put to bed. She slipped out again and looked for the room they slept in, briefly checking on them. Sanna smiled with a warmth as she saw them sleeping peacefully, then closed the door and went back to Venser's room to finish preparing for bed. She'd worn the thong he'd given her all day and as she slipped out of the dress she blushed upon seeing it, chuckling. "I suppose I forgot to take it off," she murmured as she brushed her long hair down her back, careful not to undo the beautiful braid that Lucinda had made a few strands of her hair into. Her eyes searched for her lover's presence in the room but couldn't quite see him off the first glance unless he was in bed, so she decided to admire the thong in the mirror for a moment. She ran her fingers over the material and smiled, biting her lip a little as her fingers slid forward and lower... Just barely brushing over her clit. She bit back a moan as her other hand came up to cup her breast, then slid down to her belly. She wouldn't know if she'd conceived yet or not, not until her bleeding came and passed... Or didn't. It was in a few days, but... Still...She wondered about his reaction on the matter, chuckling at her own thoughts. He'd already mentioned he wanted another, and wanted her to bear it. She swayed over to the bed and laid atop the sheets, one hand still squeezing that perked breast.

"Having fun?" Venser asked suddenly lying beside Sanna in bed, as if he had been there the whole time. He wore nothing but a leopard print thong. He smiled and leaned over to kiss her, placing a hand on her stomach. "How did treating the girl go?" He ran his hand up her stomach, up her sides to stroke her hair. "Lucinda did a good job with your hair."

She started a bit as she noticed him lying beside her, giggling some as she returned his kiss and rested her hand over his. Shivering as his hand ran up her stomach and into her hair to stroke it. She pressed another kiss to him tenderly. "Yes she did... Your children are wonderful. Treating the girl went well, she was simply fearful is all. The injuries weren't truly terrible, though she had two broken ribs."

"They are very much indeed." Venser said pulling the sheets up to cover them as he wrapped an arm around Sanna and pulled her close. "Glad it went well, and I'm sure she'll be fine with some more care." He nuzzled her head and closed his eyes. "How do you feel?

She nestled up against his form as he wrapped an arm around her, nice and comfortable as he pulled up the sheets to cover them. She nodded in agreement with Ven and kissed his shoulder softly, nuzzling in return. "I'm feeling well. My bleeding comes in only a few days, so naturally I've been a bit tired but I'm not affected in any other way."

"Part of being a woman right?" Venser asked casually. "I'm sure I'll fear the day when Lucinda gets in and hormones act up."

She nodded a bit, then made a soft "aww" in response to his woes regarding his daughter. "I understand. Perhaps if you'd like, I can be here to help ease some of the burden."

"She's got another..." Venser paused for a moment and chuckled. "Never was good at mathematics. Ten eleven." He shrugged as Sanna cuddled against him.

''Tell me more about your home?''

''Boats.''

''Boats?'' Sanna raised a delicate brow.

"Boats, before whale oil was discovered you'd just have to row it all on your own, some still do. Whale oil can make boats motorized, and make them move straight without rowing or sails. Some years later, people have made flying machines. Zeppelins, aeroplanes. But zeppelins are more preferred. Like, giant floaty things that float from isle to isle and over to the continents. In Pantia especially, they favor magic black crap that comes out of the ground to power everything."

"Zep... Pellen?" She tried, though nodded at his explanation of what they were. "It seems as though you and I are from different worlds entirely... You are so knowledgeable about the world."

"Yeah. I grew up in that world." He said getting out of bed, walking over to the wardrobe. There were many dresses sticking out of it for whatever reason, and they looked like they weren't touched in months. "Read about it, saw all that stuff, shit like that. While it's unlike anything you've ever seen or heard... It suffers from too many people, too many social problems, urban decay, stupidity and declining sense of dignity, not enough work, and leaders that never do anything and make the rest of us suffer... I still take my children there like I did earlier but eventually it's going to stop. I don't want them to know such a world... Only Laguna. Where I come from originally I try to talk about less and less... Unless you think it's all a jest." He then began to search through the wardrobe, giving a chuckle.

"Maybe it is, maybe it isn't... Flying boats!"

She nodded a bit with a gentle smile, a concerned frown only appearing for a moment as her beloved rambled about the negative aspects his homeland as she sat up and watched him, tilting her head. "Looking for something, dear one?"

"Don't wear this anymore since having weapons kinda offsets the customers. And..." Venser said holding up a leather leg holster, with a dull, metal grey curved club about a foot and a half long. He removed the metallic, double barreled sawed off shotgun and held it up in front of Sanna. Pausing for a moment. Lately, with being taken into service by God Queen Y'vonne he had been trying to remove all references to his past. And his homeland, on another plane of existence altogether in a vast multiverse, just sounded crazy.

"This." He offered it to her.

Seeing him remove the strange 'weapon' she tilted her head with a gasp, curiosity at its peak as he offered it to her. She took it gingerly, her fingers avoiding the curve that was known as the trigger and instead wrapping around the stock and the barrels, holding it. "What a strange weapon… What does it do?"

"It blasts." Venser said. The weapon itself was badly aged, mostly made of metal the sides were beginning to rust both due to neglecting to clean it and the various exotic environments it had been on to. A faint, "JA" was carved into the shotgun, on the stock close to the trigger.

"Blasts… Like a fireball?" She asked, blushing a bit as she examined it. "I ask too many questions; I fear… I've never seen anything like this before, as you know. You're always teaching me new things," she chuckled, setting the gun down on the bed gently before cupping his cheek and kissing him softly.

"Close." Venser pressed his lips against hers and smiled, looking back to the shotgun and picking it up. "I try to live a lot simpler now." He said standing up to put it back in its place. "Much easier, in a land like this, there are way more interesting things."

"Are there?" She asked as he stood to put the gun away, chuckling some as she slipped out of the thong while his back was turned. She never slept with clothes, and she wanted to surprise him a bit.

"I'll show you tomorrow. It's late and we've had a long day, you especially having to patch some- Ooh…" Venser put it away and turned to Sanna, admiring her naked semi-golden body. "Now that's my girl…" He said slipping his down, so that she may look at his muscular naked body.

Sanna smirked a bit as he slipped his thong down, standing from the bed to wrap her arms around him, fingers snaking down his back. "We both had a busy day. You got to be with your children, and I helped someone with your help. I appreciate everything you've done for me…" She murmured as she kissed his chin lightly, pressing herself against him.

The bearded man smiled and kissed her nose, slapping both hands on her rear, squeezing it as he looked down to her. "And I'll be doing more to make you happy." He said nuzzling her head, giving her rear a few hard smacks.

Sanna gasped a bit as he slapped both hands against her ass and squeezed, biting her lip with a soft moan as he smacked a few more times. "You already do so much, my love…how can I repay you?" She asked him as she ran her fingers in his hair, one hand sliding down to wrap around his shaft.

"Your love and loyalty. Nothing more." He said as he began to stiffen up.

"Both of which you shall always have," she said as she slid to her knees, kissing the tip of his stiffening cock. "Let me prove that," she smirked with a whisper as she wrapped her lips around it, taking him in as much as she could, an inch or so away from the base.

CHAPTER NINETEEN: THE NEW BARBACK

The Dragon's Head Tavern and Inn, Vorland, 1436 ATC

The twins were still shy asleep in their beds, nuzzle up with their pets. The ears of Lucinda's little white bunny perked up and its head shot up, sniffing the air and looking at the twin's mother, who was a young woman in her twenties, with a candid complexion, icy blue eyes, and hair so blonde it looked white. Almost like a porcelain doll in appearance. It then jumped out of bed and hopped past her out of the room. "Mr. Bun..." Lucinda said softly and tiredly, her eyes fluttering open.

Kari almost stepped on the rabbit as it dashed by, but managed to avoid the mammal's massacre as she set down the bowl of stew on a small bedside table. It was too much to try and eat now. Her stomach was turning wildly with her stomach pain, her eyes threatening to brim and spill over as she sat on the end of Lucinda's bed, stroking her hair gently. It helped to relieve her of her tears, and soon her eyes were drying as she leaned down, one hand on her belly, to press a kiss to Lucinda's forehead. "Good morning, sweetie..."

"Mr. Bun... We need to catch him!" Lucinda smiled and sat up, jumping up to give Kari a quick kiss on the forehead before hopping off the bed. "C'mon mommy! Wake up Soawin!" She rushed over to her brothers bed and began to shake him.

"Sweetie, you-- Luci! Not like that-- Oh!" Kari hopped up and gently pried Lucinda away from Soarin, smoothing out the boy's hair and rousing him. "Luci... Don't hurt yourself, but go on. Soarin will catch up to you, I'm sure. He's fast." She pulled off Soarin's covers with coos and kisses, pinching playfully at his nose. "C'mon, sweetie. There's a bunny hunt afoot."

In the tavern area, a patron named Valka furrowed her brow before tilting her head to the side. "Indeed, but a guard? What makes you need one?" She'd sip her mug once more as she leaned up straightening her posture. The arrows in her quiver rustling a bit as she let her fingers brush through the ends of her locks. "I hunt in my spare time, but got caught up in some bandits. And well, here I am. Other than this. I'm just a girl who lives in a town far north in which female are to do nothing but cook, breed, and take care of the house and children." Her eyes would slowly roll over to the man. Her eyes widened, hearing the voices of what seemed to be children.

Soarin mumbled in his sleep and flailed his arms a bit in front of him, giggling a bit as a little girl with shoulder length black hair in a white nightgown began to chase a bunny around the bar area while laughing. "C'mere Mr. Bun!" Soarin opened his grass green eyes and smiled up to Kari, yawning.

Then, their father, a bearded man with emerald slitted eyes in a red rubber suit appeared out of a puff of thick red smoke, a bandage covering part of his neck, a tri cornered hat on his head tipped back a bit, and he looked completely restless. "Someone say breed?"

Another patron, a fancy dressed man named Jace looked to the lady and smirks saying." Oh I run a dynasty and we are recruiting warriors and guards. Though mainly guards at the moment for we aren't big enough for an army yet." He chuckles as he listens to what she said and said." Well looks like you took care of those bandits with a few scars to prove it." He chuckles as he says, "It's a shame you seem like you could handle your own." He smirks thinking he should ask her to come with him as he heard the male speak after hearing breed and shook his head." Oh just as sure as the rooster crows."

Kari smiled back, forgetting her troubles from before as she scooped up the boy and set him on her hip, pressing kisses to his nose with all a mother's affection as she carried him out to the bar. She set him down. "Help your sister catch Mr. Bun, and then we'll have breakfast."

Valka's eyes would look to Jace's facial features, a soft smile filling her cheeks. "I can." then before she could continue her eyes rolled to the man who magically appeared from red smoke, along with his words speaking, "Breed." Her eyebrows would scrunch up never seeing someone like this before. "Yes, breed." She said simply.

''I don't think that's how a dynasty works…'' Venser dismissed the man as crazy. More like the leader of a band of mercs that wanted to be at the top and in the favor of many local rulers, there were too many of those roaming Posiil. The man wobbled back and forth as he removed his codpiece and tossed it aside, pulling down his suit. "Well we can breed right here..." The voice trailed off and he slumped over, hitting the ground again. "With smoothies?" Soarin asked as the bunny ran underneath the woman's chair. Lucinda dropped down and tried to grab him, but the bunny ran underneath the other chairs at the bar too. "Mr. Bun!"

Kari nodded down to him. "Definitely with smoothies..."

Thunk.

She rolled her eyes. "... If your father can stay awake long enough to make them, that is. Help your sister, sweetie. She needs an extra set of hands, it seems..." Kari shooed him off before she slipped behind the bar, picking up the codpiece and laying it over, erm.... Venser's more delicate parts. She rolled her eyes, but straightened him out on the floor, not unkindly, and held his chin between her fingers. "Venser," she called to him softly. "Hey, bearded horror, wake up..."

Jace looked to the male who seemed to like breeding like a rabbit and shook his head and said." Mate better not take more than you can handle." He smirks looking at the woman's features." Even for a warlock." He shakes his head rubbing his muscles his legs relaxed as he stands up." Though I doubt she would take someone like you." He looks to the woman and says, ''If you are looking for a place to come to for work come find the Thelmuz Fang Dynasty." He chuckles as he turned around and leaves a leather sack of silver coins on the bar and leans down grabbing his steel sword stained with old blood attaching it to his side.

Venser quickly jolted up, and slammed his fist down on the bar. "Come work for the kingdom of..." He fell asleep again and slumped back for a few seconds, before he raised a finger and uttered. "Our kingdom is recrui... Zzzzzzzzzzzzzzzzz... Tsk! That sword looks too brittle since blood can do that... Zzzz." Meanwhile the twins were still chasing the bunny around. "Got him!" Soarin yelled standing atop one of the tables.

Valka would turn her head back to Jace, raising her eyebrows nibbling her inner lip a bit as he spoke to the man. Turning her head back to him. "You know, he's right, I wouldn't take someone like you." She'd laughed a bit, with a soft smile shortly after. Her eyes would then wander back to Jace. Nodding at his offer of the words about his kingdom. "Of course, thank you." As he began to gather his things she'd turn in her seat. "Leaving so soon?" She'd chuckle slightly as she leaned back her elbows against the counter, her torsos abs tensing up a bit as she then crossed her legs a bit.

Kari jolted as Venser awoke, leaning back in before jolting back AGAIN. She seemed hesitant to do so a third time, but after gently poking his cheek she deemed it safe. Her fingers toyed with a curl of black hair even as she heard Soarin's victory. "Good job, sweetie," she called out, but remained by their father, looking down at him with a mixture of loving familiar affection and concern. Their relationship in a nutshell, she supposed.

Venser snored and leaned up against the wall, muttering in his sleep. "Zzzzzzzzzzzzzzzzz... Soda water... Zzzzzzzzzz... In place of vodka... Zzzzzzzzzzzzzzzzzzzzzzzzz..." Lucinda tugged on Valerie's dress and said. "Smoothies now? Daddy is asleep and nakie!" Soarin jumped off the table and scratched Mr. Bun behind the ears. "Mommy I know that you have to wear a dwess to cover your milk makers." The bunny wriggled in his arms and sniffed around, leaning over to smell the two patrons at the bar.

Jace chuckled and said. "Sadly yes many leagues to travel and villages and kingdoms to visit." He shakes his head as he taps his feet on the ground." Besides if I stay here then I may just end up in trouble with love." He smirks and says. "You are welcome to join me if you want." He looks to her wondering what it was like where she came from." We could go to your home kingdom." He looks at her as he was finished preparing checking his throwing knives as he traveled extremely light waiting on her answer.

Kari sighed, nodding and hiding her slight frown behind a smile, one saved especially for Lucinda. "Smoothies now," she confirmed, and directed the shadow tendrils to make up the twins some smoothies and their breakfast. Picking up the little girl, Kari struggled to her feet and blushed as Soarin spoke, spluttering for a moment. "Well. I mean... Yes, I suppose that's true... " She sniffed, pretending to be fancy if only to forget about Venser behind the bar. "But I think I look rather lovely in dresses. Your father wouldn't, of course. He doesn't look as pretty in dresses."

Valka would breathe out slowly before smiling. She'd push herself up from the bar, wondering over to where he was. Tilting her head as her hair fell from her shoulder. "Then you must be on your way." She'd blink a few times, lifting her arms and crossed them against her waist. "My home town isn't one where you'd find people you're looking for in. but maybe someday I'll show you." She'd turn her before walking back to the bar. "you'll see me sooner or later." She'd glance over her shoulder, "I got by Rhue." She said simply with a kind smile. "Happy Travels." And walked back to the bar taking a seat.

"We need to make him try a dwess!" Nearby, the shadow tendrils placed a few plates of bacon and eggs down on the table, along with some orange smoothies. Out of nowhere, Soarin asked. "Mommy where do babies come fwom?"

Jace nodded looking at Kari and her mate as he smirked and said." Well I bid you farewell and have fun!" he boasted as he looks to the woman and grabbed a map and throws it to her." That directions to the kingdom come when you're ready." He turns around as he opens the door and walks out making taking a deep breath as he made his way towards his next destination.

Valka would reach out catching the map, with a smile nodding before putting the in her small pouch, which rested on her hip. She'd exhale, picking up her ale taking a soft sip, looking to the ceiling before looking at the children and the bunny that was referred to as "Mr. Bun".

The blonde woman carried Lucinda to the table that the tendrils set and put the child down on one stool, nuzzling a kiss into her hair as she moved to pull out the stool for Soarin, and, yes, Mr. Bun. ''Oh, dear gods… Kari's cheeks went from rosie to pale in a matter of moments, a hand pressing tight to her belly. Her throat went dry. "Well…." Dear gods, dear gods, don't panic. Not here, not in front of the children. Their mother sat down. "…When a man and a woman love each other… They choose to make a baby. And it's a very secret process with a secret recipe. Like making a smoothie that's JUST right…"

The little girl picked up her smoothie and began to drink it down. "Mmm…!" Soarin blinked his grass green eyes. "How's a smoothie made?" He walked over to the woman at the bar and rugged on her dress, looking up to her. "Do you think there will be more babies than gwon ups and the babies will take over the world?"

"I'm sure your daddy does," The blonde cyromancer mumbled softly to herself, but let him go and speak to the lady, keeping a close eye on him as she stroked Lucinda's hair. "Don't forget to eat your breakfast too, sweetie."

Valka would glance over to the female whom had stormed off earlier. "Question, is there a bathroom where I can clean up…?" She'd raise her eyebrows leaning over to the small child, her smile filled her cheeks, though her canine teeth were sharp, like a vampire's. "I believe that anything your heart wants could happen."

''Down the hall… Left hall, turn to the first right." Venser mumbled shifting against the wall, snoring more. "Gimme five minutes…" Seeing the sharp teeth, Soarin screamed and ran away from the lady. "Mommy! Mommy!" Lucinda nuzzled into

Kari and smiled, her smile died as she watched Soarin run quickly over to the table screaming.

Kari's head shot up as quickly as if she'd felt Soarin's own fear, and with Lucinda in one arm she scooped up Soarin with the other and held him close to her side. "Shhh, shhh, sweetie... You're fine, it's okay..." She held him close, along with his sister, and ignored a slight flash of pain behind her navel. She imagined it to be stress, and winced as she held the children closer, soothing Soarin as best she could. "Shhh..."

Valka raise her eyebrows and shook her head, sliding off the stool. "Thank you drunken warlock." She'd grab a bag that was tucked away underneath her quiver and made her way to the washroom following the drunken man's directions. As she entered the room she'd look around and took her bow and quiver of dropping it to the floor, along with her belt, and then moved onto her boots. tugging her top off, letting her breasts free, and then fiddled with the belt holding her bottoms on, looking into the water as she did, quietly.

A pair of bright blue eyes gazed upon the doors of the Dragons Head Tavern, those hands then carefully took ahold of the door hand and pushed/pulled it open to peer inside again. This would be the second time she came within the Tavern's small little source of comfort, for the first time it was last night, late and had to aid an injured hunter. Now, she was back, feeling a bit more confident in her freedom and felt like she knew what she wanted to do. So, walking inside of the warmth and closing the door behind her, the pink haired elf carefully went up the wooden steps towards the bar area. Again, she was barefoot, wore a short white dress/tunic and her flesh was like ivory. The bells around her ankles and ears jingled lightly with every movement she made. Kira, stopped in front of the bars counter. She was quite small in height, but she had a great rack and a wonderful set of hips. Those lips were rosy in color while those cheeks held a trace of pinkish hue. "Uma. Hello?" She spoke up, her hands gripping the counter top as she stood on her tippy toes to appear taller.

The twins hugged her tightly. Venser wobbled back and forth behind the bar, yawning. "Yeah, what do you want kid?" He asked the short woman, knowing she was not actually a child but deciding to mess with her anyways.

Sedna stepped out to the brink of the forest and stared at the open plains and marveled at the openness of it compared to the forest. A nearby tavern cast twinkling lights across the plains, making them look magical in the midnight blackness. A cool breeze blew around her, making her raven hair dance and her black cloak flap lazily like large wings. An impatient nicker startled her and as she turned, she saw that the forest horse she had caught earlier was pulling at the tree she had tied him to. He pulled on the rope as if wishing he could cast off the rope that this strange woman had tied him up with and disappear back into the inky blackness of the forest he loved. Clicking to him, the woman untied the rope from the tree and leaped up onto his back, spurring him towards the building with twinkling lights. As she neared the tavern, the horse became spooked by the many lights and whinnied in fear, rearing and bucking in a futile attempt to throw her off. Clinging tightly to her steed, the huntress turned him away from the lights and comforted him, stroking his neck and murmuring in soft, calm tones. Untying the rope from around his neck, she thanked him for accompanying her and sent him back to the forest with a sharp slap on the rump. After ensuring that her bow and quiver of arrows were unharmed, she walked up to the building that she now recognized as the tavern she called home. Pushing the doors open, she stepped across the threshold and stared in awe at how little the place had changed.

Kira bit her bottom lip slightly, the elf peered up at the bar keeper with those innocent blue eyes for a moment, then tippy toed up against the bar table to where her chest barely rested on top of it. "Kid? Beg your pardon sir. But I am not a child." she spoke in a light sweet tone and cleared her throat. "I ... I was in this tavern last night. and the place seems interesting. Would this place be hiring?" She tilted her head to the side a bit, hopefully that she may be able to get a job. It would be better than the last place she came from, and she would be able to keep what she earned. "I am a good worker, a healer, and also... I know how to cook, bake, make teas, clean.... Anything." She lowered herself to where her feet were now flat on the wooden floor. Then, she gazed over her shoulder as a new faced patron stepped within the Tavern.

"Welcome to the Dragon's Head Tavern and Inn!" Venser called out hearing the front door open, flailing his arms with a yawn. "Ah right shit my balls!" He slammed the whole upper part of his body down on the bar. "So you have loads of experience eh? You sound right up the ass- Er, alley for the job- Heh heh. Sorry... Just... I get delirious when I'm tired. Been trying to make a virgin out of my booby. So miss... What position would you best prefer mainly?"

Valka would hear the voices out in the tavern as she shook her head standing naked now, pushing her hair off of her shoulders and would step into the tub of water, slowly lowering herself down in it, letting her shoulders sink under the room temperature water, that sent goosebumps across her flesh. Her hands would rub down her thighs as she exhaled and began to relax. Cupping a bit over water in her palms and water her face. Rubbing off the dirt and blood from her eyes and lips. pulling all her hair over one shoulder-

Kira the elf hopped back for just a moment, the bells giving a sweet soft set of jingles once more. She then stepped forward to lower her head to meet the bar-keepers face... Whom had slammed his whole upper part of his body down on the bar. Her hands placed on top of the bar table as she lowered her gaze a bit to meet his. "Yessum." She answered to the experience question, then looked puzzled at his next choice of words. He spoke of being tired, and how he was trying to make a virgin out of his booby???? "Virgin out of your booby?" Kira then could not help but glance to his chest. even though it was now down on the bar. Men have those? She then glanced down at her own as if curious if theirs looked alike... Then snapped back into reality as he spoke again. "Sir... I would prefer any position your willing to give me." She leaned forward with a begging face. "Also, I can help you re-energize if you would like. My tea making is superior. I was taught by..." She paused, and cut herself off immediately. Last thing she wanted was to blurt the fact that she came from a slave house... A whore house. Yes, she was still PURE, but at this particular establishment, the women were trained to tend to the men who were willing to pay a handsome set of coin.

Sedna heard Venser's familiar welcome and time stopped completely. Those were the very words hollered at her when she first came to the tavern, by the same man. Pushing the door shut, she went into the kitchen and began preparing the rabbits and fowl she had caught. He'd probably acquired a new healer for the tavern, and the anger she felt at being forgotten was taken out on the dead rabbits on the chopping board. Wiping her face and sighing in frustration, she pulled out her coin purse and walked upstairs.

Venser snorted and rose up. "My signature drink, my magnum opera that trumps the house special is called Pink Footed Booby. And I've been..." He fell asleep for a few seconds before straightening up, resuming his sentence. "Trying to make a non-alcoholic variant." He was really interested in her tea making skills. "Hmm... The shadow tendrils usually handle the hot drinks. But if you claim so..." He looked deep into her eyes, her begging face. "Ya know I started out as a barback for my friend Thorn..." He fell asleep standing up again. Somehow.

Valka started running her hands up and down her body cleaning herself up before standing up and stepping out of the tub of water, letting herself drip a bit. Taking out a brush and brush her hair and pulled it up into a hair tye. Pieces of her hair would fall forward. She'd then pull out a dress, and some jewelry, normal attire. She'd slowly dress herself putting her slipper lip shoes on and stuffed her other ragged clothes in her bags. Throwing her bag taking coin and walking back to the bar, her shoes tapping against the wooden floor. "Venser? Could I have a room for the night?" She'd curl her lips with a soft smile.

As Venser rose up, the elf could not help but gaze at his 'boobies' to see if he had any... and sure enough that positive face went from enlightened to puzzled even more. A hand covered over her lips a bit as those eyes squinted. "Huh. so he does not have boobs." Yet, he clearly explained what exactly he was referring to and her face lit up in understanding. "Pink. Footed. Booby. Interesting name." Kira nodded, then clapped her hands together, "I can do anything. any household chore. Whatever this place needs I'll work hard I promise." then she moved her arms to rest behind her body and nodded, "Barback you say?" she questioned, but the bar keep kept falling asleep. "Would you like me to make you some tea? I can make some Ginseng tea." she was checking again if he wanted it. hH was falling asleep every two seconds. Then a lady with a very pretty dress came out of one of the rooms, gracefully making her way towards the bar. Woaaah! Kira was not really into women. but she did appreciate beauty one could bring. She was beautiful! Another lady was making her way up stairs, just as graceful and beautiful as well. But this one seemed... Kinda. not happy.

"Zzzzzzzzz.. Nugh huh? How the fuck do you know my name?" Venser said with a nod falling back, accidentally knocking a few bottles down from the shelves. "Fuck that's coming out of my pay!" He fell to his knees and then began to search for the room cards to see which rooms were occupied and which ones weren't. "Yes yes, go make some tea. The best possible! I have... Zzzzzzzzz..." His head slumped against the bar and a small thud was heard. "Nugh! No doubt of your abilities. I've been needing a barback to help me out and talk to the customers." He stood up, looking through the room cards. "The shadow tendrils do a very great job, but you know what the shadow tendrils don't do?" He slid a small, silver key to the woman. "Ten gold a night, miss."

"Oh!" He slapped himself across the face. "Right hall, third door on the left."

Valka would raise her eyebrows as she slowly reached for the key, nibbling on her inner lip a bit as she rolled her shoulders back a bit. Laying out twenty coins for two nights on the counter for him. She'd smirk to him and turn wandering back to the room he had given her the key to. She'd exhale sitting on the bed. Glancing around to see what was in the room. Crossing her arms, a bit sitting thinking to herself.

Noticing the other patrons in the Tavern, Sedna the huntress lowered her gaze, and sat in the furthest bar seat away from everyone. Pulling out an old length of leather that had coins dangling from it, she began retrieving the new coins she had collected, as well as a very blackened needle. Holding the needle over one of the candles that adorned the bartop, she glanced around at the other patrons, quickly taking in appearances and scents. The young-looking one, obviously not human with those ears. She didn't smell right, that was what gave her away. She smelled like outside and herbs, and something that made her think of glass. The other patron smelled like dirt and expensive clothing. And then there was Venser. He was still a fool, but he'd clearly been concocting again, probably making a virgin version of one of his more potent drinks. The needle in her hand glowed white from the heat, and she held it against a gold coin in her hand, the smell of melting metal bringing back memories she'd rather not remember.

At the words, the elf rubbed her hands together and gave a proud happy nod. Her eyes of blue seemed to sparkle and shine with enlightenment, excitement and bliss! Yet the bar keeps seemed to be having a rough time keeping awake, so she hurried behind the bar to pick up a few bottles that had not shattered, then asking, "What don't the shadow tendrils do?" She asked while stacking the bottles back onto the shelf. Her face was a bit alarmed in worry for the guy.... Jeez. He was really having a hard time today. Glancing towards the unhappy looking lady, she then eyed the other who gained the room key and made her departure for now. "Let me go ahead and make that tea." she spoke so the guy can at least gather himself. "The kitchen is downstairs correct? Unless you have a kettle here. I don't need a stove..."

'Well hello beautiful..." Venser said brushing back some of his messy black hair back, the tricornered hat accidently fell off his head. "Been a while since, ya know." He made one hand into a circle and thrusted his finger into it. "Ahhhh..." He snorted like a pig and looked to the elf, glad she was picking up the bottles. "They don't make conversation. Bartenders have to get to know the regulars, talk people through problems. That cliché about bartenders dispensing a lot of wisdom along with drinks is ALL true!" He flailed his arms again. "What did you say your name was?"

As the young one got up, the breeze she created made the huntress' candle gutters and go out. Cursing under her breath, Sedna removed her arm covering and conjured up a small flame, not realizing where she was, or who she was around. Speaking to the young one she replied in a voice that was as light and sweet as a spring breeze. "I have a kettle on me, if you want to use it. I'm not going to be boiling any tea tonight, not until I replenish my herb stock."

Valka would shake her head and would lean over onto the bed, as her eyes grew heavy before falling asleep.

Those blue eyes peeped from over the bar counter and a bright smile would present itself on those rosy lips. "Aye! Thank you miss!" Kira placed her hands then in front of her person and gave a bow in thanks. Then would carefully clear some room from the bar, then would lower herself onto her knees to dig for a couple of cups. Her movements were easy, quick and with a bit of jingle because of the golden bells on her person. "Those tendrils still seem like they offer a lot of help." she said gently, finding a few cups, took a stand and placed each neatly on top of the bar table while waiting for the kettle.

"They are. You'll find everything you could possibly need in the kitchen downstairs. Seriously though, what's your first and last name?" He asked the elf, looking to Sedna and waving to her.

The pink haired elf would freeze her actions for a moment and looked up towards the bar keeper in silence. Then would answer uncomfortably, "My name is Kira. I was never given a last name." She tilted her head a bit to the side while she cups her hands together before her chest. "Apologize if that makes me questionable." Another patron made his way into the tavern, quietly slipping up to the stairs and sitting down. She had not been given permission to actually work here yet to her understanding. Only to make some tea. Stepping away from the bar and waiting patiently for the tea kettle, those blue eyes lowered as she spoke honestly. "Whore houses do not care for last names. The one I was born into definitely didn't."

Nodding at Venser, Sedna let go of her needle and fished around in the many pockets of her cloak. Retrieving a small, battered and blackened kettle as well as its stand and handed it to the young one, pasting a small smile on her face.

"Doesn't sound like any I've been- Oh. You were born into one... Hence no last name." Venser said giving her an odd look. Not as odd as the one he gave Sedna afterwards. "Don't recognize me, how could you not? Do I have to sing my song?"'

Those blue eyes widened as she got ahold of the battered, small kettle in her soft hands. Again, the elf bowed in great thanks, "Thank you so much! I shall make some wonderful tea with this." she smiled up to the women, then looked at the bar keeper one last time. "Aye." She answered while turning to head towards the kitchen and make that tea.

Laughs and shakes her head at Venser. Same old Venser, the drunken idiot who could barely keep his pants on. "No Venser, I remember you quite well. Although, if you wish to sing your song, I won't be the one to dissuade you."

Venser set a mug of mead down in front of the man. "Two silver." He said clearing his throat. "After song we'll have to catch up." Venser cleared his throat more and sang, "No onessssssssss slick like Venser, no one's quick like Venser, no one's dick is as big and as incredibly thick like Venser's! There's no one in the country half as manly! Perfect, a pure paragon! You can ask any Kari, Alex or Thorny, and they'll tell you whose side they prefer to be onnnnnnnnn...!" That was only the start of his song.

Kira moved swiftly to the kitchen with the bells ringing joyfully with each step she took. Pushing aside a green heavy curtain, she peered inside the kitchen. admiring all the utensils, and the large stove that took up a large portion of the area. Here, there was food, herbs, etc. All glistening. Placing the kettle upon the iron plate, she then would point her finger towards the log. Her palm, turned fiery hot, thus causing the log to gently smoke then eventually catch on fire. Retracting her hand, she then would point an index finger towards the kettle and wiggle her nose. At the very tip of her index, water sprouted out to fill the kettle up.

Sedna smiled and covers her face with her hands. She couldn't believe she almost fell for him. Admittedly, he was very good looking, and his humor and wit were second to none. But he was the biggest fool this side of the Slender Sea. "Venser, shut up. You're scaring the guests. Nobody wants to be greeted by a harpy!"

A little girl with shoulder length raven black hair walked out into the bar area, yawning and rubbing her eyes. "Daddy will you read me and Soawin at bedtime stowy." She said walking over to Venser, holding her arms up to her. "I need to drill Kira on some things and read the kids a story." Venser said looking to Sedna, chuckling at her comment. "We'll catch up later, yes?" Lucinda wrapped her little arms around her father's neck as the two disappeared in a puff of thick red smoke. They suddenly appeared right behind Kira in the kitchen. "How badly do you want to help"

Next, the elf found some fresh root within a jar, taking one in particular and a knife, she begins to cut it into the thinnest shavings. She then would take one tablespoon of the shavings and put them into a couple of metal tea balls. She waited patiently for the water to come to a boil while doing this. As a couple of minutes went by, the elf could hear some loud obnoxious singing from upstairs. Was that... The barkeeper? Those blue eyes went wide for a moment as she wanted to get a better look, but the water began to boil which grabbed her attention. Moving to the kettle, she then moved it off of the heating plate and set it off to the side. From there she moved about the kitchen to find a tea tray and a couple of tea cups. Setting everything neatly on the tray along with the metal tea balls. As she then turned to make her way out of the kitchen, her vision was blurred by a puff of smoke and there the barkeep stood with a child in his hands. This honestly scared her, making her jump back, and almost dropped the tray.

"Oh Paradise of the Gods!" She gasped. Then answered, "Ah... Yessum! I wanna help!"

"I'm going out on a limb here and trusting you to run the bar tonight. You listen to me, if you don't know how to make a drink, clap twice and tell the shadow tendrils to do it. All the money we make goes in the big, seemingly bottomless payment jar, and if one wants to rent a room you have to look through the room cards and pick a room that isn't occupied. And anything and everything you do I'll know about. The shadow tendrils report everything that happens in the tavern to me and the rest of the staff." He cleared his throat and the little girl looked to the elf with happy, tired, icy blue eyes.

"Hi!" She waved and said in her tiny voice, "I like your ears!" Venser moved closer and looked down. "Well then, let's try it, shall we?"

As the barkeeper spoke towards the pink haired elf, her hands carefully set down the tea tray, placed a metal tea ball in one of the cups and began to pour the water on top of it slowly while she listened. He wanted her to run the bar tonight?

"Nani?" She spoke out in surprise, then glanced around the kitchen. She probably could do so. But then again, she was not too familiar with this place. But according to the bar keeper, the tendrils will help with making drinks and such thankfully! "Yessum." Kira nodded lightly, those blue eyes of her own looked patient now and shockingly calm. Then would shift her gaze upon the child, who commented on her ears. "Thank you." She spoke, then nodded again towards Venser. "I'll do my best. If I make a mistake, do what you will with me."

Venser picked up a cup and took a sip, nodding in affirmation. "Exquisite. I hope you can brew more... Exotic tea. Never was one for ginseng but this is pretty good." He looked to his daughter. "Do you want some?" She shook her head. "Maybe tomorrow. Maybe... Sleepy time tea. Now, I gotta put Lucinda and her brother to bed. Good luck, alright Kira? If Roselie or Syn or Thorn or anyone else who works at the bar asks about you, you say I put you up to it as on the job training. Night!" He then disappeared in a puff of thick red smoke.

CHAPTER TWENTY: SANNA'S ANNOUNCEMENT

The Dragon's Head Tavern and Inn, Vorland, 1436 ATC

The rays of the beautiful sun cascaded down upon the snow covered land, and through the blinds of the room Venser and Sanna shared together. He was not to be found in the room when she had awoken. There was a box of assorted chocolates on the nightstand, with a good morning note. "Meet me here as soon as you wake up. Love you. - Venser" with a map draw of the tavern, through forest, to some cliffs overlooking the lake.

Sanna's bright green, intense eyes opened to an empty bed, a soft "mmm" escaping her lips as she stretched out and sat up nude in the sun rays. Combing out her hair with her fingers, she noticed a box of chocolates and blushed darkly, covering her mouth as she read the sweet note on the nightstand. She pressed a kiss to the words before taking up the map, looking over it as she got dressed for the trip there. Taking one of the chocolates she popped it into her mouth before slipping the box into her coat, wanting to take some to share with him as she exited their room and went out into the tavern area to head downstairs and outside. She of course made sure everything was in order first. She followed the map until she reached the cliffs, eyes searching for him. "I got your note and your gift, love," she called out.

At the edge of the highest cliff, Venser stood there with his battleskirt blowing in the quiet wind. He had the ivory pipe in-between his lips and a match in the other hand, puffing out whitish green smoke and coughing. "Shit. I haven't done this out of a pipe in almost a decade!" He almost choked and fell back on his ass on the partially snowy grass. He groaned and looked to Sanna with a weak smile. "Morning love. The kids are with their mother."

The golden gypsy saw him puffing away at the pipe she'd given him and smiled warmly, gasping a bit and walking over as he fell over with a laugh. "Are you alright? Seems like an interesting way to start the morning, aye?" She leaned over to kiss his forehead.

"Uh huh." Venser didn't look at Sanna. merely stared off into the great blue lake that was starting to ice over. "Haven't been up here since me and my friend Sedna went hunting not long ago. Back there a bit away from the cliff is my favorite camping spot." He sighed and puff in more smoke. "This is some really dry shit." He said reaching for a canteen on his belt. He let out a harsh gasp and asked, "How do you feel?"

The tanned woman tilted her head some, not understanding what he meant by the tobacco he was smoking being dry. Usually tobacco was rather moist, so it flew over her head a little. After ensuring he was alright she sat beside him, and the question was asked, how was she feeling. She seemed to pale a bit and then blushed, looking out to the water and unable to look him in the eye. He could tell that something worried her, but..."I'm feeling alright... You seem as though something bothers you, though." A redirection for now, but she knew she couldn't avoid what she had to tell him.

"Trying a new type of weed. This stuff sucks and I'll punch anyone in the damn face who tries to put this stuff in a cigar." The bearded man emptied out a clump of burnt, dry green leaves into his hand and tossed them off the cliff. "It's like going into the pantry, grabbing some cinnamon or paprika, and just eating straight from the container."

"Weed? As in the weeds that kill other plants?" She asked with a tilt of her head, examining the clump he emptied out and tossed over the cliff. Sanna giggled at his explanation of what it would taste like and shook her head some. "I wouldn't know what it's supposed to taste like, the men in my caravan were the only ones to smoke that particular herb."

"Ya gotta try it at least once. I'll cut up one of my cigars for you and dump the contents into the pipe, here, hold it." He said offering her the ivory carved pipe.

She held the pipe in her hand, nodding. "Is it safe for the body?"

"Of course! Safer than alcohol, dries up your throat quickly though so you always have some drink nearby. Safer than tobacco too." Venser said taking a small silver tin from his belt, opening it up while pulling a dagger from his boot. "Heh, haven't pulled this in years.'" He muttered pulling out a light green cigar, cutting off the end.

"Oh wow, that's actually really nice," she said in intrigue as she watched him open up a dagger and cut off the end of a strangely colored cigar. "Venser love, after I've tried this herb, I'd like to tell you something important. Is that alright?"

"Do it now." Venser said pinching some of the bright green herb into a ball, placing it in the center of the pipe. He sighed and brought his knees to his chest "I've had a glimpse into the past. And I... I... Just came up here to think."

Sanna watched as he put a small ball of the herb into the center of the pipe, then frowned a little as he brought his knees to his chest. She rested her hand on his shoulder, then nuzzled against it gently in an attempt to comfort him. "Just know that even if the past haunts you, without it you would not have met the people you know today... Right? You would not have met me, not had your beautiful children...Or have become a father-to-be." The latter part was softer, but it was enough. Her cheeks went bright red as she fell silent, waiting for his reaction.

"I know." Venser said with a shrug. "My life is fucking great now compared to my late teens when I lived in a small, shitty duplex in Pantia trying to make a decent fucking living for me and Her. Trying to make it as a fucking thespian. Oh whatever... No one knows a duplex is." He jumped up holding a match, looking down to his lover.

"I sing, I act, I tell stories. I'm a born entertainer! I've got the mug of a pretty lad I'm handsome," He gave out a frustrated grunt and kicked at the snow, sitting back down. "I try hard not to think about the past. And it just crossed my mind... I never focus on the past. Or the future. Just today, Sanna."

"You did what you could... I know you did," she offered as he jumped up with a match, listening as he told his feelings and kicked the snow in apparent frustration before sitting back down. She rested her head on his shoulder once more and smiled faintly, knowing that perhaps he had not understood what she meant... Then again, it was not easy to tell him that he was going to be a father again, or her a mother. It was terrifying, the aspect. Sanna looked into his eyes. "There will always be a day when our mind drifts to the past... We just have to remember how far we have come when it does, and if that doesn't help to seek out comfort in reminiscing. Don't let it swallow you, but... Remember enough to comfort you." She kissed his nose lightly.

"I love you, Venser... And you are a very good man. A good father, a wonderful lover... A man I don't want to be without, especially..."

Venser didn't say anything and nodded his head. He closed his eyes and nuzzled her forehead. "I think I'd just like to lay in bed and rest. I can't get my mind off of some things from my past right now..."

"Well if you'd like, I can make you something warm to drink and we can just relax," she nuzzled him back gently, running her fingers through his hair. Sanna closed her fingers around the ones that held the pipe, squeezing just lightly. "... Did. You hear what I told you?"

"I'm a good man, lover, and father. And you love me despite the short time we've been together." Venser said falling onto his back, starting up at the bluish white sky. He smiled weakly and took her hand, squeezing it gently.

Sanna fell onto her back beside him before rolling onto her side, squeezing his hand in return. Sanna nodded with a sweet smile before pressing her lips to his briefly, looking into his eyes as she whispered against his lips only loud enough for him to hear. "You are going to be a father, my love."

"I already am a father." Venser casually said with a sigh, kissing Sanna back. "Wait." he squeezed her hand again, looking into her eyes. "Are you pregnant? Already?"

Sanna flushed darkly as he kissed her back, and then squeezed his hand in return as he looked at her. She only gave a nod, in truth she didn't know how, but she'd always had a quicker breeding cycle than other human women. She had the blood of a phoenix in her but she figured it only affected her in the way that she gained its abilities, but apparently it allowed her to breed quicker as well. "I am still coming to an understanding, but... Yes."

"It's only been a couple days..." Venser sounded astonished looking up to her. He rubbed his face with his hands and sighed, smiling. "I... I'm glad." He wastes starting to stumble on his words and his smile grew. "You're going to be a mother Sanna!"

Sanna blushed and smiled, kissing his growing smile. "I have to admit that I am nervous, when the wise women told me I had the phoenix blood, I only thought it affected me by giving me the ability to heal and use fire. Apparently it does so much more than that..."

"How do you feel? What do you want the baby to be? What do you want to name out baby? What else does phoenix blood do? How short do you think the pregnancy will be?" Venser spout out his words like machine gun fire, sitting up to place a hand on her wise, looking Sanna in the face with one big smile.

The tanned woman giggled like a madwoman and rested her hand over his, thinking over each question before answering while still looking into his eyes with a shy smile of her own. "I feel good so far, I don't feel ill like the women described. I have always wondered what a little girl would be like though I wouldn't mind either way, so long as the child is healthy... Names... Hmm.., Perhaps Vansurr for a boy and Leilinda for a girl. I know that the phoenix blood allows me to use fire and my tears to heal others, but I don't know much else... I hope it is a healthy pregnancy, though I've no idea how short or long it will be. I wish I had all the answers," she giggled as she finally took a breath and kissed his cheek.

Venser shook his head. "Naw. A little girl... Hmm... Rowena? Jessamine after my great great great great grandmother?" He shrugged and gave her a quick peck on the lips, playfully flicking her nose. "No more drinks for you missie."

"Rowena... What a beautiful name! Jessamine is so pretty too... Oh, I can't wait to find out!" She laughed softly as she pecked his lips back, nuzzling his neck. "I won't drink, my love, though you deserve one as a father-to-be. What do you think?"

"Later... Rowena Karkaldwin. Nice ring to it? Or a boy... Elijah Karkaldwin. No no no not Elijah not that name..." He shrugged nuzzling her back. "Back at your caravan, what were some names people had over there?"

"Oh, the names were so diverse there... There were so many people from so many places, so to remember them all... I earned the name Sanna from them, actually. I don't remember the name I had before." She chuckled softly. "Rowena Karkaldwin... It's perfect. Oh gods, what if it is twins? What if my body can't?" She paled a bit, frowning in worry. "I know not if I am fertile enough to create multiples in one birth."

"Kari is smaller and thinner than you, and she gave birth to twins." Venser said wrapping his arms around her. "And she was nineteen at the time. If she could give birth to twins, why can't you?"

She smiled softly and kissed him, nodding in agreement. "You're right. I am not only older, but the women told me I have a high chance of... Not having problems in birth. I shouldn't be so worried... Thank you, love." She nestled into his arms softly, her skirts riding up to show her calf some. "Shall we head back home?"

Venser nodded and stood up. "Let's walk home, love." The bearded man reached out and took her hand in his, first kissing her knuckle.

She stood as well and held his hand in hers, smiling softly. "I'd love to, Venser. Always. Though I was thinking maybe we should look for an actual home too?"

CHAPTER TWENTY-ONE: THE MAGIC BEANS

The Dragon's Head Tavern and Inn, Vorland, 1436 ATC

The bearded barkeep sat alone at a table in the corner, unmoving and staring off into space while holding one of his usual, light green cigars. There were a few empty cider bottles on the table as well.

Sanna the tanned gypsy had been folding clothes at the foot of their bed, but now set down the dress she was working on in order to check on Venser. Walking from the bedroom to the main bar area she spotted him in the corner and tilted her head a little, wondering what it was he stared at and why he seemed to be as still as a statue, all while smoking the green cigar. She knew what was in it thanks to the rather humorous day she told him about their little surprise, and couldn't help but allow a smile to tug at her lips. Folding her hands over her abdomen that had the tiniest of bumps, she walked over and kissed the top of his head gently. "Are you alright?"

After several long minutes, the bearded man finally said, "I'm bored." He took in a puff and looked to Sanna, a blank expression on his face that barely recognized her. "How are you doing love?" He asked patting the seat next to him, urging her to sit down beside him.

The soft smile turned to an expression of increasing worry as she sat next to him, resting her head on his shoulder. "I'm doing well, though I'm merely worried for you..." She trailed off, smiling a little as she rested her hand on his knee.

Sedna the huntress woke from her fitful slumber and sat up, hitting her head on a hard object. Puzzled, she looked around and saw that she had set up a shelter outside the Tavern in a drunken state of confusion. Collecting empty bottles scattered around her, she stuck her head outside and smiled as a bitter chill swept past her face. It was going to snow, either today or tonight, she could feel it in her bones. Just in time for the winter solstice. As she started out of her shelter, a chill on her midriff alerted her to the fact that her dress was missing. Scolding herself and her love to drink, she wrapped some of her furs around herself, securing it with leather and throwing her cloak over herself. Walking up to the doors with her empty bottles in hand, she swung open the doors and walked in.

Venser wrapped an arm around Sanna, resting his head on hers. "I'm fine." He placed a hand on her stomach. "By how are you doing, I also meant... Ya know."

At the bar Kira the new barmaid's hands resting upon the counter as she watched people come inside from the chilling cold.

The smile returned and she slid more so into his arm, nuzzling his cheek gently. She was a little relieved thanks to him being alright, and when his hand rested upon her belly she blushed a little and kissed his cheek while placing her hand on top of his. "The little one is growing well. The sickness hasn't been too bad, and with you beside me I sleep well." Sanna chuckled softly. "I don't think she's big enough to move yet, though I wish she was. I've heard so much about what it feels like when the little one kicks inside a woman... What is it like, feeling it against your hand?"

Venser shrugged. "Odd. I can't describe the feeling when Soarin and Lucinda were still being born." He sighed and closed his eyes. "The snow has pretty much melted outside due to the rain, and I have something to show you later."

Sanna nodded in understanding. It wasn't a sensation one could easily describe, and she knew that. Squeezing his hand as he spoke, she tilted her head in wonder as to what he'd show her later.

"Oh? It's good that the snow is going down some, it seems to have been so cold lately. A change in weather should brighten things up a little, yeah?"

"I was born in the winter. I run hot blooded, I'm used to it. Actually, I was born right near the end of winter... Just before spring, like, only a week away from spring." He said staring off into space again, recalling his early years. "When do you think the baby will be here?"

As the huntress moved quickly through the tavern to the kitchen, where all this started, she quickly looked around at the other patrons, taking in appearance and smell. Finding her dress, bow and quiver, she ran into the secluded part of the kitchen to quickly change.

"I was born a little toward the summer, when the heat just started, though in my home country, I'd imagine 'heat' takes on a new definition." She chuckled a little as she looked around for a moment to assess the visitors. Nothing odd. When he asked when the baby would be here, she thought for a moment. "Hm... I think the only way we'll truly know is when she comes, but I would say in the late spring much like myself. The baby is growing faster than I've seen in other women, so the only way we'll really know is by watching."

The pink haired elf placed her hands behind her back as she listened to his request. "Aye, right away." Taking the coin in exchange for the drink to a random patron, she hurried forward towards the bar in order to whip out the bottle of Black Devil's Whiskey and poured the contents within a glass. Then, she carried it over to the male patron with a bow. "You are in luck, last bottle."

"Aren't you worried it might come too fast? Like, start of spring? I don't know." He sighed and rubbed his temples. "Aren't you bored, Sanna? I've been wanting to go out and do shit. Alex went out to deal with some of her old friends and told me not to follow..." Upon closer inspection, his hair had faded to pitch black with a green tint, and there were a few faint bruises on his head.

This time Sanna wrapped her arms around him. Worrying... Was something she was good at hiding. Of course she was worried, she just didn't want him to. "I do worry about those things, yes... But I know it'll be okay." As he started rubbing his temples, she let go and kissed one of the bruises very gently. "It would do us both good to go out and have some fun. It seems we've not been able to do so in such a long time."

Walking up the stairs to the bar, watching the patrons interact. More to the point, watching Venser and another female patron interact. Seating herself at an empty table, she drummed her nails on the wooden table, wondering where to go after here.

Kira gave another nod, "Yessum, uh huh, leave the whole bottle. And not a problem. Thank you." She laughed a bit and then moved over towards a female patron that was indeed familiar. "OH!" she gasped in realization, and then quickly moved back behind the bar to fetch a clean black kettle. Walking back over to the huntress, Kira placed the black kettle on the table. "I remember you, you let me borrow your kettle. Here you go, and thank you again for letting me use it. Could I get you anything to drink?"

Pulling out a ragged map, a small book, a quill pen and ink, Sedna began poring over the map, writing in the places she'd been in the little book. Muttering to herself, she looked up to see the short elf woman she helped a few nights ago. "Hello again. Please, keep the kettle, it's yours now. I won't be needing it anymore. I'd love a pint of fire whiskey, if you still have any. I may have drunk you out of house and home last night." Smiles sheepishly and pulls out her coin purse to pay the short pink haired elf.

"Damn right." Venser said kissing her back. "We've been planning one going..." He went still into another one of his comas, staring off into space for several long seconds. "Going ice skating for a while. Anyways," He reached into his pocket and pulled out a small, burlap bag. "I went into the market earlier, and I bought beans for half of my weekly pay. The man told me the beans are magic!"

The tanned woman's smile brightened as he mentioned ice skating and she nodded, tilting her head in interest as he produced a burlap bag. "What sort of magic are they? That's incredible!" She said with a grin. The pay was not a true concern given she had a little money stashed over for them both, and the beans could be worth quite a bit, as well as what they would potentially produce.

"I don't know!" Venser got up and took her hand. "Shall we go test them out?'"

Kira looked surprised again, hearing that she could keep the kettle. Picking the item up and hugging it close to her boobies, she bowed to the woman in great thanks. "Thank you so much. It has served me well making tea so far. And let me double check to make sure if we have any Fire Whiskey. If we do, I'll be sure to bring you some." Kira gave another bow, and moved forth towards the bar to check through the bottles and to set the kettle back under the bar carefully.

"Sure! I wonder how fast they grow." Sanna squeezed his hand gently, standing with him wearing the biggest of childlike grins.

Smiling at the elf's antics, the huntress went back to examining her map. She began muttering in a foreign language.

Venser led his lover out into the middle of the bar area and looked to Kira behind the bar. "The fire whiskey is-" He paused noticing the huntress at the bar. Going into another one of his comas where he stared off into space. "Umm... Ummm..." He looked to Sanna, then to Sedna. He looked to Sedna, then to Sanna. "... I have to piss on her..."

Kira blinked as she paused her hands from searching amongst the shelf, she was rather confused as Venser did not finish his sentence. "Where?" She asked again, still leaned over to glare at the bottles, not quite seeing it available to her eye at the moment. Then, a light bulb went off in her memory as she forgot the Venison. "oh no.." she peeped while her cheeks flushed a pink color. "E... Excuse me!" She shouted, running away from the bar, down the stairs and into the kitchen.

Now that was a new one. Sanna went scarlet and her tone went to a hush as simply asked "what for?" as she looked in the same direction as he did. She saw a woman that was dressed like a fighter, or maybe one of the hunters from nearby. Yeah. Either way, she couldn't make sense of the reasons why he'd need to piss on her.

Still muttering away, the huntress leaned forward and knocked the inkwell off the table. Jumping up with a stream of curses that would make any sailor blush, Sedna whipped out a piece of leather and began cleaning the table and floor before the ink set, still cursing away.

"Uh! I mean, I need to piss in a bit! Come Sanna." He led her down the stairs by her hand and looked back to Kira. "Beneath the bar in the drawer beside the room cards!" It was somewhat soggy outside, but still cold as they left the tavern.

Now Sanna giggled as she followed him down the stairs, using the other hand to lift her skirt enough to not trip over it as she walked. When they left the tavern the cold didn't seem to bother her, and thankfully her clothes were warm enough to keep her belly comfortable. Not that cold temperatures were an issue anyway. "Where should we plant them?" She asked him, looking around for a patch of ground that wasn't too cold or snow coated.

"Thorn always kept a small garden behind the tavern, near the barbecue pit I built after Tempey left me." Venser said looking back to Sanna, stopping in his tracks. "Are you warm enough love? Do I need to get you a scarf or something?"'

Resurfacing from the kitchen, Kira heard partially of what Venser spoke of. Then had a clue that he meant the fireball whiskey. Fair enough, she will get it in due time. For now, she had a hot plate of venison ready to give to the male patron. Moving over to the table, she sets the food down in front of him and apologizes. "Deeply sorry, but here is your food." She then moves back over to the bar in search of that Fire Whiskey. Lowering herself to a squat, she spotted the drawer beside the room cards and pulled it open to pluck the bottle from within. Setting the bottle then on top of the counter, she picks out a suitable pint glass and fills it up.

Then eventually she moves towards the huntress and places her request down, yet it would seem there would be but a mess. "Oh! Please let me get that for you."

Sanna extended an arm and opened her palm, producing a small balled lick of flame in its dimensions. "I'm made of fire, beloved, and these clothes are of a very thick material. I'm just fine." She kissed him gently with a giggle as the flame extinguished, leaving her palm pleasantly warm and not burning hot like one would expect. "What about you?"

Venser looked down to the red rubber suit he always wore. "What do you think?"

"I'm thinking the suit would make you colder, silly," Sanna chuckled as she wrapped her arms around him. "But I can always warm you up when we get back."

"I know love... Heh heh, it actually gets quite stuffy here." Venser said kissing her arm, hitching his back and picking Sanna up, carrying her on his back as he walked behind the tavern. "Later I want you to meet Kira, my new barback. She's a nice girl, and she's doing a fine job here so far. Better than me when I first started here! Although, I haven't seen her mix any drinks yet. She makes a good tea though. Expertly."

"Oh? How does i-yaa! Haha!" The beautiful gypsy squealed a bit as he picked her up and carried her on his back as they walked behind the tavern. She was quite light and her legs wrapped around him easily, her head resting on top of his. "She seems to be doing really well from what I saw. I'd love to meet her!"

Still scrubbing at the floor, the huntress waved the elf off. "Thanks, but I've got it. That was the last of my ink, so there shouldn't be too much of a stain." Curses again and begins to wipe the table, ensuring her map and book were unharmed.

Venser arched his back a bit for Sanna to get off. "Here's a good spot!" Thorn's garden was pretty much barren, the cold having killed off many of her plants. Nevertheless, since the ground was fertile in his spot, anything else could be grown.

The short, pink haired elf stepped back for just a moment as she listened to the huntress deny the need of help. "Alright... Would you like some more ink at least?" Kira rose a hand to press slightly against her lips as she felt helpless right now.

Sanna slid off easily as they came to a patch, nodding a bit as she lowered to one knee to feel the ground. It didn't seem too cold, but she could see that the snow had killed off the previous growths that had been planted. Her touch alone warmed the ground enough that it wouldn't freeze-shock the seeds and turn them into duds, so that was an added bonus. Sanna stood again. "I can plant them with you if you'd like," she offered.

Conjuring up her shadow, she put it to work scrubbing the floor while she did the table. "I'd actually love some more ink, if you can spare it. I'm leaving soon, and I need to keep a note of where I've been. I'm so sorry about the spill, I'm not usually not this clumsy."

"If these beans really are magic, let's just try one." Venser dug a small hole into the dirt and dropped a seed in, covering it and pouring a few drops of water from a canteen he carried on his belt. He took a few steps and watched. "Any minute now... What do you think will happen Sanna?"

The elf's worried expression changed to instant happiness that she was able to help. "Yessum! We have plenty of ink to spare." She then hurried behind the bar to dig through a particular drawer to pull out a jar of black ink. Holding it in both of her hands she then moved quickly to give the ink to the woman. But sadly, her feet caught him of her skirt sending her flopping to the hard wooden floorboards with a thud. "Oh!" She gasped in surprise as the impact almost knocked the wind out of her, thankfully her boobies were a suitable cushion to lessen the fall. The jar of ink though, luckily landed right on the table untouched.

"Perhaps it is like the stories and a gigantic stalk will grow, though I'd worry about it taking out a good chunk of the tavern," she giggled a little. "I don't think such a thing could be that large, then again." Her eyes drifted to his crotch for a moment before she blushed and shook her head. Her gaze fell to where he'd planted the seed, pun not intended, and she watched with intrigue. "Do you think it will grow before our eyes?"

Venser let out a sly laugh and a smug smile came across his face as Sanna said 'large' and looked to his crotch. He did a few pelvic thrusts in her direction and looked to the spot where the magic bean was. "Maybe." When he said that, a good red geyser burst from the ground and sprayed continuously in the air. Those inside the tavern could easily see the big geyser in the windows behind the bar.

The thrusts had her blushing even harder and she smirked at him playfully, then a squeak came from her as she stepped back to make room for the geyser that had simply begun to erupt. "Good gods, what is that?!" She laughed as she watched it go, knowing fully well that it soaked her dress as well as him.

Venser licked some off his face and lowered his eyes, walking over to the geyser and cupping some of the blood red liquid in his hands. Upon closer inspection it was actually pretty bright. He sipped some and exclaimed, "It's cherry soda!"

The huntress watched in frozen shock as the elf tripped, almost certain that she would hurt herself or that the ink would be spilt. Seeing that neither happened, she returned to her scrubbing.

Sanna watched him cup some in his hands and sip at it, raising an eyebrow as he called it a soda of some kind. She did the same as he and cupped some in her hands, taking a sip. The flavor was amazing, and it seemed bubbly in her mouth. "Whoa... It feels like a thousand bubbles in my mouth at once. You called it soda?"

"Cherry!" Venser dove into the geyser and drank a lot of it as he was swept into the air, at the top of the geyser he was thrown off and ended up hitting the ground really hard. "Ow!"

"What in Laguna?" The short pink haired elf whipped her head around in time to see a crap load of red being shot up from the ground. "What is that?" she questioned as she stepped closer to the window, then eyed the patrons to see if they caught wind of this.

The tanned woman gasped as he jumped into it and almost reached out for him, too late as he was already swept up into the air. He was thrown up quite some distance and she winced as he hit the ground, running over and kneeling beside him. "Are you alright?! You dove in and then you went up in the air and... Where are you hurt? You landed hard."

Finishing with the floor, the huntress walked over to the window with the elf and watched the bright red geyser spurting liquid everywhere. "It's not blood, otherwise Venser wouldn't be playing in it. His female seems unconcerned, so I would assume it's a drink of some kind. Maybe the bean he planted stretched its roots down to the cellar and broke barrel of wine?"

"Now that shit is good." Venser said sitting up quickly, holding his side. He laughed and said, "We need to get some of that to sell at the bar." He waved to Kira in the window and yelled. "Come outside and bring some buckets!" He jumped to his feet and stumbled. "Let's try another! Another!" He dug a quick hole in the earth, dropped a bean in, and repeated the process again.

Relieved he didn't break anything, she giggled a bit as he sat up and then jumped to his feet to plant another seed. Sanna nodded as he flagged down Kira from inside to bring buckets, wondering if she should go herself, though the excitement from seeing what the first seed brought was giving her conflictions.

The pink haired elf watched as the blood like red rained down, splattering against the windows and painting the ground. Glancing towards the patrons once more, the male questioned what it could be. Blood, red wine, or cherry soda. The huntress came up to even comment, saying it was not blood, but a drink of some kind. Giving a slight nod in both their considerations she answered, "I have no idea what cherry soda is, and I hope to mother earth that it is not the last option you spoke of." As Kira continued to watch, she spotted Venser flagging her down. Wanting her to bring buckets. Looking down at her already stained dress, she then gave a shrug and went to go fetch as many buckets as she could from the kitchen. Carrying at least three by the handle in each hand and one in the mouth, she moves out of the tavern to where the red geyser was sprouting.

"Here are the buckets."

Going with the elf to get buckets, the huntress realized how rude she had been. "Kira, is it? I'm really sorry, but I haven't introduced myself. I'm Sedna. Sedna of Kynareth" Walking outside with Kira carrying some of the buckets, she stopped in awe of the red geyser. "Gods Venser, what shenanigans have you gotten yourself into now? This corner of the tavern will be stained red if you can't tame your squirter."

After a minute, more than a minute. Absolutely nothing happened. But then, a squirrel came along, looked to the spot where the bean was buried, then quickly dug it up and ate it. The little squirrel grew a thin, very narrow moustache that grew downwards in two long tendrils from the upper lip.

It looked up at the three and began to speak in the voice of a wise old sage, "My articulate friends, through many trials of meditations I have gained knowledge from beyond. Everything, from the realms beneath us to the peaks of the heavens above. I am skilled in every field of knowledge imaginable. So ask. If you have no questions, then I will give you hints to a very powerful artifact hidden deep in these woods."

Venser merely fell over, laughing hysterically and pointing at the talking squirrel. He didn't even hear the others who spoke to him

Sanna saw that nothing happened but then noticed the strange squirrel that came to them, dug up the seed and ate it. At first she was about to protest but then her jaw dropped... As the squirrel spoke and grew a moustache. "How... I... Whoa. Love, I think I inhaled a bit too much of your green herb," she murmured as she watched him laugh hysterically at the squirrel, her own eyes wide and dumb-founded. She knelt down to the little creature.

"Are you real? As in I'm not seeing things due to the little one?" The tanned woman chuckled.

"Lovely to meet you, Sedna. And thank you for helping me with these buckets." She spoke as she placed the rest of the buckets down upon the ground and peered up at the red geyser, painting the walls of the tavern red along with those once clean windows. She has never seen a geyser of any sort up close, so this was indeed interesting.

Now, the pink elf got the hint that this drink... Is wanted for the tavern. So, she unbuttoned the blue dress carefully to peel down the blue layer of the dress to only be wearing the black. Then rolled up her sleeves while hiking up her dress skirt. The dress was beyond damaged now so no point in trying to save it. Taking a couple of buckets, she gets ready to battle with this red geyser to get some of the red liquid in the containers. Then, she could hear a rather elegant voice from behind, and looked over her shoulders as a squirrel had a mustache, and was speaking rather intelligently. "How odd.... Interesting but odd." She then turned her attention to filling those buckets.

"I am indeed very real, my articulate friend." The little squirrel with the Mandarin like moustache said, looking up to Sanna. "Do you, or do you not wish to ask me anything your heart desires? I have seen all, and know all." Venser let out another snort and sat up, waving his arms. "No but we'll take the location to that arti-fact you mentioned!" The wise sage squirrel looked at him curiously, then to the others. "Are you certain?"

The tanned woman smiled to the small creature and offered a hand for him to hop up on to look at him more closely. "The artifact's location would be wonder-ful, but if I may, I have another question for you if you are able to answer it." She blushed a bit. "It concerns the little one. Do you know if the pregnancy will be like that of other humans or if it will be faster? We've both been curious, given my... Odd blood. I have the blood of a phoenix within me, and the ability to use magic with it as well as a different lifespan. He and I have wondered if she will come sooner than a normal child."

Hanna's weary feet trod the accustomed path to the tavern door, she paused momentarily at the threshold listening for familiar voices within and she pulled her stained travelling cloak closer about her against the bitter northern wind. Hearing the voice of the always welcoming barman of the hostelry she entered quickly, slamming the door behind her against the wind. She looked about her, letting the warmth of the interior embrace her frozen limbs and drew deeply of the delightful smell of stale ale and human sweat. "It's been a good few days since I left this place but nothing seems to have changed. She strolled to the bar and helped herself to a flagon of wine, leaving some gold coin on the bar and taking her drink to a nearby table where she sat down with a sigh and shrugged off her travelling cloak.

Smiling at the exchange between Venser's female and the squirrel, Sedna went back inside and resumed poring over her map and books. She began muttering to herself, not realizing what she was saying. "If I leave tomorrow, I can board the ship to Arinova, and then travel on foot to Kimlascar, bypassing Engeve. I wonder if I'll be allowed to hunt there."

"The pregnancy will be shorter than other humans, as you have the regenerative, monocyte blood of the phoenix. However, the child's magical abilities will be limited regarding it's... Mixed blood." The wise sage squirrel replied to Sanna.

Pulling out her coin purse, Sedna flipped to a page in her book where she had many currency conversions written down. "So, if one silver here is worth half a silver in Arinova, then I'll have to sell some of my belongings here. I'll get more for my stuff here and be able to buy it back in Arivona. There's still the problem of coming back."

Sanna bowed her head in respect and pet his head. "Thank you very much, though I've no idea what to call you by." She looked over to her lover and chuckled, shaking her head. "He's likely never seen such a thing before, neither have I... Give him a moment to breathe. Venser, love, are you able to breathe?"

"Vagrant." The squirrel said. Venser sat up and nodded his head. "I've got seven beans. Let's try another love!" He let out a laugh afterwards. "Isn't this fun? Oh! Did Kira get the buckets filled like I asked? Sorry I didn't ask earlier." He looked around for her.

''Nghn!'' Kira approached them carrying multiple buckets, setting them all down. ''Oh gods all of this is all heavy.''

''We'll be drinking good for weeks! Ha ha!'' The bearded man ejaculated sticking his face right into the fizzy red geyser, much to everyone's amusement.

CHAPTER TWENTY-TWO: THE DYAD

???? ATC

"Metalratnothingscavangerwhoareyoufluidsfluidsfluidsqhatisthatsoundletsgpu toverheregotitcsughtinthefrickwhydoyouevenexistinyourenotasyflasherrenew aloucancomeonyoubeaneightthiswatironactiongoodjobquinnrayherofestseventeenbrigendheywhoareyougethimsforgeofnarscalicehisneckishinakusichimwhatafunnyfellow." Voices. Voices. More voices. Silence.

The silver haired half elf exhaled as he laid in the warm waters of the bathtub, muttering to himself and rubbing his forehead, trying to cope with his recently found psionic abilities. It was the largest tub he had ever seen, as it was the size of a small swimming pool. It was circular shaped and it was made of the smoothest white porcelain and sat alone in the middle of a giant room that looked like a gallery in a museum. The high ceilings were covered in the stars, the sun, and the moon and they were surrounded by chains of golden roses. Against each of the walls, which were papered in elaborate swirls of turquoise, pink, lilac, and gold, was an oversized, lavishly carved wooden armoire. Primo closed his eyes and sank into the bathtub, the water was up to his buff chest. This was peace. Back in Nomerhia in the bigger cities hearing everyone's thoughts almost became overwhelming. This was wonderful. Where he came from people killed each other over water all the time, which was essential for all life. Now, he could just relax in it. And here in Kundaland he had all the water he could possibly have.

He was set for life.

The water helped silence his own thoughts, the thoughts of other here was actually quite few. Here in this strange island. In the space between spaces. And at the same time. He found the silence eerie and discomforting. Enough to hear his own blood rushing through his veins.

The regal neko girl swayed amongst the hallways, her slick tail danced behind feeling over every familiar crack in the stone floor. It was windy outside, the trees blew with the wind, the air humid and thick, a storm had passed over and thankfully missed Kundaland, she couldn't stand a storm. Heading to the door Fleur pulled it back, hair blasted over her eyes covering the perfect sparkle of her opal hues, wind slammed the door shut behind as she decided to take an unusual stroll outside. Skin pricked with cold her arms raised to cover her exposed shoulders, the wildlife which blessed the land had retreated until a calmer weather arrived. Digging her heels into the ground she mindlessly strolled, even though she'd seen this place a thousand times if not more she was constantly fascinated with the beauty of her home. Knowing Primo was relaxing away she pulled out a crude roll up from between her breasts, taking it to her lips a fire shortly followed sparking the end. Sweet smells of green whisked past her as she indulged in the spliff.

Thankfully, the bathroom was perfectly intact, so Primo was unaware of the weather outside. "What a lovely day." He thought opening his golden sunset eyes, using his hand to skim the surface, parting about five inches of frothy bubbles. A pillow sized sponge bobbed up. He grabbed it and used it to scrub his face, then he stood up in the bath and began to scrub down the rest of his body. "Wait..." He tossed it a few feet in front of him and closed his eyes, placing four fingers to his temple, focusing on the water, the sponge. Trying to lift it with his mind, and as he did all the previous thoughts of all the minds he had ever read came flowing through him like a mass cacophony.

Fleur's ears flicked back and forth, the sound of footsteps was noticeable as there was no one else with them. Sneaking round the back of the building her natural instincts kicked in. The back door in the bathroom seemingly blew open with the wind, but her body streamlined for a moment, slipping between the open door she entered the room unnoticed. Now standing behind Primo her cheeks gradually turned bright pink with a blush, she expected him to be dressed and was going to surprise him, but the sight of him cleaning his body, well, made her shy. The smoke drifted in front of her from the half smoked joint between her lips, she covered Primo's eyes with a smirk and spoke.

"Guess who!" Her voice seemed different, not the usual thick Kundaland accent but a 'put on' masculine voice.

As Primo scrubbed down the slick sides of his nude body, he could smell the weed from several feet behind him. He knew instantly who it was. "Oi-" He said about to turn around after he covered his bare crotch with the sponge. Upon having his eyes covered he fell forward into the water, his hand shot out and he tried to grab

Fleur to pull her into the water too.

Opal eyes widened Fleur tried grabbing hold of him, slipping on the water below she also fell straight into the bath. Surfacing she gasped for air, the joint hung soaked and limp in her mouth as she looked to him. Brushing her sparkling lilac hair out of her eyes Fleur chuckled to herself, sending a wave of water towards him.

"Oi! Oi! Oi!" Primo exclaimed floating back about a foot, creating distance between the half elf and the cat like shapeshifter. He surrounded himself with bubbles so she couldn't see much. "What awe you? Some kind of pervert?" He asked matching his eyesight with hers. "I don't have no cozzie on no nothing. I'm bathing here!"

Her bright opal pupils were wide and she was clearly baked, grinning to herself she stood up. Her body dripped and clothes clung tight to her frame, the whiteness of her top became rather sheer without her notice. "Ahh, best give you sahme preevahcy " The regal neko's tone was playful, stepping out of the bath her tail swayed sending another bout of water over him to wash the bubbles away. "Ahnd whaht ahre your plahns fahr tahday zen?" Fleur asked, smiling and narrowing her eyes a bit, recognizing his abilities and now trying to reach into his mind.

"Crikey..." Primo mumbled to himself gathering what few bubbles were left to cover himself up in the bathwater. She could easily see his barrel chested torso and much of his upper body and his legs, but not much else in the lower area of his body. "Once I dry off I'm going to get a flatwhite and go back to looking for the Sand Stalker." He swam forward a bit and pushed the few bubbles along with him, which were breaking up into nothing. "Again, I can't thank ya enough for..." Splish splash. "Alla this. I know where it sank... Just need to go and raise it from tha dephs."

"Just like you? A psion."

A nod of understanding. Though, the look in the half elf's eyes were uncertain, meaning to ask more about such abilities.

"Noooo prahblem, m'hearty." Turning round Fleur winked, her hair tumbled over her shoulders and down her back before she made her way out of the bathroom, hoping to roll another joint as she'd just so tragically lost one in the bath. She pulled her top up, not used to having company it was slung to the floor. Her upper half was cold and bare, she searched around for a replacement. "Dammit." She mumbled, pulling the thick wet slap of trousers from her legs, it was a struggle as they were already so tight. Trying to keep her balance Fleur pulled the material down.

"Wait a mo, Fleu." Primo said quickly in his strange, thick accent rising out of the tub, quickly grabbing the pillow sized sponge and using it to cover his crotch. He got up out of the bath and walked after. His eyes widened a tad seeing her pull her top off and attempt to pull off her pants. "... What are ya doing?"

The neko's tail straightened out like a flat board, freezing on the spot Fleur heard Primo's voice and realized he was directly behind. Now trying to pull the trousers back on quickly she struggled to keep balance. Hopping about the place she panicked. "Sheet, sheet, sheet, sahrrrry! Fleur called out in her famously thick accent, spotting a blanket thrown down the back of a drawer she pulled the crimson thin material up with lightning speed. Draping it over her slender figure the fabric just about covered her breasts. She turned around, taking a deep breath. "Oui Primo?" Fleur smirked, trying to keep her gaze from his strong torso.

"... What are ya doing?" He repeated watching her quick outburst, raising a silver brow. Primo didn't quite catch the meaning of the smirk.

"Well, I wahs hahpeeng to get out of zose wet clahthes, I like wahtair... But I dahn't lahve eet." Fleur shook her head, sending lashes of cold droplets over to Primo, the kitty's eyes now covered by the once soft bouncy hair now strewn across her face, her ears flattened.

"... Alright then mate..." Primo said looking away from her over to a table with a coffee brewer and some fine tea cups set out. "I dragged those in from tha kitchen. Plentya room in here." It was true, the bathroom was rather large and looked like a gallery in an art museum. "Would ya care for a cup of flatwhite?" He asked looking back to Fleur, matching his golden sunset eyes with hers.

Her opal hues revealed as she moved her hair away, as if brighter than ever. Fleur's eyes set upon the tea cups, the memories captured her mind, people flooded the halls all sharing tea and chatting away. She could hear them, looking around the vision of her mind seemed real, distracted for a moment her gaze drifted around the room before resting back to the cups. "Oui. I'd lahve one." She said with a smile.

"It's top drop, I don't know where ya got it but Numerites would give an arm an' a leg for just a sip of this." He said looking over to a wall which was papered in elaborate swirls of turquoise, pink, lilac, and gold. "Would ya kindly look over thea until I tell you?" He asked. "I'm going to get dressed."

The regal neko girl nodded, calmly sitting herself down beside the table her tail coiled up and around her thighs. Still sat in the fabric something about it felt so comforting as the soft materials grazed her skin. "You like ze painteeng, yes? Fleur asked.

"Fair dinkum." Primo said with his back turned to her, he walked towards the opposite wall near the coffee brewer to another table where a towel and his outfit sat. He threw the pillow sized sponge back into the water, grabbed the towel, then began to run it through his messy, wet silver hair.

Looking back to the painting he once looked at a smile drew across her lips. She remembered the time she'd been balancing on ladders, swiping the paint brush across the wall vibrant streaks of color followed. "Hm, perhahps time fahr a new one." Fleur thought gazing to an untouched patch of wall in the corner, wandering she lost track of what was going on around her, instead her mind was filled with ideas, those very ideas leaking into the mind of her half elven friend.

Primo's armor was practically falling to pieces and carefully maintained to prevent further damage. Over his light grey armor that was starting to darken he wore another set of leather armor that was tattered and stained with unnatural fluids and dirt from all his travels. "A new whaaaaa... What?" He asked sliding the many plated, rune scarred bionic arm over his left one. He moved his fingers about and extended his arm. "There we go." Once dressed, he began to pour them both coffee. Rubbing his forehead and staring past the regal neko, a small smile coming across his face seeing the visions her painting away "Elf bean, did ya say this was called?"

"Eh, sahmetheeng like zat." She replied, watching the steam dance from the cups her ears perked up. "Ahnd just ahbout ahnahthair painteeng, fahr zat wahll." Gesturing over into the corner Fleur's lips hovered above the warmth from the cup. Her ears batted back and forth sending lilac hair flicking across her face and a wiggle of her nose.

The silver haired half elf inhaled the rejuvenated and soothingly dark roasted funkiness with hints of milk and sweet sugar in it. "Elf bean it is then." Primo said carrying two cups over to Fleur. "Too right. Soooo... Who painted that?" He asked, despite knowing the answer and sitting down, handing Fleur her coffee.

"Zat would be moi!" She exclaimed, reaching out and making the cup float with her mind, taking the coffee with a thankful nod.

"Ahnd so whaht ahre your plahns tahday monsieur?" She took a sip, her shoulders lowered relaxing over the rich nutty taste of coffee. Leaning back into the chair, her eyes drifted trying to spot the little tin she carried about, having just a coffee in her hand didn't seem right. A smoke would settle as a fit compliment. "Unless you wahnt sahme of ziss?" Darting away, barely noticeable her body streamed across the room and returning within a single moment. In her hand she now clutched a small brass tin.

"I thought I already told ya larrikin." Primo replied sipping on his coffee. He jumped a bit seeing her dart off quickly and coming back with a small brass tin. "Lovely. We can drink and have a rollie at the same time."

"Oh sheet yeah..." Shaking her head Fleur's memory wasn't, well, at its best currently. But that thought came and passed as she opened the tin, pulling out the components to roll their joint. The aromas of coffee now swirled with the bitter lushness of weed, buds crumbled out on the table it's crystal like texture caught the lighting.

"A cahffee weethout a smahke ees naht a cahffee aht ahll, well, so I say... " Taking a sip every so often to the hot drink on the table she twisted and turned fine papers, curling them up and filling them with the herb. "Plus you tahtahlly ruined my lahst one " Fleur chuckled and winked her kitty tail swishing about

Primo licked his lips at the sight of lush leaves and licked his lips. "My apologies." He replied, he paused and set his cup down. "When I get tha Sand Stalker back I can try to merge the thing that brought me hea with it. Now I have a way of getting ho..." He stared off for a couple of seconds, his mind filled with an overlapping cacophony once more. "Home."

This took her thoughts away from the rolling, the joint jolted as a little sprinkle of weed fluttered back onto the table. "You're going hahme?" She didn't mean to sound so surprised, but the thought hadn't crossed her mind of him leaving. The company had been so welcomed and they got along so well, her ears gave it away, lowering without her notice Fleur's head tilted aside awaiting an answer. Him leaving was normally impossible after the events of the Cataclysm. Though, sometimes other pieces if other planes of existence this one.

"You sound surprised Fleu." Did this get on her nerves? Never saying the R's at the end of almost every word. He saw her ears lower and the neutral expression on his lips sank. "Not that I don't like it here, but the experimental interdimensional device allows me to travel anywhere fast. I can visit other kingdoms, and go home. And I'd like you to come with me."

"Venture down where ya don't go yourself. You've been here for Lhikan knows how long, never leaving."

She wanted to travel, so badly, and with him it'd be different to those times she'd left the kingdom before. Always ending up in some form of trouble. But she returned for a reason, she wanted to build up her homeland once more and in all honesty she hoped. She hoped that those who left would once return, that the sound of laughter and chit chat would echo through the halls again. Her lips pursed, eyes drifted as she fought internally. "I would lahve too, but I've gaht to stay." Those opal hues of hers grew bright as she looked up to him, almost reflecting all the colors of the spectrum as the light hit them. "I'm sahrry Preemo. but, I cahn help you learn how to ahctually... Hahndle leeving ahs a psioneec. I know how overwhelmeeng eet cahn be. Ahnd I cahn teach you..." She made her own teacup levitate in front of her, sipping it with no hands. "To prahperly cahntrol eet."

Absent mindedly he began slipped down his leather armor and began to undo the top part of the metal armor underneath, looking to Fleur and saying nothing.

The regal neko didn't understand this silence, confused and looking around she finished rolling the joint. "Tell me, where exahctly do you plahn to go? Ziss plahce ees just a leettle bubble een ze vahst multiverse. Eet ees so much beeggair." Taking a final sip of her coffee she placed the joint between her lips, sparking the end with a light she pulled from between her breasts.

"It would be good... Yes. Especially during the times I space off." Primo stood up and began to strip in front of her. This was very unlike him, as he was often quiet and reserved, and still somewhat of a loner. But he had the small feeling that Fleur was into him, and she couldn't keep her off of him taking a bath. He was unsure of this, as few women had been so affectionate towards him in his twenty-nine years in existence. But this was just a shot in the dark. "I was going to show you my world. Just drive around in the wasteland a bit. I'm not fond of tha cities."

Fleur coughed, smoke puffed from her rich lips and cheeks brightened with pink as she watched him undress. "Your wahrld huh?" She asked, clearly distracted as her brow raised curiously at what he was doing

The half elf was done now seeing fleur's cheeks brighten. "Nomerhia. Land of the fallen stars." Primo said putting his armor back on.

"Fahllen stahrs " This caught her attention, she loved the skies and the way they sparkled at night. Biting on her bottom lip almost hidden from view she was trying to keep her thoughts to herself. Staring back into the empty cup of coffee she handed the joint over to him.

Nodding Fleur stood up, stretching out before realizing she'd simply had a blanket around her. Eyes widened with horror as she exposed herself she was then no longer to be seen. Crouched down and hiding behind the drawers across the room Fleur poked her head out. "Umm..." She was too embarrassed to speak but she gestured to the pile of clothes in the corner.

His eyes widened at the sight and he was unable to say anything for several long seconds. His mouth opened, and no words came out. Finally, he said, "Now you know how I feel. Let's get a move on." Primo said turning his back to her and walking towards the exit of the bathroom.

"Well charming." She said, creeping from behind the drawer. Scurrying over to her pile of clothes she grabbed another classic white vest top with darkened trousers. Fighting to pull the tight fit on she just about managed it. "Que vais-je besoin?" Fleur called, completely forgetting he didn't speak her tongue.

"What was that now?" He called standing in the doorway.

"Oh... Whaht will I need eef we go?" Turning around she just about had time to completely cover herself and not frightfully exposed to the poor man again.

It was a good thing the leather that made up a majority of his armor, some of it was reinforced with metal, because thoughts of Fleur naked, spread out against a bed began to invade his mind. Or in the bath, her pale frame wet and naked while she shaved her legs. Primo rarely had such thoughts and had no idea how to deal with them but he could feel himself getting a stiffy. "Nomerhia is mostly a desert land full of junk. So proper attire."

Primo shook his head a bit and grumbled, pushing the thoughts of Fleur out of his mind. "Water." He said loudly after seeing a brief vision of a nude Fleur, pressed into the front of his body caressing him gently.

"So chains ahnd leathair zen?" As he looked around somehow Fleur had managed to roll and light a joint, she was never too far from one. Bending over she rummaged through the pile of 'stuff' clothes thrown behind her almost hitting Primo in the face. Colored lace panties darted by like a javelin landing perfectly on the door handle beside him. "Huh?" The word water confused her a little, there was plenty of that around why would they need to bring any. Brows furrowed with confusion she turned round to him.

He silently raised his hand to catch the clothes before they hit him in the face, but he was able to stop it with his mind. Primo looked in awe and rotated it in the air. The weed helped the headaches he had been having since he arrived in Kundaland. The voices in his head, and the random telekinesis he would display by accident. "Wata. It's hard to come by where I'm from."

The joint fell from her lips as she watched, fumbling to catch it the hot end poke at her delicate little hands. "No, no, no, no." She panicked, trying to stop it from falling to the ground she eventually caught it. Not the way she hoped though, more from instinct. Opening her hand, the end sizzled against her skin, her opal hues flickered in pain for a minute before returning the unlit end to her lips. "You've been keepeeng zat quiet." Fleur walked amongst the levitating clothes, her fingers pawed at them, palm clearly sore with a red burn.

"You've never been to a desert, have you before, Fleu?" He asked looking at her palm. "Are you going to be alright?" Primo asked not changing his almost blunt tone. His hand reached out and grasped hers. She held her palm hand in his and examined the burn. He lost his concentration and then accidently dropped all of Fleur's clothes on the both of them.

She'd lost concentration for a moment also. Suddenly she squeaked and become bundled under clothes, she'd tried gripping Primo's hand tighter in an attempt to not fall. A thong hung from one of her ears as it flicked back and forth. Grabbing it she stood, kicking the pile away. "I'll be fine." Fleur said laugh. "But first... You know."

Primo held Fleur's hand in his and picked a silk thong from off of his shoulder. He threw it on the pile of Fleur's clothes. "Is yoah hand good?" He asked.

Turning it over in his palm she shook her head, ears flattened against her head. "Guess naht." Fleur took the joint from her lips and put it against his. "Wahnt sahme?" They were standing close now, her eyes seemed wider as she looked up to him. Her slitted eyes narrowing. The half elf reached out for it, only for the regal neko to pull her hand away and stick her tongue out. "Cahme on m'hearty. Reach out."

The half elf flung his hand out as fast as he could, but Fleur dodged with feline reflexes. "No Preemo! reach out weeth your minddddd. " She went and sat back at one of the tables a few feet away from him, raising the spliff to her lips and inhaling. "Wait. I've gaht a good idea! we've gaht cahffee, spleeffs... now ahll we need ees spahnge cahke to dunk een our cahffee!" She clapped in a giddy manner.

A few minutes later...

Their side of the bathhouse had been cleared of its furniture, sans on table far against the wall. The silver haired elf and his lilac haired neko friend sat across from each other, eyes closed sitting in lotus position.

"Ugh." A frustrated sigh from Primo. "Tha mind is such a noisy place..."

"Eet ees. But through medeetahtion, slow breatheeng... Cahlmness. Cahn we quiet eet. breath een... Breath out. Eemahgine yourself wahlkeeng ahway frahm zose zoughts. Mhmmmm... Yum... Mhhhmmmmm... Yum." Fleur raised a hand to her chest, her hand glowed a bright lilac, before she lowered it down and breathed out, and the light disappeared. Before she repeated it. "Peace. Fahcus on ze now. Reach out to ze lahnd ahround you, reach out to Mahthair Lahguna. Ahnd tell me whaht you see."

Primo focused. He saw her land. He saw the endless ocean around them, and he saw the space between spaces. He saw calming waters and waves that seemed to break forever. And focused on that.

The neko popped one eye open and smiled, watching her friend concentrating now. "Good, good. You found your fahcus point. Hahve a spahnge cahke!"

Using her mind, she made a bite sized piece of sponge cake float, dunking it a few times in their coffee and floating it near his mouth.

A few more minutes later...

The silver haired half elf lay spinning on her back on the wet tiles of the bathhouse floor, struggling to keep several old wine barrels afloat at once.

"Eef you wahnt to leeft your Sahnd Stahlkair... You need to use telekinesees. So useful... Here, hahve ahnahthair cahffee cahke."

Dunk dunk.

Primo grunted as she set the wine barrels down, struggling with balance. He levitated the upside-down cupcake into his upside down mouth, noisily eating. It wasn't everyday he had readily access to food. Sustenance was precious.

"Wine time." Letting Primo practice with the other wine barrels, she focused on a single one. She flipped forward on her hands, touching down nose first on the ground. She extended her full body length upward, so that every ounce of her body was being supported by her nose, using her tail for additional support. She closed her eyes and stuck out her tongue, a tiny bit one wine dripping from the floating barrel and she started lapping at it. Before the sweet liquid stopped and the regal neko channeled all her focus and energy through her with full confidence.

The wine barrels rose into the air as one, orbiting her body in a perfectly circular orbit. The orbit was slow, and each one that stopped in front of her tipped a bit, spilling droplets of wine into Fleur's moth as she sampled every single one.

"Crikey... How... How are you doing that so easily?" Primo asked, mouth agape in disbelief. "All without like, extending your hand out., or just... Like you ae right now."

"Prahctice, time. Bahdy, Speerit... Ahnd mind. Being een tune weeth zose three ahnd Mahthair Lahguna, who ees ahll ahround us... Here, hahve ahnahthair cahffee cahke! Hee hee." Dunk dunk dunk dunk dunk.

GLOMP!

A satisfied grunt.

Swallow. "Wait, wait. So yes. This is a form of magic? Like nature magic?"

"Yes ahnd no. Seemply being een tune weeth nahture, ahnd een tune weeth yourself cahn you truly fahcus. Observe ze eenhahle. Nahtice ze exhahle." Fleur gently set all the wine barrels down and rolled over on her stomach, stretching out just like a regular cat.

After a full minute of contemplation and observing, Primo turned to face Fleur, mouth set in a grim, determined line. A few incoherent voices entered his mind, but he quickly replaced them with the sounds of the rolling waters of Kundaland.

"I'm ready to understand this meditation stuff fully now, My Queen."

It seemed like it was another lifetime ago that she had been called that. To the point where it felt strange to hear someone refer to her as that. Blink blink. "Mood, m'hearty. I hahve ahn idea. We cahn go to your hahme weethout ahctually leaveeng Kundahland."

Primo blinked his golden sunset eyes. "How?"

"Seet weeth me ahnd I'll show you ahnahthair psion ahbeelity. You, me. Our minds one ahnd tahgethair... A dyad."

The two sat directly facing each other, legs crossed as Fleur took Primo's strong hands in hers, pressing her forehead against hers. "Crikey... Hea goes nothin then eh?"

"Shhhhhhh... Ze quietair you becahme, ze mahre you cahn hear."

They both entered Primo's own mind. And the land they found themselves in was bare. Dusty golden abounds, piled in softly undulating dunes. There were no trees in sight, the only vegetation was a few cacti and spiky, brown plants growing out of the sand. The nation's capital of Cometfall lied in the center, outside of it was Shining Mount, a jagged, metallic peak that is the largest of the alien starships that crashed in Nomerhia during the ancient event known as The Starfall, and small communities, with some small towns. Other than that, there were no other civilizations. Just the dead plains of Nomerhia's heart. Still, explorers, travelers, and scavengers alike arrive daily, hoping to strike it rich by finding new technologies hidden in the far reaches dozens of crashed spaceship ruins. It was a very clear night, and all the stars in the sky were visible. And the moon shone bright.

The kitty's eyes widened. Reflections of large metal pieces glittered in her opal hues and reflected all outside. Fleur's tail swung about, then her eyes set on the moon, her pupils widened as she glanced in awe, her chest warmed as she zoned out "Eet's ahmahzeeng! Look aht zat!" Fleur pointed at the moon, her tail curled and swayed happily.

"It's just a big rock in tha sky." Primo's voice echoed.

"A beeg rahck?! Zat's la lune! Look to la lune!" Drifting once more to her native tongue she looked around puzzled at the difference in fascination.

Inside their mind meld, the starry night in the desert was suddenly fused by a vision of a beautiful garden, and the sky split half. One half a stretching night, and the other a long clear blue sky. The garden was well tended, with the softest grass that isn't scratchy, and a slight wind which brings out the beauty of this garden more. There was a white rocking bench, with a beautiful snapdragon painted on it. And there were lilies, snapdragons, roses, and lilacs everywhere, with a few other unnamed unique, beautiful flowers. There were also a few nice plants. And there are trees surrounding the garden. The air was warm, but worth it. The view was gorgeous. The trees were filled with the colors of summer, as if they had been painted. Their leaves were scarlet-red, orange, bright green. The beauty overwhelmed the half elf as the rushing water tumbled over the glimmering stones. Everything seemed to be right with the world, and in that moment, the half elf's breath was taken away by the pure beauty of the scenery, he had forgotten all my troubles for the mere moment.

"Oh my... Fleu. Its... Its... Perfect."

The man was lost for words and had completely zoned out. Completely captivated the swirls of rich colors dancing in the wind and not a single drop of darkness decayed the site. Fleur approached, standing on the edge of the dark land of fallen stars, eyes nearly matched the wideness of the alien moon, her fingers tapped on the petals of rich lotus flowers, her touch delicate and forgiving. This represented Fleur's love for nature, how she spent endless hours tending to the gardens within her home.

Light and dark came together, the two met where night and day were fused together. Golden sunset eyes met glimmering opal eyes.

Blood rushed around the neko's body sending a warmth throughout, knees weakening she looked to Primo with an unfamiliar gaze. Eyes glittering like fireflies, flashbacks came when they were in the kingdom, his frame in the bath and stripping figure at the coffee table. She bit her lip, the little clarity left in her mind was simply confusion, why the sudden hot rush? Her body slowly drowning with a needy want for him." Preemo..." Fleur whispered, her accent was unusually thick, the Kundaland tongue rolled like honey as she looked once more over to him. The handsome silver haired half elf was bathed a ray of light above the garden and the bright turquoise sky. Truly incandescent, glorious like a blazing sun that would never set.

Primo's breath became heavier as he looked Fleur over, examining every curve and feature of her body. Visions of her slowly stripping in front of him appeared to him. He shook his head and tried to control himself, but her beauty overwhelmed him. "Fleu..." He said in his thick strange accent walking towards her slowly. The shadow of the night and the moon illuminated her dark beauty. She was the moon, and he was the sun.

Her eye's doe and innocent, the kitten's ears fluttered back and forth as she took a more submissive appearance. Looking up to Primo her mind clouded and body burned more, desperate to be touched. "Oui, Primo?" Tilting her head aside hair rolled over her eyes, batted away by her thick lashes.

Primo's breathing slowed as he wrapped an arm around her waist and pulled Fleur towards him. Pressing his body into hers. He closed his eyes and leaned forward, licking his lips before he pressed them against hers.

His rough touch was so welcome, pressing her slender frame against his Fleur kissed him back. Her hands trailed up his neck, nails scratching the skin softly as she completely succumbed to the handsome rugged man.

The silver haired half elf locked his lips with Fleur's and planted a kiss after gentle kiss on her lips, then he stepped back. Fleur's hips swaying her tail dusted the floor behind. A purr rumbled through her chest as she felt every movement of his. Her palms cupped his jawline as she planted more kisses on his lips.

The mind meld between the neko half elf dyad broke and they were back inside of the bathhouse, standing up and holding each other close and tight. Outside, the weather began to improve, sunlight leaking through the windows.

Purring a little louder she arched her back up into him, pressing her chest against her nails harshly clawed down the front marking the skin as she snapped her teeth playfully. A naughty expression sparked in her eyes.

Primo's hands became shaky as he held up both of his hands, staring down at her bare chest that was pressed against his. He arched back a bit as well and brought both hands up to fondle her breasts gently.

Fleur let out little moans as his fingers pressed against her chest, teasing the skin it drove her wild with lust. She brought herself up to his lips, letting them meet once more as she kissed him harder and deeper than the first time. Breaking it, she whispered. "Do you wahnt to tahke ziss outside? Eet ees so nice right now. Eet's... Perfect."

"I don't mind..."

Fleur smiled, whapped the half elf in the face with her tail, and then telekinetically pushed Primo back a few feet, scampering away and out a pair of doors. "Cahtch me eef you wahnna keess me, m'hearty!"

Primo chuckles and gave chase, both of them leaving their troubles behind. The moon now had her sun to brighten her sky as they went running towards a brighter future.

CHAPTER TWENTY-THREE: FAME JOY

The Dragon's Head Tavern and Inn, Vorland, 1436 ATC

The golden gypsy sat outside to watch the stars, bundled warmly as she looked up into the night sky. A beautiful full moon shone back on her face, a rare occasion given the time of year, with the backdrop of a clear and starry sky as its company; this was a night she didn't want to miss. She caressed her rounding belly for a moment before going inside after a small prayer of thanks to her gods, looking around for Venser. Her redheaded and rough girlfriend Alex was inside, asleep at one of the tables and wrapped in a blanket, having knocked herself out with too many whiskey sours.

"Hey." Venser said meeting Sanna right at the door. "I was going outside for a smoke but, did you see the moon? I wanted to go out and see it for myself too."

"I was actually going to ask if you'd like to come see it with me. Read my mind," she smirked as she took his hand and kissed his cheek.

Venser chuckled and squeezed her hand gently, kissing her back passionately on the lips. "Let's go outside then..."

She turned round after returning his kiss, licking his bottom lip softly before starting to walk outside with his hand in hers. It was a cool night but she had warmed herself plenty by the fire inside already and would take a bath later. Still, she remained bundled to keep herself and the child inside warm.

Out behind the tavern was an ordinary picnic table along with a brick barbeque pit, a few feet in front of it, up against the tavern was a bench. Venser walked Sanna to the bench and sat down. "What a lovely night... Back home in Pantia, the pollution from the whale and earth oils make the sky blurry at times. But this... Is true beauty..." He never liked to speak about where he originally came from, and only spoke about it briefly.

She settled next to him and rested her head on his shoulder as they sat at the table, weaving her fingers in his as he spoke of his homeland. "I'd love to see Pand... Pantia someday, if I could... But I wouldn't trade the nights here for all the world."

"You don't want to see Pantia. Kupidnos though... That's what you wanna see. Maybe It's paradise... But..." He wrapped an arm around Sanna and smiled, feeling so relaxed beneath the mood, surrounded by the faint sounds of crickets. "That wise talking squirrel said we'd be having a girl... And I'm certain our little girl is going to love seeing a moon like this for the first time."

Sanna seemed to struggle with the pronunciation, but she attempted saying Pantia again under her breath before giving up on it. When he mentioned Kupidnos, though, she lit up and rested into his arm as it wrapped around her. She faintly kissed his jawline. "I truly look forward to seeing you hold her for the first time... To hold her myself, to see her face."

"We're going to have a beautiful child." The bearded bartender said moving his head to the side, nuzzling her head, blinking his slitted emerald eyes a few times. "Just a few more months..."

Sanna blushed as she felt a flutter, a tiny one but it had been there. She rested her hand on her belly and beamed, nuzzling back. "You're going to be a wonderful father... I hope that I will know what I am doing as a mother when the time comes."

"If Kari is available... When she's not busy being the protector of a village I'm sure she can offer advice and stuff. Heh, most of the employees with kids have left. Like Eza and her two kids... Soarin and Lucinda's nanny doesn't have any kids... Not so much older than the twins last time I saw them. Which was years ago." He shrugged and rested his hand on hers on her belly. "Who knows? It may be just instinct..."

Sanna nodded a little and she felt the flutter again, directly beneath her hand. She squeaked a bit and looked down, tilting her head. "Something moved, Ven..."

"The baby." Venser said with a smile. "She's kicking... The baby..." He repeated. "Have we settled on a name yet?'"

Sanna grinned in wonder and awe as she felt a couple more tiny flutters, one against his hand. "I'm not sure, though I'd love to hear your ideas... I would love her to have your last name, just as you gave me yours."

"You said either Rowena or Jessamine were good..." Venser said resting his head on Sanna's, kissing her hair. "Have you thought of any suggestions lately?"

The woman crooned a bit and smiled fondly. "Rowena... Still a beautiful name. Yes... Like the Queen Rowena Grigori of Grigwald, across the sea from Pryldahn. Yes... Her name meant fame joy? Famous joy? She'll be a famous dancer when she grows up! And Jessamine... The only suggestion that seems to call to me is a name I haven't heard spoken in... Many, many years. There was a woman of different blood that was a friend of my birth family, but I only got her first name from the stories." She chuckled a bit. "I'm sorry If I seem a little all over the place right now love."

"No, don't apologize." Venser kissed her softly. "And what was her first name? From these stories." He asked.

"Sephira, Sephiria, something like that. Long name, but rolls off the tongue." She answered him, frowning as she tried to remember.

"I wouldn't say it does honestly... Rowena is easier. Much easier to say." He said with a chuckle kissing her again. "Rowena Karkaldwin... Sanna Karkaldwin..."

She chuckled and nodded in agreement, kissing him back once more. "Rowena, Venser and Sanna Karkaldwin. Sounds like a lovely little set of names for a family." The tanned woman smiled and placed both hands on her stomach, imagining their happy future as one big family.

"Rowena, Venser, Sanna, Kari, Soarin, Lucinda, Alex, Nivarah Karkaldwin... And many more to come. Oh you've no idea."

Sanna chuckled and cuddled into Venser, basking in his warmth, trailing her golden hands over the new outfit he had finally decided to put on. "It's going to be a full house... Tavern!" A giggle.

Venser really needed to look into some property now. The bungalow near the lake did not count. Nor his room in the tavern. Nor the other rooms that his many other lovers usually rented, or that he rented for them.

It was time to scrape some money together... It was time... For an adventure!

CHAPTER TWENTY-FOUR: THE VEIL TOWER

1436 ATC

Somewhere, deep within the marshlands and swamps deep past the forest of the veil. Deep within the swamp shows signs of a once different time. A time where the land was livable. A time where people inhabited a once beautiful land that had now changed over the years. Standing tall in some still waters of the swamp deep behind some withered willow trees stood an abandoned tower. It stood tall but at a slight tilt. The door on the front was rusted at the hinges and the door nearly fell off the tower. As one would climb the steps they would feel an erry draft as the stones of the wall were loose. Coming to the top as there would be another door, this door in better condition than the last. The door was a glass door with black steel details.

Opening it the room anyone would enter would be in shambles. A sofa ceil was in front of a window, vines grew creeping along the window frame. To the right of the room when coming in from the door was an old sofa, both ceil seat and sofa decorated in skull and rose pillows. In the middle of the floor a broken chandelier had fallen, its beads scattered across the floor. An old skull of some unknown person sat there with a crow named Bosco. He would occasionally hide his next meal in the eye sockets of the skull. Above the sofa an old dry rotted wooden cloak hung and next to it in the corner a birdcage with the creeping vines from the window grew onto, beautiful blossoms bloomed on these vines. To the left of the room were some old lights and a mirror and on the wall a candelabra. On the floor scattered around the room were old candles as well. As if this had been someone's secret hideaway. Oddly enough for the visitor, all the candles were lit but no one was there except a cold chill clinging to the air around them.

A man sat on a branch of a dead tree, scouting out the area with a silver spyglass he held to his eye. He wore a crimson and turquoise tunic with baggy red pants and bright red boots caked with mud from the swamp, along with a black cloak and a hood draped over his head. "Odd. Nothing out here but this tower." He muttered. "Can't really see a way in..." He disregarded that thought spotting a door in very bad condition that blended in with the tower. He disappeared in a puff of thick red smoke and reappeared several feet ahead of him, right at the door.

Ven cleared his throat and slid the spyglass into one of the many pouches of his belt, pushing the door open. It creaked noisily and he was quick to step back, ready for anything to jump out at him. He was met by a chill, and a hollow silence. "Exciting. Filled with... There's got to be something valuable, at least." The man said with a small smirk, stepping inside, his right hand grabbing his odd, blade-less sword that hung from his belt. The hooded man climbed the stairs slowly, wary of his surroundings and keeping both ears attuned. So far, nothing. His mud-died boots squished against the stone steps and he shuddered, reaching the top. Eying the glass door he raised a brow. "Is that a..." Could someone be living here? He approached it slowly, raised a fist, and knocked once, before quickly pressing his back up against the wall away and out of sight of the door. Best to knock, as there could have been something dangerous on the other side lying in wait, and it would be best to know before he opened the door and it left at him.

BUMP!

The sound of the knocking fist resonated throughout the murky insides of this estranged tower, seeming to rock the foundation of the building itself. In fact... It did. The door would fall from the bronze, rust laden hinges to hit the ground, another thud finding purchase to the ears of all involved. That all being one... Or was it? Further auditory prompting came from snapping support beams, shifting stone. It was like an earthquake, but confined within this tower.

To any with any sort of knowledge, it was rather apparent. The Tower was col-lapsing, right around the footfalls of this rather... Eccentrically dressed traveler. Ahead of him, right before his eyes the couch fell through the roof, as the solitary nesting crow fell underneath a crashing block of oak. The floor, from his behind, toppled to the floor, ten stories below. Dust, mold, and displaced stone filled the air, creating a choking, oppressively atmosphere to breath in... There wasn't much time before the entirety of the structure would fall, and take this explorer with it, to be buried under a surplus of limestone and steel.

The only glow in the room was that from the burning candles, smoke scenting the air, but there was another smell here. Something rotten. Something old. Per-haps it was the mold? Perhaps it was something else? As the man entered the room looking around the air grew colder, denser. Something was here. A being who could not be seen or heard formed from the smoke of the candles and she stretched yawning a bit. She blinked her ghostly dead white eyes stared at the intruder and she huffed. The Tower Keeper floated over towards the male circling him. He couldn't see her but she could see him. She circled him more before she leaned in towards his ear.

Her cold breath gently brushed his ear and a small whisper came out for him to hear, "Beware... This place is not for the faint of heart..." She spoke softly.

"Ahek! Ahek!" The man coughed several times and swore underneath his breath, throwing himself forward through the door when the hall behind him fell. Now in the room, he moved about slowly in case the floor would collapse again, looking about for any kind of valuables. So far, no threats aside from the environment itself. He clipped his strange folding sword, named Whalebone, back onto his belt and sighed, coughing a bit more. Or was someone here... Once he saw the lit candles his hand went back onto his bladeless sword. "Ah!" He jumped at the voice that whispered into his ear.

"Who's there?" He called out. Reflex kicked in, and he twirled his hilt and a short blade extended. With the faint lighting he did something he didn't often do... Placing the sharp blade in his left hand, he slowly dragged it across his palm, his mark glowing greenish white as he coated it with blood.

Zzzrt!

A very brief crackle of magical green lighting erupted from his fingertips and onto the blade. Zzzrt zzzrt! Waving his sword around, the blade now glowed bright green and crackled with unstable magic lightning as he used it like a torch.

Each step the male would take would result in the floor directly adjacent to him collapsing, falling down to the ground, with each and every second, more and more cracks formed in the foundation. He was now caught in a circle, gradually decreasing in size. There was not much time left... And not much visibility with all the smog clogging the air around each and every inch of his visuals. Oh, what is one to do in this situation? Another voice chimed into his ear, on the other side. Less quiet, but far raspier..."But...perhaps it's a bit too late for that...."

The Veil Crescent looked up to see Veil Dusk floating there with her examining the male who had invaded their home. She looked at Dusk licking her lips. She was hungry. She hadn't fed for a rather long time. Veils were interesting creatures,

Night Terrors. Hallowed out Souls who fed on terror and fear and insecurity. But they had a special ability. What one Veil fed on and collected in negative energy they could share with one another. She was sharing with Dusk, but she hungered for more. She reached out her long black eerie narrow finger gently brushed across the male's cheek and she pulled her hand away, he would barely feel her a streak of cold brushing against his cheek. She wanted to feed and she waited for her senior Night Terror to give her the okay.

"Too late for what?" He asked aloud moving to the center of the room, besides the broken chandelier. Whatever entity, or entities hovered around him, he assumed they were tied to the tower. If it fell apart, then they would vanish. "Too late for you too..." He said raising his left hand, and the mark on the back of it glowed greenish white, emitting steam. He moved back sharply when something touched his face and backhanded the air in front of him, blasting it with a powerful gust of wind.

The Hand, thrusting outward to lash at the air... Would find itself caught in the grips of a decomposing palm, nails hinging on last lines of putrid, green flesh, maggots wrenching from the muscle and bone. To shift one's eyes lower, would result in seeing the source of this extremity... A rolling, black mist, with nothing visible within its depth, save for the rising hand... And two, pupil less, blank eyes, bloodshot, and milky, pure white. The gusting wind would fall short as a light breeze generating from his digits, and from that same fog, which encroached all around his feet, more degenerating limbs rose to grasp his limbs. The Veil Dusk shifted his silvered eyes over to his fellow Night Terror... And offered but a nod in acceptance.

The wind did nothing and once she got the okay for the feed she smirked widely. She also felt it funny that this man assumed they were bond to this tower, thinking it was to late for them. Yes, she supposed it was too late for them, they died and turned into something less than a spirit. Something much more terrible. But they were not bound to this tower. This tower acted as their headquarters for many years. Floating behind the man she placed her two index fingers into his temples.

The Tower Keeper would not make him a host, only a surrogate until she found a proper host to feed from. He was her snack. Her index black fingers slipped into his temples, it would not hurt but he would feel a cold caress against his temples, and as she did this suddenly his darkest fears would come up to his mind staring him right in the face. She began to whisper in his ear, the eerie voice of a dead girl speaking, "I warned you..." She spoke softly.

"Oh by the void!"

Some adventure this was. Here Venser had recently kicked his heroine and Grey Amber addiction and was getting out of his usual dojo to travel and this went south fast. Then again, he knew the risks of adventuring. He nearly vomited at the sight that looked him in the face. He tore away from it, only for limbs to reach out of the floor and grabbed his legs. "Oof!" He tripped backwards and quickly disappeared in a puff of thick red smoke, reappearing against the wall. "Still think something here is of any value?" No. He had to- Everything froze and went cold. And his back arched and he heard a snapping noise as his mind fell away to the things he feared most.

With the male crumbling away to his fears, and with the Veil Crescent feeding, the use of further illusions was minimal...Veil Dusk released his hold over this tear between the realm of nightmares the corporeal existence, the tower losing its dilapidated state, and making a display of a well upkeep area. Of course... The male in red wouldn't quite see this, even if Maxx had lounged against the couch to watch him shrivel away in a corner.

"Enjoying your meal, Keeper?" His voice would only be heard to The Tower Keeper, conducting the 'soundwaves' solely through the fourth dimension. Anyone in earshot would merely get a strong sense of dread, given his nature... Though that would be useless information, to someone battling it out with inner demons.

The Tower Keeper felt his mind go towards the darkness of his fears and she smiled brightly. She began drawing the negative energy from his mind taking away his fears as quickly as they came feeding off his energy. When she was finished she floated over to Maxx touching his arm and sharing some with him, "Taste for yourself... It has a tangy taste if you ask me." She said happily glancing over at the male. Her words could only be heard by Maxx at the moment, "What should we do with him? Why do you think he came to this place? Is there a way we can probe him for information?" She asked glancing at Maxx who lounged on the couch. She floated around him before taking her own seat on the ceiling watching the male cower against the wall.

Anaxximander just shrugged his shoulders, now lounging along the couch, all in a relaxed mode. "Honestly, once he comes to from this fit, he'll more than likely leave. If he sticks around, we just hit him again, get a bit more food. Carboload and all that...No telling when my laziness will subside, after all..." Maxx offered his compatriot a slight smile. "Thanks for sharing... Nice job on that one, by the way. He seems to be really out of it... He's attuned to otherworldly and other dimensional forces. You can tell by that mark on his hand... So it makes sense that he probably has more fears than those within the mortal coil."

Hallucinations appeared. "Pryldahn was so beautiful... Both inside and out. It would make travelling to work so much easier and all of the children could play together, when the baby grows a bit of course." A woman with flawless, semigolden skin and warm, loving green eyes said smiling warmly and pressed a tender kiss to Venser's lips then, nuzzling against them. "I love you, Venser...Thank you for the life you've given me." Beside the woman in the comfort of turquoise silk sheets inside the Dragon's Head Tavern and Inn, laid the man himself. "Yeah... We can just walk to work every day, and we can have Kari and Alex watch the kids." Venser said smiling as he took Sanna's soft hands in his, rubbing his thumbs over them.

"I love you too Sanna. So so much." He nuzzled her head, and she did the same. "Thank you for the life you've given me." Her words echoed in his head as the hooded, bearded man lay still against the wall, staring up wide eyed and unblinking at the ceiling. His head fell forward and his vision blurred, everything went white and he saw a figure approach him. One... Familiar.

The Tower Keeper frowned a bit looking at Maxx, "He fears loss of love I believe..." She spoke, "I wish I could have sympathy for him.... But I have never experienced love... I was alone when I was alive.... And now I am dead...." She spoke sighing, "I almost forgot what it's like to be alive... Really the only thing I remember is my pain..." She said floating towards the male who seemed to be in a cold sweat and she felt bad. She knew she needed to do this for survival, but when she wished to plague all those others who hurt her, she didn't think it would be at the cost of plaguing everyone who came around.

"Ven-" A blocky, beautiful voice said as the figure approached him, the figure being human and wearing a simple white sundress, but the light blocked out most features.

A year ago... "Tempey's gone!" Venser yelled at the top of his lungs dropping all the bottles he held and pushing his dear friend away. "What was it she said? She doesn't love me anymore!" He shoved his head back into the garbage and wept before falling over. "Oh well... I can always have female company at The Golden

Minx. Or The Witch's Wiggle!" He jumped up and faced his bard friend Juliette. "We could have those orgies they have every three months! I've taken you to No Name Port right?! Orgies Julie! Orgies! Orgies!" He kept yelling that one word and flailing his arms, making a huge commotion in the middle of the tavern he lived and worked in. The children hated seeing their father like this. "Reeky what does orggie mean?" A little boy with messy hair so blonde it looked white with grass green eyes asked in a tiny voice a nearby succubus.

Further back... A woman seven-foot-tall, beautiful despite the odd marks etched into her skin, mismatched eyes, and muscular appearance was not sure how she felt but she gave him a kiss back however it was far less affectionate and she cut it short. "Maybe." The half giant stated and then she walked out the doors. Once she headed down the stairs Venser walked over to the railings and silently watched his love exit his life. The door shut and was easily heard inside the empty and quiet tavern. "I love you." He said sadly shedding more tears slumping down against the railings, looking through them with his hands on them as if they were prison bars. "I love you..." She didn't have any second thoughts as she got her horse from the stable and began on her new journey, a healthier one. "Tempey..." He croaked. The figure moved closer, and closer. "You can't help yourself, can you?" The female voice was clearer now and he tensed up.

The Tower Keeper watched the man relive these painful memories and she frowned. Her effects never lasted this long on anyone before and she feared his mind unraveling.

Suddenly a loud voice of a dead girl boomed out, "STOP!" And the tower quaked at the voice as if it were alive. Veil Crescent watched the man cry and break down on the floor and she decided to do something she had never done. Suddenly the small ghost girl stood before him in plain sight. She was a small girl only five foot four. She was slender, as if deprived of food and even affection. She had black hair that faded to white and she had white eyes. Her skin was pale with a black line across her face and black lips and black shadows around her eyes. Her fingers were black and slender and she was dressed in a plain black shirt, black skirt and black sandals shoes. Around her neck was a Crescent choker which gave her, the Veil name of Crescent.

The man carried loss and regret on his shoulders like no other. On the back of his left hand, were the letters "RG" branded there. On his right palm was "AK" and on his right wrist was "TD". On his left palm was "AV" and on his left wrist was "AN". "Aytu. Angel. Tempey. Alexis." The ghostly figure that approached Venser was close enough to show her form. It was a woman around the same height as Venser, shorter, and wore a simple white sundress. She had shoulder length black hair with a pink streak in the front, azure eyes of deepest summer, and a kind smile. "And you." Venser said aloud. His lip quivering at the sight of the long dead woman before him.

"I tricked you to fall in love with me. And... You killed me." She spoke strongly and sternly, her gaze matching his. "I'm so sorry..." She frowned. "You should be." She disappeared along with the white light. Instead, he envisioned himself covered in blood, holding the bodies of his children close to him. Their eyes blank and lifeless. "No... No..." He began to sob as he held them close, nuzzling into their heads. They disappeared and before him stood an unfamiliar woman touching his forehead. Reflexes. He lunged forward and let out a savage, angry yell that held a saddened, stifled sob of pain. "You took my children away from he!" They figments all but disappeared, and he found he had wandered into a long hallway of the tower. "It's not real... No. No. All this can't actually physically hurt me... I'm sure."

As he lunged forward he would go through her and onto the ground. The Tower Keeper frowned and turned around and shook her head, whilst she pitied him, she needed his energy. "I am hungry... Let us delve deeper into your fears... Now, show me what you fear most." Her voice was cold, dead, meek. Not nearly as scary as she wanted to be to people to see her, but it was not her they had to be afraid of, it was whatever was within their own minds.

Venser cautiously walked down the corridor, his crackling green lightning sword providing a good source of light in the darkness. And then... At the end of the hallway, his greatest fear rounded the corner.

A large, bulky figure stood at the end of the wide hall. He looked like he had just been ripped from the ground, stains of dirt were splashed all over his dark green jacket. From knapsack, a bandolier across his left shoulder, aged trousers, a military belt with several fastener pins and studded pinholes, and combat boots adorned with weathered gaiters, and medals pinned to his chest that bounced as he moved closer and closer. Blood was even visible on his uniform. His skin was a dead grey, and covered with lightning bolt shaped burn marks and veins that glowed a supernatural orange. The broad shouldered undead soldier had very short wispy brown hair, long eyelashes, a strong clean cut jaw, and a mouth that was stuck in a permanent scowl.

In his hand, The Revenant wielded a claymore, it's very blade blazed a molten orange as if he had just pulled it out of the core or a forge. The claymore flowed through the air, leaving a trail of misty steam. At the sight of the familiar bearded man in front of him, The Revenant's eyes flared red with blinding hatred, his volcanic veins that covered him turning the same color and pulsating. Behind him, it seemed as if several shadowy, vine like tendrils were attatched to his back akin to a puppet, and behind him the thin silhouette of The Revenant's puppetmaster, the one who had raised him from the dead as this monstrous minion, the witch Louise Lampshire.

Venser breathed slowly and held his sword in front of him, listening to the cracking if the unstable lightning that coated the blade, able to see the strings and the shadow that represented the controller. But it was only for a fleeting moment, as the very familiar soldier lunged at him and the shadow disappeared.

"ERRRRAGGGGGH!"

CHZZZZT!

Sparks from the hot claymore and the lightning infused sword flew everywhere as Venser was knocked back barely off balance blocking the during blow. "Ah! No!"

With an incoherent roar of rage, The Revenant launched a vicious, all-out assault. Venser was able to keep up with the strong pattern of attacks, simply dodging as many as he could. Gripping his sword in one hand, bright green lightning erupted from his fingertips, crackling and sputtering at the soldier, who gripped his magic claymore with both hands and absorbed all of it, simply flinging it off to the side and blowing a hole in the wall.

"YOUR LIGHTNING WILL NOT CUT ME DOWN TWICCCCEEE... VENSERRERR."

"I don't want to fight you. No. Not again." The bearded man said shedding a single tear, moving back. In response The Revenant narrowed his glowing red eyes and held his glowing hot claymore up, prepared to strike again. His mark glowed greenish white and emitted steam and he disappeared in a puff of thick red smoke but found himself dragged back to the hallway and pulled forward.

The Revenant had the very same mark, and an ethereal green chain now bound them together in The Veil Tower, and the only way out was death. There would be no teleporting out, nor running away, lest the undead soldier dragged along. As their duel progressed down the long hall, the bearded man found that he could still anticipate the familiar soldier's offense, but could not find any openings to strike back. All he could do was block his enraged blows, sending sparks flying all around them. Venser could feel his energy falter as he kept dodging and attempting to block the heavy claymore. "Hoo... Hoo... Hoo!"

After blocking for what seemed like forever, Venser lunged again, but The Revenant was ready, bringing them into a blade lock. The tall, bulky undead soldier shoved hard breaking the lock and forcing Venser back. The Tower Keeper watched the two duel with great interest, a smile across her black lips clearly entertained and feeling her strength return from the man's fear. Sweat ran down the man's handsome visage as he held his sword in front of him, and then, as a desperate measure he drew his strange twin tubed device, aimed, and fired.

KERBLAST!

The Revenant recognized the device and threw his left hand up just in the nick of time, a burning orange shield appearing in the palm of his hands and absorbing all of the projectiles, all of them coming together to form a molten ball of metal.

"HERREGH!"

Thinking just as quick Venser did a fast back hand motion and knocked the molten ball back at the undead soldier, striking him in the chest and the heated ball lodging itself in his chest. "Ha!" The bearded man closed the distance, spun his folding sword around and gripped it with both hands, summoning all the strength he could and swung at The Revenant's neck, slicing it clean off and sending it flying.

Thunk, thunk.

The bearded man dropped his sword, letting it clatter against the stone floor beneath, and not too soon after he dropped to his knees beside it. Emerald green eyes filled with tears, brushing them away and tightening his fist watching the illusion fade away. Overcome with regret, and reminded of what had become of that familiar man, what he had done to him, reminded of where he came from and a past he ran far away from, caused him to briefly break down. He did what he had to do, forced to kill him once again. It was simply a ghostly illusion, but it all felt too real.

The Tower Keeper almost felt bad for the bearded adventurer in the crimson and turquoise tunic, and simply allowed the rest of the wall to crumble behind him, revealing a small space filled with the pale bones of other long dead adventurers, victims of The Tower Keeper and her cohorts. Their treasures ripe for the taking.

"Take what you want… And go. You have greatly entertained me." She said fading away along with her demon cohorts, leaving an eerie silence behind in The Veil Tower.

A few coin purses filled with silver, old equipment mostly steel and simple leathers he chose to leave behind, a ruby pendant, an intricately cut red crystal stuck in a strange stone base, a small leather sack filled with diamonds that would fetch a fine price. All quite boring so far, but would do the job in helping pay for a big home for his family.

"Now this looks interesting…" Deep in the pile was an old bottle of elven wine from the Alfonse Islands. Called Alfonse rose wine, the bottle was of silverbough wood, crafted by a 'Shape Wood' spell and appearing as a delicately crafted rose, with the date and winery listed in the elvish along the stem. Rose wine is a brilliant red in color, delicate and dry, with the flavors and scents reminiscent of spring and life. The grapes for rose wine were only grown in those far off southern islands that he himself had never been to, and such an aged wine was surely very expensive and very tasty, and the man loved traveling around for exotic wines and liquors. This was a perfect find, and now planned on sharing it with his lovers when Rowena was born.

The man collected all of these items in a leather sack and slung it over his shoulder, and made for the entrance with his bounty, vowing never to return to The Veil Tower.

CHAPTER TWENTY-FIVE: THE OTHER NEW BARMAID

The Dragon's Head Tavern and Inn, Vorland, 1436 ATC

"Welcome to the Dragon's Head Tavern!" The raven haired huntress Sedna exclaimed taking the silver from a random patron and placing it in the seemingly bottomless jar of coins behind the bar. Setting the shadow tendrils to work on the fowl in the kitchen, she began lighting the candles in the tavern herself. Sedna Rosarian was quite the regal looking lady despite her furs and leathers, with high cheekbones, a slightly pointed jaw ending in a delicate chin, full pink lips, straight black hair, and eye color of an impossible shade of turquoise blue.

"That's my line." The bearded bartender said from beside Sedna, as if he had been there the whole time. "I don't remember you working here."

Sedna smiled at Venser and steps away from the bar, seating herself. "Kira asked me to be barback while she and you were gone."

Sanna would walk down the dirt road that obviously had to lead somewhere, going for a relaxing walk alone earlier today. She gets to the door and pushed it open hearing the greeting and the voice after that seemed to follow it. She wasn't from around here and you could tell that from her clothing. She was tanned skin and her curvaceous figure held her breasts and hips nicely. She'd step up the stairs quickly as her bare feet tapped against the wood panels. She'd walk up to the bar. Her ravenous hair fell over her shoulders and down her back. The tanned woman gave them a smile. "Thank you for the greeting ma'am." She'd bow her head to a random patron, before going to the bearded bartender and giving him a soft and loving kiss.

"Kira? She doesn't have the authority. The shadow tendrils can do the job in her place." Venser always had a red beaked hood attached to his suit, and he always kept it down. But for the first time in years he wore the hood over his head, shrouding some of his face in shadow. He sighed and took his usual place behind the bar, looking to the tanned woman and returning the kiss. "So, what can I get you love?"

"Do you serve a certain drink here? It's non-alcoholic... And... Hard to explain. It's sort of like a beer, but made from the sassfras root." She'd asked curiously, leaning into the bar, her elbows propping her head up as she blinked a few times staring at the man and his attire. "You're wearing that again? Why?"

The bartender in the red rubber suit with rubber nipples an oversized codpiece, completely out of place in an establishment like this burst out laughing for a few short seconds. "Errrrrrr... I know exactly what you're talking about but I can get it later. Can I get you something else in the meantime? Juice? Water?"

Sanna just nodded and smiled. "Water will do nicely then." The tanned woman leaned farther in as she looked over the counter a bit and would let her lips curl into a smile. She'd smile reaching up stretching her arms as her shoulders cracked a bit. She'd drop them down glancing around as the quietness of the area. She bit onto her lip a bit, breathing out quietly.

A regular named Lynn noticed a woman enter the tavern and turned to face, "Greetings" she said as the woman asked about wine. Her eyes catch Venser and looks at him before turning away and looking around the tavern to see who all else was around. Seeing not too many more had entered she returned to her tea and took a drink of it.

Venser pulled down his crimson, beaked hood, revealing messy raven black hair that had a dark green tint to it and really needed to be cut again, fair skin, and a handsome human face mixed with eyes that looked like they were plucked from the skull of a snake. He had strong arched brows and eyelashes so thick it demanded confidence, strength. Attack eyebrows! A prominent jaw curved gracefully around and the strength of his neck showed in the twining cords of muscle that shaped him. "Coming right up." As he grabbed a glass and a pitcher he looked to Sedna and asked, "How you been doing lately?'"

Looking sheepish and slightly jealous at the beautiful gypsy woman and the handsome bearded barkeep, Sedna played with her hair as she answered Venser's question. "I've been alright. Hunting for the tavern, mostly. I have to leave at dawn, though. The ship will arrive at the docks at around mid-morning, and it's a long walk. How are you both?"

Sanna would glance at the female whom had been staring at her. Blinking a few times before smiling a bit as Venser placed her water in front of her. She'd take the glass and raised it to her lips taking a sip, exhaling from the sweet taste. "Mmh... Very refreshing after a threshing."

"Good, good." Venser said leaning against the shelves, looking down for a split second. "Ooh!" He exclaimed and quickly grabbed a bucket from below the bar, chugging a bright red drink from it. "Ah that's good... You been vomiting or anything, Sedna?"

Puzzled at Venser's question she put her head to one side. "Vomiting? No, not really. I had food poisoning last week, I think. I was really sick. But I haven't been vomiting or anything out of the ordinary. Why do you ask, Venser?"

Lynn kept drinking her tea. Her eyes looked up in time to see the woman look at her, "Sorry for staring but you do leave little to the imagination." She said bluntly.

"Well that's a good thing." Venser said hearing the woman's comment. "Well, considering it's been cold out lately, and raining. Maybe not. But if you ask me, people should just be naked all the time. Unless you're like, eighty-two." He cleared his throat and looked to Sedna and said, "The hunting trip."

"The hunting tri... Oh! The hunting trip! Yes, no, nothing like that. I'm still all in one piece. No vomiting for Sedna. That's why I'm travelling."

Sanna's eyebrows would scrunch up as she listened to what the female said. "Is that a bad thing?" She asked, tilting her head a bit before sipping her drink once more.

"I won't argue the point she does have a good looking body." Lynn giggled. "But if she didn't want to be stared at she could have at least put on a bit more."

The tanned gypsy shook her head and would chuckle a bit before finishing her drink. Her other hand against her chest fiddling with the fabric a bit as she glanced out the window. Leaning against the bar counter. Her back curving smoothing, her thighs filling the whole bar seat as she placed her hands on her pregnant belly.

"I meant how we ended it." Venser said with a short, seductive growl looking to Sedna before looking to the other two women at the bar. "Yes, yes she does have a good looking body. Compliment."

Breanna Rowland entered the tavern with a confident exhale and stepped towards the bar with purpose. She had grown tired of travelling, and now that she's found a good town to put down roots in, she was now on the hunt for employment. She was experienced in bartending and general inkeepery, but wasn't opposed to anything like farming or tending to crops either. Mainly, Breanna just needed the money. Approaching the barkeep with a smile she asked, "Good day, might I ask if you all are hiring new positions? Other barkeepers, perhaps?" Her voice was pleasant, as were her kind hazel eyes. She tried her best to exude warmth and hospitality.

Sanna slowly turn her head to her beloved in the red outfit, blinking a couple times. She'd wiggle her toes a bit before, shifting her arms on the counter glancing at the two. "So many wanderers. "

Lynn nodded her head hearing the female's answer. "Yes, and eventually the wanderer become regulars." She said with a small laugh.

He brushed back some of his messy tinted green raven black hair and turned to the girl with a blank look. "Uhhhhhhhhhhhh... Well fuck. I just took a barback under my wing to train her to become a bartender. But lately it's just been me, Thorn and Kira. And Thorn has a bad tendency to disappear." She seemed nice enough. "Have a seat, and tell me what are your qualifications?"

"Taking all the pretty young ones, eh, Venser?" Sedna asked, Sanna blushed a bit and watched them all. Leaning up as she stuffed her hands between her thick thighs.

Breanna nodded and smiled, placing her folded hands on the bar and leaning on them a little. "There's an inn out in Placerville called the Sulking Badger that I served at for around five years. Three as a bar maiden and two as the head barkeep." Her accent was incredibly southern, but her cheerful demeanor contrasted it in an almost comical way. She raised her eyebrows in surprise and then a slight pink rapidly crossed her fair cheeks. "My name is Breanna Rowland. I probably should've started with that. My apologies."

Venser took the glass of water from the shadowy hand, and it retreated back below the bar. He took a sip and said, "Venser Kaldwin. Or Venny, or Ven, or Handsome VenVen, or My Little Vensie." He nodded his head listening to her. Years of experience, and once a head barkeep like he was currently. "What happened at your last job that's making you seek out a new one?"

Breanna shifted in her seat, switching how her ankles were crossed. "While I was head barkeep at the Sulking Badger, I was not the innkeeper. His name was Ellis Eoin, and he was ancient. I'm talking very, very old." She furrowed her eyebrows subconsciously as she recounted the past events. "Anyway, he married a young lass o' twenty-something; and when he passed, sure enough, he left the inn to her. Well, the girl had no clue in Summerland or Eternal Darkness on how to run a business, let alone an inn!" Brianna met eyes with the woman named Lynn who was now watching her tell the story, and she started to address her as well, thinking of her as an audience member. "So, the Sulking Badger finally had a reason behind why it sulked: it sucked." She shrugged and re-crossed her ankles, brushing back her shoulder length sandy blonde hair. "I left. There was nothing for me there anymore."

Sanna would exhale a bit. "Yes far west were the warm and sand is." She'd smile warmly. "I was apart of a gypsy troupe, more like a pack. The cold doesn't bother me." She said quietly. "Weirdly enough I naturally have no problem staying warm in the cold.

"It went under and you were out of a job?" Venser asked turning his head back to the hazel eyed blonde woman. "And now you're here, trying to get a job to replace that one. Excuse me a second, Brea. I can call you that right? Okay." He disappeared in a puff of thick red smoke and reappeared beside his gypsy wife, leaning forward, running a hand through her hair and gently caressing her skin. "Sorry if this seems weird."

Watching the dark night begin to lighten, Sedna took a walk around the tavern and inn, avoiding the rooms that were occupied, taking in the sounds and smells that made the Dragon's Head one of a kind. Pausing at her own room, the one that she'd had on reserve for a while, she took one last look at the bed she'd called her own, and grabbed all her knick-knacks and threw them into a large trunk, which she picked up and carried on her hip.

Walking out to the bar area, she set the trunk down and raised her hand a little, saying goodbye to those who noticed. Carrying her trunk to the kitchens, she wrote a note to Kira, and walked over to the main doors. Turning back to look up at the main bar, she watched the sun gave a soft glow to the room. Raising her hand again, she turned and walked out of the doors, wrapping her cloak around herself.

Breanna nodded. "Take your time, sir." She then moved her folded hands from the bar to her lap.

"Oh no love, you're good." Sanna felt his hand brush through her hair and against her flesh. "Hmm..." He took her hand and extended each of her digits individually, before lolling his tongue out to lick her hand. He teleported back in front of Brea and asked, "Where were we?"

Breanna met his eyes once more, and stuck out her fingers to count. "Uh yes, you can call me Brea. Inn went kaput and took barkeep job with it. I found a town I like, aka this one, and am looking for a job so I could live here." She put her hands down in her lap again and half-smiled, her shyness getting the best of her. For the moment, at least.

Sanna would stare to Venser, her eyes widened a bit as he licked her hand. Her eyebrows slowly relaxed a bit before, he disappeared. "Hm." She said softly, "Aren't I a lucky woman?" She'd laugh a bit before glancing over to Lynn once more, "My apologies." She'd laugh a bit, her lips curl into a smile.

"What do you specialize in? Making tea? Mixing drinks? Just being quick and efficient?" Venser asked rapping his fingers on the bar as he looked her in the eyes. "Kira, my current barback is quite helpful but excels in making tea. Normally, since I wind up running the tavern alone the shadow tendrils fix hot drinks downstairs. Alright but not the best. Are you particularly best at something?"

Breanna's face quickly filled with a grin in response to his question. "I was the head barkeep for a southern inn. I'm good at making and serving tavern fare as well as pouring ale. I'm particularly quick in getting food out, and I don't take no bunk neither, sir." She added, bright hazel eyes getting serious to match her tone. "If some drunkard is raisin' trouble in the bar here, I can kick him out no problem." She nodded with a smile and a wink.

A mysterious black mist would begin to conjure off in a quiet corner of the tavern, slowly becoming thicker as it came to form of a petite female's silhouette. The smoky mist would subside just as it came revealing the demoness and marking her arrival. She let out a soft sigh whilst lifting back her right boot to rest against the wall behind her, the rest of her figure leaning back softly to rest against the wall as well. She chose to remain silent for the moment as she began observing the other patrons of the tavern.

"Hmmm..." He nodded his head and rubbed his chin. "I'm going to have to ask Roselie... She hasn't been around in a while. But like with Kira, I think she's a good asset. And I'm sure you will be too. Let's test you out, shall we?" He stepped out from behind the bar and gestured for Breanna to join them in their work.

The woman's eyes sparkled and her grin broadened. "Thank you sir! Thank you." Brea nodded each time she thanked him, and took his previous position from behind the bar, adjusting to the new atmosphere and getting back into her professional state of mind that she had adapted all those weeks ago.

Venser appeared right beside her in a puff of thick red smoke, nudging her a bit to the right. "You can get to work right now. The girl against the wall." He whispered, teleporting into a seat at the end of the bar.

The puff of smoke startled her. The girl with sandy blonde hair and hazel eyes stumbled for a second but caught herself on the bar. Once she had regained her composure and balance, she lifted her hand and realized it was a little sticky. "Yessir." Brea responded as she wet a rag and went to cleaning the bar, starting with the strange sticky patch. She lifted her head when she heard a new creature enter the bar. "Greetings." She called from behind the bar, the warmth in her voice matching the sparkle in her eyes. The traveler still seemed pretty far away, so she thought it best to wait for them to approach closer before she asked if they needed anything. That way she wasn't yelling across the room.

Breanna was quick to put some now-clean tankards back in a neat little row, then took her clean rag and tossed it halfway in the drawer, letting it partially hang out to dry. She looked at her shiny counter and smiled, then raised her eyes to meet the guests. "Can I fetch anything for anybody? Mead, ale, wine?" She suggested, looking for something helpful to do.

The pink haired elf had been absent for about a good hour, and came back to the bar floor of the tavern wearing different attire from her last. After fighting the geyser for the 'cherry soda' her dress became scrap, and her hair needed an extremely good washing after the color stained her 'pink' hair. She had taken the fabric from the dress, re-dyed it, and fixed it to where it was more suitable. "Lynn Lynn!" The elf piped up, running up to her friend with a bright smile. "Took your advice!" Kira rose up her slender arms to show her creation.

"So, Brea, I take you already know the basics of this positions? I mean of course, stupid question." Venser asked looking to her. "If so then I'll just need to get you a room and show you around the tavern." He pointed back at the little pink haired elf. "That's Kira, my barback, apprentice, whatever. You both will be helping me run the bar and running it when I'm unable to. Honestly, a lot. Since lately I've been off on so many adventures."

She nodded, "A king can't say I haven't seen many of them but non the less it sounds a bit annoying." Lynn wasn't one to take orders very well or even listen to advice. So something like a council of advisors would drive her up a wall. Lynn turned to look at Kira as she showed her dress off. That is a beautiful dress you did good cutie." She smiled warmly.

"Heh. I might be able to take some time off to spend with my family and do some merc work here and there... I mean... More!"

"It's a pleasure to meetcha, miss!" Brea added as she turned to Kira with a hand outstretched for a shake.

Clapping her hands together with a bit of hop in her step she then swayed back and forth feeling the attire on her form. "Thank you!" She spoke up with more pep in her step, then turned to greet the new employee of the Dragons Head Tavern. Feeling... Hyper?

Kira scooted closer to the girl and glanced up at her face, "Hello! Nice to meet you, Breanna! Brea!" Taking ahold of her hand she shook it happily.

"I could not live that way no personal time no offense but being royalty is not good at all." Lynn said. She took another drink of her tea finishing the cup off. She turned to look at Kira and smiled, "Could you make me some more green tea?"

Brea giggled, but it was more like a guffaw. She then laughed without abandon, no matter what the cause of the laugh may be. "Pleasure's all mine." She answered, putting her arms back by her side.

This was more of an exciting day, another employee for Kira to speak with! This was going to be a blast! The pink haired elf beamed that brilliant smile of hers, and once she heard Lynn request for some more green tea with honey, she placed her hands in front of her person and said, "Aye aye! Right away." Then rose a finger, "Oh and Venser? The 'Soda' has been all placed in large glass jars in the cellar for whenever you want to sell it." with a hop in her step she darted down the stairs and into the kitchen to get some hot water for the tea.

Brea smiled as she watched Kira skip off to complete her task. She stepped back from her place at the bar to survey her work, and the guests that sat in front of her.

Venser stood up, thinking about how he would pay them both. He was sure it would be no problem as Kira had been a good worker lately and stayed around. There was nothing he really wanted and only needed money to feed his kids and buy gifts of affection for his lovers, and he drank a lot from the tavern's stock which came out of his pay. Well, now he had to think of a proper home. That was it! Fifty, twenty five twenty five. "Excellent. When you're down with the tea I need to take control of the bar!" He called, turning to Brea. "Lemme show you around."

"Well, shadow tendrils can run the bar and everything all by themselves. But you know why I don't like the shadow tendrils?"

Brea looked at him and nodded. "Very well, sir. And why?"

"They can do everything, cook, run the bar, clean the floors, but not talk. You know that trope of bartenders being wise and always give good life advice? Well it's true. You need to be social on this job."

Venser clapped his hands twice and the shadow tendrils manifested themselves into a shadow duplicate of himself, rubber suit, cape, battle skirt, shoulder pad everything. "They can mimic my voice, but they're limited in words. I've been trying to teach them how to dance but it's been fucking hard.

Being in the kitchen was perhaps Kira's favorite part of the job, she liked to cook, make teas and... It was simply quiet and she could be in her own little world. She literally took the liberty to restock the herbs, and the basic foods, along with cleaning the entire kitchen to where it sparkled in her eyes. She knew where everything was and made sure to keep it organized. Even though the tendrils could do the same thing, Kira just liked being hands on. After a few moments, Kira came back up with the 'tea tray' which had the hot water in a black kettle, a couple of tea cups and a few jars of herbs in case anyone wanted a different tea. Walking her way behind the bar she quickly began to produce the green tea carefully, and with an extra spoon of honey added. "Here we are, Lynn." The elf spoke, sliding the tea cup to the woman.

Brea followed him completely, but giggled at his dancing remark. "Now that's a damn shame." She added, watching them with an added amusement.

Lynn turned to look at Kira and smiled as Kira slid the tea to her. Lynn took the tea and brought it to her lips taking a sip of it. As always the tea was great. She gave a pleased sigh and paid for the tea.

"See that?" Venser asked pointing to a medium sized jar on one of the shelves. "That is the payment jar. It's bigger on the inside, and everything you get paid goes in there. Except for tips." He pointed down to the floor. "Below us is the kitchen, and beside that is the alchemy room."

The sandy blonde girl nodded, mapping it all out in her brain, seeing it all in her mind's eye as a 2D blueprint, almost. "Okay." she said, signaling for him to continue when he was ready.

The bearded bartender stepped back and pointed off in the directions of the hallways. "On the right going into the halls are the bathrooms, on the left down the halls are the rooms. On the right is the shower room. Come come, let's walk down them."

The brand new barmaid followed behind him, but the more he explained what things were, the more often she slowed down, as to map them out. She heard him beckon her again, and she found herself heaps farther behind than she had previously thought. "Coming, sir!" Brea called, lifting her dark green skirts and hurrying after him.

"Tell me, what race are you?" Venser asked as they walked down the hall of the rustic tavern, a window was at the very end of the hallway and it seemed longer than one would think.

Kira stood next to the bar with her hands in front of her person, she could not help but hum to herself as she swayed. Perhaps some of that soda seeped into her pours and made her overly energetic this evening? Maybe she should try a sip of whiskey? Standing now in front of the drinks, the elf peered up at the many choices beside whiskey as well. What would be a good start than Venser's ass kicker of a drink? She was small... And. Did not drink often. "Lynn, what would you advise drink wise for a lightweight?" She asked.

Brea sighed. "Human. But I can hold my own just like other races, I assure you, sir." She added hastily. Often it felt to her that many opposed humans in comparison to other races like demons, elves, Pryldahnians, and shifters and the like. So, when it seemed necessary, she would defend humans. Now, she wasn't one hundred percent sure if it was necessary, she really just used it as a defense mechanism.

"Any special abilities? Can you use magic?" Venser asked stopping at the sixth door on the right. The door was like any other, only with several scratches on it and a crude drawing of Venser and a large breasted naked lady carved into the front of the door. "If you ever need to clean or anything, don't go in my room. If you see a rubber codpiece on the door, then don't bother knocking or anything. Got it?"

Wind blew through the door of the tavern as a young woman walked through. She was an odd thing, the demoness wore all black clothing, her hair was dyed purple, she had a bow and quiver on her back, but perhaps the most peculiar thing about her was that across her face sat a blindfold. She walked in slowly letting her body shift and adapt to her environment. She walked forward with confidence as if her vision was not impaired at all. She climbed the stairs to the top floor without missing or guessing a step, and walked up to the bar. She turned an ear toward the bartender and pounded the bar, signaling that she needed something to drink. She reached into her pocket and pulled out a coin, setting it on the bar then tapped it with her fingers impatiently.

The pink haired elf quickly turned around from gazing at the liquor bottles and instantly greeted the newest Patron that stepped into the building. "Welcome to the Dragons Head Tavern! Please make yourself comfortable. I am Kira, and I will be glad to fulfill your wants and needs. May I start you off with a drink?"

Brea nodded and clasped her arms loosely in front of her. "I am a sort of a witch. Self-made and taught. I can cast self-made spells and things of the like. Defense or offense. It's rather helpful, I must say."

Lynn looked at Kira, "I would start with a weak ale or something." Lynn wasn't much of a drinker so she really had no clue.

Kira nodded in response to Lynn, thinking that may be a good idea. Weak ale. Lynn always seemed to have the best ideas. "Right, I'll get myself some." She then dug into her dress pocket to pull out her tip money.

The girl placed her head in her hands and shook it, she pointed to the coin on the counter then to the bar behind the bartender violently as if to say, "There, right there, that thing on the wall, that is what I want." she continued to tap the bar impatiently.

"Lovely! And I've decided you'll be bunking with Kira. So you two can get to know each other." Venser said. "I showed you the basics, oh! The basement is rather large, half is a wine cellar and a training room. Go see Kira at the bar and I'm gonna go get some rest. Long day on the job and never a dull day at the Dragon's Head!"

Kira looked towards the coin, then to where the patron pointed and spoke, "Oh, yessum." Pouring the patron, a drink, she sets it down before her.

She smiled and curtsied as he turned away. "Aye, and thank you again, sir! Thank you kindly." Brea bid him farewell before going back towards the bar. "Well, it looks like most things are settled!" She said, stopping right beside the counter and allowing a yawn to take over for a moment. The brand new barmaid blinked for a moment before stretching. "But if it's alright with you, I've done quite a bit of traveling these past few days, and I think it'd behoove me to get some rest." She curtsied and to Kira and then inclined her head in farewell to the guests. "Good day all!"

Venser teleported right behind Kira with his arms crossed. "She was once a head bartender at another tavern. You and her will be learning a lot from each other." He moved around the bar and looked to the gypsy woman who had slumped over a bit and struggled to keep her eyes open at the bar, shifting a bit and being careful to pick Sanna up in his arms, bridal style with surprising strength.

"That is great, I am super excited to work with her." Kira nodded.

The demoness pulled down the cowl that was in front of her eager lips as she gripped the handle to the glass and brought it up for a swig. She coughed a bit and let out a relaxed sigh. "About damn time..." Her voice was pleasant if not overtly aggressive. "I know bartenders don't exactly get the best of educations but one would think when a patron places money on the damn counter the idiots would know what to do." She took another swig and slammed the glass on the bar. Her demeanor was definitely rude and crass, she was that kind of person, young, impatient, assertive.

This particular patron did not seem in the best of spirits, and kinda lashed out, causing the elf to shrink back a bit with her hands cupped within one another. This patron was indeed rude, but because of Kira's mistake. The pink elf was now deemed an idiot. But this was not the first time she had someone spit in her face without a second thought. Taking in a deep breath, Kira let it out smoothly. "My apologize for my foolish mistake." Her good mood seemed to have continued in spite of this particular customer.

"Anyways, good luck tonight. I'll be asking about your progress tomorrow." Sanna stirred in his arms and fluttered open her intense, bright green eyes, wrapping her soft arms around his neck. "Ven... I'm tired... Take me and Rowena to bed?" The tanned woman rubbed her belly.

The bearded man leaned to kiss her on the lips gently, and she rested her head in his barreled chest as he carried her back to his room, disappearing around the corner and down the hall.

CHAPTER TWENTY-SIX: THE TALL TEMPTRESS

The Dragon's Head Tavern and Inn, Vorland, 1436 ATC

Nestled in the shadow of a great volcano sat a homely tavern. Inside the tavern sat a black haired beauty with medium golden eyes. All titty, six feet tall, a nice bouncy ass. Her name was Ceirra Dusk, and she had a bad habit of stumbling into places she ought not to. She was dressed to emphasize that beauty. Her amazingly long legs, were exposed as her dress was hiked up to her knees, the ends dripping with melted snow. "Oh, for Kore's sake. This is a bloody fuckin' mess, that's all this is." She muttered, brows furrowing into a deep, angry wrinkle. Fuck winter. Nothing good ever came from it. All you got was hypothermia and pointy nipples. She huffed, scooping up her skirts to her thighs and waddling to the bar. "Hello lovies," She purred, her voice surprisingly high pitched. Plopping her round rear down onto a stool, she let her skirts fall with a good thuwmp. "Drinks all around, yeah?"

Venser eyed some drunk woman at the bar spouting nonsense. He exhaled greenish white smoke from his cigar then jumped at the woman's impact on the lower floor. "By the void what's been going... Welcome to the Dragon's Head Tavern and Inn! And what would you like sir?" He looked to the girl who requested something with rum and waved her off. "Can I interest you in my signature drink, Pink Footed Booby? It doesn't have rum in it but I can tell you it's the best drink you'll ever put in your mouth." Like most nights, it was decently busy, and he had trouble paying attention to most patrons.

A regular named Hanna made as if to speak. She wanted to assure Venser she was as confused as he was, but her words were silenced by the sight of the woman showing a great deal of cleavage who had sat down beside her. She gulped and drank more wine.

Wiggling her brows at the lass next to her, Ceirra made grabby hands towards the barkeep. "Love, wet my aching whistle, won't you? Anything with a high alcohol contact will do." She winked at the wandering eyes, a grin splitting her face. "I'm looking to get a little foolish tonight."

Hanna stretched languorously thinking it was high time she took to her bed but enjoying the companionship at the bar too much to move right.

Jezebel pulled a few strands of loose hair out of her face as she entered the building, shivering a bit from the cool air she had left outside. She should have brought a shawl, but, it didn't dawn on her until it was far too late. She looked around the building, smiling at all of the eyes on her as she walked up the stairs, her hips swaying from side to side in perfect rhythm. She raised a brow as she saw Ceirra, rolling her eyes as she noticed how drunk she already was. "I thought we were trying to cut back on the drinking, Legs," She murmured in Ceirra's ear as she finally made her way up the stairs and to the bar. She realized that all of the seats were full, and wandered over to one of the empty tables. Sliding down into the seat, she smoothed out her dress skirt, her eyes scanning the room as she waited for a reply from her.

The bearded bartender cracked his neck and rubbed his hands together. "Time to get to work." He snapped his fingers and summoned two snaky, shadowy hands beside him, then he began to list off a few ingredients for the shadow tendrils to get. "Lemon juice, grenadine, and whiskey sour mix." He grabbed two silver cocktail mixers and slammed them down on the bar, grabbing a bottle of vodka and a two other bottles, one being whiskey sour mix. He mixed the three into one cocktail mixer with ice and added a drop of an unknown glowing pink liquid from a vial on his belt. He shook it up for a few long moments and then dumped it into a glass, resulting in a glowing neon pink drink. "Ta da! Pink Footed Booby! Not the actual name. I just like to say booby." He passed it to the tall golden eyed woman and smiled, brushing back his messy black hair.

"Five silver ma'am!" He turned to the other woman and said, "Gimme a minute to finish your rum cocktail."

Hanna rose, bidding a drunken adieu to the company she went to her bed.

The handsome barkeep grabbed three different kinds of rum off the shelves and had the shadow tendrils put the other ingredients back, mixing the three into the other cocktail mixer followed by lemon juice and grenadine. "Ice." He told one of the shadow tendrils, who dumped a fistful of ice into the cocktail mixer. He picked up the cocktail mixer and shook it for a bit, straining it into a glass and passing it to Khal "There ya go ma'am. Four silver." He cleared his throat and leaned against the bar, looking out to everyone. "Anyone need anything? I may have missed som- What the fuck did I do with my cigar..."

The tall temptress grinned, thumbing her coins before tossing them onto the bar. "I love saying booby, too." Ceirra wrapped her thin fingers around her drink and slipped off to join her dear, dear friend. "Why, Jezebel. It's been ages. I haven't seen you since, well, yesterday." Settling onto a stool with all the caution of an old woman, she flashed the girl a grin. The two were peas in a pod, though they often squabble like siblings. The cigar, left unattended on the bar, she slipped between her lips, the smoke curling above her head in neat little patterns. "I say I'm cutting back on a lot of things... Alcohol, sex, thieving tendencies... You of all people should know that's all talk."

The bearded bartender's light green cigar had an earthy smell and taste to it, with a hint of citrus. And it would quickly make her throat dry, but also dull her senses and calm things. The glowing pink drink itself would begin to warm her from the inside when she tasted it, and when she did she would find it tasted exactly like a Strawberry Starburst. Only liquid.

"Of course. I'm glad you've been cutting back on the sex however. Wouldn't want to catch anything else, now would we?" The demoness Jezebel Dusk asked, smirking. "Besides, your daughters want to know if they should be expecting to see you in another nine months or so, it's been a while, no?"

"You're so full of shit, it's a miracle it isn't spilling out of that mouth of yours. 'Course, a hearty chunk of man meat is usually stuffing that whole, among others, isn't it?" Ceirra rolled her burnt golden eyes. "Isn't wise to joke about children. "Sides. What if it hurt my feelings for you to say such things? I can't have children. You know that. Broke my mother's dark, shriveled up heart." She, the trained alcoholic she was, threw back her drink in one long, slow pull. Shuddering with the bite of the alcohol, she grinned. "How's your life then, demon?"

"You may." Venser said rapping his fingers on the bar and then brushing back his messy black hair that had a slight green tint to it, waiting for an order. He took the time to examine all the patrons present, how great in number they were. "Now is a good time to recruit..." He thought fumbling around in the many pouches of his belt.

Roselie had made it very clear to Venser over the years that there was a no smoking policy in the Dragon's Head. And having to run the bar alone most days, Venser treated it like his own dojo. Which he was, being the head bartender when Roselie was not present. He would just flat out disregard the no smoking rules. He clapped his hands and summoned the shadow tendrils. "Open the windows." They did so and Venser pushed the coins back to the girl. "Keep em, the man right there paid for you and everyone else." He said sliding the sack of coin to him, throwing it to another snakey shadow hand. "Put that in my room."

A wave of serene calm washed over her, though it did little to mute the sexual ferocity growing low in her stomach. The tall temptress was used to a usually high libido, but, jeez, this was ridiculous. "Aye, lovey, what in the name of The God Emperor's firm cock did you put in that drink?" She lifted herself from the table and reclaimed her spot at the bar.

Venser began to pour himself a glass of the glowing neon pink drink from the silver cocktail mixer as he looked to the woman, raising a brow. He highly suspected she was a succubus, which he always welcomed here. The handsome barkeep did love the succubi race very much so. "What did I put in it? Well, vodka, whiskey sour, watermelon pucker, and a secret ingredient I shouldn't be talking about." He replied grabbing a metal tankard, walking over to a barrel at the end of the bar and dunking it into a bunch of turquoise liquid that had somewhat of a sparkle to it for some reason. "Blue Lagoon, six silver." He said passing it to the man.

Gia giggled at the stranger who watched her hips swaying while she made her way up to the front door to the tavern before blowing a kiss towards him. She pressed her hands against the door, opening up enough so she could squeeze her body in. She bit down on her bottom lip, pulling her skirt up as she climbed the staircase to reach her cousin Ceirra. "Oh hello dear, I've been searching for you for quite some time."

Eyes threatening to do a complete three sixty in her skull, Ceirra's face fell into a deep frown at her cousin's arrival. "Maybe it's been a task for you because I have no interest in being found." Scooting her stool away from Gia, she gave the bar keep a desperate look. "Something stronger. I want to black out and possibly asphyxiate on my own vomit. Liver damage at the least, please, my love."

"And the Pink Footed Booby isn't huh? Well good thing that the Blue Lagoon is the strongest thing we have available here, seconded by Winter's Dragonfire Whiskey." Venser said grabbing two tankards to dump in the barrel, as he filled them he muttered. 'Which I'm not allowed to sell..." He set the tankard down in front of the man, and the other in front of the supposed succubus. He was about to ask her name but a woman had come to speak to her first. "How bout for your lovely friend here? The same for her?"

Gia Dusk rolled her eyes before chuckling. "I'd like to have the same please, whatever she's drinking," she stated as well towards the bar keep. "I didn't know my cousin Legs here was going to be an angry drunk today."

"I'm not angry. I'm absolutely serene." Throwing a handful of coins on the bar, the tall temptress sighed. It wasn't that she didn't enjoy her family's presence, it's just she often felt like the second fiddle around them. Not that she necessarily minded, but eventually it became really, really annoying. Thankful for the drink, she busied her hands and her ill-tempered tongue with it.

Venser nodded in affirmation and proceeded to get Gia a tankard of Blue Lagoon too. "She's only had one from drink from what I saw. And she pocketed one of my Kulleros..." He said setting the tankard of the turquoise liquid down in front of Gia, swiping the coins away. "Six silver from you, miss." He looked to the two who were family and asked, "So, what are your names?"

The tall temptress smiled, thumbing her tankard. "Ceirra Prytania Dusk, and that cigar you abandoned on the bartop begged me to take it in. I couldn't abandon an orphan like that. Would be heartless of me."

"Thank you, and it doesn't take much for her, or anyone in our family for that matter," One of the demon girls giggled a bit, taking a sip from the tankard. "My name is Gia, by the way. Gia Dusk. She replied to his question, pulling out a bag full of coins and setting them on the counter.

"Consider it a gift then, my fair lady." He said with a chuckle raising his glass of Pink Footed Booby to his lips. "True, those things deserve to be enjoyed. Especially while drinking or laying around and relaxing." He looked to Gia and said, "Well good! I love women who can't hold their drinks well. Anyone really, I mean, people are a lot more fun when drink. You get me? I know that drinking a lot on duty." He swished the drink around in his glass and said, "Drinking... And lust. No one can match me in such things. I am the god of tits and wine and beer and brandy and ale and mead and cider and sprites and schnapps and tits and whiskey and wine and gin and... ''

GASSSSP. Had to take a breath before he passed out on the spot.

''What haven't I said yet?'' He gave a small smile, raising his thick attack eyebrows a few times.

Gia raised a brow at the bar keep as he rambled on, "I believe you said it all," she murmured before taking another drink.

"Oh, baby, I love when you talk dirty like that." Ceirra Dusk grinned, sipping from her drink like the classy woman she was. "Tell us more. What's your name, darling?"

Downstairs, Roseanna walked into the tavern and looked it over with a bored expression. The four foot nine dhampir headed up to the bar and spoke in a clipped tone. "Red meat. Rare as possible. Bloody! Ale." Before more or less slamming coins to pay for it on the counter. The woman sat nearly as stiffly as she moved and had overly large deep blue eyes and the aura of someone who practiced black magic regularly.

"I don't think I have." Venser said in response to Gia, clearing his throat for something... Interesting. He clapped his hands twice, summoning a snakey, shadowy hand. "Go get her some of that elk that was hunted earlier today. A rare steak." The bearded bartender proceeded to pour her a tankard of ale and passed it to the woman. "Two silver." He looked to the tall temptress and put a finger on her lips. "My name? Well, my dear... Hush those lips and I'll you about myself..."

She glanced over the man and sneered before turning to the barkeep. "For a plate o' rare meat and an ale? That's bloody robbery!" She tossed silver down in the place of a bunch of coppers. "It'd better be rare as hell and FRESH." She snarled.

He took his finger off Ceirra's lips and spun around behind the bar. "No onessssss-sssssssssss slick like Venser, no one's quick like Venser, no one's dick is incredibly thick and big like Venser's! There's no one in this town half as manly! Perfect, a pure paragon! You can ask any Alex, Sanna or Thorny. And they'll tell you whose they'd rather be onnnnnnnnnnn!" He disappeared in a puff of thick red smoke and reappeared atop the bar with waving back and forth, a swagger in his step with a glass of his signature drink in hand. "No one's been there like Venser, no one's hunky like Venser, no one's got a lovely smile like Venser! As a specimen yes I'm awe inspiringgggggggggggggg! Give five bravos and twelve encores! Venser is the best and the rest are all prickssssssssss!"

In spite of herself a small smile formed at the corners of her mouth. The dhamphir liked odd people. Always had.

Ceirra Dusk clapped wildly, her face split in a wide, laughing grin. Bouncing in her seat, she yelped out an "Encore!" Though she suspected he owed royalties to the original owners of that tune, she appreciated his show very much. It wasn't often she came upon a man with a humor similar to her own. It warmed her black little heart. "Venser, you absolute dream, you. You are entirely too entertaining. You must sing for us again, my love. You must." She laughed to herself, relaxing back in her seat. She needed another drink. Fast.

"No onessssssssssssssss handsome like Venser, no one's charming like Venser, no one's muscles are incredibly strong like Venser's! In a sparring match nobody spars like Venser! For there's no man as lusty and amazing! As you see I've got plenty of facetime to spare! There's no lying, he's clearly no weakling. No ma'am I give it my all I solemnly swearrrrrrrrrrrrr....!" He held that note for a while and flexed his arms for Ceirra. Venser himself was a man in his early thirties, with fair skin, messy black hair that was tinted green, a neatly trimmed beard, and unnatural serpent like eyes. He hopped off the bar and playfully flicked her nose. "I am an absolute dream..." He said as the shadow tendrils set down a plate of very rare steak, bloody down in front of the woman as she enjoyed her ale. "So," He said with a pause straightening himself. "What brings you to my comfortable little dojo, Ceirra?"

Meanwhile, the dhamphir tore into the steak. It was good... Not quite what she needed but it would do. She wasn't the type to go in and just announce that she needed blood... Not many places carried it and frankly it could frighten the locals.

Ceirra Dusk leaned forward, her chin balanced in her hand, burnt golden eyes glazed over from the cigar she had snatched and the multitude of alcoholic beverages sitting comfortably in her stomach. "My love, I've been wandering your damned forest for quite a long time. A woman like myself can only go so long without the lusty company of others. So many bloodsuckers here tonight..." She winked, though a great mop of hair flopped down and covered her face. She was hammered, as announced by the flush in her cheeks and the slight slur to her speech. "Plus, I heard the alcohol was strong here. That, I see, was not a lie."

"It must feel terrible. Being deprived of both things for such a while..." He refilled her Blue Lagoon, moving a bit to the left away from the girl who pretty much tore her steak to shreds. "Well, good thing you're here at the Dragon's Head. Ya know, I got this saying," He said with a pauses gesturing to the drink he had in his hand. "One I invented like I did this drink. Sex everyday keeps the gloom away."

"It's a complication." Roseanna said dryly before taking a swig, looking up from her meal "You have more meat?"

Ceirra laughed, sliding her fingers through her hair to push it back in place. "Well, love," she purred, avoiding the bloody scene next to her, "If your sex is anything like your drinks, I'm sure it hits the spot."

The dhampir felt her eyes drawn to it before roughly throwing a bandage at the man's head. "Would you wrap that up? It's not sanitary to let it bleed."

"Oh it is indeed..." Venser said with a seductive growl looking deep into her burnt eyes, matched his slitted emeralds. Clapping twice again, the shadow tendrils took the woman's plate away and replaced it with a clean one, with another fresh, bloody rare steak on it. "Since you've been wandering, I take you need board?"

Roseanne the dhampir nodded and confirmed. "I am." Before tearing into the steak and placing more coin on the counter.

Ceirra leaned forward now, hands folded in her lap, breasts pushed into the lime-light. His growl stirred something inside her, her own eyes slitting like those of a snake. "Something like that, yes. If you've got room, I won't be staying long. A day or two, perhaps."

"A day or two? Shame." Venser bent down to retrieve the room cards and chuckled. "Not a good way to let it out of your system!" He called standing back up, searching through the room cards. "What the void..."

"That is the most idiotic thing I have heard today you moron. Intoxication does not work that way." Roseanna snapped at him.

Ceirra chuckled, low and soft. "Maybe three, maybe longer, if the company is right." Shifting in her seat, she wiggled uncomfortably. The damn bodice of this dress was far too tight, not that she had packed any roomier clothes in her pack. All she had left was another soft, blue dress and her leather play outfit, which, unfortunately, was not suitable for a crowded atmosphere.

"Well it alllll depends on the person!" Being located where the tavern was located, the red rubber suit with rubber nipples and an oversized codpiece was far from suitable. And most saw it as unusual. "Ah! By the void... We have a lot more people staying here than I thought." He passed a small, silver key to Ceirra Dusk. "Ten silver a night. Right hall, sixth door on the left. And I happen to be right across the hall..."

Roseanna shrugged. "I am from a land several weeks travel from here. My uncle and his men taught me... How do YOU know how to fight?" She then rounded on the one that was like her. "Misjudge?! Hardly! Do you KNOW what you're doing aside from causing your hunger to grow, endangering yourself, and creating a mess?! Absolutely NOTHING! Gods have you ANY concept of what someone like ME can do with just a drop of your blood? What someone worse than me WOULD do? Obviously not!"

Eyeing the mouthpiece next to her, Ceirra slid from her stool. "Well, my love, I ought to take my things to my room." She dropped a hefty pouch on the bar top, enough silver for four or five nights. She smoothed her gown, a naughty grin curling the edges of her lips upwards. "I certainly hope I won't find myself lonely this evening."

"Remember, I'm right across the hall." Venser said with a sly smile swiping the coins away. "By the void what time is it..." He handed the shadow tendrils the room cards and walked over to the open window, closing it to block the cold air. It was pitch black out. "Heh... Note to self. Buy a clock to hang somewhere in here..."

Ceirra Dusk, warm all over from the alcohol and that ridiculous man's reminder, stumbled off to find her room, her beautiful long legs giving her lengthy strides. Crowds be damned, she was changing into something more comfortable. Perhaps by fault of the alcohol or her own natural ability to get lost, she just couldn't find her room. Instead, she sat down on one of the staircases and started pulling chunks of black leather out of a deep red sack. If she had to strip in the open, well, the alcohol told her it was alright to do so.

Roselie Talemn had be absent from the tavern for quite a while, she had wanted to get an order for certain berries and sadly had to travel to do so, and wanted to put it in before the weather got too bad to travel in plus in her growing condition she didn't think her off and on lover Atsu would like her straying too far from the tavern. She did leave him a note saying where had gone and the estimated time coming home, but knew he still would be worried about her and would make sure she was alright once she got back. The carriage she took made its way slowly up the dirt road and to the back of the tavern, Old Joe opened its door for her as she emerged from it taking a deep breath pulling the hood over her head as she walked to the tavern entering through the backdoor that led through the kitchen and pantry area. Still a bit cold she left her fur trimmed coat on over her dress, and headed upstairs to the bar grabbing an apple along the way and munching on it looking around.

Roseanna glanced at him coldly. "Oh poor you. Shall I fetch you a tissue, then? Your lot is what YOU make it. Get over yourself. If one side despises you then find a new one. Christ it doesn't matter who or what hates you so long as you stand for what's right."

"Hey boss!" Venser yelled, appearing out of a puff of thick red smoke in front of his boss. "I don't believe Atsuma is up! Or... I dunno. He might have gone out to the town. I dunno honestly, don't see him much anymore. I thought he was with you!"

Only a short moment later, the six-foot-tall temptress who was all legs returned, boots cradled in her arms. Otherwise fully clothed in her so called 'play outfit', black leathers that clung to her skin, she made her way back to the bar. Making sure she looked good for the handsome barkeep before claiming the seat she had previously occupied.

"Wrong is death, destruction, and the things that haunt the darkness ripping apart those that cannot defend themselves. Do not fight for fame, fortune, acceptance, or gain... You'll never find them. Instead stand as a light where there is shadow. So what if they hate you? They live. Someone get the idiot a steak... He needs to replenish a few things, I'll pay." The dhampir said coldly. "The thing is the best I can do is defend those who are what I cannot be. Nice, innocent, and good. I need nothing from them and expect no care nor acceptance. Why should I need it? I do the best I can and move on."

"Evening Venser." Came a slightly muffled response, as Roselie chewed on her apple, nodding to him.

Clearing her throat, Ceirra set a couple silver pieces on the bar. "Something a little less strong this time, perhaps?"

"We need to chat, Roselie. I've hired help, good help without asking you first because I'm often alone and I get so busy some days. And... I need a raise." Venser said to Roselie. A snaky, shadowy hand set a bottle of cider down in front of the tall temptress. Venser's usual preferred brand he had overstocked at this tavern.

Rose blinked a few times, looking to Venser nodding that she was alright with him getting help for himself. "A raise?"

"Much thanks, love," The tall temptress smiled at the shadowed hand, flicking an extra cold piece in its direction. She kept her gaze away from the woman who had snapped at her, careful not to attract any more of the woman's temper. Ceirra, simply enough, was not the fighting type. She much preferred the quiet, fun atmosphere the tavern had had earlier in the day.

"Yeah. A raise. I work hard here most of the time alone with only the shadow tendrils to help. They do a good job, but still. Actual workers are much better for the sake of conversation and... Personality." Venser explained. "And I know it's a lot to ask, especially with the new barmaids I hired on to help out around here." Looking at the bar, to a new woman who had found herself talking to the gorgeous golden eyed beauty.

Ceirra grinned, obviously pleased with the compliment. Damned flirt. Soul finding a familiar presence, she scooted her seat closer to the apparently elven woman. "Bloody pissing match we've got here. Panties all twisted up in a wad over who's more disadvantaged."

"Huhu... Seems to be." She drew her attention to the girl next to her, Ceirra. "I never properly introduced myself. Khalyst, call my Khal if you want." She held out her hand, while the other threw four coins out to the bar table, and grabbed ahold of the cocktail, sipping it politely. Her skin was made perfect, and was obviously touched by the sun, though she did not have the glow humans often had. Hers was more of an airbrush type of effect, though, her perfection wasn't something you could just rub away with some soapy water. Her lips were what stood out about her skin the most, they were quite pink. Although being on the more chubbish side, her waist was quite small to compare. The rest was actually quite busty. Her body was decorated in beautiful leather. Even with the bra absent, which she usually never wore, she was perky. Her dark hair was quite long, even with it being tired in a ponytail around itself, it still hung down her back. She had a liking towards piercings, and she had many on her, and in possession. She had about nine of each ear. Her eyes were much like ice. A crystal blue, shimmering even with no light.

The shadow tendrils manifested themselves into a silhouette version of the head bartender himself, with the suit, shoulder pad, battle skirt, shoulder cape, and everything. It fixed the "Hurricane" Venser had served her earlier and passed it to Khal. Venser teleported himself to Roselie again, leaning up against the wall and said, "I am looking to buy a home. A proper home... A farm north of here, over the border of Vorland and in the capital Pryldahn. For my children, and for my lovers.

For us, as a family."

Roselie clicked her tongue at him. "Venser, if you need the money for something that important, your children or something like that... I understand completely. And when I count the tavern's earning as a whole, do inventory, I'll see what I can do." She offered a kind, almost motherly smile and looked to her new patrons.

"Ceirra Dusk," she purred, clasping her hand around Khal's. "It is a dream to meet you, Khal."

"Oh, thank you Roselie. Thank you! I appreciate it greatly." Venser said with a calm smile, nodding his head as the woman walked away, picking up the coin jar from off the shelf behind him and walking off.

Khal gave out a petite squeal of excitement. "Your touch entices me. I bite, if you're not careful, love." She twiddled her thumbs beneath Ceirra's, all while holding eye contact with her. "'Tender, do you sell food for particular individuals?" She rose Ceirra's hands with her own, placing kisses upon her knuckles.

With a wicked sort of grin and a mischievous wink, Ceirra wiggled her brows. "I have always liked a nibble here or there." She laughed, light and airy, giving the girl's hand a gentle squeeze.

"Yes we do!" The shadow version of Venser nodded in affirmation. Before the real one appeared out of a puff of thick red smoke in its place. "Shadow tendrils will serve! Well, the owner is here... But, yeah. Have a lovely rest of the night folks! I have to go check on a few things." The emerald eyed bartender locked eyes with Ceirra for a long moment. "I'll be seeing you soon..." He then disappeared in a puff of thick red smoke that quickly disappeared.

Ceirra licked her lips. "I can't wait to taste him..." Reaching a hand into her dress and pinching a nipple hard until her eyes watered a bit in pained pleasure, biting her lip at the same time.

CHAPTER TWENTY-SEVEN: CEIRRA DUSK

The Dragon's Head Tavern and Inn, Vorland, 1436 ATC

Later that very same night... Someone knocked at Ceirra Dusk's door four times. When she opened it, she would find the handsome, serpent eyed bartender in his usual outfit, holding a fine bottle of wine and two glasses, a sly, seductive smile spread across his face.

Her blankets wrapped around her, she pulled open the door. Ah. So, she would have company that night. Good. She did hate being lonely at night. "Venser, my love. What brings you this far across the hall, hmm?" She eyed the wine with a naughty grin, stepping further into the room to make space for him to come inside her room.

"You, of course." He said stepping into the room. The bearded man didn't wear his usual gloves or gauntlets, and the mark on the back of his left hand glowed greenish white, emitting steam. The door knob was trapped in a green aura and it closed behind him as Venser slinked over to the bed, sitting down. "Are you thirsty, dear?" He asked popping the lid off, pouring them both a glass. "Kupid Red, the real vintage... The best wine money can buy back home..."

The tall temptress smiled, sliding onto the bed next to him, her blanket wrapped around them, long, beautiful legs laid across his. "My, how you spoil me." She took her glass, sipping from it as she watched him, her burnt golden pupils narrowing and growing vertically, mirroring the snake-like slit of Venser's own lovely serpentine eyes. "I was hoping you'd show that lovely face of yours. A girl gets lonely, y'know."

The bearded bartender chuckled and moved closer to Ceirra, wrapping an arm around her as they sat side by side. He raised his glass and said, "You won't have to be alone tonight. Cheers..."

She settled into his embrace, her hair falling down her back like a thick, ebony-black waterfall. "Cheers, love," she purred. Setting her glass aside, Ceirra took his glowing hand in hers, a curious sort of look spilling across her face. "Now, this is interesting. I don't recall this part of your song." She pressed her lips to his knuckles, the blanket slipping ever so slightly from its pinned position under her arms.

Several drinks later...

"Yer sexy..." He slurred brushing back her long, ebony black hair. His mark stopped glowing as he squeezed her hand, before wrapping his arms around Ceirra's waist and pressing his lips to hers, kissing her roughly before he exhaled and moved back, then placed his lips on the ride side of Ceirra's smooth neck. He began to kiss, suck, and bite on a certain spot as he moved his hands up and down her body, feeling every curve of it. "Mhm... Let's get these clothes off... Hic! Clothes are a prison..."

The tall temptress chuckled, her blanket long forgotten. "Mmm, darling, you're the one who's wearing a prison. All's I've got are these damned pants." She slid her fingers in his hair, her breath coming out in warm, lusty sighs. "Kiss me again," She murmured, guiding his face to hers with her unoccupied hand. Everywhere he touched was ablaze with the fires of lust. Her blood tingled, her body craving him so desperately.

The handsome bearded barkeep raised his left hand and undid his red rubber suit from behind, then removed the maroon colored codpiece he wore and threw it away. He wrapped his arm around her again and locked his lips with Ceirra's, his kisses ranging from soft to rough. He suckled on her lower lip as he trailed his other hand up her leg, then he began to rub two fingers against the outside of her pants where her crotch was. "Yea... You like that... Don't you?" Venser asked in between kisses as he rubbed her slowly.

Deep, soulful moans slipped out of her, her fingers sliding down from his hair, his chest, to the meeting between his thighs. His fingers were pure bliss, her body responding before her mind could fully comprehend it. "Mmm, Ven," Ceirra sighed, her fingers working their way towards dangerous territory. It was her turn to kiss and nibble at his skin, her lips finding home on his collar bone, his neck, the soft bits of his ear. She slid off the bed, pulling her leather prison pants off her legs. Then, her hands splayed across his chest, she pushed him back onto the bed. The six-foot temptress was done talking, preferring to put her mouth to work elsewhere.

"Oh yes..." He ran his hands up her body, placing them on her breasts. He fondled them gently and tugged on her nipples, pinching them once or twice. Venser wiggled a bit, pulling down his red rubber suit as best he could. From where Ceirra sat, she'd have to help him get out of his clothes.

She chuckled, though it was heavily laced with lust and desire. "Prison break, hmm?" With swift, careful hands, she freed him from his suit, her lips immediately pressing kisses to his hips, her hands busy at work. Ceirra would need to tie her hair back, or else have him hold, perhaps give it a tug. She shivered, the fire blazing bright inside her. Replacing her hands with her tongue, she looked up at him as she wrapped her lips around him, taking him deep inside her mouth.

Without his suit, Venser's body was muscular, and barrel chested, with his chest being covered in faint scratch marks that ran all the way down to his stomach. The sight of Ceirra's perfect breasts, and the beauty before him made him very hard. His member stiffened up and was a bit more than average when it wasn't, six inches at least. He moaned and arched his back when she took it deep into her mouth. "Mhm... That's it... Lick the tip and go right down on it..."

The tall temptress hummed softly, his moan only making her more needy. She did as he requested, her tongue sliding over the tip slowly, then down the shaft, his length impressing her. As she worked him with her mouth, she guided his hand to her hair, her fingers pushing her hair into his. Pausing to give her jaw a short break, Ceirra kissed his thigh, "Hold my hair, love, or else it gets it the way." Then, back to work she went, up and down on his member, until her patience grew thin.

Venser sat up on the bed and grabbed Ceirra's head, pressing it down on his nice, thick cock as he held her hair back with his other hand, slowly moving her head down on him. "Sex is always better with anticipation..." He said with another seductive growl.

Gods, that growl. She moaned, her hands sliding up his thighs to cup the base of his cock. She wasn't sure how long her patience would hold, her body twitching with anticipation. Mmm, no. She couldn't wait. Ceirra pulled herself up from her knees, her hands sliding up to push again back onto the bed. This time, however, she climbed on to his lap, her lips planting kisses across his neck once more. "There's only so much anticipation a girl can take, Ven. I need you now," she murmured in his ear, moving to slide onto his thick member. As she did, a deep, loud moan slipped out from between her teeth, her fingers curling into skin ever so slightly.

"Ahh...!" Venser groaned in bliss as his member pushed its way into her entrance, the inner walls of her cunny hugging his cock in a way he had not felt before. "Mhm!" He bucked his hips up and down as she sat on his lap, his hands were placed on her sides. He held her close and placed his lips on her collarbone, and like a vacuum he sucked and bit on her collarbone, leaving a nice love bite behind. "Oh void you're tight Ceirra!"

Her nails dug into his shoulders, her hips rolling as she rode him. Never before had she felt such euphoria as a man entered her, his cock filling her in a way that was so very satisfying. "Mmm, Ven. Gods above, you feel so good." Ceirra Dusk nipped his ear, his neck, kissing and nibbling as he rocked her core over and over again. Pulling his body with her, she flipped them over, her legs spread wide to allow him more room to work his way inside her.

"Oh!" Flipping them over with surprising strength. She reminded Venser of himself. Grabbing her neck as he kept on pushing in and out of her at medium speed, he licked her lips and held his face close, breathing heavily. "Yeah, you like that fucking cock inside of you?" The sounds of his pelvis smacking up against hers as he rammed into Ceirra's filled the air, and Venser loved hearing that, combined with his moans and his dirty talk. "Mhm...!" He pressed his lips against hers again and moaned into her mouth, before pulling back. "I'm just going to fucking fill you up and make you mine..."

Her back arched, his fingers around her neck sending a delicious tingle down her spine. "Mmmm Ven, harder, " she pleaded, her nails dragging down his back. The tall temptress needed him, all of him, right then. His moans, his hot breath on her face, his thick cock filling her, she needed it all. Grabbing his head, she smashed her lips against his, sucking and nibbling at his bottom lip.

"Gods, Ven," she moaned, her hips bucking hard against his. She moved a leg to his shoulder, desperate to get him deeper inside her. She wanted him, needed him, to send her over the edge, to make her vision blurry with pleasure.

He nodded in affirmation and held Ceirra's arms down as he rammed in and out of her, speeding up his thrusting. He arched his back and gave her his all, the bed creaked furiously as they went at it. "Ah! Mhmm." He breathed quick and hard looking down to the tall temptress, his eyes filled with lust and desire. "Ah...!" He moaned again. "Any long you're going to milk me!"

"V-Ven!" She semi-screamed with her surprisingly high pitched voice, careful to avoid alerting the other patrons of the party going on in her room, though it was likely they already knew. She never was a quiet one. Ceirra was close, so close. Her breath came in quick bursts, her cheeks flushed and eyes locked on his. She kissed him, hard, her hips rising to greet his with every thrust. Closer and closer she came to the spilling point until, finally...

"Ah! Ven..." The succubus screamed, and, in a great wave of pleasure, she came, her thighs trembling like trees in a storm.

"Ah!" At the same time, Venser gave her one last, hard thrust and his hard shaft spasmed inside of the tall temptress, firing glob after glob deep inside her while love juices soaked his cock. "Oh... That felt so good..." He felt himself go weak as he laid on top of her for a second, then he rolled them over on their sides, Ceirra's inner walls felt like a warm blanket wrapped around his member. He kissed her on the forehead and asked, "Have fun?"

"Mmm," she sighed, a content smile curling her lips up as she nestled into his chest. "More fun than I can remember ever having before. Thank you." Ceirra kissed his chest, gently, as though she were afraid to break him. "Just like I said earlier, you are a dream." She chuckled lightly, her fingers lightly sliding up his side, tracing odd little patterns on his skin.

The handsome barkeep yawned and nuzzled her head, closing his eyes as Ceirra's fingers glided down his side. "I should have brought you to my room instead... My bed is queen sized, with pure silk sheets. And the pillows have some really nice furry gold throwovers you'd love."

Ceirra Dusk smiled against his chest, fumbling blindly for a blanket to pull over them. "Sounds expensive... This'll do for now. I'm not sure I could make the walk over there, anyway." Her body hummed, warm and satisfied and content. Gently, she tilted her chin up to press a kiss to his jaw, her eyes heavy as sleep called her name.

"It's only across the hall... But... Yeah. We could do it again in my bed tomorrow..." He said, snuggling into Ceirra's tall naked body, and wrapping the covers close around them as he slowly drifted off.

"Yes, tomorrow," She murmured, sleep pulling her into its dark embrace, Venser's body wrapping her in a sense of safety.

Several hours later...

The rays of the beautiful sun shone through the windows of the room, lighting it up as Venser held a naked Ceirra close to him as they slept together beneath the sheets. He thought he had heard a crash in the distance, causing him to flutter his eyes open. He yawned and sat up, stretching his arms out as he brushed back his messy raven black tinted green hair. "Bah... Need a haircut again..." Venser mumbled to himself falling onto his back, staring up at the ceiling. He yawned a second time and ran a hand down his chest and stomach, feeling all the new scratches and bruises made on his body last night.

The morning light hardly registered to the tall girl, her head buried in the little space between Venser's body and the bed. When he stirred, she rolled onto her other side, back to him, and yawned with all the innocence of a newborn. Her hair was a dark mess around her head, it's tendrils knotted in places from the night before. She lay there quiet for just a few more quiet moments until she rolled back over, brows furrowed just slightly.

"Always hated wine hangovers," Ceirra murmured, shielding her eyes from the sun by pulling the blankets over their heads.

The bearded bartender turned his head to her and smiled, stroking her hair gently. "You get used to them." He planted a soft kiss on her lips as they laid beneath the blanket and asked, "How are you?"

"Mmm," she purred, resting her head on his chest. "Besides the hammering in my head, I am wonderful." Ceirra's arms snaked around his middle, pressing her body closer to him. "And you, love? How are you?"

"Wonderful." He replied wrapping his arms around her waist, holding her close. He sighed and nuzzled her head. Venser really loved the feeling of her breasts squishing up against his chest, he pressed her body into his further and said, "Well, here I am relaxing in bed with a very sexy, wild lynx. We're both nice and warm and relaxing in each other's comforts... Who could ask for more, honestly?"

Ceirra chuckled, her fingers reaching up to stroke his hair. Eyes still gazed ever so slightly from the romping around they had done, she looked up at him and pressed a kiss to his nose. "It's been so long so I felt this much peace." She tucked her head into the space between his shoulder and head, planting little kisses to his neck. "Thank you."

"You're very welcome Ceirra Dusk." Venser said with a smile kissing her hair rubbing her back. "Huh... I gotta admit it's a very nice name. It all just really rolls off the tongue and sounds awesome. Why don't we go back to my room? You can make yourself comfortable and I'll cook breakfast for you..."

"Sex and breakfast," she grinned, rolling away from him to stretch her muscles. "You spoil me, Venser." Ceirra gathered her hair to the side, her fingers making quick work of securing it back in a braid. Still finding her sea legs, she slid out of the bed and looked around for her clothes. The room was a mess. Clothing was strewn everywhere.

"Looks like a small tornado ripped this place apart." She picked up her pants with one hand and nudged the pile of red suit parts with the other.

"You should see my room... Heh." Venser hopped out of bed and wrapped his arms around Ceirra from behind, slamming his pelvis into her rear. "Why not just lay around naked?" He kissed her neck roughly and said, "I'll gather them up and go cook... I'll bring you into my room. Have you ever teleported before?"

A grin split her face, and as he held from behind, she gently rolled her hips against him. "Mmm, no. I don't think I have. Is it safe, love? I don't fancy losing any of my... Assets... In a cloud of red smoke when I could just scurry across the hall." She turned in his arms, pressing a kiss to his jaw.

"It is. Just stay calm and hope you don't get sick." His mark flashed greenish white and the two disappeared in a puff of thick red smoke, reappearing atop Venser's queen bed in his room. Venser's room was fairly big. A queen sized bed lay by the windows, and it was covered in turquoise silk sheets and he had about a dozen pillows all with furry gold throwovers. Off to the left was a wardrobe with a few dresses hanging out, some spilt onto the floor. Beside that was a naked mannequin wearing a white porcelain comedy mask. To the right of the bed was a desk with a bag of silver in it, a mirror, and a few pieces of jewelry and some small boxes. Right beside it was various papers and pieces of art. Above Venser's bed was a multicolored painting of a woman's vagina, and below that his signature double bladed sword, the Dual Personality. On the wall in front of the bed was a lovely painting, showed a woman descending naked into a bath, the painting showing mostly the curve of back and neck and the elegance of her arms rising up to unpin her golden blonde hair. He kissed her back on the jaw and said, "Stay here." He then disappeared in a puff of thick red smoke.

"Mm." She loved the sounds he made. Each little moan of his sent a shiver down her spine and made the space between her legs damp with lust.

"The sun warming our skin and the sand between our toes... I look forward to it, love," she purred, looking deep into his beautiful, serpentine eyes. "Wait... Why don't we go right now?" He suggested, looking deep into Ceirra's burnt golden eyes as he leaned towards her face, feeling her warm breath against his lips as he used two fingers to spread her slit open, stroking the inner walls of her.

Her breath caught in her throat, leaving her as a deep moan. "Ah. Ven..." She murmured, one of her hands leaving his member to wrap around his waist and pulled him close. She rested her forehead against his, eyes closed in pleasure. "We seem to be a little occupied right now, love."

"You have got to try fucking on the beach sometime..." Venser said letting his fingers explore Ceirra's womanhood, his index and middle finger slip inside her wet opening. He twirled them around inside of her like a little screwdriver and made the low, seductive growl she loved while his forehead rested against hers.

Her back arched, pressing her against him as she shouted out her pleasure. This was paradise. She opened her slitted eyes, glossy with lust. That growl, that beautiful, sexy growl of his. Ceirra kissed him hard, the hand she had been using to work his member leaving to get lost in his green tinted hair.

"Mhmmm...!" Venser groaned into her mouth with ecstasy, wrapping his arms around her. He raised his hands up and ran his fingers through her hair, then grabbed her cheeks and held her face close to his as they kissed. He breathed heavily and slide his tongue into her mouth.

"Venser," Ceirra moaned, her lips parting to let his tongue into her mouth. Her body trembled with anticipation and need, her breath coming in heavy bursts. Swinging her leg over him, she climbed over his lap, her knees keeping her just above his stiff cock. "The beach?" She sighed against his mouth.

"That can wait I suppose..." Venser said licking at her lips, grabbing his cock and positioning it right at her entrance. He delivered a nice, playful smack on her bum, watching it jiggle. "You're not allowed to leave this bed until I say so." He gave her another playful kiss on the cheek and said, "You're my prisoner."

Ceirra slid down onto his cock, the ecstasy of it pulling another low moan from her. "I haven't even been a bad girl yet," She murmured, rolling her hips against him. She kissed his collarbone, nipping and sucking until a neat little love mark was left behind.

"Good! Good!" He fondled her breasts more and tweaked her nipples, breathing heavily as he ran his tongue down her back again. His hips slapped hard against her nice, round rump as his shaft was buried deep inside her. "Ah! Gotta cum!" He groaned firing the sweet, sticky love juice deep inside her. "Mhmm...! Ah!"

The man sent her over the edge, her orgasm coming in heavy waves, pulling a scream out of her. Collapsing on the bed, Ceirra Dusk breathed heavy and hard. She pulled his hand from her breast and brought it to her mouth, kissing it gently.

Venser pulled out and collapsed next to her, groaning and stretching his back out to relax in bed. "By the void you're amazing... What race are you again? I really think you're a succubus."

The tall temptress lay still on her stomach, a smile spilling across her face. "You shouldn't judge someone just by the quality of their sex." Ceirra chuckled and pulled a pillow down from the head of the bed, burying her face in it. "That was amazing..."

"So are you?" He asked reaching his left arm out. Venser trapped his belt in a green aura and pulled it over to him, then pulled out a silver tin from one of the pouches. He opened it and pulled out a light green cigar, along with a match. He relaxed back on a pillow and lit it, inhaled some, then breathed out greenish white smoke. "Ah... Cigars after sex. Amazing."

Ceirra rolled over, snatched the cigar from his fingers, and took a drag from it. Handing it back, she blew the smoke out of her nostrils. "Yes, love. I am." Resting her head on his chest, she traced little patterns across his skin. "And you? I don't think most humans have the powers you do."

Venser snapped his fingers. "Ah! Knew it! A sexy succubus walked into my dojo, I wanted her, and I got her." He took the cigar back and inhaled some of it. "Human. Didn't always have my powers though."

"Oh?" She asked, propping herself up on her elbows. "Did you fall into a magical pool of water that granted you these powers, or did you sell your soul to a demon like me?"

"Why did you sell your soul to a demon?" Venser asked looking over to her, dodging the question. The cigar had an earthy smell, with a citrus hint. "Do you have powers too that I haven't seen yet?"

Ceirra winked, kissing his cheek and rolling onto her side, back to him. "Some secrets you'll just have to learn with time, my love."

"Yeah... You're right. Only the second day we've known each other..." Venser said rolling over, spooning Ceirra from behind. "We should go out and do something later."

"Are you asking me on a date, love?" She wiggled against him, pulling his arms tight around her.

Venser chuckled and rubbed her stomach. "Yeah... If we can actually manage to get out of bed. But I think we already have an idea for our date... My favorite nude beach."

Ceirra yawned and reached around for a blanket to cover them with. "I think that sounds wonderful." The tall temptress flipped around so that the two faced each other and kissed him hard on the mouth. "You spoil me. However will you get rid of me now?"

"Why would I want to? If you'd want to leave it'd be on your own accord..." Venser said wrapping the blanket around them, kissing her back. "Admit it... You're addicted to me already..."

She rolled her burnt golden eyes, tucking her chin in against her chest, her head buried under his chin. "I'm fond of you, yes. I think I'll keep you around. Your good company." Ceirra yawned, interlocking their legs and wrapping her arms around his middle.

"Succubi, so secretive about your feelings..." He wrapped his arm around her again and pressed his body tightly into Ceirra's, kissing her forehead. "See this? You can't help but latch on to me like a barnacle... Proof you can't keep your hands off of me."

"I could if you tied them up," She grinned sheepishly, kissing his chest. "I meant to ask, love, these marks are not all from me." As she spoke, she ran her fingers over the scars on his chest, her touch light and careful.

"Maybe I'm an incubus... Ha ha. Oh! I have something for you." Venser said sitting up a bit, running his hands down her side, stopping at her thigh. He rubbed her sides a few more times rapidly "Hmm... Can you get off of me for one minute?"

Ceirra Dusk looked up at him, pouting just a bit, though she then peeled herself off him. "Something for me? Love, we just met last night!"

"Always be prepared, I was a scout when I was young and that was our motto!" The handsome bearded man said hopping out of bed, stretching his nude muscular form and popping a few joints, all looked well in the afternoon sun. He walked over to his wardrobe and filed through a small box inside of it. "Ah!" He tossed her a red lace thong with the words, "Venser's Property" in green on the back. "Try it on." He said with a smile looking to her.

The tall temptress examined them with a careful eye, neatly plucked brow arched high. "I hope these aren't used, love." However, with a shrug, she slid out of bed, wobbled on the spot for a moment, then slipped them on, enjoying the soft fabric as it traveled up her long, shapely. Turning, she held her hands out to the sides, posing for him. "Well?"

"None of those in the box are." Venser said walking over to Ceirra as she posed for him. "Mhm..." He gave her a playful smack and said, "It suits you perfectly... How does it feel?"

Ceirra Dusk chuckled, pulling him close to her so she could kiss him. "According to these, you now have yourself a succubus. How does THAT feel?"

"Absolutely wonderful." He replied locking his lips with hers, grasping her ass in the process, giving it a nice, hard smack.

CHAPTER TWENTY-EIGHT: THE DRESS SHOPPE

The town of Aline, Vorland, 1436 ATC

The bearded green eyed man laughed as they linked arms and walked down the street of a cozy little place called Aline a mile and a half down the road, looking about the town "I haven't been here in months, even though this is the closest town to the Dragon's Head." As they walked he stopped a few feet away from a woman with a strange eyepatch and pointed his cane at a particular building. "Wait no. I did recruiting in that tavern a few weeks ago. Their cider is under par if you ask me." He looked up a bit to the tall temptress holding his hand beside him, wearing his black hood over her head, cloak about two inches off the ground. "Are you alright?"

Ceirra Dusk nodded, bumping his hip with her own lightly. "Teleporting gave me a queasy stomach, but I'm alright now, love." She looked up at the building, taking a glance back to the wandering woman that passed. "Not every tavern can serve the same high quality booze as yours. How unfortunate that they embarrassed themselves in front of the inventor of the Pink Footed Booby himself." She shook her head with a little laugh, straight long raven hair bouncing, fingers lacing between the spaces in the bearded man's hand.

"You get used to teleporting." Venser said with a laugh at her last comment. "Yeah... Last time- Wait no it was. I invented the Pink Footed Booby last time I came here. Right in that tavern over there inspiration struck me! They walked and he kept looking around. "My it's fucking busy today... All we gotta do is find that dress shop now." As they walked he looked up to his newly acquired lover who was about two or so inches taller than he. "Before you got lost in the woods the other day, did you wander from a town like this?"

"Similar but not the same. I'm from Driggs. Nearby. The sister town that over-shadows Aline, sort of. Like, I swear this one is just a smaller version of Driggs."

She hung close to him, the height difference becoming more noticeable as they walked. Goddamn, she had long strides. Ceirra was pretty much all legs anyways. Stubbornly, she pulled him back to a slower pace. "How'd you even come up with the name Pink Footed Booby?"

"Right over there sir!" Venser said pointing his cane, the handle carved and shaped like a whale, in the direction of the tavern as they passed another random passerby who seemed lost and thirsty. "Well, I like boobies. I like saying booby. Blue Footed Booby is a bird. One of those very same birds once just flew right into my face whilst I was walking down the street here. It has booby in the name. The drink is pink. Hence, Pink Footed Booby." He slowed down and they passed by a shop with a lovely red dress in the window. "Oooh...!" It was a well maintained building, above the door an intricate designed sign that read "The Dress Shoppe."

Ceirra released his arm and pressed her hands against the glass, the very tip of her nose brushing it gently. "It's so beautiful. Look at it, Venser." She reached back and grabbed his hand, pulling him closer to the window. Her burnt golden eyes widened looking to the bright red dress with the short skirt and an opening that would expose the navel. "Mhmmmm... And to think it's actually displayed like this. It's so naughty!"

The red dress in the window was a symbol of elegance. The lustrous, pearl beaded fabric of the dress glinted, light reflecting from the sun that shone through the glass. Venser squeezed Ceirra's hand and imagined her wearing the dress. "Heh... I think you'd look absolutely lovely in that... Do you like the color?" He asked turning his head to her.

She nodded, still staring at the dress as if it were the last piece of bread and she hadn't eaten in days. "I have too much ass to fill it out, but it's so lovely. Look at the beading. It's so delicate and beautiful."

"The ass to fill it out?" Venser asked looking down to Ceirra, still holding her hand. "Don't know what ya mean... But I'm sure they have one in your size." He gave her hand a tug and pushed the door open, "Come, let's go inside and check it out. Maybe we'll find you some nice jewelry too!"

Ceirra followed him, shaking her head and muttering something about men under her breath, which was pretty noticeable given her high pitched voice. "Think they sell it in... I don't know. Big and tall size?" She mused, giving his hand a squeeze as she followed him into the store.

As they entered the dress shop, they passed a steel gray silk dress trimmed with onyx beads as they looked about. "Go look for a dress, I'll ask that woman at the counter if they have that red dress in the window in your size." The bearded man gave her a quick peck on the cheek and walked over to the bored looking blonde woman at the counter. "Hello again Mister Venser." The sales associate waved over to him.

The tell temptress nodded and bent down a bit to plant a kiss of her own on his cheek. Releasing him, she went off to further examine the gray dress they had passed by on their way into the store, her fingers sliding over the slick onyx beads. Beside it, there was a soft blue dress with sparkling silver adornments. She smiled thoughtfully, fingering the fabric carefully.

"Seventy-five silver huh? For a dress? By the void..." Venser muttered speaking with the woman at the counter. She rolled her eyes. "The local dressmaker was an apprentice to the royal dressmaker for the king of Vorland remember? We sell only the finest garments, and I figured you'd remember that by how often you used to come, sir." He rubbed his temples and disappeared in a puff of thick red smoke, reappearing about two minutes later, much to the woman's surprise. He set a big bag down on the counter. "Alright sir, I'll just need to measure your friend's waist and bust." The woman said in what sounded like a mid-Atlantic accent. She grabbed a measuring tape and looked to Ceirra. "Step in front of that mirror please."

Ceirra turned, brow arched. "I take it she had the dress?" She looked to Venser, then, following the woman's request, stepped in front of the mirror. "And she knows you? I'm not the only woman you've bought a dress for am I?" She clicked her tongue. "Venser Karkaldwin you strumpet! I knew all those dresses in your wardrobe weren't yours." Giggling to herself at the thought of the handsome bearded barkeep crossdressing.

"Yeah. And boy... Ahem." Venser leaned against his cane. The woman moved all around Ceirra, measuring her, grabbing her arm and holding it straight out to measure it. "Yes. A strumpet I am. I have kids and other lovers... Sanna and Alex are both visiting my love Kari and our kids and Kari's adopted sister and her mom." He had failed to mention he was sleeping with Kari's adoptive sister, Marvella, but in truth he had a lot of women to mention and it would take much too long. And would be much too awkward.

"That sounds... Complicated. And I thought I really got around! Are you sure you secretly aren't an incubus?" Ceirra teased and watched the woman work, comfortable enough to let the woman's hands go wherever they needed. "Did you say something else, Ven?" She was focused on watching the woman measure and write down numbers.

The bearded man walked over to the window and looked out of it, not being able to see much from where he stood. "No.... Um, how's it coming?" He asked spinning around. "I'll be able to get her the correct size dress shortly." The woman said.

"You're done measuring then, yeah?" Ceirra slipped away from the woman and crossed the store to join Venser by the window. "I've forgotten how beautiful a town Aline is. Thank you for bringing me."

"Could be better. Capital De Seraphim has it beat." Venser said walking over to the counter as the woman disappeared into the back room, rapping his fingers on top of it, playing with a fine pair of scissors that was left there. "I mean; it could be Crown City. Or Capital De Seraphim. Ya know... When we get home I'll have to tell you a story about my home." He said turning to Ceirra. "Maybe." It was not wise to keep talking about where he came from. But he supposed most people would think of it as crazy.

The tall temptress smiled. "Could be worse, too, love." She leaned on the counter next to him, her hip cocked to the side. "Could be some filthy little village with no clean water and pigs running around after their women with their pants halfway down their legs." Ceirra turned, pressing her stomach against the counter now, her body still sore from the work out earlier in the day. "I mean, look at me." The red dress went up above her knees and just below her crotch.

"Ya know that last part doesn't sound too bad, actually. Women running around with their pants... Yeah. Are you gonna wear this around town today?" He asked, and she responded with a nod, looking at herself in a mirror with pride. "Despite how... Ya know." Another happy nod. Soon enough, the blonde shopkeep handed him a large white box with two blue ribbons wrapped around it and took the silver that the bearded man had paid her. "Come by our boutique again sometime." She said with a soft smile. Venser walked over to Ceirra and took her hand as they exited and kept exploring Aline.

The two spent their time slowly walking through shops and stalls, taking in what's available for purchase and trade. Being careful moving through overly active areas or really crowded places but seeing most just sold basic supplies such as dried rations, tea, and adventuring supplies in various shops.

Ceirra held the box containing her old outfit to her side, and kissed him hard as they briefly stopped, her hands gently holding his face to hers. "Thank you. You didn't need to do this for me, love." She glanced down at her red dress, her lips turned up in a smile.

"Seventy-five silver... It looks great on you." Venser said with a smile caressing her cheek, giving Ceirra a very sweet smile. Before stepping back and stretching his arms out, then began to pace about in small circles."I feel like running." She watched him pace, shaking her head. He was a mystery to her. "I mean; you'd want to run around after spending half the day in bed right?"

"Yes." The succubus nodded, and couldn't help but look down again, it's beautiful red fabric. The back would need to be pulled tight and tied, however, she'd need Venser's help with that. Pulling her hair over her shoulder, Ceirra turned to him. "Would you mind lacing it up?"

"Of course." Venser said moving behind Ceirra, lacing up her dress and straightening her hair so that it hung down from behind.

She turned, slowly, with her hands out at her sides. Looking down at herself, she smiled. She loved it. "Well?" She looked up at him, giving a slow twirl. "Tell me you love it again."

"I love it... Again." Venser looked at her with his mouth open a bit. "Wow..." He sat up slowly and walked over to her, placing his hands on her side and moving his hands all over her body. "This is fine material... And it makes you look so beautiful."

Despite herself, she blushed a deep red. "Well, for that much silver, it had better." Ceirra wrapped her arms around his waist, pulling him closer. "Thank you, for this dress and for everything else. I feel like I've been living in a dream since I met you."

"Despite the fact it's only been a day?" He asked feeling her up, the material of the red dress. "Or, less... Today isn't over yet."

The tall temptress nodded. "It's been a good day." And it had. However, they had spent most of it in bed. "Still feel like running? You've been stuck in bedrooms for most of the day."

"Yes. Yes, I do." The bearded man wriggled out of her grasp and gave her ass a playful smack, running down a nearby alley between several cramped buildings. "Come and catch me!" He called, causing the tall temptress to giggle with amusement and give chase.

Only to be stopped in the middle of the long alleyway accosted by two brigands. One wearing simple grey wool clothing and other simple leather armor, steel blades gleamed menacingly in the sunlight from above. "Not your lucky day both of you. Now, I'll make this quick." They grey one demanded impatiently as he nervously brandished the dagger.

"What do you want?" Asked Ven standing his ground when Ceirra caught up to him, looking beside her to his lover who was armed only with a cane despite all of the vials of liquids and knickknacks on his belt.

"Your belt, your fancy cane, and your coin purse and whatever the lady has in that box will do." The one in leather armor said with a confident smirk, smiling behind his short brown beard. "Now I think I'll take that for myself." The grey brigand pointed his dagger at Ven, making sure he made no sudden moves. A third robber dressed in a dull green wool outfit armed with a cleaver emerged from behind them.

Then, the tall temptress placed her long fingers into the front of her dress, showing the two her lovely, bountiful breasts.

"Heh. Nice titties tall-" Venser charged forward, knocking the dagger from the grey brigand's hand.

"What the?!"

Venser's mark flashed greenish white and he made a quick backhand motion, the grey brigand found himself blasted by a powerful gust of wind and placed on his back several feet away. The leather brigand was taken out with a groin kick, then a smash with the bottom of his cane to his head, which rattled his dome, and dazed him. He crumpled to the ground before Venser spun around and pointed his cane to the last one, spinning around on his left heel. "I yield! Fuckin..." He said, dropping his Ceirra, which caused Ceirra to smirk. "Didn't think that through, did you?" The green brigand crouched down hands above his head, looking up to them both, and quickly he lowered his hands, and went for a knife in his boot, unsheathe it and tossing it straight at the bearded man. The thin sharp steel flew through the air and the tall succubus moved with lightning reflexes, catching it before it stuck

Venser.

"Too slow for even the circus." She said, blowing a small, sarcastic kiss to him, before raising her middle finger with her free hand. Ceirra dropped the throwing knife and rushed the man, grabbing him by the throat and choke slamming him to the ground, before picking him up against with surprising strength and slamming him into the wall.

"Alright! Alright! We'll leave you be just let me down!" He cried as Venser approached them both, checking out the other two downed robbers. Her thick raven hair hung it loose curls and fluttered as she ran, her burnt golden eyes stayed fixed on the frightened robber's neck. Ceirra's blushed lips parted into a sinister smile, one that showed her subtle fangs. Her urge to taste blood left her searching from town to town for a distraction or to take it out on something more deserving. Sex was one thing, being a succubus and all but the taste of blood was on a slightly higher level. Yet she couldn't stand being alone, she not only craved blood, she craved company even if she didn't show it. Though, in her heart she had the strange feeling Venser changing it all.

"Are you going to shake him down or something? Just knock him out and we'll be on our way." The bearded man said gesturing to the green brigand's unconscious friends. "See that? That's what happens when you try to mug us, and next time, it'll be far worse." Venser wandered around the alley, disarming the men. "I hope you've learned your lesson."

"It will... And you will never mug anyone ever again." Ceirra Dusk said narrowing her burnt golden eyes, her fangs extending before the man's fearful eyes, and they grazed the flesh of his neck, drawing a few tiny droplets of blood.

Her nose twitched at the smell as it got stronger, going in to take a bite.

CHAPTER TWENTY-NINE: FOR SUMMERLAND'S SAKE

Capital De Seraphim, Pryldahn, 1436 ATC

The sounds of two pairs of tiny feet echoed against the stone walls of the castle, traversing the red carpet they stepped on. "Dis place is bigggggg!" Exclaimed a little boy with messy hair that was so blonde it was white, he also had grass green eyes and wore a red sweater and black pants with boots. "Daddy!" A little girl with raven black hair and the same grass green eyes wearing a white sweater and blue pants called out down the hall.

You could find Y'vonnne, second child to the great Dragon Emporer, asleep in her bed. The fireplace had died, a small trail of smoke rising from the still warm firewood. Her obnoxiously tall and thin body was still. Unnaturally still, except for the small rising of her chest, indicating that it wasn't a statue that laid in the bed, but a being. She made no noise, but the same could not be said to the creature that laid curled on the floor beside her bed shirt. It's breathing was like the sound of something crackling and raging, but ruffling snores belonged to Gummy, the woman's pet miniature wyvern, and companion for life. Von did not seem to be bothered by his snores. She was use to them, growing up with the boney reptilian since a very young age. However, a sound she was not acquainted with found its way to her sensitive ears and pulled her from her slumber with a grumble. The soft padding of feet made the woman toss over to her opposite side of the bed, a grumble a sleepiness and annoyance bellowing out from her throat. Then she heard an excited voice.

It sounded young.

Young?

A child?

For Summerland's sake why now?

Von buried herself into her pillow, pulling the covers over her head in hopes she would fall back asleep again. But, she knew it was pointless. Once something woke her, it was almost impossible for her to fall back asleep again. She threw the covers off of her in a huff of annoyance and tumbled out of her bed. She wore a long gown, her hair completely down and messy. She walked over to her door, swung it opened walked into the hallway, her back hunched in all of her grumpy glory. She yawned and silently cursed all the people who would want to get up this early. Especially people who would WAKE someone up this early. Curse them. Curse the sun. Curse this wall. Curse everything.

"Lady have you seen daddy?" The little girl asked running up to Von, giggling at the sight of her hair. "Poofy!" The little boy, both of them were twins ran up beside his sister. "He's biggggg and he's red!" His sister pitched in, "And he's wearing a silly green hat!"

Von stopped in her tracks as two children came up to her. Figures. Of course it was children. Von sighed and tucked her hair behind her ear.

"Your father?"

Big and red? Hmm, that sounds awfully similar to her own father. Von chuckled to herself and shook that image to herself. The only person that came to her mind was... "Venser?" She said to the child that spoke to her, her hands trying to calm the 'poofy-ness' that was her hair. The comment from the child was not appreciated.

"I have not, but I am sure he will stand out based on the description you just gave me." Her tone was passive and unemotional, like she was talking to another adult. It was apparent that Von was not good with children.

The children still smiled up at Von without a care in the world, listening attentively. 'Will you help us find daddy? We're playing a game!" Exclaimed the boy. "Can I braid yo pretty hair later lady?" The girl asked before she loudly gasped. "Awe you a real live queen?"

"Define "live", child." So, these were Venser's children. How quaint. She was still tired and waved off the girl with a small gesture of her hand. "Perhaps later you can play with my hair little one." Trinity, it was too early for this. "Sure, I will help." Why not? The God Queen was already dead inside.

"Are you a qwueen?" The little girl repeated again. The boy smiled reaching up to take Von's hand. "C'mon lady!" As the twins pulled the princess down the hall, a loud scream came from one of the broom closets far away from them. "Ah! Someone help me!"

"I-I am child. Why are you two traveling alone-" Once the boy took hold of her hand she stopped mid-sentence and allowed herself to be dragged down the hall. His hand was small, and soft. And oddly cold. Von's eyes shot up immediately as the sound of a scream erupted from a broom closet and she halted, pulling the boy that held her hand behind her. She stopped the girl, placing a hand on her small shoulder and guided the girl to stand next to her brother. Why, WHY, in the morning? The world just hated her, that's what it was. "Stay behind me children." The woman said without looking back at the children. This could either go two ways. A terrible accident or one of Venser's tricks. Either way, she wasn't sure the children should witness either option.

When Von would open the door, she would find Venser sitting up against the wall wearing some sort of weird device over his eyes with a slot where one would slide pictures or pieces of paper down into it. There was also a fake ass made of the same material as his strange suit, only more realistic. "Ah! Someone help me I'm trapped inside a sex dungeon! I'm trapped inside a prison of my own design! My own, dirty kinky sexual design!" He then began to cry inside of the thing that covered his eyes while squeezing the fake ass. The twins stared at their father wide eyed and confused. "Qwueen what's daddy crying about?" The little boy asked looking up to her, then to the device covering Venser's eyes. "What are thoseeeeeeee?"

You know what? She wasn't even surprised anymore. She just stood in the doorway, her eyes heavy lidded and her face wiped clean of any emotion. "Being a jester." She replied in a stoic tone. And, once she spoke those words, she reached her hand over, grabbed the door knob, and slowly closed it until the door clicked. "Perhaps it is better to leave your father to his work, agreed children?" Y'vonne wanted to pretend like she didn't see anything, and so that's what she did. She casted her electric blue eyes down to the two little ones and offered and simple smile. The best one she could offer while not being fully awake.

The twins smiled back sweetly and their father appeared out of a puff of thick red smoke right behind Von, facing completely away from her. "Hey sorry you had to see that just got so bored in there!" He was still wearing the giant goggle like device that blocked his vision. "Ya found me kids!" He exclaimed getting on his knees to hug his children, the kids cheered and ran around into Venser's arms. He wrapped his arms around the two lovingly and protectively in his embrace.

"Couldn't hide foever daddy!"

"Indeed..." She responded and stepped aside. He was a good father, or at least he tried, no one could deny that. The woman yawned again. "What you do in her personal time is none of my concern." She said in between her yawn. "Though, do keep an eye on your children. They could disturb some of the inhabitants while they sleep." Like me. They disturbed me, she finished in her head.

"What time is it?" Venser asked removing the headpiece, turning back to look at Von. "Me and the kids only got here twenty minutes ago before they suggested a game of hide and seek."

"The sun has barely risen." Too early, she said in her after thoughts. "So... I honestly do not know." Von leaned her weight onto another foot, pulling her wavy hair off one tanned shoulder onto another. This would honestly be the first time Venser has seen her in pretty much her underwear, for she always made sure to dress properly during other affairs.

"Twenty minutes? I assume you came from your tavern, yes?" She eyed the odd green hat he wore and blinked slowly.

"What?" Venser didn't have much reaction to the sight of Von wearing nothing but a gown. He had seen countless women wear less before. Void, he even saw her naked once. He stood up and nodded his head. "Actually we came from their mother's place. I have them for a few days." The little girl hopped up and down with her arms extended up. "Up daddy! Up!" Venser chuckled and picked up his daughter, who rested up against his chest and batted at the bells at the end of the tendrils of his jester hat, giggling as she played with them. The boy just ran down the halls giggling wildly. "Look pwincess!" He ran a few feet towards her and attempted a somersault, he fell forward and landed on his back. "Ta da!" Venser chuckled again and said, "Good job Soarin!" He looked down to his daughter and said, "Lucinda, you're getting too big for daddy to carry." He poked her nose playfully and said, "But one day you'll be able to carry me!"

Von sure felt the difference or rather, lack of clothing. She shivered, her bare arms suddenly erecting a wave of goosebumps. She rubbed her arms with her hands to generate heat. She wasn't use to standing anywhere outside of her room with her nightgown on. Nope, this sure was a first. "Lovely." The woman said in a scratchy voice. "Do they need a nanny? I could perhaps have a servant watch them for you while they are here." Von watched as the boy performed what could only be described as a clumsy tumble. As he landed on his back, she arched an eyebrow. What should she do now? Should she praise him? But he accomplished nothing. "Uh...mhm." Yeah, that was safe. Von was more than out of her element here.

"No, they already have a nanny. Though Valerie isn't... She hasn't been well lately." Venser said patting Lucinda's back as she wrapped her arms around her father's neck. "I miss nommy..." She said sadly. "Nommy will manage to stay awake longer than a minute eventually, princess." Venser said kissing Lucinda on the forehead. "You sure daddy?" Soarin asked looking up to him. "I'm certain, son. You, your sister and nommy and mommy will be able to play and run all you like!" Soarin began to jump up and down in front of Von. "I like running!" He chirped. "Do you qwueen? Do you like fried chicken too??"

The God Queen's brows furrowed as she listened to their banter. She hoped things were well with them. From what she could tell this 'nommy' was a mother figure to these children. Von found herself staring at the little girl that sat so comfortable in her father's arms and smiled. There was nothing like a father's embrace that made you feel safe and...at home. But, her eyes soon fell on the boy as he jumped in front of her, stealing her attention. "Running? I'm afraid I'm not very athletic. Ask my sister, she was a physical one." Fried chicken? "Fried? What is... Fried?"

"It's like, really cwispy chicken! And tasty too!" Soarin chirped again before taking off running down the hall as fast as his little legs could carry him. Venser moved close to Von and said quietly with a sigh, "Nommy. Nanny plus mommy. And she... She's just been passing in and out of a terrible sickness."

"Heavens, has she seen a physician?" Von watched as the boy took off again down the talk and gasped as he almost collided with a servant carrying a tray of cups. But, the servant barely missed him and Von heaved a sigh a relief. The servant wasn't relieved but confused, staring at the boy as he ran boy without stopping and then turn their gaze to the princess who merely shrugged at them. The servant shook his head and continued on his way.

"She is. She's getting better." Their father set Lucinda down and said, "Go play with your brother." "But daddy..." She whined. "Go, go. Your brother is probably running around outside without clothes and you need to watch him. Do it and there'll be candy..." At the mere mention of candy, Lucinda squealed and ran off to catch her quick brother.

Sanna stood beside a tree to allow Venser and his dear friend to speak alone of things she needed not to be informed of, smiling a bit as she looked upon the falling leaves with a hand to her rounding belly. The baby kicked every now and then lightly as if to greet his mother and she'd chuckle a bit, rubbing her thumb over the spot where she was kicked before beginning to hum a soft tune from her homeland. She already missed the tavern a little, but this area was absolutely beautiful. Mountains and green as far as she could see, and the castle itself was grandiose. Well decorated within, she'd only seen a little bit as she'd closely followed Ven on their way past the doors before deciding to step outside for conversation's sake, but by now she figured that they would be alright with her ear around. "Come little love, let's go see what your father's up to," she cooed to her kicking unborn as she turned from the tree to venture the steps toward the door.

The doors open, and a semi-golden skinned beauty walked in. "Well hello beautiful..." Venser said with a seductive growl, brushing back the tendrils on his bright green jester cap. "Y'vonne De Seraphim, that is my lover, Sanna."

"Give my regards to the children's nanny." Von replied and watched as her friend strode over to a woman with a welled belly that came into view. Oh... Dear. A new guest and she was hardly dressed. Von combed through her hair a bit, flattening it down as much as she could and patted down her night gown. One guest or a hundred, she must be presentable. "Greetings, miss Sanna. And, you're welcome." Von did a curtsey in one graceful movement, her voice was formal and practiced, very well pronounced. "It's always wonderful to meet Venser's companions. Do forgive my attire my dear, an early rise was not something I anticipated." She gave a small laugh, though it held no true warmth.

Upon the growl she heard from him she blushed a little, offering a small smile as she once again took her place at his side. She herself was only garbed in a green mother's dress and her hair had been brushed back behind her shoulders, matching her bright and intense green eyes and accenting the tanned skin Venser loved so much. She gave as descent of a bow as she could with her condition and her smile was heartfelt, a genuine greeting passing from her lips. "Greetings to you, m'lady. It is a pleasure to meet you as well, and don't worry. I normally am not so casual myself." She chuckled a little. "I fear I will have to forgo formality for comfort soon enough."

Venser wrapped an arm around Sanna and kissed her on the cheek, trailing one hand down her stomach to feel her bump. "Sanna wants to work here as well. Why don't we discuss it over breakfast? We can give you time to get changed and for the servants to whip something up."

The God Queen smiled and tilted her head at the golden gypsy, her eyes squinting in amusement. "I do not blame you, my dear. I'm surprised you have not fallen to the whims of comforts, you hold yourself quite well." Von began to absent-mindedly rub her bare arms as her tanned skin began to give rise to goosebumps. "That sounds lovely. I would like to change." Looks like this will be an early start. "Please, excuse me." Von bowed her head and made her way off down the hall to her room to slip into something worthy of a princess. She sighed to herself as she walked, her arms held around herself as the weight of the early morning started to crash down on her like a wave. Like it's been mentioned, she was not a morning person.

Sanna had nodded with a bit of gratitude to Von's statement that she held herself well, bowing her head in respect. Weaving her fingers in between her beloved's fingers she waited for his lead as they'd mentioned the preparation of breakfast; she didn't realize how early it was and indeed was quite awake despite this, a little used to the whims of early risers. This was an oddity given how prone to fatigue a mother-to-be usually was, but she didn't mind. She watched as Y'vonne walked to her room and smiled to Ven. "Everything alright?"

Venser nodded his head in affirmation, the bells of his bright green jester hat jingling as he did. He took her hand in his and said, "Everything is good, my love." A small voice was heard from behind the two. "Hi Sanna!" Lucinda stood there with her brother, who promptly moved to Sanna's side to take her hand, while his sister moved to Venser's side and took his hand. "Eat?" He nodded and led his family into the giant dining room. "Yes, eat." He said with a chuckle after ordering some servants to prepare breakfast. The kids scrambled into their seats as Venser pulled out a chair for his lover. "You look so wonderful in that dress Sanna... I mean, I think green is really your color!"

Von gave a nervous laugh and cleared her through as she hugged herself tightly, painfully aware of her attire. From a standpoint, her gown wasn't revealing at all, but Von herself just felt uncomfortable wearing it around guests. "It... Was not proper."

Sanna nuzzled against Ven's cheek as he assured her all was well though turned to the sound of the little voice, smiling brightly to see the two little ones standing as her lover's son moved to take her hand. She took it and squeezed gently with loving eyes, following as Venser led them all to the dining room and taking a seat when he pulled out a chair for her. "Thank you, my love. I'm quite fond of the color and always have been... Such a healthy, natural one. Aye? Reminds me of forests."

The servants brought plates of cheese, bread, smoked salmon, and salted fish with some fruit to the table. A few more began to set it. "I agree completely, Sanna." Venser said taking a seat right beside her. "How are you? And the baby?" He held off from eating for now, slightly concerned where Von was and f they should eat without her or not.

I've been doing really well, especially with your help, and the baby is nice and active. Seems we're going to have a healthy son." She smiled softly as her hand once again began absently rubbing up and down her bump. "I wonder if the other is alright. God Queen Y'vonne."

Venser stared at Sanna for a few seconds, blinking as the children began to serve ourselves. "I recall the wise talking squirrel saying we were going to have a daughter."

"AH HA HA!" Y'vonne cackled, getting a good laugh out of that surprisingly. "Ohhh... That was out loud. I apologize." She swayed a bit, try to blink away the urge to fall asleep but she soon yawned.

"Ah... Oh goodness, pardon me I..." She yawned again and sighed and began to stumble. She fell forward a bit. "Must, get dressed and attend... To the... Guests..." Y'vonne sat beside Ven and slumped over onto him. The crimson haired woman had fallen into the man, asleep. Asleep now. Completely gone. My, that was quick. But it was so, her breathing even slowed down to a steady rhythm and her face was relaxed now. The woman was obviously more tired than she had lead on.

"Talking squirrel?" Lucinda said popping a piece of fish into her mouth before spitting it out. "Yucky. Too salty!" Venser patted her head and Soarin eyed Sanna's stomach suspiciously. "Yeah, right. A daughter. Glad you remember that now. Yeah... We will have a healthy, perfect daughter..." When the conversation ended they all looked to the sleeping queen beside him.

Sanna blushed at forgetting their child's gender, lowering her head in a little embarrassment. "My memory has been terrible, love, forgive the mistake." She squeezed his hand a bit and smiled apologetically, nodding as she listened to him and rose to greet Y'vonne again, before she sat down and passed out. "She seems very kind. Do you think she will like me working here?"

"Oh of course. The people at the tavern love you, and she and all the other people here will love you two." Venser said placing a hand on her cheek, rubbing it with her thumb before leaning in to kiss her gently on the lips. "Is he your husband?" Soarin asked in his tiny voice looking to the two while they kissed.

Sanna returned his kiss and leaned her cheek against his rubbing thumb, smiling tenderly to him for a moment as she nodded. He always found a way to ease the nervousness she felt around new people, even if it went unspoken by her own mouth. When Soarin asked if they were married she turned a dark shade of red and looked to Venser for a moment, trying to hide a smile as she answered. "No, dear, but I... Well... It's something we haven't talked about yet. I love him very much."

"Hold on. Be right back love." Venser said pulling out The God Queen's chair and picking her up. Her head was pressed against Venser's shoulder as he kept her close to him. Moving the door open more with his foot and walked to the large bed that laid up against the wall, he was quiet, not making a sound and was careful with the woman. Not knowing if she was fragile or not, either way he was going to do this. As he put her down on the bed he wrapped the covers around the obnoxiously thin woman. He stared at her for a moment to make sure she was okay, he hesitated and moved his hand to her cheek to brush the hair behind her hair as she laid resting. Venser nodded and took a step back away from the bed, turned around and whispered "Good night. Er, I mean morning Y'vonne." He walked out of the room and silently closed the door behind him.

CHAPTER THIRTY: THE WATCHER IN THE WINDOW

The Dragon's Head Tavern and Inn, Vorland, 1436 ATC

Sanna had followed her lover's return back to the tavern and was now preparing for bed, sliding her hair into a braid section by section as she sat upon the mattress and hummed quietly to their child. She wasn't too sure when he'd come down from the bar but didn't mind; she was in a particularly interesting mood tonight and she wanted to surprise him, though she hoped her knees would allow it. What she wasn't aware of, though, was the faint figure of a pale skinned woman with dark lips and dead eyes that watched the pregnant woman with a longing and sadness that seemed to be ancient and not caused by the sight in front of her. She was just veiled enough to not be seen behind the curtain and if one did see her, they'd know she was merely a phantom and no threat to anyone anymore... But one would be damned to say the woman wasn't beautiful. Sanna seemed not to notice her as she finished with the braid, wincing as she cupped one breast. She'd have to learn how to ease the ache in them soon.

"Da da da!" Venser slinked into the room, shaking his hands like a runner does before a race. He was wearing nothing but a leopard print thong and he began to sway his body slowly in front of his lover as she lay on the bed. He gripped the front of it and began to pump his body up and down, his right hand slipped down inside the waistband of it. "Like what you're seeing here?" He asked spinning around, wagging his ass at Sanna, just as ignorant as her of the ghost in the mirror.

Sanna had she had long, glossy black hair, an olive complexion that made the woman look gold at times, and a slim but voluptuous physique with a baby belly. While her lover had a strong arched brows and eyelashes so thick it demanded confidence, strength. Attack eyebrows, eyes like emerald pools. A prominent bearded jaw curved gracefully around and the strength of his neck showed in the twining cords of muscle that shaped him.

The golden gypsy heard his voice first and then squeaked with a dark blush and a grin as he stepped into the room in nothing but a thong, swaying his body in front of her as she lay comfortably. She couldn't help but bite her lip with a seductive look in her eyes as he gripped the front of it and pumped his body, fighting the urge to lick her lips as his hand slid down inside the waistband. She laughed as he wiggled his ass and gave a playful growl, and the phantom's reaction to all of this was to watch on with a rather impressed look in her eye. "My love, you look ravishing enough to devour..." Sanna purred, the boldness of her statement surprising, admiring the muscles of his athletic physique.

The bearded man's erection was very prominent inside the leopard print thong as he growled seductively in her response to her playful growl. His fingers dipped further into his thong, slowly pulling them down inch after inch, very, very slowly... He slit id down over his thighs for a very brief moment as he pushed his hips forward. Climbing onto the bed he swung his hips from left to right making his penis sway back and forth as he hummed "The Stripper."

This time the phantom's jaw dropped a little and she slid past the wall, staying behind the curtain and keeping herself as translucent as possible, after all, even a spirit didn't want to be caught as a peeping tiffany. A fang bit into the woman's lower lip as she watched Sanna moan a little at the sight of the hardened cock inside of his thong, very obviously fighting restraint as he slid the cloth over his thighs for a moment and pushed his hips forward. She sat up and moved to a position where her face was near his cock as it swung back and forth, licking her lips again while looking into his eyes. "Mnf..."

He sat on the bed now, showing off his muscular frame and barreled chest for his tanned skinned lover now and grinned, looking down to her before backing up. Venser hopped off the bed, rubbing his hands up and down his body, occasionally gripping himself squeezing slightly before rubbing over it and throwing his head back with a soft moan like he was going to have an orgasm.

The tanned woman grinned right back at him and as he hopped off of the bed she watched eagerly while her own hand seemed to wander to her breast, squeezing as gently as she could before wincing a little in some discomfort. It was then she couldn't help herself and she got on her knees for him, weaving her hands over the hand that rubbed over it as she gave a long and loving lick to the head of his cock. That alone caused her nipples to harden so much that they strained against the gown she wore. "Please, Ven..." Was all she could say, and by now the woman in the window was fervently watching the young couple all while chewing on her bottom lip.

"Mhmm... Please, what- What the fuck is that!" He moved back, his cock throbbing a bit at the lick as Venser gazed to the woman in the window. Though, he didn't see that the woman was actually IN the window. "Get out of here pervert! If you want a show you're gonna have to pay for it! Or at least let us know first!"

Sanna froze and squealed in embarrassment as he yelled out, standing quickly and hiding behind him. The woman stepped from behind the curtain, though didn't really... Step. She glided, more or less, and her translucent form was obvious. She wasn't alive. "I'm plenty sure that you cannot force me out given you can't actually touch me, but feel free to try. In either case, your girl is quite beautiful and you are well endowed..." There was a scent, distinctly a vampire one as she passed by the couple as though to go toward the door. Upon closer inspection she had the same curve of hips as Sanna had pre-pregnancy, the same shape of breasts... The same long, black hair, but with brilliantly pale skin and black lips. Further features were hidden by a black gown of lace.

"I knew it, a ghost. I dealt with these in that cursed tower..." The handsome bearded man said shielding Sanna from her, he didn't even bother putting his thong back on and stood completely naked with his cock fully erect. "What do you want? Why are you here?" He asked examining her closely.

"There's no sense in asking that, dear, you should already know considering how hard you still are. I'm just a woman long dead who likes to watch once in a while... From both sides of the spectrum," she purred as her eyes fell to the woman's swollen belly. Sanna blushed and buried her face in his shoulder from behind, shaking her head fervently. She didn't want to believe she'd been peeped by a ghost.

Recently Venser had thought that stripping would be a good source of on the side income for he and Sanna, and Rowena when she was born and had decided to test it out for Sanna. Then he'd go to Alex's room next and try it with her. Then Ceirra. And then his other lovers in the tavern if they were in. Though he didn't expect some long dead woman to show up watching the two. "She looks like you." He said still looking to the ghost. "Did you die inside the tavern?"

"I died as lunch for a panther person, but not here. It was actually quite far from here," she answered plainly. Sanna looked over the woman for a moment and nodded in agreement. "Paler though," she whispered in her lover's ear.

"Do you know her?" Venser asked looking back to Sanna. "Distant relative? Ancestor?"

The tanned woman shook her head. "Isn't familiar to me, truthfully," She answered her lover as she came back around and hugged him from the front. It was mainly to cover his cock from the phantom's view. "She doesn't know me; girl hardly knows herself. I'm a bit older than that. The name is Sephiria Trepahs."

"Sephiria... Never heard that name before." Venser said placing his scarred hands over Sanna's, looking the ghost dead in the eyes with pure confusion in them. "Again... What do you want? This is a very very awkward situation."

"I wanted nothing more than to see two people in love," The spirit chuckled as she moved closer to the door. "I apologize if I intruded and made things rather... Unfavorable." Sanna squeezed his hand lightly and nuzzled his neck, trying to keep from looking at her. Meanwhile, Sephiria seemed almost sad at the sight of them, but the only indicator of it was her gaze. She smiled through it, it would seem. "You chose a good woman."

"I did indeed." Venser said nuzzling Sanna's head back, kissing her cheek and taking Sephiria away from his gaze. "... Pervert."

"Dragon cock." The golden gypsy retorted back with a wink as she phased through the door, and Sanna sighed with relief. Thank the gods, the creature was gone. "I didn't even see her here! Gods above, I'm drawing the curtains before bed next time." She murmured against his shoulder, nibbling playfully.

Venser's cock began to go flaccid as he stood there still as Sanna nibbled on his shoulder. "I feel so... What the fuck? Yeah, draw the curtains..." He now had lost the motive to continue dancing for Sanna. "Probably won't help but... Whatever..."

She hurriedly moved to the window and drew the curtains closed, moving back over to the bed to sit down with her hand upon her belly. She patted the bed gently after sliding under the covers, blushing a little. Yes, it had off put her mood, but she couldn't help that she still desired him... More specifically to taste him, but she was a bit too shaken to full-on instigate. "The way she stared at me was disturbing..."

The bearded man merely nodded his head and crawled into bed with Sanna, slipping underneath the covers next to her. He sighed and placed a hand on her stomach, rubbing the bump.

Baby Rowena gently kicked her father's hand as he rubbed and joined her mother on the bed, and Sanna smiled faintly with a gentle kiss to his cheek after nestling closer. "Tomorrow will be a better day..." She tried in an effort to help with his mood.

The bearded man nuzzled her head and chuckled as the baby kicked. "Springtime soon and we'll have a healthy, happy baby... I was thinking... What if we had our own home? Outside of the tavern."

The tanned woman nuzzled against him in return and relaxed as she felt the baby play against his hand, listening to him as he asked about a home of their own. "That would be wonderful...a space to raise our little one and spend time with each other," she answered with a smile.

"I took you to Pryldahn the other day to meet God Queen Y'vonne. And you went outside to check things out. Imagine it... We have a little home just outside the castle, with a big yard for the kids to play in!" Venser said resting his hand on her stomach. "Big enough for them, big enough for our other lovers."

"Pryldahn was so beautiful... Both inside and out. It would make travelling to work so much easier and all of the children could play together, when the baby grows a bit of course." Sanna smiled warmly and pressed a tender kiss to his lips then, nuzzling against them. "I love you, Venser."

"Thank you for the life you've given me."

"Yeah... We can just walk to work every day, and we can have Valerie or Alex or their Aunt Marvella watch the kids if I talk her into living with us. I mean, Kari too... But yeah." Venser said smiling as he took the golden gypsy's soft hands in his, rubbing his thumbs over them. "I love you too Sanna. So so much."

She leaned down to kiss the tops of his hands as they held her own, giving his lips another lingering kiss. "Is it a bad thing that I crave you every day? Even just a touch, like this... You drive me wild in more ways than you know. Your dancing was very arousing... I was very much intent on bringing that beautiful cock to my lips and sucking with all my heart." She blushed a bit, her voice shy as she spoke.

"No no... It's not bad. I get it... I mean, you love me so much." Venser said taking her hand and trailing it down his chest, stomach, and down to his cock. "And I'm unlike any man you've met before."

"Of course you are...you were my first, beloved, and my only." Sanna shivered as he took her hand and trailed it down his chest, lower and lower until it slid along the length of his cock. The tanned woman bit her lip and pressed her lips to his, gently squeezing as she rubbed up and down along the length of him. Sliding to lay on her side so she was more comfortable and continued stroking slowly for him, kissing his chest softly. "I cherish you with every part of me."

"The first man you ever met?" Venser asked with a chuckle, licking at her lips.

Sanna purred softly, nibbling his lower lip gently as she gave another teasing squeeze. "The first man I ever let close to me, the only man I've ever made love to, and the only man I've ever loved and ever will love."

"Oh..." Venser began to stiffen back up as he kissed her softly back, placing one hand on Sanna's cheek and turning his head to the side, kissing her neck with a seductive growl. "And ever will love... Hm..."

"I said man. I never said anything about loving you and other women..." The golden gypsy moaned softly as he kissed her neck with a growl, finally sliding down his form while trailing kisses down his chest and belly. "Mm.." She purred a little as she reached his navel, swirling her tongue down to the base of his cock before sliding up along it.

"Yes..." Venser said stroking her hair softly as she went down on him.

Finally, Sanna reached the tip of his shaft and she rolled her tongue around the mushroomed head, giving a soft whimper as she finally wrapped her lips around it and sucked gently. Then she slid down a little further before sucking back up, then down while sucking up again...until she reached about halfway down. It was at that point that she suddenly slid down all the way to the base and held him there with a soft moan, her nipples harder than rocks as she slid slowly back up until he was fully out of her mouth.

"You taste so good, my love..."

CHAPTER THIRTY-ONE: THE HOUND

The Dragon's Head Tavern and Inn, Vorland, 1436 ATC

A very strange patron dressed in crude, spikey improvised armor stopped at the bottom of the stairs, and stared up at her, "I don't want it! What is it?! Who are you?! What's your name?!" He shook his masked head, and ran a hand through his black mohawk, "Here.... Let's start over, yes? I am Hound, or Rabid Dog Man. The deadliest knife-for-hire on the continent!" He pressed his right forearm against his waist, and pressed his left forearm to the back of his waist as he bowed low, "Pleasure, to meet you." He grimaced under his mask as he fought back a shudder. He stood up straight, and stared up at her, "You are?"

Floppy, elven-like ears twitched to the male's words, as she sat on the stairs, causing obstruction for anyone who wanted to use them. "Hound." Thorn the pink haired demoness barmaid nodded then giggled. "Like, a dog?" She then held the coin purse out him a little more, wanting him to take it. "Take one, Thorn makes them special." She completely ignored the male's questions. "Yes? No? Take it!"

The golden gypsy was driven by way of carriage back to the tavern after a brief visit with her family in the caravan, bidding them goodbye with hugs and kisses as they all waved her back to her mate. She chuckled and allowed the small children one more touch to her round belly as she left the carriage and walked to the door, heading inside. "Venser, beloved, I'm home!" She called out with a grin, carrying a small basket of gifts from her family to them both as well as some keepsakes for the baby-to-be. She made her way up the stairs slowly, making sure not to trip on her own skirt to head over to the bar where he usually was.

There was no response from the bar. For the only who were out in the open were Thorn and the one called Mutt.

The large patron called Hound sighed, and dropped his head as he took the wallet. He grimaced again under his mask as he fought back a shudder, "Thank you." He stared at the small leather sack, and opened it, turning it around and upside down. He turned the coin purse around, and stared at it through pale red eyes, "What goes in this?"

The golden gypsy blinked a bit and looked around before walking to their room, a bit of a worried frown on her expression. "Venser?" She called again, looking toward the front door downstairs.

Once he took the coin purse from her, she was able to relax, and moved to a stand, moving up to the bar, and behind it. "Money goes in that." She replied to hound, giggling.

When she would enter their room, she would find Venser wearing a giant fish costume with a maraca in each hand, the blinds were shut but the light from the angel feather on his nightstand lit up the room just a tiny bit as he slept.

Hound followed her as he slowly stumbled up the stairs, "Hmmm...." He shrugged, and sat down at the bar, still turning over the coin purse, "How it work?" He sniffed it, and opened it up fully, sticking in a finger. Hound wiggled his finger around on the inside of the wallet, and held it up with his finger, spinning it around, "Like this?"

"Oh... Awww." Sanna smiled softly and slowly closed the door, setting the basket down before quietly moving over to the bed. She pressed a kiss against one of his hands and smiled, watching him for a moment with a hand on her belly. She couldn't believe her luck in finding a man like him, along with the other women they got to know, and even more lucky that they would be expecting a daughter together. She wondered how long he'd been sleeping.

"Zzzz... Nugh?" Venser awoke with a jolt and snorted, rubbing the top of his fist costume where his head was. "Sanna!" He wrapped his arms around her and pressed a soft, loving kiss on her lips. "I've missed you." He said licking at her lips, picking up the maracas and shaking them. "Yayyyy...!"

Thorn leaned on the counter to him, nodding as he began to figure out the simple thing. "Yep! Coins, and notes." She giggled, twitching. "Maybe even some other things, like small jewels." The ditzy demoness had no idea, she had never even used a wallet either. She never carried money on her even, so it was strange how she could get away with so much and not needing to pay. "Thorn has been working on these leather coin purses for a while. Maybe I will add a zip to it." She pondered. "And make them custom, for Thorn's friends."

Hound tilted his head, "A zip?" He closed the wallet, and tucked it into his pocket, "What a zip?" He stared at her, "Stop speaking nonsense. Speak sense."

Sanna smiled warmly as he woke and hugged him tightly, returning his kiss as well as pressing another to his cheek before resting her head on his shoulder... As best as she could with the fish costume. She giggled when he picked up the maracas and shook them, giving a playful lick to his lips in return. "I have some things for us from the family, love. They gave us gifts for the baby as well as ourselves."

"Oh? Well let's see what you have." He said wrapping an arm around Sanna, looking into the basket.

Thorn blinked her mismatched hues. "Sense? What's sense?" She held up a zip all on its own, and began to move it up and down. "Up! Down! Up! Down!" She went cross-eyed a moment.

The tanned woman smiled and leaned to grasp the basket, the first of the items being a small baby's blanket meant for a newborn laying over the top. It had been handmade, embroidered with their initials as well as the child's proposed name. Underneath it was some herbs to help with things like breastfeeding, healing after birth, as well as a couple of celebratory cigars and alcohols for the father-to-be for when his daughter arrived.

Hound stared at it, and leaned in, "That is odd." He nodded, and leaned back now, "Odd. Odd is odd, but good." He picked at his barbed wire collar, and grunted as he made the barbs stab into his throat, "Stupid collar. Why do I wear you?" He shrugged, and kept picking at the collar, only shredding his throat as he attempted to get the barbs out. He growled, "Stupid collar." Despite his shredded and bleeding throat, he picked at his collar still. He finally managed to get it adjusted to where it stopped shredding his throat, and rolled his shoulders as his throat slowly started healing, "Should stop wearing this. I won't."

"Nice, nice." Venser said inspecting the cigar and alcohol, holding up the blanket. "This is really cute! By the void... Rowena is going to love this. Who made it, Sanna?"

The golden gypsy smiled and kissed his cheek. "The eldest woman in the caravan, the woman who saved me. I am like a daughter to her, and she is very happy for us. She says if we need anything, to let her know."

Curious, Thorn became interested in the barbed wire collar Hound wore, since she had never seen that type of wire before. "It tears the flesh from bone?" She pondered, before shaking her head. "Thorn read about it once, but she has never used it for her experiments." The gore, she loved it. Just when she was about to speak, she paused, then twitched. "T-... Tombstones!" Twitch. "Tick-tock!"

"Saved you from what?" Venser asked rubbing her stomach a bit.

"From the slavers in the west where I worked. I was pretty much on the market stage when she was kind enough to purchase me and take me with he." Sanna answered, the baby inside kicking and rolling against his hand as though eager to play with her father.

"That's good..." Venser smiled warmly feeling the kick. He got off the bed and then got on his knees, kissing Sanna's stomach. "Hello Rowena." He nuzzled her stomach and looked up into her intense bright green eyes. "You never did tell me about your parents. What are they like?"

Sanna grinned as he kissed her stomach, nuzzling and speaking to their unborn daughter. She ran her fingers through his hair gently as she thought on his question, then spoke again. "I can barely remember, but I do know that my father died as a soldier. My mother was a singer and was very popular, and I learned my performance from her for the most part. A lot was taught to me after I was taken from her, though. I can't remember what they looked like."

"At least little Rowena will be able to know her mother and father." Venser said, most of him blocked by his fish costume.

"Yes. And I look forward to it so much," Sanna said in a softer tone, and it became apparent in her expression as she looked over her belly and her lover that she really was truly happy. She seemed absolutely serene, her thumb absently rubbing along her bump and another having moved up to caress his cheek. "I wonder how soon it will be..." She said softly, and it was clear that she was daydreaming a bit about meeting their little one.

"Month or two... At least." The bearded man said. He was also guilty of daydreaming a lot about meeting their daughter, holding her in his arms. He stood up a bit and placed a hand on her cheek, kissing Sanna softly again. "I've missed you..."

The golden gypsy kissed him back, eyes watering a little bit with a smile. "I missed you too..." She said, pressing another kiss against his lips as well as a gentle nuzzle. "You really do make me very happy, you know that?"

"You do the same for me." Venser said nuzzling her forehead. "I'm still trying to find us a place in Pryldahn for our family..."

Hound watched her, and smiled a little under his mask, "Does the lady want some barbed wire? I will gladly give her a bit. I have plenty of it." He shuddered slightly at the weird feeling that passed through his body. Was he being kind and offering to give away something for free? Abnormal, even for him and his royal disdain of acting like proper royalty. He shook his head, "I will give you some." He twitched a little, and reached into his pocket, pulling out a round tin. He opened the tin, and started pulling out while unwinding the barbed wire that lay inside. He pulled his mask up enough, and bit the barbed wire, shearing it cleanly at the length of a yard. He set the barbed wire on the counter, and covered the tin. He pulled his mask back down, and put the tin in his pocket. He picked up, and held out the length of barbed wire. "Here you go, play with this." he said as another shudder ran through his body. Was he still being kind? Something must have taken over him to make him be this way. He shook his head, and smiled under his mask.

"Have fun with it."

"Lemme get out of my costume. I was entertaining the kids at Soarin and Lucinda's play school earlier." He said standing up, walking over to his wardrobe. "Why don't you go out and have a glass of water or something?

Fantastic! Barbed wire all to herself. "Ah, danke!" Without hesitation, Thorn grabbed the barbed wire, feeling it tear in to her skin the moment she grasped it. "Owwie!" It did not take long until her blood started to pour on to the counter top, because the more she struggled, the deeper the wire went in to her skin. "It clings! It stings! It bleeds!" She began to run around behind the bar, back and fourth, yelping as she shook her hands about. "Nyaaah!"

The tanned woman chuckled a bit and nodded, standing as well while leaning a bit against the bedpost. "Alright, I will meet you out in the bar area, love," Sanna called as she gave him a quick kiss before heading out of their room. She walked out to the bar and looked around, leaning back a little with her back to the bar's counter to not put pressure on her belly. What would normally startle her in regards to the woman running around behind the bar actually didn't for once, and instead she seemed a bit worried. "What's wrong?"

Hound nodded, "Bite." He watched her, and paled, "Aww, fuck." He quickly threw himself over the counter, and stood there. He lifted his mask to just above his mouth, and held out his scarred hands, deep scars curving upwards from the corners of his mouth, "Be calm. I'll remove the barbed wire from your hand."

Thorn snatched her hands away from him, as they continued to bleed and become tangled. "It hurts, don't touch it!" She twitched. "Bleeding!" She squealed.

Even with a frown, the scars at the corners of his mouth gave him a permanent smile, "I just want to help. Allow me to help. Will you?" He reached into his pocket, and pulled out a small leather pouch. He opened the pouch, and pulled out a piece of sap candy, "You'll get this whole pouch of sap candy, if you'll allow me to help. You want it?"

Thorn paused, mismatched hues now on the couch of sap candy. "Is it good?" She asked, cocking her head to the side. "If so, then Thorn will let Hound help." She smiled at him, holding out her bloodied hands to him, the wire in rather deep.

Hound nodded as he set the pouch on the counter, "It is good. I wouldn't have it, if it was terrible." He gently took her one of her hands, and slowly pulled the barbed wire away from it. He bit it, and continued until that hand was free and the barbed wire lay on the floor in bits at their feet. He did the same to her other hand, and pulled out a roll of wool bandages from his pocket. He wrapped her hands in bandages, and picked up the pouch. He held the pouch out, despite his hands, mouth, neck, shoulders, chest and stomach being covered in blood, "You've earned this for being good."

As he began to remove the barbed wire, Thorn squeaked, and gritted her teeth as it slid from her skin. ".. Owwie." She frowned, the pain shooting through her hands, until they were finally free. As he wrapped bandages around the wounds, she winced and hissed a little. "Does Thorn have to wear these?" She took the pouch with her mouth, since she needed time for her hands to heal, which would not take long.

Hound nodded and smiled.

"What's this?" The bearded man asked suddenly, standing off to the side of the bar area, dressed in his simple crimson and turquoise entertainer's tunic, watching as the scene went on.

"VenVen, Thorn does not get the candy unless I do all of this!"

Disgusted at the scene, both of them covered in blood, he approached slowly, looking to the taller mohawked man. "Get out of my tavern. And leave Thorn alone."

"Ha. Puny man. You don't scare me. I won't. I'm having fun with my new pet here..."

"Won't, doesn't apply here. Get out before I throw you out."

Hound gave him a sinister, toothy grin, drawing a large dagger, it's blade coated in flaky, dried blood and dulled by it. "Let's see then, shall we?"

Not wanting to get any more blood anywhere, and to avoid killing an abusive nut job in the Dragon's Head, and not wanting to play or challenge himself, Venser disappeared in a puff of thick red smoke and appeared in front of the rabid dog man, tackling him to the floor and gripping him tight. And with that, they both disappeared in a puff of thick red smoke.

Sanna screamed and moved back. And just next door to their room an auburn haired woman opened the door to her room and peeked out, a pink haired naked elf seen here in bed.

"Oh gods... Thorn what happened?!" Alex exclaimed quickly putting on a robe and grabbing her saber, rushing out of her room followed by a concerned Kira a few seconds later. The ditzy demoness was munching on the candy, looking out the window. Thorn twitched, and shook her head, hopping around on all fours. "Tsh-... Tsh-... Ba!" She blurted out, waving her arms above her head, before falling on to her rear with a small thump. Her spiny tail swishing around. "VenVen went to fight the scary man!"

A little more than a mile behind the tavern was a great blue lake that Venser, the patrons, and some villagers often visited in the warmer months to swim and boat. Often used for recreation and fishing, it was a truly wonderful place.

"Oof!" Hound found himself being flung at a thousand miles per hour and then suddenly slammed headfirst into the ground, falling onto his back, the world spun around him as he quickly shot back up. " ARGHHHH...! I'LL RIP YOUR FUCKING THROAT OUT!"

FFFFZZZZZZZZZZZZZZZZZZZZZ!

Every brain cell inside of Hound's brain lit up like a firework as Venser blasted him with a continuous burst of magical green lightning that emanated from his fingertips. The next short few seconds were very painful, the rabid dog man flailed around on the ground, his convulsions wild and prolonged.

Breathing slowly Hound raised a finger, smoke coming off of him, burnt flesh filling the air. "I'll come back to cut open your woman's belly... Heh heh heh heh heh..."

FZZZZZZZZZZZZZZZZZZZZZZZZZZZZZZZ!

The bearded man knew exactly his kind the moment he saw Hound. No one hurt or threatened his friends and loved ones, especially Thorn, a woman he considered almost like his own sister. Now he just had to go make sure she was okay, walking away from the smoking corpse now. No. He turned to it, and had to dispose of the man's body first. Somewhere in the forest, in a ditch to be forgotten about.

To make sure the tall man with the mohawk and improvised armor was dead, Venser delivered a hard stomp right to the front of his face. A sickening crunch. The so called rabid dog man was dead.

CHAPTER THIRTY-TWO: SEPHIRA

Castle De Seraphim, Pryldahn, 1436 ATC

God Queen Y'vonne, for once, could be found outside of the castle, her pet dragon Gummy lingering close by her side like he always did. She sat on the stairs, her knees bent and her face resting in her open palms. She looked rather... Troubled. Gummy sat, curled near her feet, sniffing about and on the watch. Alert for anything, while the sad little God Queen sat, wallowing in her somber mood.

A yawn was heard behind her followed by the soft pattering of maroon leather boots. "Evening Vo- Y'vonne." A familiar voice said from behind her. "Evening... Er, Rex?" Venser sat down beside the obnoxiously thin God Queen, wearing his unusual rubber suit with rubber nipples and an oversized codpiece he wore less and less these days but with a fruit hat made of real fruit on his head and he was carrying a bone white guitar. "You look troubled." He reached up and plucked a grape from his hat, offering it to her.

"Want a grape?"

The woman acted like she didn't even notice as the odd bearded man with a hat made of random assortments approached her and sat by her side. "Hello." She said with a small smile She took the grape without even looking in his direction and slowly placed it in her mouth and chewed it quietly. "What makes you think I'm... Troubled?" Gummy just moved out of the way now to give Venser enough space to sit, though he did it with an annoyed growl as he settled on the other side of the woman.

Venser extended a gloved finger to her face, twirling a bit. "The face. You look... Drunk? No- Fuck. Blurry. Fuck- I mean the word you said. Troubled! Heh heh, lost the word... Sorry Y'vonne. How could I lose such a word?" He popped a grape into his mouth and added, "And you're sitting here staring into nothing. C'mon, something serious is on your mind."

The obnoxiously tall and thin woman groaned a bit and glanced over to her side where Gummy sat. "It's... Nothing. Just, something I am mildly concerned about." Y'vonne extended a delicate hand and started to pat the skulled head of the miniature wyvern and it gave a soft whine of approval. She didn't like to talk about her problems. Just something she never did with others. No even with her family when they were actually around.

"Like what kind of problems?" He asked biting into a green apple he had plucked from his hat as wall, watching her closely as the juice dribbled down his bearded chin. "I also noticed you weren't there when I was entertaining the staff. Besides, talking about your problems always makes you feel better."

Finally.

Y'vonne turned her electric blue stare toward Venser, cringing a bit at his lack of manners but was also appreciative of his company at the moment. "Eh... It's just... This Taitasu fellow that's been staying here recently..." She began to rub the back of her neck a bit hesitant about talking about this subject with well... Anyone.

"Who? Eh?" Venser asked with a mouthful of apple. "Is this guy bothering you? Was he in the dining hall earlier?"

"Not... Directly no." Y'vonne groaned and covered her face with both of her hands now, which now caused her voice to be muffled slightly. "He acts very strangely. He's a freed elf fellow who follows me around like a lost pup." She began to run her hands down her face, dragging her skin a bit as she did so. "He's odd, socially incorrect, and..." She turned her head sideways and leaned a bit toward her dear friend and spoke lowly. "And he actually murdered a resident here because the poor man said something inappropriate to me." She closed her eyes and inhaled. "Strangled him to death he did."

"By the void, like one of the servants?" Venser said frowning as he looked to her. "Alright, Y'vonne. I may not talk to you like I should since you are royalty, but I talk to everyone the same but by the void... I'm sorry you had to see that..." He sighed and rubbed his eyes. "Perhaps we need to double your bodyguards? Or make you more aloof?"

He snapped his fingers. "We can disguise you as an octopus next time he comes around!"

"I... Do not see how me dressing as an- Oh never minded."

With a roll of her eyes, the woman shook her head back and forth. "A man came to speak with me regarding some things some things and… He said something rather vulgar and this elf man comes up from behind him and…" The God Queen exhaled out in frustration and stood, her light footsteps tapping fast against the stone as she began to pace. "I just don't know what to do with him. He's odd and strange but yet sweet and harmless. I do not know what is wrong with him. It is like he does not know how to act around people!" Gummy tilted his head at the actions of his master and whined in what could only be described as an agreeing huff. "He says strange things to me and I want to call him out on his place but I have no place to give. He is a guest here and I do not rule this castle, therefore I have no true power here…" She was gesturing wildly with her hands, something she often did when she wanted to get a point across. "At least until my father returns from above."

"Sounds like me when I was young. Before, "He paused and gestured to his face, the scars hidden beneath his beard and his eyes, and the fruit hat he wore on his head. "Clearly there's something odd going on in his head. You know, Y'vonne, you may not be the god king but you're his daughter. You have SOME power if not all of it. You are pretty much my employer since our God Emperor doesn't have the time of day for every single servant, employee and family member."

Y'vonne eyed him, now truly taking in the scars that were on his face. "So…You know what he is going through perhaps? What do you think he could be thinking?" A chilly gust of wind suddenly blew across the castle causing the princess to shudder and hug herself. "My power is useless in this castle." She said in a whisper. The jester was right though, and Von knew it deep down. "Even if I did have power I would know how to use it." She shook her head again. "Maybe he'll leave soon and not cause any more trouble than he already has." Not likely, based on the type of luck she's been having. "Funny, I oversee all of Pryldahn while my father is away… And yet, I don't oversee the very walls in which I reside."

The bearded man waved his hand in a dismissive manner. "I'll have words with him… Thinking he can strangle someone and get away with it…"

Sanna rested in one of the chairs inside, having fallen asleep whilst humming to the young one inside of her belly, but she wasn't the only one that had come to visit. Beside a tree that the golden gypsy loved so much, the ghost that had watched them before now stood leaned against the trunk. She seemed more… Solid this time and upon distant viewing one would confuse her for being alive, but she was a woman who was long dead. This time, though, she had silvery hair. Beautiful, pearlescent, shimmering locks that flowed down her back and swayed freely in the wind. Her eyes matched their hue, looking out upon the sun whose warmth she would never feel again... Never did, but now she could at least look at it. Her soft singing carried on the wind, the language an old one, but familiar to the father-to-be. Sanna couldn't hear it, it seemed, and slept on dreaming pleasantly in the chair.

The bearded man slowly plucked a few strings on the guitar he held, listening to Y'vonne. "You do have power; you just don't know how to use it. Ordering your servants ago is the first step, though. It sounds to me he has quite the liking towards you. The second step, all the paperwork and what ruling you actually do in your father's stead..." Venser was ignorant of the ghost watching them while Sanna rested him inside after his performance. "Wait... Listen Y'vonne..."

"Wha? Likes me?" She snorted, which was out of character for her. Though now, her sensitive ears picked up what sounded like singing. It was a gentle voice, and Y'vonne almost wanted to stop and listen but then shook her head and decided to ignore it. "... Is that. Your lover, Venser?"

After a few moments the singing stopped, the figure turning away from the tree to walk toward the open doors of the castle. The woman glided as she walked but as she approached the doors she didn't enter, her fingers grazing the door's frame but never entreating past it as though something held her back from doing so... Perhaps the fact she was more than a mere spirit due to what she was when she passed, or perhaps because of the sleeping woman she watched with saddened eyes in the chair. She glanced over to the other two for a moment before turning away again, simply stepping away from the door and leaning against the side of the wall away from them. She was not playing coy, but rather avoiding any awkwardness due to the fact she'd caused some earlier. She was at least glad the mother-to-be was sleeping well.

"Yeah. I mean, when I was a young creepy bastard with poor social skills that's what I did. But that was long ago and a time I prefer not to remember." Venser said with a pause shooting up. "Holy shit I think I'm being stalked by a ghost that wants to suck my cock and take advantage of me!" He then proceeded to make his way inside the castle, pushing the heavy iron doors open to go check on Sanna. "Not like... I mean, as much as I love, ya know..."

"Ah, I see..." Von thought on this for a moment and then physically cringed as Venser shouted his next choice of words. Yah know? She might have preferred the company of the murderous stalker over Venser right now.

"If that man would calm down and ask why I'm here, he'd find I'm not in the slightest interested in sucking him off. Aside from being dead, I also would much prefer his wife." The woman spoke as Venser made his way inside the castle and she gave an apologetic look to the other. "We met under rather... Embarrassing circumstances. Embarrassing for him, anyway." Sanna was fine but as he came inside the castle she stirred a little, rubbing her eyes. The woman approached the other and bowed her head respectfully. "I was here to watch over the young mother."

"Says the woman who watched us for who knows how long as we... As I... Whatever." The bearded man said still holding his guitar as he looked to the ghostly woman, skin the same color as his instrument, speaking loud and clear enough to wake Sanna. "Why?"

"I was only there for a few moments. I had already been there to watch over your wife, and your sudden arrival somewhat stunned me. As far as why I watch her, she carries that which I have lost time and time again. She's young, innocent and does not know herself. I was already inhabiting the Dragon's Head to a degree before her arrival or even yours... I simply chose not to let myself be seen." Her gaze was serious, none of the playful wittiness in them anymore. Sanna woke to his words and instantly moved a hand over her belly, standing slowly to approach Venser.

"We're not married. Not yet, anyways." Venser said watching her with serious eyes. "So... You watch her because she's young and innocent? And that's what you lost? You still look young to me... Serph..."

"Sephiria. Ah, I thought you were. She seems to adore you as a wife would a husband." Her silver eyes shifted to crimson and she gave a gentle nod to the golden gypsy, who squeaked and hid her face behind her lover. "I am far from young. I only look like this because of what I was... And it wasn't my youth I lost. It was my innocence and my children."

The bearded man sat down next to Sanna, wrapping an arm around her protectively. "What happened to you, Sephiria?"

The golden gypsy nestled into his arms and the baby kicked gently, bringing a little smile to her face. She wrapped her arms around his waist and kissed his cheek as if to assure him she was alright, and Sephiria seemed to stiffen for a moment... Then relax. She folded her hands in front of her, sitting down a little to their right but not too close. "A lot happened to me, young man. Too much to recant. Miscarriage, stillbirth, murder, rape... Just to give you a taste of it. With what I was, my being a target came as no surprise."

"Oh I'm so sorry... And it must be horrible to wander now as you are. A ghost. Having to remember all that." Venser said with a sympathetic look softly taking in everything she said. "No wonder you watch my lover here..."

"The hilarious part is that I died in combat... An honorable death, but still disgraceful. Eaten by a Pardusese, can you imagine it? Cat food." She chuckled, seemingly light hearted about her death and having accepted it, but there was definitely something still keeping her from passing on. Sanna listened to the woman and seemed to relax, looking up to Venser before finally speaking. "What are you?" Sanna asked, her tone shaky though she couldn't help that. Sephiria looked to her near-identical counterpart and smiled a little, brushing a silvery tendril behind her ear. "I was one of the first of the Transcendents. Blood sucker, bat bitch, witch, whatever you will... Nonetheless, we were the dhampir. The Trepahs bloodline."

Venser was so unsure how to feel about Sephiria as he looked up to her, picking a few grapes out of his hat and popping them into his mouth. "How does a vampire dying after being eaten by a panther man become a ghost... Never heard of the Transcendents. Or the Trepahs bloodline."

The golden gypsy perked an eyebrow toward Venser as he popped grapes from his hat into his mouth, shrugging it off as she spoke again. "Even I do not know the answer to that, especially considering said dragon devoured my soul first before my body. As far as the Transcendents and the Trepahs, it's a good thing you've not heard of them and it's best you forget the name. There is a lot of bad blood, no joke intended, with that name. What I can tell you is that a Transcendent Vampire, which is what I was, is as close to a god as a vampire can become. We can live for up to a million years or more, and our abilities are very strong. Alas, there is only one left that I know of, I was with the vampire's child when I was killed."

"Then shouldn't you be trapped inside the belly of the panther man?" Venser asked listening to her. "Interesting... I sort of know what a dhampir is either. So many varieties of vampires! Ya know? Where I come from such things are myths."

"You would think so, but again; I do not know nor understand it. Perhaps the little one?" She wondered to herself, shaking her head. "Impossible." Sephiria continued muttering to herself in debate about it and Sanna looked in Ven's emerald slitted eyes. "She's not going to hurt us, I don't think. Even though I've never seen her kind before, but the name is familiar. There were only stories of her, though."

"I am only here to watch. I apologize, again." Sephira said fading away, much to the confusion of everyone present.

CHAPTER THIRTY-THREE: TAITSAU'S CONFRONTATION

The farmlands, Pryldahn, 1436 ATC

Discovering that this freed elf who had been stalking the God Queen, Taitsau Selkanor had a decent bounty on him and apparently had strangled several men in the area, Venser stood in front of the mirror examining a new outfit he had bought. A simple grey woolen tunic and a darker waterproof leather poncho with an asymmetrical cape. Akin to what smallfolk mostly wore and along with the cape, along with the utility belt he had added, it had style. His classic outfit, the red rubber suit with rubber nipples and an oversized codpiece stood out way too much. His entertainer tunic did as well with its colors. This one, rather drab, drew less attention.

He pulled his grey hood over his head, and followed it up with something that would draw attention. The porcelain theater comedy mask with a wide smile. An odd choice, but not like it would matter in the end, anyways. The bearded man made sure his wrist bow was secure on his left arm, and made sure he had his strange folding blade with him. Not only would he ease the God Queen's worries, but also snag himself a fine bounty.

The elven man began shuffling his feet through the plains around Castle De Seraphim, footsteps growing heavier with each step. He was wandering for a mere few months, and it was lonesome and tiring but he trekked forward, low on supplies he knew he would have to stop soon. "Possibly at this little cottage..." He thought to himself, only having about twenty more steps until he reached, seeing a modest cottage with a small garden on the side and a horse hitched to a post atop a small hill. Once finally atop he was welcomed with a gentle breeze, whisking his hair in a sly wave. Grinning and closing his eyes while this happened... He enjoyed it when the elements decided to be friendly. The man reached into his pack and pulled out a half-eaten biscuit which he had finished, it being the last portion of his food with no water left in his skin already. The fog was slightly heavy but finally moved itself from the hills and mountains. He had grinned and rested for a little under ten minutes before returning to his trek. His ears perked, twitching against the air as they picked up on some commotion coming inside. His stomach dropped and he began feeling eager and nervous with each footstep he moved himself to the front door, removing his studded belt and kicking the door open, stepping right into an argument between a farmer and his wife. The middle aged couple stopped and looked to him.

"I need your horse, your food, and your coin everything you have hidden!"

He reached to his shoulders to unclasp his long fur like cape, removing it from his form and held it in his arms... Letting it drag on the floor slightly as he took a few steps more around the place, making himself comfortable. His forest green eyes shot from one area to the next to take in the settings to again. Enjoy it for the moment he was there, he wasn't expecting to stay long unless he had a reason. And he didn't. Glancing down to the corpse of the balding man against the wall, his wife bound and gagged and terrified beyond all belief he sighed. First, he would rest, eat, and then strangle the woman, watching the light leave her eyes. The farmer, put up a quick resistance and Taitsau quickly put an end to him, slashing him across the stomach with his short katana before stabbing him through the heart. Much too fast for his taste. The wife, he was going to go slow with her...

Until a voice came from the front door, a voice that was deeper and richer in a soothing and yet intimidating way when spoken in the right tone.

"Tittysoup Sulkanor, I presume." Said Venser, hood up, the sun casting a shade hiding his eyes beneath the hood, smiling mask covering his face.

"What the... How'd you find me so fast?" The elf asked, scowling and rising from his seat, drawing his short katana. "Whose helping you track me?! What other bounty hunter? Severus of Pryldahn? The Hound? I think he was actually a demon!" He spat on the ground.

"All me. A freed elf walking all the way from the capital to the farmlands dressed like you... I just asked around if anyone had witnessed you. And I was planning on coming out here anyways looking for property." Venser said with a shrug, glancing down to the blade on his belt for a second, then to the short blade the elf held in one hand. He looked again to the corpse and the terrified older woman, face stained with tears and screaming for help beneath the gag in her mouth.

"No more innocent people are going to be strangled to death just for the fun of it. Or be tied up or be afraid of you." Venser boldly boasted promptly, causing the elf to laugh.

"What? Seriously? Pffffft... Ha ha ha... Next thing you're going to tell me is that you're going to be the first man on the moon. Smug piece of trash!" Taitsau hissed, lunging at Venser with surprising speed.

"Argh! Fuck!" The short katana left a shallow cut in Venser's left shoulder before he could repulse the elven strangler's attack.

The man in the grey tunic jumped back, reaching his left hand out to pull a garden hoe to him in a green aura, holding it with both hands and using all his strength he tried to counter the elve's quick strikes. Every blow the man tried to make himself was instantly blocked, though with each block he seemed to knock him off balance as they took the fight outside.

Taitsau started hopping around now like a deranged spider monkey, trying to confuse the man in the grey tunic. Venser wasn't having it. Why was he even bothering playing with this man? The man threw the garden hoe at the elf and extended his left hand, his mark flashing greenish white as forked green lightning burst from his fingertips, causing the elf to fly back into the garden and writhe in pain.

The elf had a surprisingly strong resistance to the supernatural lightning, rolling around in the dirt and hopping to his feet, drawing a dagger from his boot, recovered from the waves of raw alien magic he had just endured. Or at least, he tried his best, he was starting to falter, panting heavily.

"How about this? We make this fair. No lightning, no weapons. Just good ol' fisticuffs, man to man!" Venser proclaimed, holding both hands up, palms facing towards Taitsau.

"I don't think so!" The elf made a dash towards the man in the grey tunic, only for Venser to disappear in a puff of thick red smoke, the scent of wine and freshly cut roses filling the air. In a second he appeared right behind Taitsau, grabbing him around the waist, lifting him up with all his strength, and rolling backwards to slam the elf's head onto the ground, the angle seriously damaging his skull and neck.

Taitsau gave a violent twitch, trying to get up, recover, do something. Gripping his blades tight, he pushed off the ground, only for Venser to deliver a swift kick right into his face. "Gahhhh.... Argghhhh!" Choking up blood, the elf swiped at the man with his short katana, only for the man top stomp on his hand and kick his weapons away. Clearly dying, Taitsau lay face down in the dirt and closed his eyes.

"At least I... I..." He went silent as Venser came up from behind, choking him until he expired with the end of his asymmetrical grey cape.

"To think Y'vonne didn't order the guards to skewer you when they... When she heard about that man you strangled in the castle. And he wasn't the first... Bah." Venser dropped his body into the dirt of the garden and picked up the short katana, letting out a sharp sigh and looking to the wound on his shoulder. It didn't matter right now. He cut the farmer's wife free and wrapped her in a blanket, leading her outside to her horse and telling her to get to the capital as fast as she could.

His emerald slitted eyes watched as the horse rode off as fast as it possibly could, carrying the distressed woman while Venser sat with the corpse and awaited the guards to tell them more of the story and so he would claim the bounty.

Once he gave his report to the local guards and made sure the farmer's wife was compensated for her loss, he would go to his dear friend Y'vonne and inform her she wouldn't be seeing that creep Taitsau again.

CHAPTER THIRTY-FOUR: MARVELLA

The town of Montpelier, Vorland, 1436 ATC

Inside their modest two story home on the edge of town, Kari Fullbuster had been sitting in the kitchen fixing from food in her sleeveless black dress and black stocking with white ugg like boots on. Her white blonde hair was bouncing on her shoulders as she moved around.

Someone lifted up the back of her dress from behind. "Nice dress. I think you'd look better wearing nothing at all." Venser's voice said, as if he had been there the whole time, his voice richer and deeper than most human's, much to the blonde girl's delight.

She looked up and turned to him and smiled. "Thank you, and of course you would think so." She winked an icy blue eye at him.

"So, the twins. Where are they?" He asked smelling the food. "What's cookin'?"

Kari smiled. "I'm baking cookies, and they should be playing in their room right now."

"Excellent. You know, it was their fourth birthday recently. And I've been busy as of late. Did you do anything?" He asked walking over to the oven, opening it up to look at the cookies. "Hm." Venser walked behind Kari, and then placed both hands on her breasts, fondling them. "You've gotten bigger..." He opened his mouth to speak, but forgot what he was gonna say.

Kari smiled while shaking her head. "Maybe a little. I've gotten them both a gift it's on the table." She pointed at the table.

"Really? Just one gift each?" Venser asked placing his hands on her waist, and dry humping her from behind looking over to the table. "I got them a few toys and some clothes, and one big present outside."

Still grinning, Kari blinked a few times and glanced at the door to the kitchen." They are playing with the other gift I gave them. It couldn't be... Put into a box."

"Hmm... What is it?" Venser asked smacking her rear, laughing a bit.

"A pet rabbit." Kari said with a smirk, leaning against the oven with a smirk. "I know we didn't actually agree to it much less discuss actually being them pets..."

"Lucinda always wanted a bunny. And Soarin a kitty." He stared off at the wall, absentmindedly removing his cloak, tossing it in the corner and pulling down his baggy red pants. "Did you get them both? Or should I go out and get a kitty for Soarin?"

"The kitty should be awake soon, it's in our room right now."

"Ah ah, good good. How have you and the children been?" He asked hiking up her dress, and pulling down her panties. Acting real casual. The bearded man let out a low, seductive growl and trailed many soft, sweet kisses on Kari's neck, and she pressed against him and smiled in response. "I think we got a few minutes before the cookies are done and they rush in here..."

"They have been doing wonderfully, even been doing good at learning how to read earlier than most children in small children's books, and I've been doing pretty good." About ten seconds later, Soarin and Lucinda walked into the room, Lucinda holding the baby bunny as they looked at their parents. "Daddy!" They cheered at him.

He bent her over against a counter near the over, grabbing his now hard cock and positioning it properly to enter Kari. Venser shoved himself into her womanhood and began to thrust in and out, holding her waist while looking down to her. "Mhm!" When the kids walked in he stopped, looking at them. "Umm... Go to your room! We're having a fight!"

Kari's cheeks burned red upon her porcelain skin as she heard the twins. "Soarin, Lucy, go back to your room please." They frowned, "Okay... We will." They said as they went back to their room and left the door open, glancing back curiously before running off again.

"Go, the cookies aren't ready yet." Venser said raising his voice, putting his hand in front of the action going on. He sighed, still inside Kari. "Umm... You don't mind this, do you?"

Kari nodded. "I don't." Giggling, she said. "You know I love stuff like this." A thin hand reaching out to turn down the heat.

"And the kids saw us going at it..." He said extending his left hand, trapping the knob for the over in a green aura. He turned it down even lower so Kari wouldn't burn her cookies. "You need a tan..." He said playfully smacking her pale, bare butt as he sped up his thrusting.

She moaned a bit, "Mhmmm I don't think so... I already look so doll like I think a tan would ruin my looks..."

Venser took himself out and moaned in pleasure, smacking his rock hard member against her soft rump. Venser turned Kari around and smiled, wrapping his arms around her waist and rubbing his crotch against hers. "Why don't we get naked... The kids can handle themselves for about ten or fifteen minutes right?"

She grinned as she kissed him, "I think they can. Alex and Marvella should be home soon."

He kissed her back, enjoying the pleasure. "Lift your arms..."

The blonde girl lifted her arms, obeying him. "Oh wait." She quickly cleared the table and leaned against it, shaking her chest at her bearded lover and smiling more.

Venser slid off Kari's black dress, and then unhooked her lacy blue bra, throwing it on the floor. He removed the rest of his outfit except for his boots, and lifted Kari up onto the kitchen table. He locked lips with her and slid inside of Kari, her pussy hugging his cock in a new way than ever before.

She moaned as he slid inside her has she kissed him.

"You like that? Huh? Huh?" Venser asked groaning a bit, rattling his cock along the inner walls of her slit. He loved how the two were naked, aside from their boots, doing it in the kitchen. He lowered his had and began to kiss her neck, then suck on it in certain places.

The younger blonde woman sighed as she moaned, letting Venser do all the work. "Yeeess, it is wonderful."

"Hmhm... Yes... We should be having an audience for this, right? Us on a stage..." Venser asked starting to get really heated up, kinda feeling the urge to cum already. As if... He was just getting started. But they did have to make this semi-quick. He placed his hands on her breasts again and fondled her, tweaking her nipples.

She smiled. "That sounds like a fun idea." She let out an adorable squeak a bit at the tweaking.

He held her waist down and began to ram into Kari quickly, moaning more as he thrust in and out rapidly. The blonde girl moaned loudly as he did so, wrapping her arms and legs around his lean, muscular body.

The bearded man held her waist down and began to ram into Kari quickly, moaning more as he thrust in and out rapidly. While they both moaned loudly. Venser fucking her on the counter in the kitchen. Those outside of it could hear them getting it on. Thankfully the kids didn't all the way in their rooms.

Kari's sister in arms, one of the other local defenders of the town, Marvella, walked into the house after a good training session. She heard loud moaning from two people as she walked in the kitchen. "My my, what do we have here?" She smirked. Kari meanwhile was moaning. Marvella Fullbuster had a slender body and noticeably thick hips, about four years older than Kari, fair skin, strange purple eyes, dark hair tied back, pink lips, rosy cheeks. A black headband with small numbers of red jewels, a pair of earrings consisting of white round with and orange border with silver chain on either sides, and a black combat uniform that seemed to be mended in several parts.

Venser stopped thrusting into his blonde lover, and pulled out, looking to the woman he didn't see as often, though they still were on good terms. Pretty good at times, actually. "Um... Me and Kari were baking cookies." Said the man who was naked except for his boots, with a slick hard on.

Kari sighed. "Marvella, what are you doing here so early?" The purple eyed woman smirked still and as she stood in the doorway. "Making cookies huh? Must be good ones.

"Yeah. Yeah. Really good cookies." Venser said looking to Marvella, then over to Kari. Absentmindedly he stuck his left hand out and began to rub Kari's bare clit slowly as they both stood sweaty and naked in front of Kar's combat partner. "Chocolate chip. And... We are making, other things right now. Yeah."

Kari sighed from the touch as the purple eyed woman walked over to them,"Mmmm, my favorite." Marvella bit her lip watching the two going at it in the kitchen.

"Right..." Venser said blushing, feeling real awkward about being caught. His penis throbbed a bit as she approached them. He still rubbed Kari's slit while he watched Marvella.

Marvella walked over and touched his barreled chest softly. "Very nice looks... Your cooking wear... Or should I say, lack thereof?" She traced a fingertip around his nipple. "I don't see aprons on either of you..."

Venser growled seductively when she did that, looking back to Kari. "Should she join us for some fun?" Venser asked with a naughty grin.

Kari blushed harder now. "I guess so since she is here now." Marvella smiled, "Sounds like fun, I know Doll there is okay with it as well." She winked.

"She is, yeah. Let's get these clothes off..." Venser said running his hands along Marvella's chest, squeezing her bigger breasts.

Marvella smiled as she slipped her jacket off while he did so.

"Kari... Go over to the table where we eat, and lay down. On your stomach, and your ass in the air." Venser said as he ripped open the front of Marvella's shirt aggressively. He grabbed her right hand and placed it on his rock hard cock, using it to rub up and down his shaft.

Kari nodded as she climbed onto the table and got on her stomach with her ass in the air like she just don't care. Marvella smiled as she took her pants off with her other hand.

The bearded man quickly pulled her panties down afterwards, wrapped his arms around her waist, and pulled Marvella into him. So that their bare skin was pressed together, and his cock poked at Marvella's crotch. She needed to shave down there soon. "Now you... Marvella." He gripped her ass with both hands. "Lay on top of Kari, on your stomach."

Marvella smiled, "Of course handsome." She lied on Kari, on her stomach. Kari looked at them both.

Venser walked along the floors of the kitchen over to them, as Marvella laid on top of Kari. He looked over both of their asses, trailing his hands down them. "Nice nice... Choices. I love choices." He said teasing Kari, rubbing his cock against her pussy before spreading Marvella's rump apart, and then sticking his hardened member deep into her. "Mhm! You feel different..." He said giving her one hard thrust, followed by slower ones.

"'Ah Ven!" Marvella moaned as she was thrusted in, Kari blushed while sighing a bit.

"Mhm! Yeah... Yeah... You like that, don't ya?" Venser asked smacking her rump as hard as he could, leaving a red hand print. He took himself out and lowered himself a bit, shoving into Kari's cunny now. He wiggled his cock around in her for a few seconds, then gave her several, slow but hard thrusts.

SHLP SHCALP PLAP.

"Ahh...!" Kari gasped as she moaned. A dumb, happy grin came across her face, feeling as if she were in blissful paradise. "Who... Ah who wouldn't like this?" she said as she touched his and her skin seductively.

PAP SCHLAP PLAP PAP.

The handsome green eyed man took turns with both of them. Fucking Kari from behind for a minute, before switching over to Marvella. Since Marvella was on top, Kari could feel Venser thrusting. All three of them started to become very hot during the fast, and furious fucking. "Yes... Mhm." He loved the sounds of his skin slapping against Marvella's as he spread her cheeks apart while thrusting quickly from behind. "You two wanna suck me off soon?"

Kari and Marvella were blushing hard and exchanging pleased moans during all the time that their bearded lover took turns with their holes. "Mhmmm... Do you really need to ask Ven?" Marvella asked.

Venser slowly pulled his cock out of Marvella, it was slick from both her and Kari's fluids. He walked around the table, shaking up his can of whipped cream. "You can go first..." He said rubbing his shaft up in down in front of Kari's face.

Kari put her lips around his shaft as she started sucking on him slowly.

"Yeah... This feels good..." He looked up to the purple eyed woman. "Don't want you to miss out. Hmmm..." He grabbed a chair, pulling his cock away from Kari's mouth and sitting down, backing away from the table so they would have room. "Both of you can take turns... Share now, and don't fight you two."

They grinned as they took turns sucking on his dick starting with Marvella starting out slow and then faster each time.

"Ah fuck this is nice..." Venser said with a smile and a sigh, relaxing back, petting the two of them as they hungrily sucked on his member.

They smiled as they kept taking turns while enjoying themselves.

"Keep going..." He said looking down to them. "Harder... Deeper...'

They kept going as they sucked harder and deeper each time they sucked him off.

"Ahh oh yes..." Venser gripped Marvella's head, holding her still, he started to thrust mercilessly, making the purple eyed woman gag on his shaft. She looked up at him, with his handsome face and chiseled body, enjoying the look of lust on his face as she and her sister in arms pleased him. Kari held his ass, feeling the muscles flex, feeling how hard he faced fucked Marvella. "Hey now, don't hog it all."

He thrust his dick past Marvella's lips while she was savoring his taste and started hammering away like an animal. "Oh ahh." Kari's icy blue eyes widened watching the scene just inches away from her face. This was fine. In fact, it was exactly what she had hoped for when Ven had come home today. The purple eyed woman just sucked him down, letting him use her throat.

"Yes. Yes. Yes!" Venser shuddered, stroking Marvella's dark brown hair worshipfully. She raked her nails over his thighs, belly, and ass. The softness of his body wasn't bad. Whilst Ven trained a lot, not often as her, she thought of him as a bit little bit of a teddy bear, really. Fun to stroke. Fun to squeeze. Marvella could easily beat him in a spar, she was sure. But soon her hands were pulled away from that lovely body as Kari took his cock now.

SHLK SHLP SHLP SIP.

"C'mon, we gotta make this fast..." Kari said while Marvella rolled her eyes. "I know. Fine."

Marvella pushed two fingers against her clit and two more up into her cunny. Delight filled the blonde girl as Venser tangled his fingers in her hair and drove his hips forward. Sweet, hard flesh pushed past her lips and into the top of her throat.

She welcomed it, doing her best not to gag, lest she threw up or something. Beside Kari, her sister in arms pushed her fingers against her clit and pushed the fingers inside deeper. Her pussy flexed and twitched in response to her touch. "You two are naughty..."

Soon, he began to shake. Kari pushed him back, so that only his flare was in her mouth, stroking his shaft as fast as he could. The flare spread, filling her mouth from side to side. Venser's tightened, and he started shaking uncontrollably.

SHF SHF SHF SHF SHF SHF.

"Oh, that's it love!" He ejaculated, as hot, musky love juice started to squirt in Kari's mouth.

"Mhmmmmm...!" The blonde girl groaned around the mouthful. She loved the taste of Venser's seed. Did it taste good? Well. Not like you'd want to drink a cup of it. But it was his seed. It meant her handsome love had had a good time with her body, and she loved it for that. Though, for a brief second Kari felt sad, reflecting on the fact after giving birth to their twins, Soarin and Lucinda, the birth was so traumatic that she would never be able to have children again. Either way, she loved them all.

"That was so good..." Kari said taking Venser's cock out of her mouth and standing up to quickly redress along with Marvella and the man himself. Though, Marvella couldn't help but give Venser a few more sucks, licking him clean.

"Good thing I turned the heat down. The cookies should be done now." Kari commented opening the oven to inspect her work. Perfectly fluffy and golden brown, nicely slow cooked.

"Yeah." He started to dress and the purple eyed woman touched his hip. "Both of you had a good time, right?"

The two girls grinned from ear to ear. "The best. Can't wait for tonight when the kids are asleep..."

Dressed in his crimson and turquoise entertainer's tunic with baggy red pants and bright red boots, he looked to Marvella as she finished dressing again, leaving her jacket on one of the chairs. "Hey I was going to ask, are you going to the barbeque tomorrow?"

"What barbeque?" She asked curiously.

"The one where I slap my meat against your grill! Ahahahahaha!"

CHAPTER THIRTY-FIVE: STAR LOVE

The Dragon's Head Tavern and Inn, Vorland, 1437 ATC

The barmaid known as Brea Rowland hummed a familiar tune as she climbed the stairs from the kitchen. In her hands was an overfilled tray of molasses cookies, sweet, spicy, and soft. She had them stacked in a cone-like fashion, with one single cookie on top at the point of this edible pyramid. "Good evening, Venser." She greeted with a slight bow of the head as she placed her cookie tray down at the end of the bar. By the time she had said hello to her boss, the whole upper balcony smelled like cookies.

A cardboard cutout behind the bar greeted Brea with the same arrogant, somewhat sinister smile on its face, amplified by the Glasgow smile his face that ran from ear to ear. His clean shaven, younger self. Made about when he was twenty-six. And a look he tried to distance himself further and further from these days. Growing the beard not only out of depression, but to hide the scars. And even meeting his new loves along with everything, he just decided to keep it.

For some reason, today, Venser looked a little unnerving. Maybe it was the lighting, maybe it was because she had been in that kitchen for a while. "Cookie?" She said, picking the topmost cookie off of the stack and handing it to her boss.

"Why the fuck are you offering a cookie to a cutout?" The bearded man himself asked sitting at a nearby table, slumped in his seat, bone white guitar on his lap as he plucked the strings. "Fucking thing." He mumbled to himself tuning it. "I don't know what's real anymoreeeeeeee. Oh ho ho... But there's you, and there's me. Our souls are written in destiny. How can I, disagreeeeee? Moon kissed skin, soft as silk, your arms, their holding me gently. Our love is written in the stars, don't deny who you areeeeeeeeeee. Oop!" He knocked over an empty cider bottle he had set near his feet. Venser just stared blankly out the window watching the snowfall, with a lit cannabis cigar in one hand and a bottle of cider in the other. It had been a long fall, as well as winter, and it was only one day into the new year.

Brea jumped, dropping the cookie onto the floor, letting it explode into crumbs. "Oh, I-I'm sorry sir. In my rush, I assumed it was you. It's... Very convincing." She said looking closely to the odd, flat material, picking up a new cookie and bringing it to the living and breathing Venser. "What in St. Holly's name is cardboard? Err. Are you alright sir?" The sandy blonde asked tentatively as she approached.

Venser let out a grunt of affirmation raising his cigar to his mouth, inhaling a good puff before exhaling out smoke, then took a heavy swig from his bottle of cider right after. "Blood soaked bandages over meeee. Covering my foolish heart. Cuts so deep I see into my soulllllll... Howlolol!" He set the cigar down on an ashtray on the table and let out a sigh, looking down at the table rather than his fellow employee, a pretty looking thing with big light brown eyes and shoulder length sandy blonde hair.

Brea blinked, then walked up to him and placed the cookie to his left on the windowsill. "Quite a warbler, we have here." She said, mentioning he continued to sing. "Quite a topic of choice, too."

"What are you even talking about, Brea?" Venser asked annoyed.

"The singing." She continued, pushing past his acerbic tone. "It's about some deep shit, in lay man's terms."

Venser finally broke his gaze from the rain and the storm to crane his head over to the barmaid, plucking a string or two gently before stopping. "Yeah. Yeah." He sighed and after that one word, returned his gaze back outside. "Tell me, how would you like to own a bakery of your own? It seems... I know how much you love to bake, and how much our customers love your treats."

The barmaid turned away and started walking to a table. "I'm not sure. It sounds like a lot of business, which I don't quite understand yet." She said, tugging a chair out from an empty table. "I've learned a lot from selling my pastries on the side, and from shadowing you, Kira, and Thorn." She continued, setting the chair beside his, but a comfortable distance apart. "But I don't know if I'm fully confident in starting my own business." Brea grabbed a tankard, filled it with cider, and sat down in the free seat she had made beside Venser.

"Well, if you decide to open a bakery, I'm willing to invest my coin into it." Venser said taking a puff of his cigar, followed by a drink of cider. "After I buy the farm,

I'm sure I'll have some money on the side to spare. Ya know, being an entertainer and a stripper on the side. Along with working here and collecting more and more bounties all over the continent. So yeah. Name your price."

Brea would blink her light brown eyes and look up from her first sip of cider. "Well, thank you sir. That's certainly generous. But I think I am rather comfortable where I am right now. I don't need to risk what little I have going for me." She said with a disheartened chuckle. Soon, she found herself silent and looking out the window as well.

"And how could you risk it when I'm the one investing my own hard earned coin?" Venser asked still looking away from Brea. He shook his head and sighed. "I remember a time where before I got my powers I was a thespian just trying to scrape by and make ends meet. Not the case anymore."

"Well, that's good." She said, trying to be supportive, but happy to be clear of the bakery debacle. "It's always nice not having to wonder how you'll eat next."

"And if you can pay rent, and maybe move to a better neighborhood, maybe even actually have a house of your own." Venser said holding up the cigar he held in his left hand. "Kullero cigars. The best, and probably one of the most expensive you can buy back where I'm from. And I can pretty much buy them whenever I want. I think... If I get the farm..."

"Do you want me to leave?" She asked, sipping on her cider. For a rather important question, she found herself asking it with the same intensity as a question such as "Apple juice or coffee?" It surprised her, but she didn't show it. Instead, she sipped at her cider.

Venser silently shrugged and set his cigar down in an ashtray in the window seal, and set down his bottle too before he turned around. "I've been alone for a while. I'm not too sure, honestly."

Brea nodded as she drank the last of her cider, standing up once the tankard had been emptied. "Well, thank you for the notice. I'll start looking around at different properties tomorrow." She said with a half-smile, tugging the wooden chair back to the table. Once it had been placed back in its original resting position, she returned to her usual spot behind the bar. "So, are you going to tell me what's wrong?"

"No. It's just... It's just funny how things can just... End. Go sour, just like that. One day they are here, the next..." A snap of his fingers.

The bearded man let out a sharp, frustrated sigh and stood up, grabbing his guitar and storming off. He flicked his left hand and his marked flashed greenish white, sending a gust of powerful wind at a table and some chairs. They smashed against the floor and the wooden railing, splinters fell over it and some tumbled down the stairs noisily as Venser disappeared down the hall.

The wind whipped her hair about her soft face, stinging her neck and her cheeks. Once it was all said and done, Brea poured herself another mug of cider, and leaned against the back shelf, looking down the hallway in concern. "'Blood soaked bandages over me." She sang quietly to herself. "Covering my foolish heart..." She trailed off, forgetting the rest of the words.

CHAPTER THIRTY-SIX: HIATUS

The Dragon's Head Tavern and Inn, Vorland, 1437 ATC

The rain looked like tears from the eyes of the clouds, softly falling on the ground with a light pitter-patter sound. Spring had just arrived here upon the land, and with it came with the early spring showers. As the sky wept, a disheartened Venser stared out the window of his room out to the forest, clutching a small handmade blanket to himself. No one had seen him for a while, well when they did he wasn't around long and didn't say much. How would he tell his employees, his friends that he was leaving for who knows how long? He sighed and continued to gaze out into nothingness.

Brea Rowland wasn't sure why her boss had locked himself in a sort of solitary confinement, but it deeply worried her. Venser always seemed like a social being to her; one that, without an audience or at least company, could possibly implode. Careful not to burn herself, the barmaid pulled her fig and pear tarts out of the oven. They were the most complicated thing she's ever baked to date, but she knew it would be tasty. Maybe tasty enough to knock off whatever funk was bothering Venser. Brea set them on a separate plate so they could cool faster. Once they did, she took her plate of treats to his room, rapping on the door lightly. "Sir?" She piped from the outside.

"Intrude!" Venser called from inside.

Intrude she did. Brea cracked the door at first, just enough for her head. "I brought you a surprise." It was then that she pushed the door open a little wider, just enough so that she and her tray could make it inside. The tarts were still steaming, but the pastry was golden brown and the fruit inside glistened. "Fig and pear tarts!" She said, cheerily but not overbearing. "I thought you'd like something sweet."

There was no response from Venser, who had his back turned to the sandy blonde haired girl. Upon closer inspection his raven hair had grown longer, nearly shoulder length, and on his bed was a decorative basket which contained herbs to help with things like breastfeeding, healing after birth, as well as a couple of celebratory cigars and alcohols for the father-to-be for when his newest daughter arrived.

After receiving no acknowledgement, she set the tray of treats on his bed, glancing at the items beside her. Brea wasn't a fool; she knew what herbs helped wean children and which helped with labor pains. She'd done all of it before. Covering her mouth to hide any sort of surprised noises that slipped through, she picked up a tart and walked over to Venser, handing it to him on his right side and looking out the window with him. She didn't say a word, just offered her pastry.

The bearded man merely smacked the tart out of her hand, let out a grunt, and then placed the blanket into Brea's hand where the tart once was. It was a small, pink baby's blanket meant for a newborn. It had been handmade, embroidered with Venser and Sanna's initials as well as the child's proposed name. Rowena Karkaldwin. "I'm going away for a while, Brea." He finally said bitterly. "Taking... A hiatus. To, ahem... Just wander. Make some more money for the farm. Clear my head. Yeah."

The barmaid watched as her tart, the pastry that she had spent hours preparing and baking, flew across the room and shattered into a mess of crumbs. She didn't have too much time to stare at it because soon enough, it was replaced by a small blanket. "You don't sound too happy about it. About all of this." She said, motioning with the blanket to the bed.

"What's there to be happy about?!'" The bearded man yelled spinning around to face the sandy blonde brown eyed girl, wiping away a visible tear. "I'm sorry for raising my voice like that it's just..." Sniffing, he took back the blanket and sat down on his bed, tears falling from his eyes like the rain just outside the window. "I've been taking so many other jobs just to pay for a proper home for us to raise our child but... All this coin..." He sniffled. "I mean... Ahem. Sanna... Rowena... My lover and my baby... They're gone. Passed and I wasn't even there. Don't you understand?"

Her light brown eyes widened and she gasped and covered her mouth, letting her bewildered eyes do the talking. The silence lingered briefly as she collected herself from the news. "I… I had no idea." The barmaid whispered, not being able to bring herself to full volume. "I'm so sorry." The apology wouldn't do much, she knew that, but there was nothing else for her to say. "Oh god Venser…I'm so sorry."

She could feel her heart breaking all over again.

"I had no idea either! Hence, why I offered to buy you a fucking bakery even though you knew why I was taking all these other jobs." Venser said with a half angry, half biter sob holding the blanket close to him. "Rowena was going to be beautiful... I was going to marry Sanna... We were going to be a proper family... I mean... Marry her and the others but..." The bearded man snorted like a pig and laughed. "So many women I don't know how to marry them all."

Brea let him yell. Hell, he could try and throw punches if he wanted, she knew how to dodge. And she'd been through this loss before with both of her sons. Brea opened her mouth to speak, but she didn't know what to say. There was nothing she could say that could help him. This kind of loss devastates a person; nothing is real but the loss. She stood there, dumbfounded.

"What am I going to do?" Venser asked brushing his hands over the embroidery. "I don't know... I don't fucking know Brea... I just... I don't know what I want. Just to... Be left alone maybe? Spend all the time I can with my twins and their mother? I don't know... I know in a time like this talking to others will help but... But... Ya know. I lost a child before. Vivi, and her mother... Carriage accident... But I don't... I don't talk about them... No no, don't... Don't ask me about Vivi."

"Oh dear Venser... There's a lot going on in your mind and around it, I know. And nothing feels permanent anymore." She sat on the edge of the bed, looking over the basket of things. "Talking helps sometimes, but I think it's a lot of soul-searching, too." Brea thought back to her decision to return to the tavern although her sons were gone. "The familiar is what comforted me. Patterns. Things that helped me fall back into the swing of things. But a new start could help, too."

"What the fuck are you talking about?" The bearded man asked with an obvious twang of anger in his voice hearing mention of a new start. "Our home in Pryldahn was supposed to be a new start... When we got it we were going to paint a room for Rowena- Oh void..." More tears fell as he began to weep again.

Brea bit her lip as she fought tears of her own. She didn't want to cry. "But staying is what I found helped the most. Being surrounded by what's familiar." She looked at the plate of tarts on his bed, now they just seemed sad. Her attempts at cheering him up had failed, and she felt like she had just kept putting her foot in her mouth.

"So, what- Fucking void!" He raised the blanket to throw it, but slowly set it down on his own lap as tears fell on the blanket of his dead daughter. "You, Thorn and

Kira will have to run the bar without me for... For a while. I'm sure you two will do a fine job without me." He sniffled and looked to Brea. Not making eye contact, looking at her but not directly at her. "And both of you are in charge of each other. Co-managers... Errrm. Workers."

She nodded, dark, sandy blonde strands of hair falling over her shoulders and resting around her neck. "Aye, sir. We'll keep it warm until you return." Brea Rowland said with a nod. Of course he'd be returning. He had to. Didn't he? She looked at him even if he wouldn't return her gaze. "Please be safe. And come home soon." She said as she broke her glance, getting up and leaving his room.

Venser nodded silently and stared down into his lap, letting out a saddened sigh. Blinking his slitted orbs a few times, he glanced up at his folding sword sitting on his desk. Reaching out, he trapped it in a green aura and pulled it over to him.

He twirled it around in a full circle, allowing the short blade to come telescoping out. Examining the short blade, he slid it slowly against his left palm, cutting his flesh and coating it with blood.

ZTTTTTTTT!

Magical green lightning erupted from his fingertips and struck his short sword, reinforcing it with unstable lightning. Venser stared blankly at his glowing sword, listening to it faintly crackle while he sat in the dark, soon enough, the light faded into black.

CHAPTER THIRTY-SEVEN: THE CLIFFSIDE

Great Eastern Forest, Posiil, 1437 ATC

Venser Karkaldwin sighed and peered over the Cliffside.

Below him, surrounded by the untamed wilds of the east, the great monoliths that bordered a nearby set of stone ruins were scattered. Trunks were uprooted where the blocks had smashed their way through. The ruins themselves were little more than a pile of rubble, barely visible behind a column of black cloud.

He dusted off his grey tunic and grabbed his darker grey traveler's cloak, noticing the bottom of his cape was singed. It was going to take forever to get out the soot stains, though, it didn't matter due to the color of the tunic in the long run. Still, he thought, looking down at his shining prize, it had all been worth it.

A satisfied grin came over his bearded face, Venser was about to reach down and pick up the talisman when he heard leaves shuffle nearby. He looked left and right, along the row of trees on either side.

"Who's there?" He called out. "Come on out!" Greentusks? Panther people? Bandits?

ZZTTTTTTT!

The bearded man reinforced his short sword with magical green lightning and prepared for an attack.

Nothing moved for a while. The man kept absolutely still, his mark glowing greenish white and emitting steam, ready to cast a spell at a second's notice.

The bushes erupted behind the bearded man. He only just had time to duck when something hummed over his head and struck the nearest fig trunk. The wood split clean in half. The top of the trunk plummeted down the cliff, and the man's emerald slitted eyes widened after it. Venser's head turned to face the attacker.

"Eh? Who are you?'"

"Isn't it wonderful?" The voice belonged to a hooded man in a purple robe who in one hand, gripped a rare and powerful artifact. The blade attached to it looked like a shard of stone and glowed with a pale, lilac color, and the man wielded it with disturbing grace and strength, clearly no stranger to swordsmanship.

"I've heard of many royal families owning at least one of our blades... Such a rare thing these days. This is a proud family heirloom of mine. Even after all these centuries, it's so sharp it can cut a man's head clean off his shoulders." There was a hum as it sliced through the air, leaving glowing lilac contrails. "Care to see a demonstration?"

"And I thought I spoke too much..." Venser braced his legs, narrowing his emerald eyes. He had seen one of those before. An ancient Kundalandian sword, which belonged to a long gone race of neko people who were known to create exquisite and powerful tools, weapons, and structures from ordinary rock. Their magic, the things they left behind were advanced and were always in great demand. He had had of certain royal houses that had one of these Kundalandian swords as treasured family heirlooms of their own, passed down from generation to generation and held in the highest of regard, and often had a storied history behind them as well as a fancy name.

"Maybe so, good sir." The man said. "But those are the last words you will ever speak."

The brute lunged forwards. Venser reared back, legs wide apart. His neck just avoided the very tip of the blade before he took a step back too far, before he could counterattack, and fell backwards and disappeared over the cliff edge.

''Ahhhhhh!''

Headfirst he fell, seeing the sea of green spidery leaves rise up to meet him. The bearded man grinned at the feel of his messy raven hair flopping all around his face, the wind against him. He wished sometimes that cliffs could be taller, just so that he could enjoy the rush of air for longer.

His mark flashed greenish white and emitted more steam, lighting up before he disappeared in a puff of thick red smoke in midair.

On the cliff edge, the man watched his teleportation act with narrowed eyes. Venser saw him hack at the surrounding vegetation in fury and waved down cheerfully. "Better luck next time!"

"Disappointing! I wanted a good fight!" He was only frustrated for a fleeting moment, before the strange in the purple robe gave him a simple, amused smile and placed his arms behind his back. "I will be watching with great interest!" That was all he heard before the purple clouds of sunset obscured his view.

The bearded man disappeared again, up onto another Cliffside and up into a tree, climbing it whilst teleporting onto the branches above until he reached the very top. Below him, hills and valleys of clouds spread out and drifted. It was wonderfully cool up here. as refreshing as a dip in a crystal clear pool in the tropics. He could hear the calls of a variety of forest birds as though they were all around him but that was just the echo from the canopy far below. Up here, he felt strangely at piece admiring the beauty of nature.

Venser let out a slow sigh, holding up the prized talisman, which was made of stone and lilac crystal. He knew full well what this was, and where it came from, sort of. One thing the bearded man knew for sure is that they really loved this color. And he knew this would fetch good coin from scholars, and that was all that mattered.

CHAPTER THIRTY-EIGHT: NATURE'S LOVE AND ADORATION

Great Eastern Forest, Posiil, 1437 ATC

The Great Eastern Forest ran wild with hearty and healthy animals. Both enormously huge, like the black bears, and pityingly small, such as the simple rabbits. The fertile forest hummed with life, so much so that even the trees looked quite alive, in such a way that they could start moving at any second. Near one of them, a humanoid figure emerged. The naked forest nymph had dull purple skin, pointed ears, long green hair that ended at her waist, and tiny blue dots around her similarly glowing eyes resembled bright stars. The magical being would tend to the animals that had been hurt, and would watch over their dwellings. She felt like a mother to Posiil's forests, almost as a human woman would feel towards her child.

The nymph had everything she could have wanted. A burbling stream, full of nutritious fish, several trees that provided shade from the harsh sun, even caves and deep holes for her to live in. Although she had all of these wonderful things, which she loved dearly, she felt quite alone. She would wander through the tall trees all day, trying to avoid anything dangerous nearby. She occasionally visited the frontier towns, such as Woodstrum, and had enjoyed watching all of the humans and Pryldahnians dilly dallies in their daily lives, watching from afar. She had learned of the things they usually did, and how she looked so much like them... In shape, perhaps.

Oh, how she longed to be a human, and to be able to enjoy things that humans enjoyed. She found herself studying them, and even trying to read one of their strange scriptures called 'books'. The words were nothing but scribbles. She had tried wearing clothes once too, but it felt completely unnatural. No matter what she did, or wanted to do, she just couldn't be what she truly wanted. Or at least, know what it was like to be like them, live like them.

One day, the nymph was feeling particularly depressed when she heard the snapping of twigs behind her. Startled that a predator had come upon her, she quickly hurried away to her trees, camouflaging in the leaves. What she saw was indeed a predator, but not the one she would be scared of. It was a man, dressed in a crimson and turquoise entertainer's tunic with bright red boots. Excited to have finally seen one so close, she edged closer and closer to the bearded man. He was bent over, obviously examining something on the ground, possibly some tracks. She was overcome with a strange feeling that she had not yet experienced in her life, a feeling that dwelled within her body. A feeling so passionate, she could not quell it.

"Good. Few more of these and I can get paid." Venser muttered to himself inspecting a certain herb requested by him by an alchemist in the town of Woodstrum. The man with rich, messy dark hair with a green tint and a black beard that needed a cut. He had strong arched brows and eyelashes so thick it demanded confidence, strength. Attack eyebrows! A prominent jaw curved gracefully around and the strength of his neck showed in the twining cords of muscle that shaped him.

She spent a very long time, just following the human and watching his actions. She had insisted her insect friends to try and be quiet as she was moving, for she did not want to alert the man to her presence. This went on for several hours, the man would pick at the ground a little, and then move on, sometimes stopping to lay in the soft grass and rest. The forest nymph eagerly following his every step. She loved his grace, and his intelligence of plants compared to hers. She knew every single plant that lived in the Great Eastern Forest, and it seemed he did too.

As the sun began to set below the trees, and soon falling beneath the horizon, the man returned to wherever he came from, leaving the naked purple woman all alone. She felt utterly cold and lonely during the nights, for her friend would only come out during the day. She wandered the forests all night, lighting up the trees with her bright, greenish glow. Finally, an orange light bathed the Great Eastern Forest as the sun pulled itself free of the horizons forced embrace, rising up to the Sawtoothed Mountains. The purple skinned nymph was very happy to see that the man had returned the next morning, to do the same as he had yesterday.

Happily following the man again, she once stopped to look at what he had been very closely examining. A large, human like track had been smashed into the earth, big enough to be a giant bear... But bears didn't have such toes. A long and ragged shout pierced the air, startling the nymph out of her examination. She looked up, just in time to see a tall shadow pass across her face in the direction of the man. Oh no! That creature is headed for that human! The forest nymph thought with terror, tearing through the trees towards her friend.

When she arrived at the clearing, she was quite surprised to see the man triumphantly slashing at the eight-foot-tall, lumbering greentusk, leaving long, bloody lines across the beast's deformed face, it's face was similar to a human's. Painted in watercolor, and then smeared with a careless splash, two large, yellowed tusks jutting from its lower jaw. And the greentusk's face seemed to be permanently stuck in an angry sneer. Watching in paralyzed silence from the trees, she gazed on as the man finally killed the hulking monster, leaving its lumpy body slumped in the dirt. What happened next surprised her even more than the first time, as the man extended his left hand and lightning erupted from his fingertips, traveling over the greentusk and left it a smoking husk.

The man twirled his strange short sword in a three sixty motion, and the blades collapsed inside the hilt, and he clipped it onto his belt, and then the man continued along his path, as if nothing had ever happened. He continued to examine the trees and the ground, just as he had before. Stopping for a brief moment, Venser let out a sigh, reaching into his belt to pull out a small silver tin. A few seconds later the purple skin nymph watched as he lit a strange long object in his mouth and took a puff, exhaling smoke. And she knew the smell. Cannabis.

''Wow! That man is really, really strong!'' The nymph thought in amazement. She had a newfound respect for the bearded man, knowing he would destroy any vile greentusk that beseech his path. She thought him a hero.

Like a dazed puppy, bought with treats and wonders, the naked nymph continued to follow the man through the Great Eastern Forest she knew so well, even though it took on a new air when she followed him through it. She had thought of leaving him gifts of beautiful flowers and herbs, but she couldn't think of any way to make them noticeable. Sadly, she had no other option than to follow the man without his consent. She was content just to follow him, and watch the man after all.

One day, a great evil befell the man. Although he was strong, and often surprised the forest nymph with his might, he had been bested one day despite all his strength. He had wandered into the wrong part of the Great Eastern Forest, drunk off his ass, and had been downed by a gang of bears he had pissed off.

The purple skinned nymph had never seen so many bears together, for they were often fearsome towards each other, and quite territorial. As the man's tunic was ripped from his body, long claw marks stretching his chest, he fell to the ground in a heap of humbled flesh, flinging his magical green lightning in wide arcs that went everywhere, barely hitting their intended targets. Suddenly fearing for her friend's life, the nymph lashed out at the bears, calling for an army of bees after them and chasing them away. All the animals of the forest both respected and greatly feared the one nymph that resided there, so they fled without hesitation at her appearance.

The man was terribly hurt, blood dripping from his lips and parts of his body missing its skin. And all Venser could do was laugh and smile about it, whilst laying on the ground staring up at the sky. Giving out a whimper of terror, the nymph picked up the shredded human and carried him off, towards the woods she knew best. Making haste not to waste any time, she set him down on a flat rock and started gathering herbs. She gathered as many healing herbs as she could and put them to use, mashing up aloe and rubbing his wounds. The naked nymph could not help but admire his toned, muscular body as her soft hands trailed over his barreled chest. Wrapping the man's remaining clothes around his wounds, the nymph patiently waited for him to awake.

It was a very excruciatingly long time before the man opened his eyes again, and when he did, he still looked very battered and weak. And drunk. Perhaps even high. Moaning in pain, he reached up a hand to rub at his emerald slitted eyes, seemingly able to move his body. His eyes flickered open, the man suddenly aware of his surroundings. Looking to the side of his resting place, his eyes befell the well-endowed naked purple lady that had worked so hard to rescue him. He looked quite surprised at first to see such a woman. He blinked a few times and looked around for his utility belt, and his satchel, and his boots. And his pants.

"Oh nice..." Venser then suddenly doubled over in pain, one of his old wounds opening to reveal fresh blood staining his clothes. "Heh heh oh, wow fuck..." Worriedly, the nymph drifted over to him, pressing more aloe into his wound with her smooth hands, her fingers long and spidery. He was confused and felt as if this were a dream, but relaxed some when he saw she was not trying to hurt him.

She smiled and had no idea what the man was saying, not knowing the common language, but she could tell the man was warming up to her. The naked nymph left his side to retrieve something. When she returned, she held several apples as well as some raw fish in a woven basket, setting them on the side of the rock.

"Are those for me? Thank you." he asked quietly, picking up one of the apples. Nodding her head curtly, the purple skinned nymph merely enjoyed the fact that she was interacting with the man and sharing the same space with him. She never wanted him to leave, to go back to his city full of people. She wanted to take care of him forever, just as she had for all of her animals. She wished he would love her the same way she loved him.

"Ah...well...I've never really MET a.... Forest spirit before, so... I'll just call you... Hmmm..." He noticed all of the flowers that seemed to bloom around her. She was happy that she had a name at all, for her real name was a melodic language that no human would ever understand. "I think I'll call you... Flora." Venser cleared his throat and pounded his chest, pointing to himself. "Venser. Tybalt. Karkaldwin." He extended his pointer finger to her. "Flora."

She liked the way his name sounded when he said it, and knew she'd remember it forever. She was twice as happy given a name in the common language, now that they truly knew each other now, she doted over him as a mother hen would care for her chicks. She changed his bandages hourly, and brought different animals to see him, just to show him their majesty. He seemed happy for the time being, but she knew he'd leave when he was better. Whilst, Venser knew he could simply use his magic and teleport away, but he was enjoying this. Enjoying watching the large breasted purple naked lady fawn over him. Venser flashed her a cocky smile. "I am probably the most handsome man in the multiverse. Ask any of my lovers. Alex, Ceirra, Sedna, Sanna..." His smile began to fade, reminding himself of the lover and the baby he had recently lost.

He seemed generally comfortable with her presence, which surprised even her. She just wished she could speak to him in some way, just to ask him to come visit her. Just once, even. Noticing the sadness in his face, she pondered for a moment what was going on inside his mind. Maybe he was dehydrated? Hydration was important! The naked nymph moved away and collected some stream water in a shell, kneeling in front of him and staring up at his handsome visage. And then, she noticed something. Something hard and fleshy between his legs. She leaned forward, setting the shell down, and gave it a long lick. Venser shuddered and let out a satisfied moan, causing Flora to smile more. She was making him happy!

Flora slowly brought up her hand and began to massage her breast, her showing a deep red blush as she pinched a dark colored nipple.

The bearded man sat back and licked his lips as the forest nymph slowly began to massage her breasts. Squeezing one supple breast before quickly switching to the other. Venser felt his own hand making the downwards trips as well, rubbing his hardened shaft up and down as the purple skinned woman climbed onto his lap. A trail of glistening pre-cum dangled from its throbbing tip, a sure sign of his arousal. And Flora could not wait to have him inside of her.

On the handsome man's lap now, she quickly wrapped her arms around Venser and went for the most passionate kiss she could muster. Her mouth opened as her lips squished against his. Flora could feel Venser's mouth open and she began to battle her tongue against Venser's, who was all too willing to let her in. In response, he snaked a hand downwards, running a finger over the purple woman's clit. His thumb moved upwards, dipping into the forbidden entrance. The bearded man found her scent indescribable, an infuriating mix of spice, earthy notes, and the barest hint of sweat. Making herself comfortable, Flora sat down on Venser's cock.

''Ahhhhh... Ahhhh...!''

Not only was the forest nymph delightfully snug, but her body heat was utterly divine. Giving his partner, and himself, a moment to adjust to the insertion, he slowly moved his hips back, retracting his length from her clinging snatch. No sooner had half of his thick cock pulled free, then he slammed it back in, leaving the girl to throatily groan.

Flora thought his penis was heavenly, hitting all the right places, not to mention his hands were incredible as they trailed up her body. Upon his second thrust, she rocked back to meet his movement, ramming her ass back to impact against his groin. "Ahhhhhhhh... Ahhhhhh..." The naked purple woman grunted, matching his steadily increasing pace.

The Great Eastern Forest dimmed, around them both. The entirety of the moment was just his partner and himself. Wonderfully, as she rode him, her large breasts bouncing in his face, slowly building in speed and force. As he continued furiously rutting Flora, he began to feel hot. Like, physically heated. It wasn't a bad heat, far from it. After several long minutes of passion, he felt closer and closer.

With a loud grunt, Venser came. His testes retracted, and his hips went rigid, as he hilted himself fully within Flora. Every vein along his girthy length angrily throbbed, as a veritable a river of seed cascading through his shaft. Pressed firmly against the forest nyhmp's cervix, the first torrid shots of sperm blasted against the opening of her womb.

Flora's starry eyes went wide at the sublime warmth and gooey sensation of Venser's seed bathing her interior. With a rapturous scream, she succumbed to the sinful pleasure. A kaleidoscope of blue, purple, green and red fireworks exploding filled her vision as they consummated the ardent moment, feeling him course through her very being. Their bodies tangled, the bearded man and forest nymph looked at each other, before kissing once again.

Eventually, the time came for Venser Tybalt Karkaldwin to leave her care, leaving her to retrieve his things and send him off with a kiss and a smile. He waved warmly, walking into the forest and disappearing in a puff of thick red smoke. Flora already missed him, watching him walk off towards civilization, leaving her and her forest behind. She didn't even know if he would visit her again. She tried not to dwell on it as she settled in for the night, just hoping he would make it back home safe. As a night longer than she had ever experienced passed, Flora felt fully rested and ready for another day with her friend, Venser. Oh how she adored him. Eagerly waiting for the human to present himself, she waited, and waited.

Still wandering the woods as the sun once again slipped below the horizon, she felt outright rejected by her friend, for he had not shown up. She felt such a terrible sadness that she had not seen him again, she just could not restrain herself.

She felt so heart broken. Abandoned. She felt regret. Regret for falling in love with a man she barely knew. Flora thought of the bearded man she loved. A man that had carefully walked the forests, examining plants and tracks, who wandered in thought. To clear his mind, to be at peace with nature. A man she had admired so, a man she would never forget. Especially now, running her hands over her belly, feeling the life that grew inside her now. A life she would give birth to, and love, and it would love her back and stay. Their child would be with Flora.

Always.

CHAPTER THIRTY-NINE: THE NECROMANCERS

North Eastern Vorland, 1437 ATC

Venser slowed to a crouch when he saw a large decrepit building that could only be the ruins of an old fort at the edge of a swamp. He saw smoke from a fire burning on the other side. Slowly, the man circled the ruins until he observed three men in dark cloaks milling around the fire, deciding to draw them out, Venser picked up a rock and threw it at the lead necromancer.

They charged up the hill after him and his companion, Captain Alex Bonneville, who quickly moved forward and slashed one of them across the chest with her cavalry saber, her bearded lover blasted the other two back with a powerful gust of wind to send them flying like ragdolls. One of them, a balding man rolled over and picked up a crossbow, aiming it at the two.

TWHUNK!

Alex took cover behind a tree while Venser disappeared in a puff of thick red smoke and reappeared a few feet to the right, rushing the necromancer with his short folding blade.

"Ah fuck! No!" The necromancer fell back on his stomach and tried to scramble away, before Venser's blade was shoved through his chest. "Cunt!" And those were the last words he ever uttered.

"Ugh, necromancer." Venser said with a disgusted frown, noting the crudely stitched skull on his black robe. "I fear this ruin is going to be as foul inside as it is outside."

They found the body of a bandit dressed in furs, a woman, by the fire. No doubt they had killed her to turn her into an animated puppet for their uses, the nature of which made the man cringe in disgust. Necromancers... Necrophilia? Oh no. Inside the ruins, they found stairs leading down to a set of rotted wooden doors and another dead bandit.

Inside the ruins it seemed as though a battle had been fought. Two dead bandits were close to the door. They could still smell the blood in the air. The two crept down a ramp and saw another bandit lying prone against a stone pillar. A war ax laid at his feet. The bearded man looked away from him in time to see three dark robed necromancers fighting a bandit on the other side of the large chamber. One of the black robed men was simply standing while the other two were sending bursts of fire and ice at the bandit from their catalyst wands. He did not last long. The two magic users walked away and the third simply dropped dead, mouth wide open. The two older necromancers acted as if it was normal then continued talking about how worthless these thrall puppets were as slaves. Their kind sickened Venser more and more. He could not let them get away to create more meat puppets, an utter, deep disrespect to the dead.

"EEEEEYAAAA!" Venser lept at both of them, gripping his unstable lightning blade with both hands.

"More of them!" The two necromancers ran towards them. One went after Alex and the other engaged the bearded man. Venser got one swing through his gout of fire spell when suddenly a bandit was attacking him with a pickaxe.

"Ahhhh fuck!"

Venser wind blasted him aside and finished off the necromancer with one more hit. Now that he looked at the bandit, he could see an orange glow to him. The poor man must have been enthralled. He then glanced over at the auburn haired captain and she was bending over the other mage cleaning her saber on his soiled robe.

Alex came up to Ven and tossed him a coin purse full of silver. "This was all he had on him."

He caught it with one hand and let out a sigh, looking to the robed corpses. ''Such a waste of magical talent...''

The only exit they saw was a tunnel so they followed that a short way, finding more dead bandits and one dead necromancers. Voices caused him to stop.

"Hey! Are all the invaders dead?" A voice ahead asked. "Blah... Everyone's gonna be fighting over this place!"

Venser and Alex prepared for battle. Then they heard the sounds of fighting so they slipped forward down some stairs and saw two necromancers spellcasting at a group of undead, using candlesticks to channel their spells through, as every magic user needed a catalyst and only the strongest could pull spells from thin air. Venser held up his wristbow and his choice of who to help took all of a moment to make. The first bolt embedded itself in a necromancer"s hood, as he was aiming right for his face The undead did the rest. Then they turned their soulless eyes towards the two. Venser held out his left hand, his mark glowed greenish white, and he wind blasted the undead, sending them flying back. They must have been pretty damaged already because they went down like wheat before a scythe. They checked the corpses for loot and found mostly coins and other junk but on one mage the bearded man found a spell book titled simply, "Raising The Dead". He was repulsed even to have touched the book, which I swore was made of something more... Organic than parchment. On the continent of Posiil, and even across the Slender Sea necromancy was illegal and reviled, and for good reason too. He tossed it into a burning fireplace nearby. It stank like rotting meat, somehow. Next to the fireplace on a table he found two bottles of grapefruit beer. The best kind of beer. Unable to help himself, Venser drank down one and handed Alex the other, who simply waved her hand.

"No thanks, Venser."

"What? Is there something wrong?" He asked, blinking a few times as he quickly chugged his down, throwing it nonchalantly over his shoulder.

"Nevermind." The auburn haired captain said, "I just want to help you with this and then get out of here. Let's keep going."

"Heh. Thought you always loved beer and an adventure." He commented.

They saw rooms to the left filled with dull clay urns, as they wandered, they found a set of iron doors and beyond it is an enormous underground hall.

"I've never seen anything like this." Alex commented. "Why would this be beneath some frontier fort?"

"Some kind of ancient crypt obviously... Maybe re-used by the Vorland army?"

While looking out over the hall, he spotted one skeleton walking along a stone bridge. This skeleton was quite strange, human, but with a long cat like tail, a slightly elongated skull, and long fingers. Venser bent down a bit, loading another bolt into his wristbow on his left hand. Licking his lips, he extended his left hand, and pressed down hard on the flat trigger with his middle and ring finger. The bolt hitting the skeleton in the chest and causing it to fall to pieces.

Alex was impressed. "You're turning into quite the marksman with that little thing. I'm even surprised it has that kind of range."

"Made from the finest materials and... Yeah." Venser shrugged and they moved on.

Onto one chamber where a smaller room was blocked by two stout metal gates. On the table was a chest but the only thing in it besides some gold, mining tools, cobwebs, and stone tablets with etchings of a strange, long forgotten language on it. Oddly enough, it resembled the common language but just jumbled with odd marks added in.

The path they found took them back to the hall we saw earlier. Ven noticed a catwalk that went above it so he decided to use that for reconnaissance before they just waded into whatever might be waiting. The catwalk, though, was broken in several places. The first spot he managed to jump over. About to teleport over the next one, he saw several skeletons walking around patrolling. Venser stood up and simply blasted them with a gust if heavy wind, sending them flying apart like bowling pins. He saw Alex down below looking for something to hit. She gave up and sat down on a bench to wait.

FWOOSH!

"Let's go." Venser teleported over the gap and kept along the catwalk.

The catwalk led to a room with a chest and a skeleton cradling an ancient stone ax. In the chest he gold ore and a few pickaxe heads. Good find. He stuffed them into his satchel then returned to the catwalk but he decided to jump down to another platform where he could see some gems sitting on a shelf. Ven grabbed those joined up with the auburn haired captain then went down a path towards a waterfall and pond he had spotted from the catwalk.

The path was merely a ledge and one misstep would send him plummeting into the water, which would not be so bad, unless it was shallow. "You'd think these ancient advanced cat people would have built some railings on this bridge." Ven started towards the waterfall.

"Where do you think you're going?" Alex asked, "Not that I don't think you could use a bath."

"You'll use any excuse to get my clothes off, won't you? So obvious. You can just ask, you know." She sighed and waited with her hand on her hip, adjusting her black cape lined with blue fabric.

"I saw a space behind the falls as we were coming down. You coming... With me, that is?"

Alex shook her head and chuckled.

They dashed through the waterfall and found a dark room. Alex lit up a torch and they walked towards a small table with a chest on top. The chest held only some coins and a few Kundastones and an old iron sword on the table was not even worth carrying. The small lilac stone with tiny red specs that seemed to glow with its own inner light was worth a good amount, useful too. One would break it, crack it like an egg, and then it would ignite, an almost liquid fire spilling out. An instant campfire, a fire bomb, the possibilities were many.

The rest of the area only yielded some more coins and gems. Back up in the hall they crossed the stone bridge they had killed the first skeleton on. It led to a strange room with a gate at the back, three stones in the middle, and stairs on the right. Something blue caught his eye to the left and I find a blue potion next to a couple of bones stuffed in the rocks. An arrow nicked his shoulder, and he was more startled than hurt.

"Mhm shit I really need to wear armor!" Venser ejaculated, recoiling in pain.

Alex bounded up the flight of wooden stairs and before he could reach her, she sent a skeleton to the boneyard. He grabbed its arrows and another potion nearby. Of all things, he knew arrows were always in great demand, especially for tournaments.

Down at the three stones, when the bearded man got near each one he saw one of three gates open down a hallway. Venser tried to get through them in time but they kept closing.

"Looks like some strange, convoluted puzzle. Or maybe the gates just aren't working right." Alex pointed out.

"Easy." Venser approached the closed gates and noticed a stone button against the wall with a glowing lilac crystal in the center. He took a few minutes looking past the gate and the surroundings beyond it. In order to teleport he had to know exactly where he was going, otherwise he could end up teleporting inside a wall and killing himself instantly. And that was the last thing he needed.

"Hmmmmmmm..." He extended his left hand, and disappeared in a puff of thick red smoke, appearing right in front of the button and pressing it in, allowing the gates to be raised.

The gates stayed open. Alex followed, her blue and black cape billowing behind her as they continued until we reached an odd room covered with spider webs and a tiled floor. They stepped on the tiles and they heard chittering and things moving around them.

"Die!" Alex yelled and he spun around with hands up. She was pointing her saber towards the far wall at three spiders lurking in the shadows, one of them lunging toward her, and she stabbed it through the mouth with her cavalry saber. The spiders spit down poison but they were no match for their combined strength, magical green lightning flying through the air and shocking them to a crisp.

"Oh St. Holly... Ick! Burnt spider... THAT smell..." Alex grabbed the bottom of her cape and covered her nose with it.

They kept moving forward, spying two more spiders they were dispatched quickly. Seeing no more we ran across the last of the tiled floor to a dais covered with webs and a few desiccated corpses. On one he found a lockpick and a broken knife, which he tossed away.

Then a huge spider, the size of a bear dropped from the ceiling.

"Awww shit!"

Alex covered for him by charging at it with her cavalry saber and slashing at its frail limbs. It began its attack by spitting poison at her then chomping down on Venser's arm with its hairy mandibles.

"Ahhhh! Owwww!"

Venser cut it deep in the hindquarters with his short sword and it spun around on its eight legs and hit his sword hand with poison. The green acid stung at first then burned on his flesh. It forced me to back up then it hit me again with more poison. Venser fell to the ground, gasping from the pain as it felt like his skin was sloughing off.

"Shit! Void!"

His shaking hands managed to grab a bottle of healing elixir from his utility belt, he drank it and destiny prevailed as the healing potion quickly ran its course, numbing all of the pain. Alex had drawn the spider's ire with her curved weapon. The spider looked weak and was oozing green blood from a dozen vicious wounds. Venser pressed the attack and finished the giant arachnid with a single thrust into its cluster of eyes, and then grasping the blade of his sword, sending several thousand volts of magical green lightning through it.

"Ohhhh ahhhh..." Alex was picking herself up as he walked over to lend her a hand. The bearded man gave it a swift kick and lifted both arms into the air in triumph.

"Whoooo!"

"Next time we see giant webs like this. " She said, "How about we just make a run for it?"

"You can. I thought we handled it well."

Alex rolled her eyes and sighed.

They followed the stairs off the dais to a wall of webs. Reinforcing his short folding sword with magical green lightning again, Venser cut through them and behind the webs was a door. Through the door was a large burning brazier and another gate. Then Alex and him stepped into a grand room with rectangular pools on both sides and a large stone altar in the middle. When they reached the bottom of the stairs, the ground trembled and four identical statues rose slowly out of the water. They expected something else to appear and try to stop them. When only silence greeted them, the bearded man proceeded cautiously to the altar. There were stone hands that looked like they should be holding something. A small wooden horn of some sort.

"It's one of those baskets that's shaped like a horn." Alex commented as Venser reached out to inspect it, flipping it upside down and causing about a dozen bananas to come tumbling out. "Uhhhh..."

Alex's hazel eyes widened. "What the... Did... How did all of those fit in there?"

"So it appears to be a horn of plenty! I imagine... Holy shit... Unlimited bananas!" Venser placed the cornucopia on his crotch, the pointy end erect up in the air. "Let's grab what we can and get back home."

The two began loading up anything worth keeping or selling. They rummaged through everything and they best they found were several silver and gold coins, a few Kundastones, all kinds of ore they left the ruins by the same door they entered.

It was late by the time the two breathed fresh air again and they knew the walk to the nearest town would be pretty far. Not like it mattered, since Ven could easily take the auburn haired woman's hand and teleport them both away. Stepping through the doors to the fort and past a few corpses, the auburn haired captain cleared her throat.

"Three cheers for us eh?" The bearded man said

"Venser, before we leave... Well... I felt like this is an appropriate time to tell you since we made it out... Ahem."

The bearded man turned and blinked his emerald slitted eyes a few times. "Yeah love?"

The woman rubbed her hands over the front of her blue uniform top, sliding her fingers along the golden buttons and down to her stomach, holding it with both hands and letting out a deep sigh.

"I... I'm just going to be blunt about it." Alex sucked in her breath, her cape blowing in the wind. "I'm pregnant, and this is going to be my last adventure. From the time I've spent with you. Normally... Normally I'm used to being on the back of a horse, in a battle... My father was a soldier before founding the Bonneville Brigade, pretty much still is. But... But..."

Venser let out a shivering sigh, letting the auburn haired captain before him speak, concern and uncertainty on his face.

"These past few weeks with you, with your family has shown me a peaceful life I've never known... I like it, but at the same time I don't. But, I'm going to carry Asher and when he's here take care of him as much as I can until... Until I feel like

I'm ready to go back out there and get back in the fight." Alex spoke.

"I shouldn't have even brought you out here! You could have- Both of you could have..." Venser balled his hands into fists and brought them to his temple, his breathing quickened and his cheeks flushed. "Both of you could have been killed! No! No! You suck Alex!"

"What?"

"You suck cock!"

"Well, yeah! That's not the point! The point is, I'm going to have a baby. You have every right to be mad. Mad at me for not telling you this before I agreed to come along..."

They stood about two feet away from each other, tears welling up in Venser's eyes, their capes blowing in the soft wind. Both of them silent and looking down. Alex knew what had happened recently and knew how greatly he feared and worried for the safety of the rest of his family.

The bearded man said nothing for now, walking up to her and wrapping his arms around her waist, pressing a soft kiss on her forehead.

"Asher? Him? You already know the sex and picked out a name?"

Alex smiled and leaned up to kiss him softly on the lips. "I have Ven... Yes... Yes..."

A single tear rolled down Venser's bearded cheek as he pressed another kiss to Alex's lips, sobbing a bit. "Your last adventure... I don't want to lose you... Or our son... How... How do you know it's going to be a son?"

"I just do... It's a weird, strong feeling... But... Asher Karkaldwin. I like the sound of it."

"So do I love... So do I... Let's just get you home now, where it's safe for you... For you, and for Asher."

CHAPTER FORTY: THE MINE OF INFERNAL WORMS

1445 ATC

Two adventurers stood at the twin gates of the abandoned silver mine's main chamber, one a tall knight wearing only simple chain mail, covered by a split white and red tabard, a crest of a bell crossed by two swords stitched into the front of it, along with a bucket like helmet that obscured his entire head. The other a short woman with a long, cat like tail and ears atop her head to match, long red hair, and wearing simple robes armed with a repeating crossbow, a wand sheathed on her belt.

As the worm infested, twin headed dragon moved about to do its business, the land around the mines shook little causing Aithne to stay on edge often eyeing the door to the hallway leading to the mine's main chamber which was barred. Outside the sun shone through the leaves illuminating the greens of the woods and casting an almost holy golden hue to the air. A giant wolf-like beast with grey fur and patches of skin missing lay dead and full of crossbow ammunition beside a few other creatures the two put down trying to get into the overrun silver mine. The flies buzzed around in mass and fly off as crows descended from the skies, signaling death in their wake.

"Ready to kill this scaley roarboom gone bad, Sir Knight?"

"Yes. I can't wait for everyone to hear our heroic tale back in Cold Springs, and then allllll of Grigwald and beyond! Sna ha ha!"

The worm corrupted creature scratched at the ground and tapestries on the other side in the hallway and the knight and the flame mage could hear the shredding noises, along with the sound of metal being knocked over. They could hear the roars and growls of the ungodly, corrupted creature. Certainly not a thing to be messed with. To any sane person, but these two were adventurers. And the knight, Nicholas of Grigwald who always hid behind a helmet and always went in with a jovial attitude was either brave for agreeing to fight this monster, or very stupid.

"Hmmmm... There's a set of stairs that lead up. Come on Aithne, we need to get the high ground and hopefully we can get the drop on the Roarboom."

The knight climbed the stone stairs. There were ways around this. His crossbow perhaps? He listened to the large beast scratch at the ground and tapestries, all of the shredding noises as he finally reached the roof and peered down over the observation balcony.

"Hmmmmm..."

It stood about six feet on its fours, hunched over and beneath its dense plated and deep green scales were nothing but pure muscles. Its eyes were like coin slots into a dead white nothing and this creature was so statue like. The draconic body had rotted and useless wings. It had two stubby horns on top of its heads and when it became aware of the two it turned to look at them. In both of its twin head, where it's tongue should be was only a writhing, black, worm-like monstrosity with a single red eye each. Air is sucked in from outside through the hole in the ceiling as the dragon inhales. Its large chest gets bigger with the expansion of its lungs and with a blowing noise a thin linear jet of black wind is sent upwards towards them. It only seemed to be testing them so far.

This beam of wind tried to home in on Nicholas and Aithne from its angle. The gale cut like a blade expanding as it passes through the hole in the roof. The knight was able evade with no injury but the hole in the roof was made bigger by the cursed blade winds whos impressions leave black fire burning around the edges of where it touched down. The worm dragon then laid down resting its head atop its clawed hands to relax thinking the two were scared away from its hoard.

"Oh my gods!" He had pulled a handful of black firebombs and saw the beam of wind, falling back and jumping back out of the way, dropping a few of the bombs in the meantime. The cursed beam attack cut away at the mine's rooftop, almost cutting into his boots ad he sat up and watched the stone fall down into the mine's main room. He breathed heavily and stood up, leaning over the edge again and letting out a sigh. "I'm smarter than this." This was it. Fear. He could not let fear overcome him, no. Nicholas had to confront this dark being, conquer it. And all the precious metals in the mine would be his and Aithne's. And he'd be able to bring it all home to his family, share it with the poor.

When the firebombs detonated the explosion was loud and the shockwave considerable. Aithne drew a sharp gasping breath now and looks to the door. The twin headed monster went flying a few feet back, knocking over a giant pile of silver, with a good deal of chard and broken scales going everywhere. Its smoking skin which was now mostly exposed but in very good health. It was now officially pissed off and started charging for the big iron doors to the treasure chamber. Aithne grabbed her Pryldahnian repeating crossbow and runs a free hand through her red hair and aimed down from the second floor balcony.

"Oh fuck... Here we go."

He heard the drake ram against the barred doors rummaged around in his satchel for more bombs. Four left. Maybe he had more? He let out a sigh and climbed the railing, drawing his simple steel sword and holding his badge shield close.

"Time to be a hero! I am Nicholas of Grigwald and PREPARE TO FEEL MY WRATH VILE WORM DRAGON! EEEYAAAAAA!"

The knight leapt from the balcony, striking his sword down and slashing into it's back, before failing to catch its grip and fell to the stone floor with a harsh smack.

Angered, the twin headed worm dragon shot forward, bursting through the iron doors, the flame mage used her magic to superheat the heads of the bolts, firing them slowly. She had a few good hits in the worm dragon's body fixed in there, fair, but these fuckers were more than strong enough to shrug it off. The neko fire mage on the other and didn't have such options. "Gah!" She leapt to the side, running up the stairs to reload.

Nicholas slashed at the worm dragon's tail, making sure to stay behind it while he attacked, he darted behind pillar, behind pillar, and behind another pillar trying to avoid its twin headed gaze. He peered out from behind one of them, then pressed his back against it, panting heavily beneath his helmet and trying to figure out how to play this. He reached into his satchel and grabbed a single bomb. He would go for the neck, it would be best to sever them and then cut up the demon worm creatures puppeting the corpse. "Hiya!" He wound up his throwing arm, and threw the bomb as far and as hard as he could.

It punched right through its rib cage from the side, right below the necks. Its heads went to the sides with a loud roar that broke nearby scaffolding. It was pretty mad and flails its heads to knock over some tables and its tail smacked a pillar.

With a rage filled snarl it made a one eighty, Throwing Aithne with its tail high into the air and then a dark accursed vortex of razor winds pull her in. "Auggg-ggghhhh...!" Dropping the crossbow, she flung her hands out and bursts of flame shot from the palms of her hands. Slowly she rose as the funnel constricts making the winds move faster.

"Hiya!" Charging with his badge shield in front of him, the knight charged, bracing as hard as he could, drawing the gaze from one of its twin heads. The dead mouth of the twin headed dragon opened up and from it shot a long, black parasitic worm that snaked at the man, who promptly smacked it away with his badge shield and slashed down with his sword, severing the infernal worm.

As she drifted in the wind stream like a ragdoll it looked rather peaceful but as the mini storm picked up her ears could hear the slicing of wind like blades into flesh and bone she was thrashed. The stream had drawn a multiple bisection, one across her belly, another diagonally across her chest.

She screamed and cried as flames began to burn away it's weakened scales and burning exposed flesh, before the knight took out one of the heads and she finally landed on the ground, her head bashing against a nearby rock, the force enough to leave her dazed as she tried to lift herself up enough to stand, her nose leaking and dripping blood as she grasped at her stomach. She let out a short gasp and went still, the light leaving her eyes.

The worm dragon reared its head back takes air in, letting it all out at close range like a shotgun blast, sending the knight flying back into a cart full of silver ore, blasting his badge shield in half, some of the stream punching right through his chainmail, directly into his chest. The worm dragon, while victorious in battle was heavily wounded and only wanted to protect its makeshift nest, falling for-ward, exhausted, and hungry, looking to the wounded fire mage before it. The still intact head loomed over Aithne, its mouth opened and in place of the tongue a slithering back worm that came closer and closer...

It stopped suddenly as the neko's corpse moved, flames came out of her very being, parts of her body glowing bright orange as she rose again, though she looked like she was being pulled up by a string, behind her flames manifested from deep within her body and created two massive wings and a jagged flame crown above her head.

Seeing it distracted, Nicholas gripped his simple steel sword with both hands and rose to his feet with all the strength he could muster, and began to swing it throughout the air while he rushed forward. He twirled and swirled the blade elegantly before simply planting his back foot, and thrusting forward. The point went through its body, causing it to emit a shrill, monstrous scream. In response Aithne threw out her hands again, burning the image of a sword onto a nearby boulder and then ripping it free. It floated in the air before flying straight between the worm dragon's twin heads, slicing it in half down the center.

"Ah! Hyah!" Nicholas used all his strength and rushed forward again, gripping his sword with both hands and hacking away at its exposed flesh until he severed the neck and head completely. The neko fire mage summoned great pillars of flame and burnt all of the small, demonic black worms that spilt from its body until the infernal worms were finally purged from the world.

"Hoo... Hoo..." The knight dropped his sword and stumbled back against an anvil, his head falling back as he held his hands to his bleeding chest. "Argghhh..." The eyeholes in his helmet being pitch black despite the lighting, and seemed to be always dark even in the bright sunlight. His limbs went limp as more blood poured from his chest, his vision going dark.

"I... We slayed the beast... And now... It slayed us too..." He rambled with his dying breath as the neko mage, wreathed and crowned in an ancient flame approached him. "I'm not... It's a glorious way to die... In battle... I've only seen death once and... And." Nicholas choked.

"In... In my youth we were all friends on the back of a high speed wagon ride... And there was this girl I was sweet with... Bailey... Bailey Wallace. She had long golden hair and eyes like the color of the summer sky... Cute upturned nose... And she... She fell from the wagon... Her head was bashed in and she died only minutes later... Such a terrible accident and I remember every moment of it and I wish we were more careful... It was... I wonder... I wonder if I'm going to see her soon."

A muffled sob from within the faceless knight's helmet.

"She was too young to die..."

Aithne knelt in front of the man, her giant, flaming wings rising higher behind her. Nicholas becoming extremely tired, he knew he was just a few seconds away from death as his mind entered a bright, twisting tunnel.

"This isn't it ov... The dream, that queen with the cat ears in hiding, the bells that called me to adventure..."

"Come, embrace me, Sir Nicholas. Take up my curse... Be reborn as the new Phoenix King." The neko said approaching him, embracing the dying knight.

"I grow tired of death and rebirth over and over again... Now it is your turn... Take up my curse, and use this power to return Kundaland to the world of Laguna... The visions will guide you. And soon, all will be one again..."

Aithne wrapped her burning wings around Nicholas' body, caressing his helmeted head as flames consumed them and the entire mine.

CHAPTER FORTY-ONE: ROWENA

The Dragon's Head Tavern and Inn, Vorland, 1437 ATC

Home with Venser and his children... And now, their child. Rowena was bundled sweetly in her arms as the golden gypsy made her way up the path to Dragon's Head, fast asleep against the warmth of her mother's chest while two gypsy women walked at her side, each with one hand behind her back to steady her along. She had fallen gravely ill whilst away and hence needed her family's healing efforts, but she was well enough to walk and come back home for a moderate bedrest. Plus, she'd been adamant. Sanna knew how long she'd been gone, plus she'd left without much warning. She was worried Venser would be angry with her about it, but... Sanna hoped not. She came through the doors, dressed lightly for the weather as was Rowena, still nicely tanned and with weary but happy eyes and a tired smile that grew wider with every step.

The tavern was deserted. Save for a large cardboard cutout of the man himself looking smug with a fishbowl on his head and a weird looking metal suit, beneath him the words, "First man to visit the moon! Blue Lake, the twenty third, at dusk!"

She blinked for a moment after reading the words, thinking this to be one of his pranks, but at the same time... Why was it deserted? It was literally never deserted here. "Venser?" Sanna called out, worry growing in her eyes as she started stepping away from the two women who were trying to keep up with her, spouting in a distinct forging language all the while. She checked the bedrooms first, then the other rooms of the tavern including storage, before heading outside.

His room was empty as well. And everything was pretty much the same. Though, his bed was unmade and the windows were closed. A shadow tendril manifested itself into a shadow version of Venser, handing both women flyers for the 'World's first man on the moon. From Laguna to Summerland!' Featuring, a drawing of a bearded Venser on the front with a fish bowl on his head detailing where he would be and what he'd be doing.

Sanna walked outside then, holding Rowena close as she called out his name again. She continued to ignore the yelling of the women who followed suit behind her, instead in near hysterics, no one lived to go to the moon. No one. She knew that if he tried, he would die much like he probably assumed she had. After all, it had been so long, and she was ill when he left... It was a hard but valid assumption to make. She continued to walk around all around the tavern, searching vigorously and calling out to him multiple times.

Behind the tavern was a giraffe wearing a saddle and a leash around its neck. For some reason. It ate some fruit from a tall, nearby tree and looked down at the three women, munching away. Behind it was a rather large dog house like structure.

Sanna blinked a couple of times in disbelief, but continued to look around, going so far as to peek inside of the dog house structure. "Hello?"

At the lake about a mile away... Bursts of color exploded in the skies, mainly green, turquoise and red. And if one listened closely one could hear the sounds of a crowd of people talking and laughing in anticipation. The giraffe looked in the direction of the noise while he continued to eat.

Sanna jumped a bit at the peripheral sight of color exploding skyward, nearly running in its direction while carefully holding her daughter's head. As she drew closer, she heard the people talking. Urging her on toward that direction until she approached them, looking quite frantic and exhausted.

When she would reach the lake, a cluster of men on the shore fed a young bonfire to push back the oncoming night. There were several spectator stands and booths where shadow tendrils that resembled Venser sold food and drink a plenty, a swarm of children chased each other in a nearby field while they awaited the event. In front of the spectator stands, as a giant white sheet that hid something on the docks from all sides.

"What in the name of the gods..." Sanna murmured as she looked over the spectacle, completely confused, until she noticed the giant sheet. Perhaps he was there tending to the device that would aid him in the show he wanted to give them? She had no idea what to call it really, other than a thing. Being careful not to bump into many people, she weaved her way through the crowd and headed toward the giant sheet.

Ruari, an elven patron with tanned skin, almond shaped eyes, and curly red hair appeared at the lake in a flash of light, far enough from the crowd to not startle anyone. "Huh... An event?" She asked herself quietly as she drew nearer to the crowd, looking around the area curiously.

"Can I wet your whistle?" A shadow tendril mimicking Venser's voice asked the passing girl when she walked by the food booth. Dusk was upon everyone as people started to settle into their seats in the stands. Another shadow tendril appeared before Sanna and the three women, stopping them from getting any closer to the giant white sheet. It said nothing but pointed to the stands.

"Oh! Well, sure, I guess." Ro nodded, somewhat confused as to why a shadow clone that looked and sounded exactly like Venser Karkaldwin was talking to her.

The voice surprised her the most, making her do a double take as the gypsy woman passed, only to discover it was merely a copy. When another approached to stop them from getting closer, she almost glared but instead merely went to the stands with tearful eyes. Nothing was going to stop him, was it? Sitting on the first set of stands, she simply rocked the baby as she'd begun to fuss some thanks to her mother's stress.

"What'll it be?" The shadow tendril asked Rauri. Another shadow tendril on a small makeshift stage that floated in the water appeared. "Greetings citizens!" The shadow replica of Venser spoke, his voice amplified and sounding like it was pre-recorded. "Today marks the day a mere man reaches into the sky above! Far above Summerland and touches the hands of the gods! A man just like us!" The sheet fell and revealed a giant red rocket sitting at an angle. "Oh yes indeed citizens!" The crowd began to cheer as a man in some odd metal armor with a fishbowl on his head watched across the dock to the rocket as many explosions of red and green filled the dark sky, raining down even more brilliant shades of red and green.

"YOUR LIBERATOR!" The shadow tendril's voice, mimicking Venser's voice still boomed.

"YOUR LUMINARY! YOUR LOVER AND LAB ASSISTANT AND OTHER L WORDS! THE ONE WHO VANQUISHED THE TYRANNY OF ARTUS KARKALDWIN ALL THOSE YEARS AGO! THE MACK DADDY OF THE DRAGON'S HEAD TAVERN AND INN!"

The man mounted the rocket and held on to the sides.

"VENSERRRRRRRRRRRRRRRR!"

The long eared island elf watched as the show went on, no longer confused about what was going on as much as why. "This is what all of this is about?" Ruari the islandic elf muttered before turning back to the tendril to place her order. "Rum, if you have it."

Sanna stood up then and, after making sure Rowena's ears were covered, called out again, but this time with a smile, finally crying a bit. "Venser, it's Sanna. Don't do this, okay? Rowena is with me. Just come home!" Figuring he would not be able to hear from that far away, she slumped back into the seat and just watched blankly.

The shadow tendril set down a bottle of rum down in front of her. "Three silver!" On another makeshift stage floating appeared more shadow tendrils with instruments, playing epic music. An entire orchestra. "I'm Venny Karkaldwin and I'm going to the moon!" Venser yelled as more shadow tendrils lit the fuses on the big red rocket.

"Five! Four! Three! Two! One!"

Nothing.

"Five! Four! Three! Two! One! Kablamo!"

A loud burst was heard and the rocket with Venser on it flew up nearly two hundred feet in the air, leaving a trail of white smoke behind it. The rocket did a backflip in midair and threw Venser off.

"Aughhhhhhhh!"

SPLASHHHH!

From where the spectator stands he disappeared under the rocket. A majority of the crowd, including every single one of the shadow tendrils began to cheer.

"... Holy shit..." Ruari muttered as she watched, oblivious to the shadow tendril's request for silver.

Once again, she had to kick herself. Without a word but very obviously stifling a shocked chuckle, she headed toward where she suspected he landed.

Marvella Fullbuster climbed out of her bed lazily while looking at a time with a yawn escaping her mouth. She changed into a black dress, a hibiscus in her hair, a pair of black boots with red at the bottom and chains on them, and last but not least a dark purple eyepatch over her left eye to help her aim her portal spells. She walked out of her door as she went down the hall to the bar area while looking around at the patrons, noticing they were all gone. Oh no. She napped too late in time for the event! She made haste, throwing her hand out and creating a purple rimmed portal to the lake side, jumping through it and disappearing.

"Yeahhhhhh!" The crowd still continued to cheer and several people jumped out of their seats in the stands to rush over to the shores of the lake, looking out for the man who attempted to go to the moon. "By the gods did you see how high we went?!'" One young boy exclaimed. "I want a big red firework too!" Exclaimed another. However, nothing broke the surface of the lake. But then again, it shot him pretty far into it.

As she approached the lake, the two women who accompanied her finally caught up. She handed them her daughter before diving into the lake, swimming downward. She truthfully didn't care who saw, what they thought or how crazy she looked for doing so - this was important. That, and she'd have to tease him a bit for the goofy way he fell off.

The water pushed down on him from all sides as Venser sank into the growing cold waters of the lake, and he struggled to swim with the weight from his armor. Water began to fill into the glass bowl he wore on his head. He got ready to teleport and raised his marked hand above him. Then, his mark burnt and he found himself to be disoriented. It all went dark and fuzzy before he saw a human like face come at him from the darkness of the depths. "Ah!" A moment later... The man shot out of the lake and landed on the shore. He was still and the crowd went quiet, talking amongst themselves. "Whoo!" Venser jumped to his feet and tore off the fish bowl. "Douchebag!" The crowd cheered again before blood began to pour down his nose and his vision blurred, plaguing him now with terrible visions. The world around him fell through as he went into a world inside his own head.

The next morning...

"I saw it. I saw it." He said moving around Sanna, examining her outfit, her form. The blood from his nose dripped down his beard and dribbled down his chin.

She took a bit from her cloak and held it to his nose, holding him close. "Breathe, Ven. I don't know what you saw, but I can promise you I'm real. I'm right here, Rowena is home. Come rest, you need it, you're bleeding..."

"Recently..." He said lowering his head a bit. "Let's go I guess..." Venser's tone was still neutral, an uncertain frown on his face.

The golden gypsy led him to the tavern where the two women who were with her before approached, a bundle in hand with Rowena fast asleep. She went to the bar to grab him a glass of water as well as something to clean his bloodied face before returning to his side, shrugging off the cloak. She was thinner and but retained her wonderful golden tan and thick rear end. She started to cleanse the blood from his nose, wordless as she waited for his reaction toward their child.

Venser wasn't even sure what to think as he sat down at a nearby table, looking to the two women, one of them holding a bundle as they approached. Unmoving except for his emerald snake like eyes.

The tanned woman watched his face, watched his body movements, and she couldn't help but wonder if he was upset with her, angry at her. She took the baby into her arms and bade the two to leave them, sitting beside him as Rowena rested peacefully. She had their mutual black hair, but his eyes and her skin tone. She looked about three weeks old. Sanna didn't say anything yet but just watched him as he watched them, worry all over her face. "What have I done to make you this way, love...?" She finally got out, though it was more of a raspy whisper. How long had it been? Venser didn't now. The bearded man took Rowena in his arms and gazed down to her tiny form. Carefully holding her in one hand he brushed aside some of her hair, and sighed. His expression almost blank as he held his child. For several long seconds before he smiled warmly and began to cradle her.

Sanna relaxed as she saw him smile and begin cradling her, the gaze she had upon him easing to one of love and concern again. She stayed silent for a while to allow him the moment before resting her head on his shoulder, closing her eyes with a deep shaky breath. "I missed you."

Venser went silent again but then kissed his daughter softly on the forehead and held her close. ''Hey little one...''

She kissed his neck, eyes closed as she finally relaxed. Her color started returning, her breathing slowed, and she looked healthier.

Again, Venser went silent while he held their child, pushing back her hair. He rested his head on Sanna's and sighed.

She was silent too, watching them both as they met for the first time. The two women came back with food and drink for them both.

"Who are these women? Servants? Slaves?"" Venser asked looking up to the two women, a hint of annoyance in his voice as he continued to cradle Rowena in his arms.

"Oh, sorry. They are the women that nursed me to health." She smiled.

"Members of your gypsy troop?" He asked eyeing both of them, and then the food they placed on the table before them.

"Mhmm. They are midwives."

Venser sighed and stood up, holding Rowena close to him. "I'm not really hungry... Are you, love?" A chill went down his spine and he shuddered saying that. It had been a while since he had done that, and standing up he got to fully take in Sanna's form.

She shook her head some, standing slowly while leaning against him. She stood a bit back so he could look at her, smiling softly to the other two women as she let them know to store the food for later. Once again they left the couple and their child alone in the room, and Sanna kissed their daughter's head.

"Let's go to my room." He said watching the two midwives leave.

Sanna nodded, resting her hand on his shoulder as they walked in that direction. "I think a rest might be good for us both."

"I don't know how you feel about... All this." He replied with a sigh pushing the door open to his room, eyeing the front of his bed as he walked over to it. Venser laid down and rested his back against the backboard of it and held their daughter close. ."Need to get a crib in here..."

"I could have a bed attachment made so that she can sleep beside us if you'd like, or there is the crib we used at the caravan." She said in a kind manner as she watched them, Rowena lifting her head for a moment to look at him, smile, then set her head back down on his chest in typical three-week old fashion. "As for how I feel... I am just glad to be home, to be with you again. I worry about how you're feeling, to be honest... It must be hard."

Venser smiled back at their child and he felt his heart flutter. The smile faded.

"Yeah... Really hard. A lot has happened." He then asked, "What do you wanna do?"

"Well...why not tell me what's happened? Have you been alright?" She asked, concern filling her eyes again.

"How long has it been, Sanna?" Venser asked looking up to her. The beard made him look like he had aged a few years.

"It has been four months, three weeks and two days my love."

"Why are you still standing?" He let out a sigh and rubbed Rowena's back softly, gesturing for Sanna to come lay down next to him. "Running the bar, getting into fights, getting drunk, going to adventure in unexplored lands, and going into a fucking depression. The works."

She laid next to him gently, lowering slowly and resting her head on his arm. She closed her eyes as she listened, looking up at him as he quieted. "Why, my love? Because you believed us to be lost?"

"You were." Venser said bluntly. "Alex almost become lost. I put her in danger and I had no idea she was pregnant to..."

Sanna stiffened a bit, lowering her head. "Oh dear Alex... Love, are you angry at me? For becoming ill and not contacting you to let you know I was alright? I did everything I could. I begged them to let me write more, but they refused. Kept my parchment from me as well as my quill. I was made to be in bed all the time and I hated it, hated being away. I wanted to be here for you to see your daughter being born, but they wouldn't allow it because she and I were both near death. I don't know what you were told or who by, but we're alive. We're both healthier than we were."

"Why didn't they?" He asked looking to her, scratching at his beard a bit.

"They kept telling me I was straining myself too much and that I would hurt myself. Make the illness last longer. I apparently had some type of plague."

"I would have come either way... I should have looked harder..."

"They had to take me back home. Back to Bucharest for the healing I needed, plus what was needed to save Rowena. It took a month to return from there and a month to get to a standing point, then another to have her and heal completely. The three weeks it took to travel back here were so long simply because of the raids."

There was a silence between them again. What would the future bring? What is tomorrow going to be like? Venser as of late was gone a lot from the tavern, having various other jobs, treasure hunting, bounty hunting, and just traveling. Now, he was facing a very uncertain future. But then again, he never did think of the future. Nor did he try to think of the past. Neither today, nor tomorrow. But now. Now... The bearded man looked down to the sleeping baby in his arms and said. "She's beautiful. Just like her mother..." His voice trailed off and his vision blurred, more blood pouring down his nose.

The golden gypsy wiped his nose again, cleaning his face with the rinsed-off rag she used earlier. "It's alright...why does your nose bleed this way?"

Venser didn't move and did nothing but let out a clueless grunt. Concerned, Sanna lifted his face and looked into his eyes, searching for illness. The look in Venser's eyes was blank, with a hint of distraction and worry. "What will tomorrow bring?"

"Tomorrow is a mystery and the past has already come and gone. Today is a gift... "The golden gypsy kissed his forehead gently. "So please...don't stress, my love."

"Not the first time I've heard that." He said bitterly. "I haven't been this worried in years. When I was a young man. Or a few days ago when me and Alex..."

"Tomorrow you will wake, and we will be at your side." Rowena babbled and cooed in her father's arms.

"Yeah... You will." Venser said with a loving smile, turning slightly to kiss Sanna gently on the forehead.

After he'd kissed her forehead, she lifted her lips to meet his briefly. "I am sorry I was ever gone."

"You're back now. Back in the tavern..." The bearded man said.

"Yes. Back to be with my family, with you. The family we've made together."

"I'm still making arrangements to buy ourselves a farm..." He said with a yawn.

"That would be wonderful. Do you need any help from me?" She asked, resting a kiss on his cheek.

"With what?" He asked.

"The arrangements, or even the gardening."

Venser chuckled. "Once we actually get the farm... I know Kari and Soarin and Lucinda are really going to help with that too..." He could already imagine his lovers and their children working in the dirt together, and then playing in the big yard when they were done.

The tanned woman called for one of the midwives, who set a coin purse that was quite literally packed with foreign golden coins down on the nightstand, while the usual currency was silver. "Do you think this will help at all?"

The bearded man gave them a wide, happy smile and nodded. "Yes... It's more than enough."

The golden gypsy returned his happy smile with a glad, loving one, sliding into bed beside her lover and doting over their baby daughter together, and thinking about their life and their future.

A happy future full of love and joy, laughter and smiles.

CHAPTER FORTY-TWO: CANDLELIT DINNER

The Dragon's Head Tavern and Inn, Vorland, 1437 ATC

The moon was full, and the night was still. The velvety darkness around the tavern were bathed in the pale moonlight, and outside was cool, with the occasional breeze. From Venser's room all the way to the bar area were rose petals scattered about the floor. The tavern was empty, and at one of the tables was a four course candlelit dinner, complete with steak, mashed potatoes with a lava center, lobster, and some banana bread courtesy of Brea. The man sat there waiting for his lover, hunched over in his seat and staring at the center of the table unmoving.

Sanna had just put baby Rowena to bed and dressed in a light white robe, a flower in her unbound hair as she made her way through the tavern and it's beautiful decorum. It had been so long since they'd done something like this together, and she was so glad to get to again. When she reached the table he sat in, she leaned down to kiss him gently before taking a seat across from him, giving him a warm smile. "It's beautiful, and the food smells amazing. How are you feeling?" She asked, resting her hand on his.

Venser was still unshaven and his beard and hair were very messy, and still, he wore the same turquoise and crimson entertainer tunic he always wore. Not even bothering to change out of it for a romantic dinner. Though, he did ditch the cloak, and the tunic seemed to be casual attire now. He gave her a soft, but weak smile and nodded his head. "I'm glad you like it." He said picking up a knife and fork, grabbing himself a steak for the middle. "Why don't we dig in?" Before he did he set his utensils down and clapped his hands twice, summoning a pair of shadow clones that looked like him, armed with violins. They played comforting, almost quiet romantic music while the couple ate.

The golden gypsy didn't mind that he hadn't changed, she considered the outfit charming and thought it was normal for him to wear it a lot. Squeezing his hand in reassurance for a moment, she offered another gentle smile before taking up the utensils and doing the same. She beamed when the music played, starting to eat with a vivid blush.

The bearded man's expression didn't change at all, it was blank and almost worrying. "Now that you're not pregnant you can have wine." He said pouring her a glass slowly. "Kupid Red, well, ya know." With his free hand he popped a piece of crab Rangoon into his mouth. "By the void... I loved this when I was a child, crab rangoon. In Armonia... We ate a lot of seafood, since it was a port town. The capital of Pantia." His tone seemed to lighten a bit at the food. "Took almost three hours to make..." He mumbled.

At the first bite of food, she practically made a small moan at how good it was. She lifted her glass to him after he poured it, sipping slowly with a shiver. The golden gypsy missed the wine very much. "By the gods, love, you've outdone yourself... Oh, I missed your talent. Could you teach me one of these days?" She asked, taking another bite of steak. By now, she'd almost eaten the steak and had partaken of some of the crab Rangoon as well.

"Of course." It didn't even take ten seconds for Venser to finish his first glass of wine, followed by a few pieces of crab Rangoon. The handsome bearded man stared down at the middle of the table as they ate, and it wasn't too long before he started to refill his glass of wine.

A few moments later he straightened up and let out a sign, is left hand curling up into a fist. "We need to talk." Venser said speaking up a bit.

"Certainly, love. What's on your mind?" She asked, tilting her head.

He let out a low growl and gripped his glass of wine, finally making eye contact with Sanna. Venser broke it a few seconds later and rubbed his eyes. He opened his mouth to speak, and closed it. Thought overwhelmed him. His vision blurred, and his nose began to bleed. He let out a sigh and looked Sanna in the face again. "I've had sex with several women while you were... D- Away. I mean... Er."

She blinked for a moment and seemed worried as his nose bled, reaching to dab away the mess until he made the admission. She paused for a second, met his eyes and continued dabbing away at the blood until it stopped. "I would be more surprised if you had not, my love. You thought I was gone forever. It would be cruel of me to be angry for that. If I were to pass, I would want you to move on and to be happy in life... Don't worry, my love." She eased away her hand and rested it on her cheek, giving him a comforting smile. "It's alright. I've met the women you've been with and I love them as much as you."

"I have children on the way." Venser said moving away from her hand, his tone stern and serious. "Maybe... A lot."

That did shock her a bit, enough to even make her straighten. She turned serious, but it wasn't the kind of serious that intoned any kind of anger. Instead she seemed...worried. "Are the women cared for and healthy, and will you know the children as they grow?" Sanna asked, completely serious.

"I-" Venser let out an annoyed sigh followed by a frustrated groan. He opened his mouth to speak, then closed it. "Yeah... Sure. Sure... Erm, you know Alex. You've met her yeah of course, she's lived with us."

"Aye, I know."

"I- Yeah. I fucking knocked her up."

She nodded a bit, looking to the floor for a moment and then back to him again. "What reaction are you expecting of me, love? I am not angry with you, at all. You were honest with me."

"Yeah, I figured this..." He gestured to the dinner and the romantic atmosphere. "Would have been better than you meeting some of the women in the bar and them telling you who the father was."

The golden gypsy took a step closer and kissed him full on the lips, running her hand through his hair before speaking again.

"Venser, I love you. That will never change. I would not be angry with you for something like that, especially given the circumstances, because I trust you to be honest about it. You were. This dinner is a wonderful bonus to that, and if you'd like I can always help tend to the children and the women if they would allow it. Sound good?"

Venser kissed her back softly, suckling on her lower lip before resting his head on hers, closing his eyes. "Still love me despite I've had relations with several women, and they're going to have my children. Several women that weren't you..."

"Yes...I do." She smoothed her hand over his hair, nibbling gently on his bottom lip as he suckled hers.

"Why?"

"Truthfully, Ven? Because you were the first person to truly love me. To miss me when I left home, and it shows... We made a beautiful daughter together, made a home out of this wonderful tavern, and you've taught me so much..."

"Why wouldn't I love you?"

"Figured you'd stop finding out... You know..." He said letting out a heavy sigh, wrapping his arms around Sanna.

"Never. That's a promise." She wrapped her arms around him, nuzzling his shoulder.

Venser just nodded his head in affirmation and closed his eyes again, holding her in a safe, tight, and warm embrace.

CHAPTER FORTY-THREE: VENSER'S BONFIRE PARTY CELEBRATION

The Dragon's Head tavern and Inn, Vorland, 1437 ATC

''Time to break out the rose wine!''

The twilight sky was bathed in a glowing palette of red, indigo and violet as the last traces of the setting sun left the sky. Venser watched the shimmering stars appear and the world began to darken, allowing the raging bonfire behind the tavern to burn bright. He loved the edge of night, as day became dusk, then night.

Back where he was originally from the pollution often blocked out the universe above, almost every night was a black starless one, in contrast to the simple, magical planet of Laguna.

Bone white guitar at his side, he watched his friends and loved ones sitting around the warm cheerful fire, enjoying the party he had thrown in celebration of the arrival of his newest daughter, and the other children to come.

Attending the party was Sedna Rosarian, a huntress who stood at five eleven. Her long straight hair was blacker than black. Like the void Itself lived upon her head, her eyes big blue and almond shaped, though the lids didn't fold as much as those with actual almond eyes. Added with high cheekbones, slightly pointed jaw, ending in a delicate chin, she was one beautiful huntress. An exiled princess turned huntress, but still. Such a beauty.

Then there was Alex Bonneville, a rough looking woman with ginger hair tied up, average complexion, hazel eyes, and dressed in a beige pants, black riding boots with spurs, a sky blue jacket with golden buttons, and a black cape with dark blue inner lining over her seat as she settled. When she stood, the cape would reach just below her rear, a rather short yet somewhat elegant cape. She was chatting to Sedna about hunting while on horseback, tin harmonica in one hand.

There was Kari Fullbuster-Karkaldwin, a young woman in her twenties, with a candid complexion, icy blue eyes, and hair so blonde it looked white. Almost like a porcelain doll in appearance. She sat with her children, the four-year-old twins Soarin and Lucinda, watching them run around and play and catch fireflies.

There was Brea Rowland. The latest hire who was experienced in bar-tending and general inkeepery, her voice was pleasant, as were her kind hazel eyes. She tried her best to exude warmth and hospitality. She was about five five, wore a simple green dress, and had shoulder length sandy blonde hair, and was walking about with a tray of cookies, and chatting with two women drinking cider.

There was a black haired beautiful succubus with burnt golden eyes. Fifty percent titty, fifty percent legs, six feet tall, a nice bouncy ass. Her name was Ceirra Dusk, and she had a bad habit of stumbling into places she ought not to. She was dressed to emphasize that beauty. Her amazingly long legs, were exposed as she wore a white skirt that ended just above her knees, a black bra the skin underneath her nipples visible, and a black Stetson hat she really enjoyed wearing recently.

There was Marvella Fullbuster, who had a slender body and noticeably thick hips, about twenty-five, fair skin, strange purple eyes, dark hair tied back, pink lips, rosy cheeks. A black headband with small numbers of red jewels, a pair of earrings consisting of white round with and orange border with silver chain on either sides, and a black combat uniform that seemed to be mended in several parts, she was sat beside Ceirra chatting away with her, both of them with cider bottles in their hands.

And also sitting around the fire, simply watching everyone as they interacted was a dragoness with a very humanoid shape. Her body naked and her rump very curvy. Nivarah was seven feet tall, yellow eyes, and had a mess of raven black shiny hair atop her head that resembled an undercut in between her horns. Looking over her body it was very feminine yet muscular, a small waist which curved with her luscious wide hips, topped with two plump butt cheeks delightfully squeezing her ass into a perfect heart shape. Her tail was quite long than the well trained but still feminine legs, long and beautiful. Oddly enough, no one paid much attention to the dragoness that towered over everyone when she chose to walk on both legs.

Then there were two pink haired elven looking women cooking sausages over the fire, one was shorter with blue eyes and pale skin, this was one of the barmaids, Kira. The other one, with one blue eye and a red eye and goggles on her forehead and a long, spiky tail was the ditzy demon barmaid known as Thorn. The two looked like they could be sisters and acted like it to.

And finally, sat right beside Venser was Sanna, a gypsy woman with long, glossy black hair, an olive complexion, a slim but voluptuous physique and fine clothing, leaning up against the bearded man holding their baby daughter in her arms, enjoying the pleasant atmosphere

The old rustic tavern that was a quaint little stop on the road, just a few miles away from the nearest city was lit up bright and alive with several other random patrons for Venser's party, the shadow tendrils had drinks half price and were very busy with everyone else inside. Though, it was strange no one was doing a pay-pole dance. Perhaps later.

Sanna was no longer tired; being in her home, their home had rejuvenated and revived her from her sickness. The plague had not left a single trace of its existence on her, the pallor marring her tan flesh now gone and her body glowing brighter than before. Her hair smelled of sandalwood tonight, a present from her to her lover Venser, and the low cut, figure hugging dress was an added bonus. Swept up in an elegant style, her black tresses were away from her soft face, framing it like a portrait. Her emerald eyes fell to their newborn daughter, the little one having been happily cooing in her father's warm arms.

"Dearest, you make beautiful children... She is perfect. What a beautiful celebration... All these friends!" She chuckled gently and rested her hand on his, brushing the back of it with a tender thumb. Her left leg was crossed over the other, giving a glimpse of her healthy calves due to the slit up to the hip on her gown.

"She is absolutely her father's daughter."

Rowena was a little over a month and a few weeks old, so quite tiny, but healthy. She shared their mutual green eyes and black hair. She had the skin tone her mother did, and absolutely adored anyone who came to say hello. Cooing and gurgling, as any sweet infant would.

"... It's wonderful that Soarin and Lucinda have a loving mother. They're beautiful children." The tall succubus pulled her hair over her shoulder, her fingers busy working the strands into a loose braid. Upon closer, she had changed her hair. She wasn't used to the new color yet, the red-brown hue was far brighter than her formerly black locks. Ceirra Suck tied off the braid and smiled, her legs still curled up underneath her, looking back over to Venser now when she was done talking to Kari. "Be right back..." She watched the four-year-old twins throw a disc back and forth to each other, and then approached Venser and Sanna. "You seem like an amazing father."

"Yes they are... And yes I am." Venser said with an arrogant smile relaxing in his chair lazily, nuzzling Sanna and looking down at his daughter, smiling warmly. He straightened up and smiled. Brea's cookies smelled wonderful. Best baker in the country she was. "So, weird or not weird? Seriously."

Ceirra nodded, taking her cider back and throwing back the rest of it in a single swallow, leaning down to brush Rowena's hair. "She's super beautiful too... Hi there..." She looked up to the golden gypsy and smiled. "You must be Sanna, Ven has said so much about you."

Sanna smiled and nodded in agreement with the statement made that Venser was an amazing father, bowing her head in respect to the guests that came to them both. When Ceirra approached she couldn't help but feel a warmth at the love displayed toward their infant daughter, and when she was spoken to she met the woman's gaze with a genuine and humble smile.

"Y-Yes. I am Sanna... Sanna Karkaldwin. And forgive me for not being here as much as I'd like. I fell ill, but now I am fine. It is so good to meet everyone...I hope what has been said was positive?" She teased her partner lightly, sliding her head from his shoulder to extend a hand. "Might I ask your name, Madame?"

As the sky grew dark she grinned and leaned over, the firelight adding a glow to her face, cleavage hanging low. "Ceirra Dusk." She said with a purr, her burnt golden eyes met Sanna's intense green ones. "Ven chooses his women well." The bearded man nodded a few times and kissed Sanna on the cheek. "Banging boobies ya know?" He randomly said. And the succubus chose to sit on the opposite side of Venser where people were just rotating, taking turns sitting beside the man.

"Uh-huh," Ceirra grunted, reaching down for a bottle. Sliding back into her seat. Cork gone, the bottle up-ended in her mouth, her eyes squeezed shut as the booze burned its way down her throat. With a shiver, she put the bottle down on her lap and looked back to Venser. "He's a tits man, I know. Are you a tits woman, Sanna?"

The golden gypsy faintly blushed as the fire added a lovely highlight to the woman's features, their eyes locking. She had only but glanced downward at Ceirra's ample cleavage, but immediately met her gaze once more. The kiss to her cheek surprised her a bit and she giggled at the comment, watching Ceirra sit again and take a drink.

"Hmm? I-I... Well, I know yours are quite lovely. Venser is the only man for me, but I have been curious to try a woman...if he were alright, of course. Or have we already...?" The only remnant of her plague was a foggy memory, hazy from fevered nights. It had come and gone, like a fleeting dream.

"You have, we have, Sanna. You said you find women attractive as well and you're open to sharing women with me." Venser said feeling Ceirra's long arms wrap past him and start to stroke Sanna's back, his emerald eyes reflecting in the flames of the fire. "Tits, ass... Why can't I love both equally?" Looking to the right, at Ceirra's barely constrained tits for a few seconds stuttering his barely comprehensible words. "It's a tough choice, okay? I like fondling them... And sucking on them... But asses I like to admire, and smack. And also fondle... Bah. It's too damn hard a choice! Don't make me think... Tonight is a night to drink, dance, and socialize. Tits, ass, either way... They are fun."

She rolled her eyes, pressing her breasts together dramatically. "I don't see what's so fun about these," she slurred, wiggling them gently. Ceirra slid from her chair, swaying on her feet for just a moment. "Damned heels," she muttered, kicking them off and leaving them behind Venser's chair. Bottle in tow, she ventured off to go chat and flirt with the other women, looking back to Sanna for a second to shake her large chest at her.

Rowena made a playful grab at her father's beard, before getting distracted by the incoming strands of Sanna's hair dangling as she leaned over to kiss her love's cheek back. The golden gypsy felt the tug and laughed, gently taking the strand from her daughter's fingers and kissing the tiny hand as the two spoke about tits and ass. Then she noticed Ceirra get up with a sway and made like she was going to stand and help her, but before she could the woman already wandered off to talk to the other guests. She smirked a bit at the jiggled breasts presented to her, offering a playful wink before leaning to whisper in Venser's ear.

"She is beautiful...I'm glad you reminded me that we have tried it before. I am still quite open to sharing." She playfully kissed his earlobe and relaxed against the chair she sat in with him, purring softly. "It may be time for Rowena to eat soon, do you think we have something to cover myself with as I feed her? Unless you're alright with our guests seeing me breastfeed...most are women, after all."

"And you reminded me that you love women as well... I mean, I can't blame you. Girls are pretty." He said with a chuckle when baby Rowena reached up to grab some of his beard, extending a hand out to tickle her stomach. "Who's a very pretty girl?' Youuuuuuu are! Boop!" Venser booped his daughter's nose, following it with a soft kiss. Sitting back up he smiled when Sanna kissed his earlobe. "I doubt anyone will mind if you breast feed her in front of everyone."

"Mr. Bun!" Lucinda bent down in the grass and picked him up a small animal, hugging him tightly. "Princess, not so much you'll squeeze the life out of him!" Venser called, watching his four-year-old daughter hug her baby bunny tight. It was apparent that Mr. Bun was struggling now in her arms. "Sorry daddy." She kissed the bunny on the forehead and held him, feeding him a carrot slice. After a few nibbles the little girl picked up the baby bunny and held him out to Ceirra Dusk "Cute!" Her older twin brother, Soarin was quick to come by her side. "Look at our bunny!"

Ceirra pressed a kiss to her fingers and then lightly set them on the bunny. "A kiss for Mr. Bun. He's awfully cute. It looks like you're taking great care of him, Lucinda." She smiled, petting the bunny gently. He was damn cute. What was even cuter was Lucinda and Soarin's obvious love for the creature. "Keep him safe. He'll need you and your brother's strong courage to keep him safe from the monsters. I think you'll do just fine." They both nodded and were now going around showing everyone their pet, before the twin came up to their father and Sanna and Rowena, holding the baby bunny so baby Rowena could see him. "Hi Rowena, I'm Mr. Bun!" Soarin said in a fake deep voice, holding Mr. Bun up to his face and pretending that it was actually the small rabbit that was doing the talking.

"Very well, iubire mea." She chuckled softly as she watched him play with their daughter, then looked up to see Soarin and Lucinda coming around with an absolutely adorable rabbit. When the time came and they approached Rowena, doing the funniest voice for her, they were blessed with Rowena's first giggle. It was soft and sweet, and the little babe reached to grab the soft fur.

"Oooh darling, be gentle... That's it." Sanna helped their newborn pet the creature before sliding forward to kiss both Soarin and Lucinda's foreheads, beaming with happy tears in her eyes. "It's so good to see you two." With that, she gently shifted back into a comfortable position and brought Rowena into her arms. She moved her low cut gown away from her breast, covering as best as she could from the twins' sight, and helped Rowena latch onto her nipple. She seemed to struggle a little though, and Rowena began to fuss just a touch.

"Ohh, darling, shhh... It's okay, it's alright. I'm trying, dear one."

"Hi Lady Sanna!" The four-year-old twins chirped at the same time, happy smiles on their faces and hearing their baby half-sister giggle and play with the baby bunny. Their father leaned in and gave them both a hug. "I see Mr. Bun got out again... And he needs to go back inside for the night." The little boy whined. "Awwwwww but dad he's the only bunny at this party!" Venser cleared his throat. "It's too busy out here for him and too busy to keep watch... I'll take him back inside." Lucinda gave up Mr. Bun to her father and the bearded man stood up.

"Ven, can you take my cape inside too? I don't want it accidently touching the fire." The rough woman in the sky blue uniform jacket said, making sure her ginger hair was tied up properly and handing him her long blue and black cape. "Of course Alex." Venser said taking the cape, giving her a kiss on the lips before walking back inside the tavern.

Sanna smiled and was about to answer both of them when Venser began to tell them to put the rabbit away, a further giggle leaving her as she let him do as he needed to. She managed to help Rowena attach to her breast at last and watched her suckle, not seeing the interaction between Lady Alex and her lover. The baby curled into her mother's chest, and Sanna begin to sing a soft lullaby in her mother tongue to help lull her as she ate.

"Mighty fine baby you got there Sanna. I can't wait to have a drink again when I have mine." Alex said undoing the three top golden buttons of her sky blue uniform top, placing a hand on her stomach and letting out a sigh. "Ven is a strumpet... A frustrating one, but I'm just... I'm liking this peaceful life." She said watching the golden gypsy, and the baby suckling on her teat. "I never ever expected this... To become the mother of a baby boy eventually, I'm sure he'll have the very image of his father, and the temper of... Me."

Sanna looked up to see Alex, smiling gently to her. "Thank you, dear...I don't see him as frustrating; if anything I've missed him. I know how you feel...the ease of this life, the calm...when I first met him, I applied to dance for the tavern for coin. Can you believe that? Now here we are, a child...and I hope more come. I hope your baby will be healthy and joyous, my friend. This is the happiest I've ever been."

Alex nodded and let out a sigh, watching everyone else converse amongst each other, listening to some faint violin music coming from inside the tavern. Ceirra's whiskey looked super good right now. She licked her lips and placed her hands on her stomach, her belly not yet completely swollen or that noticeable. "Tween me and him Asher might be our one and only..." She briefly moved over beside Sanna to look down at the baby Rowena. "Row row row your boat gently down the stream... God damn it." She was interrupted by the sandy blonde barmaid who offered them a tray of baked treats. "I'll just... Just have one. Thank you Brea." She said taking one of the snickerdoodle cookies, sniffing it and taking a bite.

"I do not blame you; birth was hard, and we were both sick." She purred as the woman lowered to sing to her daughter, watching as it effectively put her to sleep. She gently detached her and began to burp her, which of course irritated the little cherub, but soon Rowena was back to being fast asleep on her mother's chest. Sanna looked dreamily content, watching the goings on of the party. "So, how are you feeling with the little one?"

"Do you want a banana bread cookie? I chose cookies tonight because they're so simple and I can make a lot quickly." The barmaid Brea said with a smile, offering the tray to Sanna again as they conversed. "I mean, it's still early but I'm just having these, weird, strong feelings. The feeling of the peaceful life, living you with and Kari and the twins versus being on horseback riding into battle leading my father's company... It's..." The ginger haired woman let out a frustrated sigh. "Should have left my cocksucking cape in my room to begin with..." She spoke up again. "I'm not used to this life."

"Ah, sure... I'd love one, thank you." She took a cookie from the tray and grinned at Brea before listening to the woman tell her tale, and she leaned forward to touch her face when she was through. "I was no soldier, but I am a gypsy. We travel all the time, never settling in one place. We never lived in peace, always running from everyone who hated us. In truth, my family forbade me from leaving the troupe...but eventually they let me, and if I hadn't, I would not be sitting here with you or Venser or anyone else. I'd be breaking my back dancing for meager coin until I turned grey, or worse. I would have never found love. Your life is your own... But change is always hard to adjust to, and it does get easier. How long have you been away?"

"Gypsy, entertainer's, the lot I've heard of you people before." Alex said letting out a sigh, flipping her tin harmonica around in one hand. "Few months... Came here after being one of the only survivors of a cocksucking battle gone wrong due to my father, the commander of Bonneville's Brigade ordering me to attack a force that outnumbered ours, telling us to split up into smaller units inviting defeat until all of us were almost killed to the last man! There was no intelligence! Fucking cocksucker! My own father almost getting me killed, getting all of them killed and he had to on purpose because all of that was just fucking dumb."

The ginger haired girl closed her hazel eyes and let out a sigh, shaking her head. "I could at least use one of Ven's cannabis cigars. But..." She sucked in her breath. "I love the comfortable life here, with Venser, with you, all of them." She gestured to the party goers, Thorn the pink haired demoness was relaxing lazily against Nivarah the dragoness and staring up at the indigo sky with Kari and the children, counting the stars and pointing out the constellations. "And that one looks like... A bear! A big bear with a party hat! It's the bear's birthday!" The ditzy pink haired demoness exclaimed pointing up.

"It's just, part of me still longs to go back out there, cutting down my enemies with my saber. But, I'm going to have a son and I have to discontinue my fighting..." Alex said with a sigh.

Sanna listened carefully to the woman's tale of what she herself believed as the woman being betrayed by her own father; if it was known that it would be suicide, why call for it anyway? Perhaps that, or he was merely a fool. She gave a soft smile and reached out to touch the woman's cheek, stroking it with a thumb before lowering her hand to rest on the woman's stomach to feel the child within. "I understand the struggle you feel. I will at least be able to continue dancing after the little one is a bit more grown, but...a soldier must leave the battlefield once they have a family, lest they be killed and never see them again. I wish I knew what to say to comfort you, but...I hope that you know that you can always come to me to speak freely." She slowly got up, still slightly uneasy on her feet but getting her balance back after a moment. She shifted the infant into her arms rather than having her lean on her shoulder and chest, patting her back gently to keep her asleep.

"Would you like to help me put this little dear to bed?"

Alex nodded just as Venser reappeared. "Someone say cigar?" He smiled and handed the finger haired captain of of his cannabis cigars, and she promptly lit it on fire, relaxing back before she could answer. "Oh she's falling asleep already? We haven't even gotten to singing songs yet." The bearded man said leaning up against Sanna. Looking down at their baby daughter.

"Haha, yes it seems so," Sanna chuckled as she watched her lover reappear to lean against her figure, turning her head to face him and kiss his lips lightly. "The midwives tell me that the milk always puts a newborn child to sleep when they eat; I don't know if that's why, though. She's been quite an active little darling today."

"We will go put Rowena to bed and then come back out here for a song... And I know one that's going to involve everyone!" The bearded man kissed his beloved gypsy back and picked up his bone white guitar. "Maybe one song for Rowena, and then a song for everyone else." He said leading Sanna to the backdoor of the Dragon's Head, opening the door the wonderful sounds and smells of Brea's baked goods and the shadow tendrils cooking leaked out. Random patrons were laughing and cavorting around. It was quite a peaceful, fun night.

Sanna smiled warmly as he mentioned putting their darling to bed, following him as he led them both to the backdoor of the tavern they met in. She loved the wonderful smells that arose and the sweet sounds of laughter and banter, stroking their child's back to keep her asleep while they made their way to the bedroom. "Everyone is happy... Just like I remember. Oh, Ven... It's so good to be home."

"Nice crowd tonight. Yeah. And no fighting or anything else... Just. Good times, drinking... Brea making a lot of money selling her baked goods and stuff people reveling. I'm concerned about Rowena not being able to sleep hence why I wanted to keep her with us until we retired too." Venser explained as they went up the stairs to the bar area

Where three shadow tendrils who manifested themselves into Venser's shape served and waited tables, and one more in the corner was playing a shadow violin. Its sound echoey, a recording of a time where Venser stood there playing the same violin.

"Ohhh! Forgive me, love. I did try to keep her awake, though she was just so cute sleeping I couldn't bear to wake her..." Sanna smiled gently and kissed their daughter's head as they ascended the stairs, the sight of his shadow tendrils working the lively place one that she had sorely missed. She chuckled at the sight of the one playing the violin.

"It's almost as if time never passed."

"Hopefully all the partying doesn't wake here then..." Venser said as they made their way past a few of the tavern's patrons, he recognized most of them, like Ivy the warrior woman in her dull plate armor. For now, though, he paid them no never mind as they made a left once up the stairs, down the hall, and down at the fourth door on the right.

He opened the door to his cozy room that he owned in the tavern. They saw his queen sized bed in front of them beneath the windows, it was covered in turquoise silk sheets and he had about a dozen pillows. Off to the left was a wardrobe with a few dresses hanging out, some spilt onto the floor. Beside that was a mannequin wearing his signature strange red and black rubber suit with the rubber nipples and oversized codpiece. To the right of the bed was a desk with a bag of silver in it, a mirror, and a few pieces of jewelry and some small boxes. Right beside it was various papers and a bandoleer. Above Venser's bed was a multicolored painting of a woman's vagina, and below that was an empty display where his old twin bladed sword once hung. In front of their bed was a simple crib for their child.

"She sleeps like a dream, my love. Not to worry. They have been much louder than this and did not disturb her." She made passing glances at some of the patrons before heading to the same direction Venser did.

She saw his room and gave pause, faintly blushing at the painting on the wall...only to see the cute little crib in front of their bed. She rested her head on his shoulder and looked from it to their child, who was out like a light.

"She's ready for bed." Venser said looking down to their child with a smile, bending down to softly kiss her forehead. Stepping back a bit he mumbled to himself and tuned his bone white guitar, and then began to play a sweet, simple song. The song was ambling, sweet, but it was a song meant for family, and comforting as a result. A song that came to mind when he felt the polished wood on his hands, and he found herself humming along quietly he played, waiting for Sanna to tuck in their daughter before he sang.

She nodded in agreement and also gave their little girl a kiss on the head, walking over to the crib and bending over the rail carefully. She laid their dear one down and tucked her in, whispering a soft goodnight before standing upright once more, looking to him as he hummed and played. Sanna beamed and decided to surprise her dear one; her hips began to tick and sway to the beat, her waist undulating and rocking side to side, her hair flowing gracefully against her back as she danced for him for the first time in a long time. Her footsteps were lithe and quiet as she danced, humming along to the tune of his playing.

Venser closed the door so he could actually sing, albeit he was doing it softly.

"Lavender's blue dilly dilly lavender's green, when I am king dilly dilly you you shall be queen. Who told you so, dilly silly, who told you so? Twas my own heart dilly that told me so." A short guitar solo, he played slower, quieter, as the twangs bounced off the walls of their shared bedspace. Looking to the golden gypsy now. "Lavender's green dilly dilly lavender's blue, if you love me dilly dilly... I will love you. Let the birds sing dilly dilly and the lamb play... We shall be safe dilly dilly, out of harm's way."

One final stroke of the strings, and he stopped playing, beaming at them both. He cleared his throat. "Now you'll have to learn the words love..."

She danced to the song as it played, finding the words beautiful and peaceful - the singing glorious. When he looked to her and began to sing she beamed, winking happily at him. When the song was done she walked over, ending her dance, and kissed him deeply. "I will cherish that song and learn it by heart."

The bearded man held the guitar in his left hand, wrapping his right arm around her waist and kissing her deeply back, his lower lip suckling on hers. "We should go back out there, one more song before we come back here and sleep... Oh we'll be sleeping in tomorrow love."

She gave the softest sweet moan as he suckled on her lip in his kiss with her, a chuckle arousing in her throat as she nodded. "We should, yes... Oh, most certainly, dear. I imagine it will be needed." She winked again, pressing herself to his body before relinquishing her hug and walking towards the door with a giggle. "Come now my love, they're waiting."

Venser opened the door out to the hallway, and then offered his hand to Sanna's again. "Mhm, right they are my beloved... Right they are." Before they left, he turned to their sleeping child.

"Good night Rowena... We love you."

Outside, sitting in some deck chairs in the front of the tavern, Sedna sat there looking down to her mug of water in contemplation. "Do you remember when we went on that hunting trip? Do you remember me saying that I hadn't been feeling sick for months afterwards? I was lying, Venser. I can feel it growing inside me, a little every day. It won't be born for a long while yet... Children grow long in the womb and then grow fast from childbirth in my family, but I wanted you to know, before you proposed to Sanna. I'm carrying your child, Venser. And I want you there to see it be born." She sighed, knowing how much he slept around, how many women he impregnated, and she doubted he could ever have one woman. Sedna wrapped her cloak around her and pulled her hood over her face, hating the feeling of being so weak. She was a warrior, a huntress, and now she was just a pregnant woman who was very uncertain about the future. She sighed, looking over to Marvella.

"It's okay to cry Sedna. It takes strength to show emotion and you have a right to be scared and worried. You have a life changer heading your way and now you have a choice."

"I hoped... I hoped he would be happy with the news. When I found out, I was overjoyed. And now, I'm terrified. This will be my third child, and my first child by natural birth. I'm so scared of what may happen, and if Venser decides he wants no part in the child's life, I'll have to leave. I don't know what to do... Ever since my exile I've spent so much time moving around..."

Marvella grew silent thinking for a moment then she spoke softly after a few minutes of thinking. "What if the child was adopted or someone promised to look after the baby with you and give you a hand in raising the baby? I mean, it's what me and Kari... What we're all sort of doing. Helping each other take care of each other."

"I have been engaged three times, and have had children to two men who promised to love me forever. Both of those men decided to walk out of my life. I have given birth alone twice, raised one of my children and watched her die in childbirth. I don't think I could raise another child alone again. But I have such terrible luck with the ones I love, and I would rather die than put my baby in danger..." Sedna spoke, running a hand along her stomach.

"Elanaea."

She sniffled and a small smile forms on her lips. "Thank you. Ohh thank you so much... But... It's all going to take a lot of thinking..." Sedna Rosarian hugged her stomach, whispering sweet endearments and reassurances to the little one within.

"I think we should re-join everyone... And I'll tell him once the festivities are over. Or maybe, I'll wait a little longer."

Inside, Sanna the golden gypsy took his hand in hers as he offered it, leading them out of the room and closing the door gently. She then led them both through the hallway and bar area, descending the stairs to exit through the back door to the bonfire party.

Brea Rowland nodded, sending sandier blonde hair flying over her shoulders, as she went to fetch a certain ale from the tap. "A strong spicy, pure Pryldahnian brew, very hoppy and strong. It could knock you on your tush if you let it." The barmaid managed to fill the tankard with little head, and slid it down the bar to the guest. "Two silver, miss." She said to a woman in simple hunting leathers with the short scarlet threads, elven ears and emerald eyes that glowed and held a similar luminance.

Walking hand in hand with the golden gypsy Venser called back to the excellent barmaid he had hired recently. "You should get yourself some of that and come back out for a song! Let the shadow tendrils do all the serving today." He and Sanna disappeared down the stairs as the sandy haired barmaid blinked her hazel eyes. "Exactly what I was going to do boss!" She called back down through a smirk.

"Oh, and bring me a cider too! Er... No, just one for Sanna!" Once the two came back outside behind the tavern they sat down in wooden chairs beside each other, rejoining their friends and loved ones. Nivarah the dragoness had fallen asleep as the twins and their Aunt Thorn and mother Kari were trying to catch fireflies. "Gather around people! I have another song that everyone can be a part of."

Nivarah then woke back up and let out a yawn, rising up on all fours, watching the children run off to catch fireflies. She then stood up on both legs, walking like a human now as she walked over to Ven, bending down to hug and kiss him, forked tongue slithering into his mouth. Not a fiery, passionate kiss like before, but a tender, loving caress of their mouths, the weight of which finally crashed down upon him. It was a lovers' kiss, simple love and affection for him emanated from the mighty dragoness that towered above them, before she went back to her resting spot and smiled, ready to watch and listen.

The bearded man blinked his emerald slitted eyes a few times and looked to Alex, who was reclining lazily trying not to fall asleep. "Still have that harmonica?" He asked. "Fuck yeah." The captain said suddenly straightening up, raising her tin instrument to her lips. "What can I do, Ven? Thank you for sharing this with me." She murmured. Truly, she was honored to be surrounded by all of them, finishing the last of her whiskey.

"You can just blow onto the top of the bottle to the tune of the song!" The bearded man said. "Sanna, you can hum or something... Alex has her harmonica."

Watching Brea work was quite remarkable as they passed by her, and the gypsy couldn't help but wonder how many years of experience she'd had in the industry. She was quite quick, and knew so much about the different drinks, just like Venser. She blushed when Venser told her to bring a cider for her and chuckled, kissing his cheek, and as they re-joined their little family gathering she sat down close to him.

When she was told to simply hum, she smirked a bit. "I can do that, dear - and if you really want, I can dance to the tune as well while we all sing. What say you?"

When they sat down the bearded man nodded in affirmation. "I say yes. This is... Well, when you can hop across dimensions, planes, you pick up a lot, especially music so some of the lyrics repeat so you all can sing along too!" He traced along the neck of the guitar, humming distractedly as he began to play, stopping for a moment. "We all ready?"

"Oh love. What can I do?" Ceirra asked stretching out her long, beautiful legs and making herself comfortable as the bonfire crackled.

"You can blow the top of your empty whiskey bottle to the tune!" He responded looking to Alex. "Follow along with the harmonica..."

Sanna grinned and set her feet in position, her legs crossed and her hands on her hips as she waited for the tune. "Absolutely, darling!" She had responded to his question of everyone being prepared to sing, already humming to the little bit he had played, seeing both Marvella and Sedna approach all of them to join in.

Venser strummed his guitar and gestured to Ceirra's whiskey bottle, and she began to blow the spout to the tune. "Come gather 'round people, wherever you roam. And admit that the waters around you have grown. And accept it that soon you'll be drenched to the bone. If your time to you is worth savinnnnnn. Then you better start swimmin' or you'll sink like a stoneeeee. For the times they are a-changggggin!" Alex played along and Kari listened in and began to best in the back of a chair to the tune

Sanna was grinning happily, giggling at their sing a long and blowing him a kiss as she danced and sang along. The golden gypsy's feet began to tap to the beat as the guitar played and the bottle was blown, listening to the rhythm of the song to determine the best movements at first. She decided to mimic a delicate tribal dance of her own people, twirling about and lightly hopping in different ways as her hips swayed and her back arched. Her hair swung gently from side to side and in different manners as she moved, humming aloud to the tune of the song.

More, singing, a calm guitar solo before the twangs from the guitar sped up. "Alright everyone clap to the beat!"

The little family and their friends began to clap and sing along, knowing some of the lyrics now. Sanna began to clap as well, singing along as well. Their daughter still slept soundly, and even smiled in her crib as she could hear the soft beat of the beautiful song her father and family played.

"Come gather round people wherever you roam, and admit the waters around you have grown. And accept it that soon you'll be drenched to the bone. If your time to you is worth savin', Then you better start swimmin' or you'll sink like a stone for the times they are a-changin!" Sanna sang along proudly, dancing to the beat and clapping as well while everyone else joined her and Venser.

"All together now!"

"Come gather round people wherever you roam, and admit the waters around you have grown. And accept it that soon you'll be drenched to the bone. If your time to you is worth savinnnnn. Then you better start swimmin' or you'll sink like a stone for the times they are a-changgggin!"

Another brief guitar solo, followed by the harmonica and wind noises and of course the clapping, cheering, and then followed with everyone singing together filled the air. The energy of their togetherness around the burning bonfire was magnificent, now a few people were dancing around the maypole.

"The times they are a-changin! Yeah the times they are a-changin!" The golden gypsy grinned as she danced, her voice carrying on the wind as well as everyone else. The way that the firelight lighting everyone with an ethereal glow. Merriment was in the air, and she couldn't have been happier.

"The times they are a-changin! Yeah the times they are a-changing!"

"For they times they are a-changingggggggggggg!"

ABOUT THE AUTHOR

V.M. Mouchas resides in Boise. Idaho's coolest city, no big deal, whatever, with his thirty wives and thirty-two pickle babies. He invented walking on two legs, the bean bag chair, and the shovel. His great great great grandfather was a seasoned adventurer whose finest accomplishment was discovering Megatron frozen beneath the ice in the North Pole in the year 1897. Other than being a skilled writer, he is also a skilled wrestler and destined to be a future WWE champion. The future face of the company. All of this is true.